The Mortifications

The Mortifications

A Novel

DEREK PALACIO

TIM
DUGGAN
BOOKS

NEW YORK

Copyright © 2016 by Derek Palacio

All rights reserved.
Published in the United States by Tim Duggan Books, an imprint of the Crown Publishing Group, a division of Penguin Random House LLC, New York.
crownpublishing.com

TIM DUGGAN BOOKS and the Crown colophon are trademarks of Penguin Random House LLC.

Library of Congress Cataloging-in-Publication Data
Names: Palacio, Derek, 1982– author.
Title: The mortifications : a novel / Derek Palacio.
Description: First edition. | New York : Tim Duggan Books, [2016] |
    Description based on print version record and CIP data provided by
    publisher; resource not viewed.
Identifiers: LCCN 2015044323 (print) | LCCN 2015040881 (ebook) |
    ISBN 9781101905692 (hardcover) | ISBN 9781101905715 (trade pbk.) |
    ISBN 9781101905708 (ebook)
Subjects: LCSH: Domestic fiction.
Classification: LCC PS3616.A3384 (print) | LCC PS3616.A3384 M67
    2016 (ebook) | DDC 813/.6—dc23

ISBN 978-1-101-90569-2
Ebook ISBN 978-1-101-90570-8

Printed in the United States of America

Jacket design by Michael Morris
Jacket photographs: (top left) Frederic Lucano / Getty Images; (top right) Jeremy
Woodhouse / Getty Images; (bottom left) Peter Glass / Millennium Images, UK;
(bottom right) Lara Giannotti / Millennium Images, UK

10 9 8 7 6 5 4 3 2 1

First Edition

for C. V. W.

I have an interior that I never knew of. Everything passes into it now. I don't know what happens there.

—RAINER MARIA RILKE

THE LAND

Ulises Encarnación did not believe in fate. This may have been a by-product of the sailor's name his father, Uxbal, had given him and the fact that Ulises detested ocean horizons—they were impermanent and appeared like waterfalls over which one could cascade into death. More likely his disbelief was a consequence of how Ulises was taken from Cuba as a young boy by his mother, Soledad, as a member of the now-infamous 1980 Mariel Boatlift. Uxbal had wanted the family to stay despite their poverty. They did have a sturdy house with a garden, tomatoes when others didn't, but Soledad saw in Ulises a mind for school, and she worried about the state of young, pensive boys in Cuba. Bookworms were considered faggots, and though she did not think her son a homosexual, the state might, and she cringed at the thought of him in prison or, worse, at a rehabilitation camp.

There was also Ulises's twin sister, Isabel—or Izzi, as they sometimes called her—a young girl who sang in church, which could be done anywhere, and who seemed unattached to Buey Arriba, meaning, she might not remember much of Cuba if the family left right then. Soledad preferred to wrench two children out of one culture and into another before the Soviet Union collapsed, which she wrongly predicted would happen in 1985. Uxbal warned them they would not find a home so nice in the States. Kingdoms, he said, are hard to come by. He was so certain of his position that he'd tried holding his daughter ransom, locking Isabel inside the country house with him. Soledad was able to retrieve the girl only by holding Ulises hostage in return. Sewing shears in hand and pressed to her son's jugular, Soledad swore to Uxbal that unless Isabel walked out the front door, suitcase in hand, his bloodline would die.

It was then, at the age of twelve, that Ulises learned there were no goddesses of the loom, that people could not be, simultaneously, vessels of fate and free will. Destiny was a consequence of irreparable action and, in the case of his childhood relocation, his determined mother's forced evacuation. Outside their country house she'd whispered in his ear not to worry, but there was a blade against his neck, and why would his father have slipped Isabel so quickly out the door if Soledad had not been serious? Aboard an overcrowded lobster boat, hunched against the back of a car thief and wedged between his mother and sister, Ulises immigrated to the United States, rubbing his throat the entire time. He felt close to dying then, not sure he could trust his mother anymore, and he would forever associate that fear with the farthest stretch of water he could see over the hull of a boat looking north of Cuba, where he saw nothing but more water.

It surprised Ulises that from Miami they took a train north to what the Americans called New England. Soledad's distant cousins lived in Miami, close to Sunny Isles, and he assumed they would make a large, loud Cuban family together. This was Ulises's second train ride, the first the journey from Buey Arriba to Havana. Uxbal had once told his son a story about his own first train ride, from the farmland hills of the Sierra Maestra to the southeastern coast: a little black boy had been seated on the bench in front of Uxbal, and Ulises's father had never seen such hair before. He was five, the boy perhaps the same age, and Uxbal did not hesitate to reach over the bench and touch the tiny curls. He was mesmerized. The black boy shouted, though, and the mothers stood and grabbed for their children. Ulises's grandmother took Uxbal into her arms, from which perch Uxbal craned his neck to see his victim. The little black boy watched Ulises's father from over the bench like a boy at the zoo, Uxbal the animal in the cage. What did Ulises's grandmother say to his father? *Don't be such a shit.*

Ulises asked his mother then why they were going farther north. There are too many Cubans in Miami, Soledad told him, and Ulises, struggling to recall the point of his father's anecdote, realized how far away he was being taken and how quickly his mother wanted him to forget Uxbal.

Are we going to New York? he asked.

A little farther north, his mother said. My second cousin knows some people in Connecticut.

Are we going to speak Spanish there?

Among ourselves, she said, but English with the new friends we make.

As a young woman, Soledad had been a nanny for British missionaries. She spoke English with a comely accent.

Will you still sing to me at night? Ulises asked.

I left my voice in Cuba, she said, which Ulises understood as, I can't, because it will remind me of the island.

Do you hate Papi? Isabel asked.

I will never forget your father.

In Hartford, Ulises learned to wear a hat, coat, and gloves, but the cold didn't bother Isabel as much, and she learned to ice skate wearing just a scarf and jacket. The family moved into the South End, near a shallow pond called Opal's Lake that was reliably frozen by December. During their first winter, the first winter of their lives, it snowed twice by late November, and Isabel was drawn outdoors in a way Ulises found unnatural. Often she'd visit the pond to skate, and there she'd let the snowflakes pile onto her shoulders and melt into her hair. Izzi's gone a little crazy with the move, he thought. He told his sister, One day we'll find you in a block of ice.

I didn't think I would like it, she said. Sometimes I can't feel my neck, or my hands get numb. I forget I have a body. It's not like Cuba, where you're always sweating and the sun won't let you forget your skin. I can spend the time thinking of other things.

Ulises fought the weather by never stepping out into it. He imprisoned himself like a cloistered monk in their new house, a cloudy German Colonial with a white, claustrophobic kitchen and iron radiators. Each room in the heavy house was its own lonely cell—the doors were made of hardwood and were as dark as volcano mud—and Ulises got into the habit of closing all the doors all the time, ostensibly to trap what little heat he found steaming from the cast-iron accordions, which were in every room, placed always under a low, milky window. The house in Buey Arriba had either window screens or nothing, not the double-paned slabs of this strange New England monastery. The shifting pipes, the moaning wood: it all reminded Ulises of hurricane season, the only time of year their old house had cause to shake. He had trouble sleeping and complained to Soledad.

The house is rocking you to sleep at night, his mother said.

It reminds me of the lobster boat, Ulises said.

For work, Soledad found a position as a stenographer at the Hartford County Courthouse, and she found a Jesuit school for her children to attend. It was more expensive than public school, but Soledad possessed a bias for religious education; she thought it more rigorous and demanding and, therefore, more effective. At St. Brendan's, the priests were old white men who gave Mass in Latin every day, which Ulises found exotic and beautiful, though he was not at all interested in the actual dogma. He enrolled in Latin courses, and the old white priests believed they'd found a Spanish Lamb whom they could mold into an orator. He had a gift for the dead language, could speak it better than English, though he learned that quickly as well. At school he wrote short monographs on the value of St. Jerome's Vulgate, which the priests insisted be printed in the student newspaper. The other boys teased Ulises, but they were more jealous than condescending.

Ultimately, he was gracious with his gift, holding study sessions with his classmates to show them how certain nouns declined.

Isabel proved even more devout in her studies. She remembered her prayers from back on the island, and the nuns were impressed by the precision of her memory. In Cuba, the Encarnacións had attended Mass as a family until Soledad learned that the flat-roofed packing-house where services were held was also a rebel meeting place. It was Isabel who'd brought this, accidentally, to her mother's attention—she once carried home a typed manifesto denouncing the ills of communism, copies of which had been distributed during the adoration of the Holy Eucharist that happened after Mass the last Sunday of every month. Soledad found it ridiculous that rebels still existed almost twenty years after Castro's ascent; at that point, one accepts the world, or one leaves it. But Uxbal continued to attend services, sometimes sneaking his daughter away with him, which made Soledad furious and Ulises confused.

In New England Isabel memorized whatever new devotion the nuns taught her. By sophomore year, she was leading the whole school, grades six through twelve, in perfect Morning Prayer. Ulises would translate his sister's words into Latin in his head, and at home he would recite to her his translations, asking which she found more beautiful. Sometimes she preferred the Latin to the English, but she always finished her answers with a Spanish caveat; the Cuban *Our Father* was the prettiest song she'd ever heard. When she sang it, her eyes would close, and she would wring her hands, as if she were at Mass on Sunday and reaching for her father's palm. It was obvious to Ulises that his sister was never as happy as then.

Soledad continued her sabbatical from Mass and instead spent her Sundays practicing for the intricacies of the county court system. As a stenographer, she made a good salary; she'd been a seamstress as well as a nanny in Cuba, and her dexterous knuckles adapted well to the keys. While Ulises and Isabel were at church on Sundays—the priests and nuns kept tabs despite the five weekday services the children attended—Soledad practiced her shorthand skills on a creaky, borrowed stenotype, copying at length either Isabel's history book or Ulises's English primer. She was quick and smart, and the work and the New England cold helped her put at bay—in a manner not unlike her daughter's—the humid Caribbean climate. Yet she could not forget the region entirely. The courthouse was on Washington Street, at the end of which was Columbus Green, where stood a bronze statue of Christopher Columbus, a gift to the city from the Italian-American Society. Seeing the pale-green metal figure, Soledad recalled the famous words attributed to the sailor and taught to every child in Cuba: the island, he had said, was *the most beautiful land human eyes have ever seen*. She woefully agreed, and in those moments she suffered brief but bright memories of verdant hills, rotting fruit, overflowing rain gutters, and cowherds glistening with sweat. Hartford she understood as a machine, a contraption she might force herself into, but its clamor, all the life of the city, coalesced into a fugue noise, such that she felt herself submerged in a fugue state. This, however, provided more relief than alarm. She could move through the New England landscape without memory, a circumstance she found freeing.

More important, it was difficult for her to feel sexual in Connecticut, where the air was biting and the sky was low and gray. Soledad was never warm, and she buried herself in wool sweaters, long underwear, layers of socks, high collars, and double-thick polyester skirts. The clothing blunted the keen passes of courthouse lawyers who found her exotic, who appreciated her dark eyes and choppy accent. She made a name for herself this way, though accidentally. Her children were the shining stars of St. Brendan's School—not immigrant filth or the youngest members of the waning Puerto Rican gangs—and the courthouse administration respected her because she was lovely but not sexually opportunistic. She worked hard, and eventually the district attorney's office as well as the public defender's requested her services regularly, even for the most minor offenses.

Yet Soledad was not aware how severe her unintended celibacy was until a young tax attorney quietly asked her to dinner. She declined, saying her son was participating in a debate that evening, and her daughter needed a dress ironed for Mass the following morning. It was obvious then: she'd decided to raise her children with such devotion that she might forgive herself for abandoning the only man she'd ever loved on the rotting island she once knew as Cuba. Despite this, she sincerely enjoyed the work, and during the twins' junior year at St. Brendan's, she was promoted past court reporter and straight to courthouse auditor. The title was ominous but the pay admirable.

The following summer, at the age of seventeen, Isabel announced her intentions to enter the convent. She'd spent a good deal of time considering the possibility while gliding back and forth across Opal's Lake. Primarily, she'd wondered at the detachment she felt from her own skin. Isabel was as striking as her mother, and plenty of Jesuit boys in her class had made a point to smile at her whenever possible. She had noticed, of course, but she'd never responded. She saw in those soft faces little more than juvenile desire, which she understood as superficial, as deep as the grooves she carved into the pond ice with her skates. Eventually, what she'd previously considered a lack of interest, she now strung together as Providence. She had a higher calling, she said, which buffered her heart from the advances of all the well-mannered, pretty-lipped boys in her grade.

Despite his sister's position at school as a sort of religious wunderkind, Ulises found her insistence on divine intervention hard to believe.

Maybe you just don't like foreigners, he offered.

Here, we are the foreigners, Isabel said.

This seems rash, he said. What if you promise yourself away and then change your mind?

I don't see how that's possible. I've already made two simple vows, one of chastity and one of poverty.

You don't have any money, he said. And the other is a joke.

It's different when you say them out loud and in church. They mean something more. It's not just what I don't want anymore.

The vows are names you've given to the facts of your life, he said. They're not really paths toward God.

And that was when Isabel told her brother about Sundays in Cuba, the months after Ulises stopped attending Mass. The flat-roofed packinghouse had specialized in guava crating, which meant the work had been seasonal. The number of factory hands correlated with the number of red-green guavas shipping west.

It was a place for drifters, Isabel said. Never the same group of men working, no one ever staying.

A place for rebels, Ulises interrupted, echoing a phrase Soledad had used.

Papi was a rebel, Isabel said, and a recruiter. That's why we left. Ma found out that I was at the meetings after Mass with him, and she wouldn't stand for it. It made up her mind.

Ulises could not speak. He was not overcome by astonishment or disbelief but was awash with anger for his mother, who'd lied to him. He was also filled with terrible jealousy. Their father had never spoken of the rebel meetings to Ulises, not a word. Why had he not asked him to join the cause?

What did you talk about at the meetings? he asked.

Recruiting, Isabel said, always recruiting. They were always trying to get more people.

Why didn't Papi ever recruit me?

It wasn't part of the plan, she said. We were the plan, the daughters.

They were raising us to be rebel mothers, to someday marry and raise rebel children.

They were going to breed an army?

Something like that.

That's insane, Ulises said. They tried to brainwash you.

That's what Ma thought. But it wasn't like that. We would pray at the meetings, and then we were given a choice: we could promise ourselves to Cuba, or we could refuse.

What does that mean? Ulises asked.

It means we promised to marry whomever our fathers asked us to, and to stay chaste until that day.

And if you refused?

Nothing. But they would ask us again the following week.

Realizing that Isabel had, of course, said yes, Ulises wanted to know how many times she'd had to be asked before relenting.

Twelve times, she said.

You were twelve then, Ulises told her. It wasn't a real promise.

It was clear to Ulises then that Isabel's faith in God was nothing more than the logical attempt to keep her promise to their father. Uxbal, lost in Cuba, could not marry off his daughter. The only decent thing to do was to swear off all men and then wait for miraculous word from the island. The decent thing was to become a nun.

You weren't there, Isabel said, which made Ulises burn. The day I promised, I was filled with something fierce, and it hasn't left me since. I think I'm just realizing it now.

Ulises approached his mother right away, first out of anger, but then out of pity for his sister, who he believed was throwing away her life on a coerced promise to a madman. He gave a speech to Soledad in their cramped kitchen while she prepared her morning coffee and rubbed her hands awake. She looked tired and sat down at the pitiful table next to their ancient refrigerator. It was the first time he'd spoken to her about their exile since coming to Hartford.

Isabel thinks she's some Virgin Mary, he said.

Soledad's faced hardened. She's always been close to God, she said.

She's entering the convent because of Papi, not because of God. Do you know what she promised him?

Of course, his mother said.

If Ulises had thought his righteousness afforded him a position of power over his mother, then he was entirely mistaken. She said *of course* not to admit her guilt or treason, but to reaffirm the fact that she'd made a decision and not simply fled the island on an emotional whim. Hearing his mother's clipped response, Ulises thought of his sister, who'd made a decision, albeit a warped one, and his father, who'd decided *not* to leave with his family. Clearly, no one was in charge.

Do you think I took you from Cuba simply for a better life? Soledad asked.

It's what you told me, Ulises said.

It was partly the truth, she said. The other truth is that there wasn't even the possibility of a so-so life in Cuba. The poor were no longer allowed to just be poor—they also had to be wretched—so if we were going to live in a shack and grow our own crappy tomatoes, why not do it here? Here we can pretend to be happy, and no one cares.

Papi wanted to be happy too, Ulises said.

There you are wrong, because your father needed us to be miserable or, at least, to pretend to be miserable so that others would join his stupid cause. No one starts a rebellion when you can make salsa and brew your own beer and sit outside all night with one candle and tell stories. Revolution derives from discontent, my love.

And what about Isabel? he asked. Are you just going to let her keep living some fantasy about fulfilling her promise to Papi?

I don't think I can do much else, she said. I took her away from him once, and I think that's as many separations as she'll allow.

She's going to rot away in a habit, Ulises said. This made Soledad tear up enough that she had to place her coffee mug on the counter and scratch at her eyes.

It took everything to leave Cuba, she said. I brought her here without asking, and I don't think I can ask anything so big of her again. But the same goes for you, if that's any consolation. You can do what you like here in America, and you'll have my blessing.

I don't think that should include screwing yourself, Ulises said.

Soledad did not mention to her son that perhaps she'd made a mistake. It was 1985, after all, halfway through the year, and the Soviet bloc seemed sound and sustainable. Soledad's prediction, one of the cornerstones of her evacuation theory, had proven untrue. As a result, the mother of two transplanted Cubanos had come to believe she no longer possessed the wisdom necessary to guide her children in the larger matters of their lives. They were on their own, and they should follow fate, or whatever they eventually perceived as destiny. In any case, she would not stand in their way, which is why she approached her daughter the afternoon after her argument with Ulises to tell her: You have all my blessings. I know God makes you content.

Isabel accepted Soledad's blessings with grace but without excitement. Her decision making was an act of power, so maternal permission, though welcome, was unnecessary. Isabel did, however, request to no longer be called Izzi. She found it an infantile nickname for a young woman who now followed a higher calling. Soledad agreed, and with that the conversation was finished. In the end, the brief discussion did more to free Soledad from the guilt of her decision to leave Cuba than it did to free Isabel to pursue her religious inclinations, and from that day on Soledad no longer invested herself so deeply in her children's pursuits. She attended fewer Latin Club readings for

Ulises, and she asked Isabel to start ironing her own dresses for morning worship.

More important, Soledad met someone.

Henri Willems was a Dutch horticulturalist who, in the early 1980s, was attempting to grow Habano tobacco in the Connecticut River Valley. At the time he met Soledad, he had loose but legal land agreements with a majority of the family-farm operations southeast of Hartford. The region already had a long history of growing Broadleaf for cigar wrappers and binders, and New England Native American tribes had been growing Brightleaf for centuries. Willems thought that, with enough diligent care and oversight, one might cultivate Habano tobacco in the rough northeastern climate.

The farmers whose lands Willems had leased thought he was crazy; the Habano strand was too tropical for the temperate Connecticut weather. But Willems came from money—his great-grandfather Jacobus Willems was the first to take Sumatra tobacco to Holland, where, in 1860, he formed the Gonaïves-Sumatra Tobacco Exchange—so the growers weren't too concerned with how Henri squandered his wealth. They did, however, take issue with the elaborate shading structures Henri began to erect on their prolific topsoil. The tents were nothing new to tobacco cultivation, but together the farmers opportunistically sued Willems for breach of contract, arguing in the Hartford County Courthouse that Henri had leased the land for farming, not for construction. He'd have to renegotiate if he wanted to grow *and* build on their plots.

During the hearing, which Soledad did not attend, Willems gave an impassioned speech about honoring the agricultural legacy of the Connecticut River Valley. He spoke about his travels abroad, his search for a place where the Habano leaf could be resurrected. According to him, the plant had suffered a continual decline ever since the beginning of the deathly AmeriCuban embargo. Less tangentially, he argued that nearby landowners did not regulate the vine-staking that occurred on their leased vineyards. He finished his monologue with a plea: the Habano leaf was a masterpiece of God's creation; mankind was a better animal for smoking and cultivating it; Cuba had become a wasteland where the leaf would soon go extinct; his mission in life was to keep the regal plant from fading into obscurity.

The court found in favor of the farmers.

It was Soledad's diligence that eventually brought Henri Willems into sight, as once a week she reviewed the transcripts prepared by the courthouse's junior stenographers. At home and with a glass of white rum in hand, Soledad found the horticulturalist's transcribed story both beautiful and sincere. She was most taken by Willems's brief discussion of Cuba as a decaying wasteland, a view she shared, though it had the effect of making her both heartbroken for and disgusted with their pitiful house back in Buey Arriba. She was so moved, she attempted the following day to have the verdict overturned by discussing the case with the district attorney. The lawyer said he could do nothing, but Willems should take the ruling as an opportunity to build processing plants or whatever else he might like dirt cheap. Soledad fashioned a letter that advised the horticulturalist to do just that and included a clean set of transcripts—typed freshly on a Smith Corona SL 480 that had come with her promotion—should Willems ever need them.

Lastly, Soledad slipped a note into the package in admiration of the man's vision. She noted a romantic tone to his rhetoric—*your speech was more impassioned than most of the pleas for child custody I sometimes read at night*—and she praised his efforts to preserve something authentic of Cuba—*you're brave to save the things others would leave behind*. She sealed the large envelope with her thumb after licking the wide upper flap, but she chose, in the end, not to clean the faint smear of purple lipstick her lips had left behind. She mailed the package and waited, though not entirely certain of what she waited for.

It turned out to be a Sumatra-tobacco plant, three feet tall and rooted in a wide, circular, rose-colored cachepot. It arrived with instructions for setting the plant in front of a window receiving at least six hours of direct sunlight a day and nursing the leaf to four feet tall, at which point it should be relocated outdoors, ideally beneath the shade of an older-growth walnut. The only spot in the quaint Encarnación house for such a gargantuan weed was in the living room, and with Ulises's help, Soledad relocated the pot from the front stoop to the one window in that space not blocked by a radiator. By Ulises's estimation, the leaf wouldn't last a month.

It'll crowd out the window and die thirsty for sunlight, Ulises said. The sky is too gray here.

Some green in this house is wonderful, Soledad said.

But now the room is too dark.

Nonsense, she said. It's just breaking up the light.

Because it's so large, Ulises said. Because it's absurdly big.

Not so big, Soledad said, but certainly extravagant. Plentiful. The leaves brim over, you could say. It's like living in a palace now.

The horticulturalist and the auditor began dating immediately.

Of Henri Willems, Ulises was uncertain. The man had what his mother referred to as a country chin, a square-cut jaw that finished flat instead of round. He seemed honest, which Ulises drew from the man's routinely plain attire, a necessity of doing business in the city and walking farmland in the same day. Willems's shoes were the thickest wing tips Ulises had ever seen, and Ulises had to admit that he was impressed when the horticulturalist showed him the custom steel toes he'd had cobbled into the hand-stretched Spanish leather. Just the same, Willems was pasty white, three inches shorter than Soledad, and his Spanish, when he braved speaking it in front of the family, had the strangest accent, a lingering stress falling on the final syllable of each sentence, which gave all his remarks the sound of a question.

He reminds me of your father, Soledad said when Ulises asked why she felt such a steady attraction to the European. This could not have surprised Ulises any more than it did. At first, she said, I thought it was his demeanor. He's a very confident man, and when he talks about tobacco—I don't know—it's ravishing. And when he talks about Cuba—do you know he's been twelve times?—it's as if he is seeing the same island that I am, which is a starving place, and if only we could unearth the fields again . . . but that's idealism, impractical, which is why Henri is here with the Habano, which is why you and I and your sister are here in New England. Some things need to be saved even at the cost of paradise. Henri understands that.

You've never called Cuba paradise before, Ulises said.

Soledad thought for a moment and then agreed. It's Henri, she said. He reminds me of the treasures one could have in Cuba. I had forgotten.

That's what Papi used to do, Ulises said.

Only the best version of your father did that: the man who planted tomatoes outside our house and made salads with them at night and would eat them plain off the vine. That was the man I loved. His hands were in the soil when you were young. When we left, he was trying to grow a rebel government, a new hierarchy, and those things aren't real in the end unless everyone believes them to be. Henri's cigars are real whether I smoke them or not.

Ulises shared his mother's response with Henri himself. Measured as the horticulturalist was, he simply said, I'm a fortunate man if your mother considers me the best version of the love of her life.

I think it means she could leave you at any moment, Ulises said, and I think that would be unfair. I think she's walking around in some fantasy about who you are or, at least, who she wants you to be. I think she's feeling guilty still about leaving my father alone in Cuba.

I would expect as much, Willems said. It wasn't an easy thing your mother did. And if she ever leaves me, then she leaves me, but I'm taken with her and will believe it when she says it's me she wants.

What happens when you sleep together? Ulises asked. Aren't you afraid she might close her eyes and think of my father?

We've already consummated our relationship, Willems told Ulises. And though this is sacred ground, you've already broached it. So let me just say, she seems satisfied.

In reality, they were both right. Willems was a steady, mechanical lover, and Soledad's satisfaction stemmed from the combination of his consistency and the off chance that she might sometimes taste Connecticut dirt under his fingernails, a token of the fields and her abandoned husband, though it can be said that her concept of Uxbal had evolved into something more mythic by then, less a distinct person and more an archetype of her ideal counterpart.

Please don't think of me as the aggressive type, Willems said to Ulises, but the first night we saw each other, the inclination was mutual.

Ulises considered the history of his mother's sex life: he assumed that, since they'd arrived in the States, she'd not been with a man until Willems. That was five years of physical famine followed now by two months of feast. But how could his mother love a shadow, even a better shadow, of her distant husband without reservation? That meant moving, in some sense, backward in time. What had the gap been for if not for the last stage of abandonment? If not for forgetting? Ulises tried to imagine Uxbal during that half decade, what he must have been doing all that time. He also tried to imagine his father before they'd parted, but his memories were hazy at best.

I don't remember my father the same way my mother sometimes

does, he confessed to Willems. I don't really remember him much at all. But my mother and sister can't seem to forget him.

That's because sons have a tendency to become their fathers, Willems said. There's nothing to remember when you assume another man's life. It just becomes your own.

Ulises thought the horticulturalist was talking about fate, and he asked, What did your father do?

He was a tobacco farmer, Willems said.

A nagging fear took root in Ulises that he was headed in the same vague direction as Uxbal; that is, toward *oblivion and nothingness*, as Soledad had once described it. He was terrified not only to think that he might become his father, but also that he had no idea what that meant. More troubling was how his mother seemed so certain of Willems, the apparent resurrection of Uxbal. Ulises could not see what his mother saw: his father, as best he could remember, was a tall man with broad shoulders and a thick neck, bald from an early age, a pair of glasses perpetually hanging over his chest. Willems had pasty arms and that country jaw. He claimed to have 20/15 vision, and he was short enough to hide behind some of the more impressive tobacco plants he brought to their house, especially that first Sumatra leaf, which had grown another foot since its arrival, doing exactly what Ulises had predicted it would: crowd out the window in the living room with a set of ever-expanding leaves.

So Ulises asked Willems for a job. His logic was that he could scrape together a father, his old father, from bits of the Dutchman; he could resuscitate memories and eventually recall something of Uxbal besides the portrait lurking about his brain. Willems agreed to employ him, but only out of love for Soledad, and Ulises, like everyone else, would need to start at the bottom, working the crops in the field. So

Ulises bought three pairs of jeans and a broad-brimmed hat, and on a Sunday in August he was put to work in a Broadleaf field.

Ulises learned what his mother and sister had known for a long, long time: there is a great power in wanting. In the fields he'd proven himself almost useless; he, like Isabel, had Uxbal's long arms, but they were unaccustomed to the weight of tools, and soon he was relegated to the nearest greenhouse to sort, organize, and eventually catalog the seed inventory. He was dismayed at first, but when he noticed that Willems checked his seeds more often than he did his dirt, he thought the change fortuitous. The man was often about, and Ulises could study the Dutchman for shades of his father.

What Ulises had not expected was an industriousness to fill the hours in between Willems's visits to the greenhouse. Though the horticulturalist came in and out at least twice a day, his stays were brief, ten to fifteen minutes at most, and the hours in between became dark matter in need of mass. Into those voids Ulises thrust his energy, hoping always to accomplish some minor task worthy of Willems's attention when he arrived. Improving the already efficient operation was nearly impossible, but he did succeed in fine-tuning some minor movements of the Dutchman's tobacco orchestra: by the end of a month, he'd developed an epoxy resin with which to coat the seed bags, essentially making them invincible; after two months, he'd built a sampling box for new seed varieties, which enabled Willems to better compare texture, smell, and speculative fecundity; by three months in, Ulises had reorganized not just his original greenhouse, but all the greenhouses Willems owned in Connecticut. The Dutchman nodded his head in genuine approval of all this, and, come November, when it was too cold to work the fields any further and the sky was permanently overcast, Willems decided to teach Ulises the finer points of his finished product, to give meaning to the boy's nascent understanding of its primary parts.

What did the study yield? As far as Ulises could tell, Willems touched everything: he ran his hand through seeds, fondled the leaves of infant tobaccos, tested the weight of fresh knives for leaf-cutting, passed between his palms small *matules,* the tiniest leaf bundles, and always balanced the newest cigar on his right index finger as if the tipping point was a symptom of its quality. Willems also smelled everything; it was something to see him kneel in a row of what would become Emperor Maduros and shove his face into the dirt. Often he tasted, and sometimes he even listened, though the listening seemed less scientific; the shaking of seed bags produced a shuffling sound Willems found pleasant. In the end, Ulises determined that his mother's lover was an empiricist.

But the conclusion didn't amount to much; Ulises could have come to the same truth at the dinner table and saved himself a season's worth of time. Over pork loin, rice, spinach salad, lentil soup, and turkey breast, Willems spoke to Soledad about the pains of his day and the progress of his crop, going so far as to outline the ever-shifting agricultural outlook for the week—the leaves will swell in this sun, the dirt will dry in this heat, the humidity will thicken the stalks, et cetera. At the same time he would comment on the tenderness of the brisket or the flexibility of the asparagus or the merlot's bouquet. Ulises had trouble associating him with his father, who seemed to dwell only in abstractions, in faith and politics. He decided it was the absence of Uxbal in Willems that Soledad found captivating. She was in love with the void.

But then, on a late November evening, Willems revealed himself at dinner. As was the custom, Isabel said grace before the meal, and the others, despite being essentially agnostic, humored her, bowing their heads and waiting out the lengthy benediction. Ulises, sore in the neck from a day of tilling, looked up to see Willems mumbling under his breath. The Dutchman was praying, something Ulises had never expected from a man who routinely put his nose in the mud, and the moment Isabel whispered, *Amen,* he turned to Willems and asked, What are you praying for?

Willems looked caught in a lie, or, at least, embarrassed. He glanced at Soledad, who shrugged. The man sighed. Turning to Ulises, he said, The tobacco.

My grandfather had indentured servants, Willems confessed, former slaves and Indians, and they built our farms on the smaller islands of the West Indies. One on Cuba, also. They're the ones who picked our leaves and rolled our cigars. There was a cholera outbreak on one of the islands. According to my father, the servants would go out into the fields healthy and strong but return glassy-eyed and sluggish. A day came when twenty men and three children died in the fields. My father tried to persuade my grandfather to do something, to lug in fresh water, to clean the bunkhouses, to isolate the ill, but he refused. It was time for the harvest, and he simply imported more men, more Indians, some Chinese. The city health inspector quickly learned of my grandfather's negligence, shut down his farms, and burned all his tobacco fields along with the bodies of the dead. My father broke ties with the family and started his own tobacco company, but he would only make cigarettes. He said cigars were tainted. He said he had dreams, and in the dreams when he smoked cigars, the souls of the dead would seep out of them and haunt him for the rest of his life. I think they did anyway. My grandfather, at least, went mad. He died alone in a poorhouse. So this will sound ridiculous, but I sometimes worry that the fogs from my cigars are the souls of good people, and I say a little benediction for them.

But you're not afraid of ghosts, are you? Ulises asked.

I've inherited my father's fear, Willems said, but also my grandfather's constitution. I've yet to have my father's dreams, but I also don't want to ignore the dead. He paused. I know, he said. It's all ludicrous.

A man divided, Ulises thought, and the pain of the division was clear on Willems's face. Ulises had never seen him so uncomfortable, and it was obvious that Willems couldn't reconcile his patriarchal past with his pragmatic present: he was the most careful man on the farm, and when he touched his seeds or smelled his dirt, it was with reverence. Ulises had assumed the affection was for the product itself, the finished Colorados and Obscuros, but in reality it was for what *might* be there, what was *possibly* buried in the soil. But the logic was irregular. Yes, the Dutchman was his father's son, but these fields were not the Antilles.

Poor man, Soledad said, and her sincerity prompted a memory of Uxbal for Ulises: his father splitting their tomato harvest in two, one half for the church and one half for the family. Ulises recognized that Soledad now looked at Willems similarly. Uxbal grew tomatoes for his family *and* his revolution, and Willems grew tobacco, rolled cigars, for his livelihood *and* for fear of inherited haunts. And in that wistful look of his mother, Ulises finally understood the connection between the Dutchman and his rebel father; both men were inclined toward reason *and* fancy, and the tension of opposing forces, the power of separate wants, perhaps more powerful even than his mother or sister's unidirectional wanting, was the origin of each man's exceptional gusto.

That night Ulises and Isabel were kept awake by Willems and their mother's exceptional gusto, the intensity of their lovemaking rattling the master-bedroom door. In the kitchen, Ulises and his sister waited for the session to end, but it lasted longer than expected. In the dark, Ulises told his sister that he thought Willems and Uxbal shared the same space in Soledad's heart.

Because he sees ghosts? Isabel asked.

Because he sees something that's not there, Ulises said.

This they both agreed upon: Soledad's mad love for Willems, the evidence as loud and steady as roosters at sunrise. And they were both right. Up in the bedroom, Soledad rocked atop her Dutchman suitor with her eyes closed, and what she saw centered in that void was a faceless man rolling cigars next to a tomato vine, the symbolism trite and obvious, though arousing just the same. And, to be fair, she felt not that Willems had stepped more fully into her husband's shoes, but that he had stepped closer to the vision of her ideal man she had been cultivating ever since her departure from Cuba. Gasping, Soledad didn't know if Willems had finished with her, and so she reached for his penis, but he grabbed her hand and simply bit her neck. Over their slowed respirations they could hear the children retiring to their rooms.

For the next three months, Isabel couldn't sleep at night due to an incessant noise in her ear: the echoes of Soledad's carnal ecstasy. However, the sexual nature of the wailing didn't bother her. Since the previous summer, Isabel had spent the majority of her free time volunteering with Sister B of the Sisters of the Holy Resurrection order at Jude the Apostle Hospice Center, a restored insane asylum turned health-care facility that was a part of St. Anthony's Hospital. The center suffered a lack of funding and a transient staff, so Isabel helped Sister B clean out the rooms of the recently deceased. On more than one occasion Isabel found and then disposed of the pornography of the newly dead. Over time she saw enough *Call Girls* and *Gent* to think that the greater purpose of sex was pleasure or, at least, to hypothesize which scenarios were at the root of her mother's wailing. She had the same reaction to the magazines that she'd had to the boys of St. Brendan's, which was none. Isabel was discovering in herself a clinical perception of the body. She stopped short of associating that cold distance from passion—or her love of the cold, or her penchant for a bodiless mind and soul—with her past promise to Uxbal, though she could say, with relative certainty, which of the female or male magazine subjects were objectively plain or gorgeous.

Still, her mother's wailing never left her brain, and during the day Isabel fidgeted despite the lack of sleep. The joys of her devotion—the continued and exacting prayer, the studying of the *Third Spiritual Alphabet,* the service with Sister B, the college-level books on the evolution of Catholic theology, even the Eucharist—all seemed to lose their flavor. She maintained the same diligence in her endeavors, but they brought her no satisfaction, and she could not understand how her faith could so quickly fail her. She wondered for a time if she'd possibly misheard the Lord. She often thought back to the day she'd promised herself to Uxbal and Cuba, and she remembered the guava crate she'd stood upon, a box made of newer wood but held together by rusted tacks, and she could not recall the fierceness of her conviction.

While skating at Opal's Lake one afternoon, Isabel tried reliving the memory second by second, but after a time it changed. The pride on her father's face was transformed into disgust, and she misremembered her father spitting and raising a hand at her. She was possessed by regret and remorse—she had forsaken the cause and Cuba—and she wanted to feel the slap of his hand against her head. She did not understand why, but she felt with absolute certainty that she'd sinned against him.

But then there was a commotion at the other end of the pond. A boy had fallen through the ice, and a mob of children was trying desperately to save him. Isabel saw hands reaching into the water, and she rushed to help. The boy had fallen under completely, but he bobbed in the water, and eventually his arms and chest flopped onto the ice. The other children grabbed at his pants and belt, but it was not until Isabel gripped the boy's jacket at the shoulders and they all pulled in unison that his legs emerged. His lips were already blue, and he mumbled that he could not feel his toes or ankles. He said his chest was cold, and he'd wrapped his arms so tightly around his body that Isabel, knowing he would die if he stayed in the wet clothes, could not pry his limbs away. Two girls ran for the nearest house and phone, and Isabel found herself kneeling alone next to the boy, the other children forming a loose circle around them. When he tried to speak, the circle closed in on them, but when he started rolling around because he said he could not feel his legs at all, the children backed away.

She took off her jacket and told the boy he had to put it on, but his eyes were vacant, and he kept looking up at the sky. A film ran over them, as if all the blue in his irises had dissolved into a grayish lens. Isabel thought for a moment they might be freezing, that ice clouded them. She touched his forehead, and he blinked, but still he didn't pay her any attention. His skin was not as frigid as she expected; it felt hotter maybe than it should, as if the body was harboring what warmth it could around his brain in an attempt to keep him alive. She pulled so hard at the boy's hands and arms, attempting to loosen his grip, that her fingers started to ache. She began to plead with him.

Let go, she said loudly. You're going to die.

His eyes seemed to waver in recognition of sound, but his elbows didn't budge. Isabel knelt down and placed her lips against the boy's ear and told him again to let go. His body relaxed but still shook, though she could see some of his fingers uncurl.

Blood flooded Isabel's face, and she felt a physical excitement—the word rapture came to mind—and it sang through her skin when her lips stuck to the boy's ear. It wasn't the twenty-degree weather; she loved the cold, but here she found the other side to numbness, the very edge between a throbbing heart and a still organ, and the recognition of such a place, this borderland a single breath wide, brought her capillaries to life. She felt her blood in a way she thought her mother felt her own when naked with Henri Willems, the material body melting into a liquid form, and in her mind were images from *Gent,* women wet with male sweat, glistening white penises, stained garter belts, dirty yellow hair, and stretched thongs; it was not sex but a failing of the mind, Isabel's body knowing something her brain could not articulate, speaking in pulse and fever because there were no words for this.

Let go, she said again, and she spoke more slowly, letting her breath fill his ear, letting the throb behind her eyes endure a beat longer. The boy's arms remained tense, but the skin on his face relaxed, his cheeks drawing down and his chin coming to a rest on the collar of his thick winter coat.

Isabel removed the boy's hat with her right hand and continued to breathe into his ear, and she recalled then what Francisco de Osuna had written about God taking a rib from Adam in the *Third Spiritual Alphabet*: the Lord did not put Adam to sleep to mollify the pain of surgery; he put Adam to sleep so that his transformation was spiritual rather than sensible. The boy, she realized, was going to die in front of her, and rather than worry his final moments with the swapping of jackets, she, instead, should attend to his soul.

There's a place where it's warm outside, she said into his ear, but the ponds still freeze over, and you can still go skating. Or, if you want, you can melt the ice with a touch of your finger and swim under a hot sun. You can skate at night under the moon, and you can skate without getting tired. When you wake up again, she told him, you'll be in that place. Don't be scared.

His blue eyes looked at her, and the film was gone, but then the boy stopped moving. Isabel saw a few hot breaths come up from his mouth in miniature clouds, and soon his lips were also still. Isabel was hot all over, and she was glad she'd removed her jacket, which she laid over the face of the dead boy. Her skin felt incredibly warm, as if she'd sat too long by a radiator, and her cheeks were flushed, her fingertips swollen red.

Three of the watching girls began to cry, and it reminded Isabel of her mother's moaning, but it was nothing more than a tonal similarity, and Isabel could not be certain how alike the two wailings were, because her mother's sound had finally left her head. She heard only the crying girls and perhaps the crunch of boots in the snow, and she was sleepy and tired, which was all she could recall for Ulises and Soledad when she awoke four hours later in a hospital bed at St. Anthony's. She had a high fever, somewhere dangerously close to boiling all the water in her brain. Soledad was mortified, Ulises silent.

They told her what the policeman had told them: Isabel had passed out next to the boy, but the other children hadn't tried to help her.

They were scared, because they said she'd taken on a strange look after blacking out, and also, she'd slumped down next to the body of the boy. They also said she was brave for speaking to the boy when no one else would. But the ten minutes her naked face and neck had spent on the frozen pond gave her a chill, and now she was at the brink. Soledad told her she was strong, and Ulises said he loved her.

All the same, Isabel said she was not scared. Her family smiled and thought the fever had hindered her reasoning, because death, after all, is unreasonable.

Isabel did not die. Her fever broke the following evening, and the color returned to her face. Sister B, who'd come to visit at the request of Soledad, was surprised to find the girl awake and showing no signs of illness. She asked Isabel what had happened—comfort after catastrophe, Sister B believed, came from giving victims the space and time to categorize their pains—but Isabel surprised her again, saying she'd been hollowed out by the fire of the archangel Michael.

You suffered a fever, Sister B told her, following a tremendous chill.

My skin was on fire before I fell onto the ice, Isabel said. It was from talking to the boy and touching him when his soul was passing. I've been called to sit with the dying.

Sister B thought the girl was fanatical, but Isabel was steadfast.

When, after two weeks, she had fully recovered, Isabel knew exactly what she wanted, and she requested a new assignment: to spend her service hours comforting the terminally ill or near dead. Sister B considered denying her the post, but Isabel offered twice the volunteer hours and promised not to neglect her duties as postmortem maid at Jude the Apostle. The nun acquiesced, and a rumor started at school that Isabel was chosen by the Lord to carry dying grandmothers to their graves. The speculation was first of awe but soon was twisted by the non-devout into something more malicious: God forbid the stone-faced Encarnación daughter visit your grandfather at the hospice center or your suddenly sick aunt in St. Anthony's intensive-care unit, because there was no returning from her charity.

Consequently, Isabel became the Death Torch, though the moniker wasn't entirely accurate.

Her days began before classes, at four-thirty in the morning, when she arrived at Jude the Apostle. She traveled from room to room by candlelight, moving through the hospice center first and the hospital ICU last, praying for the souls of the unconscious or horribly afflicted. She would touch the patients on the forehead or take them by the hand or feed them ice or change the channel on the television, and her classmates never again asked to borrow a pencil or pen from her. Of course, the dying did not always die when Isabel visited, but she was so diligent that unless a body passed during the school day or at night between ten and four-thirty, she was there. By the time the twins finished high school, Ulises's sister had witnessed ninety-eight deaths.

Ulises was busy that spring and early summer working in the opposite direction, trying to draw life and tobacco from the thawing Connecticut soil. The rumors at school bothered him tremendously, and he found himself defending his sister even though he thought her habit maniacal. He'd not gone so far as to throw a punch, but once he pushed his nose into the face of another senior, a much larger senior, and said he was not above breaking the larger boy's spine with the swift snap of his neck. The classmate backed off immediately, but Ulises felt the repercussions of his brotherly love at graduation when he realized that people were afraid to approach him and wish him well—he was enrolled in the University of Hartford for the fall—with his sister at his side. There were, of course, jokes about good and evil twins, and next to Isabel in the school auditorium Ulises wondered at how the bad always poisoned the decent and never the other way around.

It hadn't bothered him as much as it might have in the past, however. The previous winter, during the time of Isabel's religious crisis and the flourishing of his mother's love for Henri Willems, Ulises had steadily lost interest in school and in his classmates. Many of them were excited to start college in the fall, but Ulises, at the time aerating small portions of Willems's frozen fields by hand, discovered a satisfaction in the tangible results of manual labor. For the first time in his life he had useful arms. They sprang out from his shoulders after three months of cracking ice, digging through frost, and shoveling snow off tobacco rows. They were not especially thick, but they were dense, something like cold rubber when he tensed, and Ulises looked forward to the new planting, imagining two seed sacks, one atop each shoulder, and the glow of the sun on his back. He strained his new muscles every day and was amazed to see how they reacted, how they grew almost overnight. For once he took pleasure in living on the surface of things. He forgot his studies as summer approached, and Latin slid away from him like an oil slick gliding down the slower tributaries of the Connecticut River.

By June, Ulises realized he would need a new wardrobe. Dressing for an awards ceremony in Isabel's honor, he could not fasten the top button of his white oxford, and crossing his arms strained the fabric around his shoulders. The ceremony took place in St. Anthony's cafeteria, which had more room than Jude the Apostle's. There, Ulises sat uncomfortably upright alongside his mother and Willems while a low-level administrator, a tall man with narrow shoulders, expounded upon the many good works of his sister. The bulk of his comments centered on what he called the little acts of mercy by Isabel, namely the scrubbing out of bedpans and the fluffing of pillows, and he seemed instructed to avoid, if possible, too much mentioning of Isabel's presence during the hours of death.

Sister B was in attendance as well, and she sat next to Isabel to the right of the podium, looking as if she might vomit into her lap. Ulises was tempted to go to the nun at one point, but Isabel was summoned to the stand to receive her plaque—the number of her volunteer hours, 944, etched onto the brass plate—and to lead the small audience in a closing prayer.

However, Isabel did no such thing. Plaque in hand, and speaking clearly into the microphone, Isabel said: I'm wasting my time with those bedpans. It's the dying who need me, not the lazy candy stripers. I am finished with these chores, which I think is fair, considering the hours on this plaque. From now on, I'll only visit with the terminally ill or those painfully on the brink. They don't want fresh pillows or clean floors or to watch TV. They want to die, and it's my responsibility to help them do so.

Sister B promptly vomited. Ulises's shirt tore, and the room drew a collective breath.

The earth, Ulises whispered to no one, *was without form and void.* It was a verse he remembered from Genesis that had syntactically troubled him for some time. Was it that Earth was without form *and therefore void*? Or was Earth without form and also—paradoxically— *without void*? But watching Sister B cover her mouth, seeing the old nun stifle the noise of her vomiting, it seemed perfectly clear that the line meant what it said, that in the moment before the universe was born—though to say that itself was also ridiculous, there being supposedly no moments before God's Universe, before God's Time—what was there was less than nothing, because nothing was an idea, was a presence, and God had not yet created it through the manifestation of its exact opposite, something.

And though the moment Ulises endured just then was rife with sounds and somethings—the muffled gurgling of Sister B, the droning soda machines along the cafeteria's eastern wall, the PA system paging doctor so-and-so, a tapping foot, the legs of a chair scraping linoleum—what was the same was the terrifying threat of a voice disturbing the halted second; the terrible idea that an awful or awesome noise would eventually flood the vacuum, and what followed could not be undone. The idea that the world could not be unmade. Ulises reached for his mother's hand, but Soledad's palms were pressed to her neck. She was saying something he could barely make out. Her lips moved in a whisper: Oh, shit.

It was a community reporter who spoke next, jumping out of her chair and asking, Does the hospital endorse this sort of behavior, Miss Encarnación? Are the hospital and the church now advocating assisted suicide? How many people have you already helped kill themselves?

The last question inspired the rest of the audience to their feet, and the head of the nursing staff rushed to Isabel's side, trying in vain to speak through the microphone over the din of the crowd.

Please take your seats, she said. Please take your seats. Please take your seats.

The administrator who had organized the event shouted over the head nurse, No one has been killed!, which accomplished nothing. He shouted, That's not what she meant!

Naturally someone shouted back, What did she mean? How does she help the dying?

Who is in charge of the hospital volunteers? the community reporter asked. Who oversees their efforts? Has anyone witnessed what she does with the patients? How many victims are we talking about? Are there other volunteers like her? How many?

A woman said, My mother is upstairs and has cancer.

My cousin's brother-in-law was in a car accident, a man said. He has a tube in his throat in the ICU.

Someone said, God save us.

The community reporter cried, Are the nuns trained to kill? Do they have medical backgrounds? How liable is the Church?

Isabel moved away from the podium, and the hospital administrator reached out to grab her by the arm. Watching, Soledad screamed, and Ulises returned to the world, rushing to his sister's side. The administrator, perhaps realizing Ulises's height or width or maybe his torn shirt, let her go.

Ulises gathered Isabel into his arms and made for the door.

Please, everyone! the administrator yelled. Please just take your seats!

At first they tried to take Isabel home, but the community reporter had made enough calls that when they arrived, a small mob of journalists had congregated at their front door. Willems drove the car in circles around the block in silence until Soledad, her face still white, asked Isabel: Love, what did you mean by all that?

Was I not clear? Isabel said. She stared blankly out the window.

What are we to do with you now? Soledad asked.

The convent, Isabel said.

Isabel was silent the rest of the way, and no one asked any further questions. Ulises and Soledad feared, each in isolation, that to question Isabel was to somehow question God, a feeling that, despite their lapsed faith, they could not ignore.

The convent was a granite building with high walls and an outer gate, stuck between a blood bank and a condemned gymnasium. The family found Sister B waiting for them in a cloister outside the convent's modest chapel. She seemed to have recovered from vomiting, and they were taken aback by the nun's confession that she'd dreamt of the awards ceremony the night before.

Not an exact vision, she said, but Isabel was there. In her hand she'd held a book the same size as the plaque, and she spoke to a crowd. Sister B blushed and said, It was too much to see it wide-awake. God has never spoken to me before, not in such a direct manner.

Ulises thought the nun had been brainwashed by his sister. Isabel could convince anyone of anything through the resolve in her voice. A book, Ulises knew, was not a plaque, and what did she say in the dream? Why would God send a message to a forgetful old woman?

Soledad, however, did not turn so quickly to skepticism; she was more concerned with her daughter than with her daughter's words or an aging nun's visions. She held Isabel by the shoulders—gently, as though the girl were a new creature, or had a new, fragile body, afraid, almost, to disturb the fabric of Isabel's modest blue sleeves—and listened to what Sister B had to say, and she nodded sheepishly at the suggestion that her daughter take refuge in the convent.

Isabel has done nothing wrong, Sister B said, but what she said will confuse everyone. If she stays here, we can protect her.

Protect her from whom? Soledad asked. The press?

The public, Sister B said. They will want to know if the Church allowed a young girl to put untended hospital patients to death.

For how long? Soledad asked.

Until they stop asking for her, Sister B said. Which they eventually will.

Have they begun? Willems asked, and it was clear that the idea of leaving Isabel at the convent was strange to him as well as Ulises.

The phones were ringing when I returned, Sister B said. And the bishop is on his way.

So began a second schism in the Encarnación family. It was swift and unrelenting. There was the geographical separation of bodies—Isabel stored away at the convent, and Ulises and Soledad back at the house—but there was also the division of blood, the son not wholly convinced of the sister's religious commitment, the mother convinced only and obsessively that her daughter's exile was her maternal fault. Soledad was a failed Catholic, but she couldn't help comparing herself to Mary, the Mother of God, a woman she thought of as stupid for abdicating her only offspring to a waking nightmare. Privately, she feared that Isabel was just as lost, that she'd watched her go without an argument.

Willems, for his part, was quiet on the matter and spent his time consoling Soledad. Never did he feel so distinct from the Encarnacións as he did just then, and it was a testament to how close and small the Encarnación triangle truly was that the Dutchman still hesitated to throw his hat into the ring. But he was determined to engage the family tangentially—namely, to distract them. He started by suggesting to Soledad that she take her first vacation. They would travel west to the Grand Canyon by train. The trip would be long, it would take them to a place as contrary to Hartford as Willems could imagine, and it would bypass Soledad's acute fear of flying.

Soledad agreed, but only if she could see the news die down in the papers. The reporters remained vigilant outside their house, lurking with notepads, cameras, voice recorders, swarming the mother and son in the street: *Are people now safe? Was the Death Torch put away where she could no longer molest the dying? Should she be put farther away, perhaps in a prison rather than a modest but comfortable convent?*

Feeling trapped inside the house, Soledad resurrected her sewing kit and began stitching a new set of clothes for her daughter. In the first week of Isabel's absence, she had tried to cart from home to convent the girl's entire wardrobe, but Isabel claimed that the T-shirts and corduroys she owned were too childish among habits and ankle-length skirts. The new wardrobe would be a gift, a reminder to Isabel that she was loved and wanted at home, and that the choice, the devotion to God, was still hers to make.

Ulises thought of his mother's actions as permissive and enabling, and he chastised her in the early mornings before going out to the tobacco fields. Willems had put Ulises in charge of four leased farms that summer, hoping to distract him with work the same way he distracted Soledad with their imminent holiday.

You only encourage Isabel when you bring her those clothes, Ulises said. She wants to stay at the convent. The Death Torch, even when the fervor has died down, will not come home.

Don't call her that, Soledad said. She needs to know that she doesn't have to choose between us and God.

She already has, Ulises said. He quoted Matthew: *Anyone who loves their father or mother more than me is not worthy of me; anyone who loves their son or daughter more than me is not worthy of me.*

Bullshit, Soledad said.

And she would say no more on the subject, would change rooms to escape Ulises's persistent nagging, and that left Ulises with no one but Willems with whom to discuss the matter of his sister. Over cigars, the two men formed an evening routine: Ulises would broach the subject of Isabel's devotion, questioning the veracity of her faith, and Willems would deflect.

We can't tell people what to do or how to live, Willems would say. We can't be afraid of what we don't understand. It's not your sister's job to explain herself.

But those careful responses even Willems grew tired of, which is how he came to bring with him several cigars instead of just two, thinking he could stanch Ulises's obsessive rants by plugging stogie after stogie into the young man's mouth. Ulises, recognizing immediately Willems's tactic, decided to coax the man into a discussion of himself rather than force one about Isabel.

It was July, the vacation now postponed until August, when Ulises, lighting a Maduro, asked, What about your mother?

She was Portuguese, Willems said. Her name was Rute. She came from a fishing village not far from Coimbra, somewhere at the mouth of the Mondego River. Her father was a merchant, and they came to the Caribbean for the same reasons most did: for easy wealth. They traded mostly sugar. My mother met my father in Cuba, where he was recruiting workers. He took her to Amsterdam for the first two years of their marriage so he could close the company offices in Bovenkerk. They were relocating the whole enterprise to Gonaïves. They had me during that period.

I like the taste of this one, Ulises said. Sweet, I think.

Willems puffed and explained, The leaves are from the base of the stalk, so it's milder. You have my taste in cigars, which is for soft.

Where is your mother now?

She passed away a few years after my father started making cigarettes. Cholera followed us between farms, and it tracked her down. Don't exhale so quickly. Take smaller breaths, and let the smoke rise into your sinuses.

What was she like? Ulises asked.

She was not handsome—neither was my father—but she was sweet and firm, like a fisherman's kid, and she could cook.

Can you bring a darker one next time?

All right, said Willems.

Ulises took a small breath and let the smoke filter through his nose. Did she share your father's fears?

No, Willems said, but she respected them. Still, she told me not to be afraid. I think now she was much stronger than I often gave her credit for.

She never thought your father was crazy?

A little, Willems said. It would have been hard to deny his paranoia. But her caution manifested itself in smaller actions.

Willems shook the ash from his cigar into a coffee mug on the kitchen table.

For instance, he said, she never smoked my father's cigarettes. In fact, she stole leaves openly from his fields and chewed them rather than rolling them. For his sake she wanted to spit souls back into the ground where they belonged.

She loved your father very much, Ulises said.

They were perfect together, Willems said, and then the Dutchman began to cry. He said, Your mother and I are not the same, though. I think I'm losing her already.

She's hurt by Isabel's decision, is all, Ulises offered.

I'm afraid your sister only intensifies a dark spot between us. I can't seem to fill it.

She loves you, Ulises said.

Only a part of her does, Willems answered, wiping his face. The other part I've never had much of a hold on. Don't you feel the same about your sister? She's two people; one you know and possess, and the other, which is the greater part, pulls her away from you.

I suppose you're right.

You should visit her, Willems said, snuffing out the rest of his cigar, adding, Sooner than later.

It was true; Ulises had yet to visit Isabel at the convent, and that night, with the cigar's nicotine buzzing through his skull as he slept, he dreamt of Willems in a field crawling away from Soledad, as if in retreat, a weak smile on his face. Ulises awoke thinking the dream a premonition. The Dutchman's words the night before were not just sad but were also a warning, something to do with cowardice and negligence.

Ulises decided he would visit Isabel.

The convent was cheerless and unnecessarily austere, like a museum, with a benchless cloister and brittle grass fading to brown. Ulises met Isabel in a small study, and she wore a sweater Soledad had knit, a dense wool top something like military attire.

Where have you been? she asked him. Her voice was unusually soft; she was almost whispering.

It's been hard coming here, Ulises told her. The press was outside for the first few weeks, and then Henri put me in charge of some fields. I'm also in charge of a group of laborers now.

You've grown.

Ulises looked at his arms. Summer in Connecticut was muggy: Ulises wore a loose undershirt and some canvas shorts, and the gray cotton was tight across his chest. I've been outside, he said.

I've been in here, Isabel told him.

What you wanted. Your speech brought this on, and, considering what you told me last year, this seems to be more of the same. Couldn't you have waited? Done this properly? You could have gotten in later just the same and kept Ma from hurting so badly.

I wasn't doing the right work, Isabel said. It was wasteful, and people were suffering when I could have helped.

How do you help the dying? They are dying. They're not going to get any better. They have families to sit by their beds.

Some do, Isabel said. A lot of them don't. But you're right. They're dying, which is why doctors or nurses can't help. They need a person to help them pass.

And that's your calling?

No, the calling was Ma that night in November when we couldn't sleep and stood around in the kitchen listening to her and Henri.

You don't have to remind me, he told her. But I can't imagine God speaking to you through Ma's moaning.

That's not how it works, at least, not for me. You think it's some message that gets sent, but it's not words. It's just a sound, and when you hear it, you can't unhear it. It stays with you and lives between your ears, and eventually you figure out how to make the noise go away by *doing* something. You do something, and the noise finally stops. I heard Ma in my head for months, and then when I sat next to that dying boy, I couldn't hear her anymore. It went away, and I was cold and then hot, but the sound was gone, and I could finally hear other things again.

You were sick, Ulises said. You were soaked from helping the boy, and an infection got into your lungs. It gave you a fever, and you sweated through some hallucinations.

I've been told that before, Isabel said.

They went for a walk, but only around the cloister and its lawn. Isabel told Ulises that she had been happy at the convent, but she did miss Sunday dinners at home. She was not allowed to visit with any sick or dying. The hospital had quietly asked her to resign her volunteer post and was undertaking an investigation to ensure that each patient Isabel had visited had died of natural causes. On occasion an ailing person came to her, though none had died at the convent with Isabel at his or her side. Instead, she was now working with deaf children, learning how to sign.

So, has the noise returned? Ulises asked. Can you hear Ma again?

No, she said, it hasn't returned.

You've gotten your fix, then.

Isabel smiled at him, and for a moment she looked like the older twin, partly because of the perfunctory clothing and partly because when she smiled, she seemed to know something that he did not, or, at least, she believed she did. Ulises thought that there was no real difference between the two, the product of both being a sense of confidence, and he suffered a pang of envy, because Isabel was moving in a strange and destructive direction but along a path that was clear nonetheless. She followed it recklessly, without apology.

The noise was a warning, Isabel said. I know that now.

Of what?

Henri, she answered. Or something like Henri—the kind of man he is and where his energies go.

He grows tobacco, Ulises said, but his heart skipped as he remembered his dream from the night before. Henri rolls cigars and goes on walks with Ma.

And that's the extent of it. He lives only in this world.

Where else should he spend his time?

I couldn't say, but don't you find it sad for him to ignore what's happened?

What's happened? Ulises asked.

Ghosts, his sister said. Ghosts in his past. His father's past. His grandfather's past. The spirits of the slaves.

He's embarrassed by it, Ulises said. Family folklore, and you saw how sad he felt about his father, who *wouldn't* ignore the past. I'd stay away from it as well if I were Henri.

He's running from it, Isabel said. What's he doing in Connecticut? There's no Dutch embargo on Cuba. He can go down there whenever he wants.

There's a communist regime, Ulises said. That's what's down there. No money in that.

Maybe. But what about those ghosts? He pretends they don't exist, Isabel said.

What would you have him do? Hold a séance? Sacrifice a lamb at the start of every spring?

I think it's eating away at him, Isabel said. You told me once it made him better at his job, which is true, but I think that's because he's scared all the time. You know why he runs his hands through the soil and touches every seed he plants? Because he wants to make sure it's real. He wants to make sure there are no ghosts hiding in the sacks or any limbs growing up from the ground. He walks his fields every day to check for body parts, not ladybugs and grasshoppers. And I was doing the same. I was changing bedpans and tending to sheets.

I don't understand, Ulises said.

I was working with bodies when I should have been working with spirits. I was sinking into this world. I was growing tobacco and rolling cigars when I should have been lighting fields on fire and letting the spirits out. I spoke with the bishop about this—snuffing out the fire of the Holy Ghost by heating too many pots with it. I'd split my flame among smaller, pointless candles.

The bishop told you this?

Yes, she said.

He sounds indulgent, Ulises said. He sounds like the kind of man who saw a sick girl and didn't want to wound her with the truth.

He read to me from St. Theresa's diary. He said my brain works in a mystic fashion. We also spoke about Joan of Arc. The French thought she was crazy at first. I'm sure it's hard for you to understand. You should read St. John of the Cross. It will help.

I understand how far away you've moved, Ulises said, and he was being honest with her. I'm scared for you and what this means. Have you told this to Ma? If not, please don't. It might kill her. And that stuff about Henri is shit. I think you hate him. I think you hate how different he is from Papi, so it's easy to twist him into a villain.

I don't hate him, Isabel said. But I do pity him.

Ulises's visit with Isabel left him with an unbearable sadness. His sister, he believed, had bought in completely to her own self-delusion, and to support that delusion she was reinterpreting the world at hand, namely the motives and psyche of their mother's lover. Worrisome also were the names she'd thrown about on her and Ulises's walk, Joan of Arc the most troubling. The saint was not only touched by God, but also called to action, and Ulises could see nothing but struggle and pain for any young girl who might answer a similar call or, at least, think she was hearing one.

In his worry Ulises immersed himself in work, which was not a hard thing to do when one worked on a farm. The men he oversaw—a band of eight Texas Mexicans Willems had hired on a recent trip he took to Houston—moved quickly and needed new assignments constantly. In the morning they would replace faulty irrigation hosing, reinforce the weaker shading tents, fertilize whole fields by hand, and sift topsoil for rows out of rotation. By the afternoon they were hand-checking seed bags for crushed or split kernels, stitching small tears in the shading tarps with travel sewing kits, and repairing patchy fences along farm boundaries. There were days Ulises invented things, not necessary but often helpful things, for the men to do. They were relentless, and the crop was impeccable.

The oldest of the Mexicans was Orozco, and he was the one to show Ulises how to roll cigars, both the long and the short ones, and how to finish flat or with a tapered snout. During lunches, huddled beneath the shade of an oak grove abutting a Habano field, Orozco gave Ulises lessons. Ulises had noticed that the men were smoking foot-longs at almost every meal break. Of course, Orozco and the other men were filching here and there from the crop, but they showed Ulises that what they took were the weaker leaves, the ones chewed on by ladybugs or altogether worthless for Willems's Imperial stogies. They cured them on the eastern windowsills of their houses, drying out the fronds in the full heat of the morning sun. Eventually, they stacked the leaves on their shaded stoops to let them ferment in the dark.

By the start of August, when Henri and Soledad were at last scheduled to make their trip west, Ulises was smoking three cigars a day, two of a rustic quality with his men at work and one of exceptional craft every night with Willems. By the time he saw them off from the platform of a train station just east of Hartford proper, Ulises was in the habit of smoking a cigarillo with his breakfast coffee, rolling a longer blonde at the same time, chewing the blonde throughout the morning, smoking the mild cigar at lunch, and taking a much longer time with whatever Willems brought over that evening. Ulises was beginning to taste the differences among the leaves and not just between plants. Soon his tongue could tell him from what part of the stalk the filler came. If it was a vague, easy flavor, he knew the leaves were closer to the ground and away from the sun; if the filler left a syrupy impression on his palate, then the leaves were from the top of the plant and had absorbed an excess of light.

He also began to speak Spanish exclusively. With Willems absent, Ulises was left in charge of everything east of Hartford and south of the river: five hundred acres total. Willems's laborers were mostly Mexican, with a handful of Nicaraguans, and all of them preferred to take orders in Spanish. Willems's attempts at Spanish possessed a formal nuance he was unaware of, but the men responded favorably to Ulises's Cuban inflection. He slipped back into his native tongue without noticing, and the men grew fond of him.

It was during Soledad and Willems's vacation that Ulises forced himself to return to the convent.

Are you trying to hurt me? Isabel asked the moment she saw him.

What do you mean? he said.

You look just like Willems, she said. Your front teeth are yellow at the tips. Your hands are brown, but your face is white. You've got dirt under your fingernails. Are you checking for ghosts while he's gone?

Maybe this is my calling, Ulises said. Or maybe I can't get your voice out of my ears, and the only time it's quiet is when I'm tending to the rows out in the sun.

Isabel shook her head.

I could do worse, he said.

They were standing outside a classroom in a small building behind the chapel. Through an open door, Ulises could see a handful of young children sitting quietly at desks and gesturing to one another, which struck him as an odd silence amid the echoes from the other rooms, which were only divided by cheap metal partitions. One boy in particular was watching Ulises and Isabel from near a chalkboard and appeared to be signaling what he saw to a few of his peers.

What's that boy doing? Ulises asked.

Gossiping, said Isabel. The nuns aren't really allowed male visitors.

But you're not a nun.

I've begun the novitiate.

You're barely eighteen.

The Reverend Mother and I have spoken, Isabel said, and I've been allowed to skip forward because of circumstance.

What circumstance? Ulises asked. That you're supposedly trapped in here? That people are worried about a killer candy striper in Hartford?

My exceptional service, she said. The strength of my calling, which is palpable to anyone who cares to listen.

Isabel blushed, and Ulises could see that he'd upset her. He handed her the clothes his mother had instructed him to bring, a new ankle-length skirt and a blouse, one dark blue, the other hunter green, and both made from a lightweight cotton fabric ideal for the month of August.

I'm sorry, he said. But you seem to be leaving us all the time.

I'm compelled, she said, and she left him in the hallway. He watched her in the classroom for a moment and saw her hands flicker in response to the silent signals from the children. He left without saying good-bye.

In the fields the next day, Ulises asked Orozco about his sister's observations. Do you ever confuse me for Henri? he asked.

No, said Orozco. Willems never smokes in the fields. He also wears canvas pants instead of jeans. And your Spanish is much better. Willems's is classroom Spanish, but you can tell yours is from a place. You sound a bit like my cousin Simón, who grows bananas in Cuba.

But are there similarities between us? Ulises asked.

You both touch everything, though you more than him, I think. You should wear a baseball cap instead of that farmer's hat. Willems wears that, but he's an older man. You look funny in it. Also, you both clearly buy your boots from the same store.

Ulises looked down at his shoes, at the boots Willems had given him for Christmas. They were still in fairly good condition compared to Orozco's, which sagged everywhere.

Ulises got his mother on the phone.

Isabel is worse, he said.

The two lovers were in Oklahoma City and on their way to Phoenix. The trip was going fine, Soledad reported, but she could not sew or knit on the train because the vibrations were too strong. She had enjoyed the South for its architecture but was happy to pass through it quickly. No one travels by train anymore, for obvious reasons, she said, and I feel a bit stupid for not getting on a plane. I could be home by now. I should be visiting my daughter.

She asked Ulises, What's worse?

Isabel has taken steps toward vows, he said.

His mother sighed on the other end. How is that news? She's been taking vows all her life, self-imposed or otherwise. I'm surprised she even bothers with the formalities of the Church.

Her stay was supposed to be temporary. If she takes vows, she'll never come home.

Did she say that?

No, but we argued over it.

If you want to blame someone, Soledad said, then blame me. She's doing what I've allowed her to do.

It's fate to her, Ulises said. A calling.

I could have done more, Soledad said. Much more. I could have, at least, taught her to ask permission before doing things like this.

She's stubborn, like her father, he said.

Like her mother, Soledad sadly corrected. But then she said, I'm sorry. I shouldn't have left you there all alone. You're out there, and Isabel, even when she's right next to you, feels far away. I didn't think you'd get lonely. You have your work, the fields.

Isabel has her prayers. Her morning Mass. Her rosary beads.

Are you thinking of going, too? Is that what you're saying? Soledad asked.

Isabel and I are different people, Ulises said, but when you left her behind, you also left me.

I'm coming home soon. Then we can really talk. I don't doubt what you're telling me about her condition.

But?

But I'm tired. And I'm afraid of your sister. There are maybe threads left between her and me. I want them to grow in my absence. But any sort of push, and I think she'd just break off and float away, without a word. Besides, she's where she wants to be, and, thank God, I know exactly where that is. I know this is an indulgence, but that's what I mean when I say blame me. It's my indulgence. Can you forgive me this?

Yes, Ulises said.

Willems, when he got on the phone, wanted to know how the August crop was shaping up. The question was a sympathetic diversion. Still, Ulises told him in great detail more than the man expected to hear, down to the color of the leaves in certain rows. Ulises, without prompting, also made suggestions for wrappers and fillers, which impressed the Dutchman.

You're learning, Willems said.

My sister thinks I am turning into you.

Willems paused before saying, Not so bad?

Of course not, Ulises answered, and yet some pity echoed in his chest. Perhaps his sister had poisoned his view of Willems. Perhaps someday he would have trouble respecting the man, once they knew all the same things. Ulises asked Willems how he thought his mother was doing. Was the trip helping? Did she seem happier?

Sometimes, Willems said. If we see something beautiful out the train window, then yes. But we've left the South now, and the land is flat without trees. It's beautiful for some but not for your mother. I'm looking forward to the desert.

Ulises wanted to tell the man to *make* his mother happy, rather than hoping for pleasant scenery. Willems was simply waiting for Soledad to remember their love. Meanwhile, Ulises waited for Isabel to listen to reason. They were two men waiting for miracles. But what had they accomplished to believe that such miracles could occur?

Ulises confided in Orozco. The older Mexican had noticed that the youthful *guajiro* was, as August wore on, chewing the ends of his cigars more and more, like a dog gnawing on a bone. While rolling cigarillos at lunch, Ulises told Orozco who his sister was: the Death Torch of Hartford. He steeled himself for Orozco's response, expecting condescension, but the laborer only shook his head.

That's a wild thing, he said. I saw her picture in the paper. She looks like you. Makes me think she can't be half as mad as they say she is.

Orozco lit his cigarillo.

I have a crazy cousin named Chuy, he said. His father was an idiot cowhand from New Mexico. He tried to abort Chuy himself, but, of course, he botched it. He scraped Chuy's mother's womb with something, but he couldn't find the egg. When Chuy was born, he was retarded, which, of course, the mother thought had more to do with the fucked-up abortion than with the pink wine she always drank. Chuy doesn't look retarded, not really, but when people talk to him, they think he's nuts. But he's good for something. Whenever his mother loses her key ring or a book or an earring, Chuy's always the one to find it. He's like St. Anthony, the patron of missing shit. Most people call him crazy. But others—namely, his mother—think he's blessed.

Isabel isn't helping anyone, Ulises said.

What about those deaf kids? Anyway, that's not the point.

What is the point? Ulises asked. That she's insane and blessed all at once?

The point is that pretty much the two are the same.

Two weeks later Orozco brought Ulises a copy of the *Hartford Courant*. The headline was Hospital Confirms All Deaths Natural, and there was a supplementary interview with the archbishop, who was quoted as saying, Of course they were natural. We knew they were all along, and it's a shame that for three months we've had to shield a devout young woman from the media because of a few misconstrued statements. We're fortunate, however, that she's kept her faith and decided to pursue it further. I look forward to blessing her first vows myself in a few days' time. She's a marvelous Catholic.

Ulises picked up the phone immediately. If Isabel was going to take her vows in a few days' time, Soledad needed to return. But reaching his mother proved to be impossible: the hotel clerk in Phoenix informed him that Soledad and Henri were on a five-day rafting trip along the Colorado River. The clerk put Ulises in touch with the park patrol, but the only promise they could make was to deliver his urgent message if a gatekeeper should recognize his mother by her description. Ulises was certain no one would. He would have to go to the convent himself to bring his sister home.

At the convent, Isabel's response was predictably diminutive. Why bother? she said. Her voice was again oddly soft and tapering; it seemed to evaporate just beyond her teeth. There's no point in going back for just a few days. Quite frankly, I'm comfortable here. I have everything I need.

Don't say that to Ma, Ulises said. And what's this business about a few days? What happened to the trial?

It's finished.

Says who?

Mother Superior, Isabel said. And the archbishop.

He was in the paper today, talking about you, Ulises said. Have you met the man? He wants to hear your vows. I think he wants to make another spectacle of you.

He's visited once before, Isabel said, and, yes, you're probably right. So why let him?

It's the only way I can join the order right away. Isabel paused for a moment. Will you come to the ceremony? she asked.

You have to postpone it, Ulises said. Ma thinks you're here out of her neglect. She'll go under if you make these vows without her knowing.

She might try to stop me, Isabel said. She'd drag me home like a child.

You are a child.

But then we'd break apart completely. I'd have to leave her out of my life. Don't you think that would be worse? To be driven off by your daughter? Isn't that worse than still having some part of your child?

Ulises assumed she meant some part of the time, and he had to agree. He couldn't imagine his mother if Isabel told her to leave her alone for good. Ma is barely afloat now, he thought to himself. And to hear Isabel say those things?

For the next three days, Ulises tried the park patrol each morning and night. Yet by the fourth morning Soledad and Henri still could not be reached, so he dressed in a new white oxford shirt and headed to the church to see his sister make her temporary vows, which, after some years, she would reaffirm as final vows.

Kneeling before the altar, Isabel swore herself to a life of poverty, chastity, and obedience. Then she swore herself to a life of silence. The archbishop looked down at Isabel and crossed one pasty hand over her face, pronouncing the verdict *in the name of the Father, the Son, and the Holy Ghost*. She stood, and the archbishop placed a necklace, a cross on a chain, around her collar. Isabel bowed and faced the congregation as a willful mute. It was over.

Mortified, Ulises scrambled out of his pew, eyes fixed to the tiled floor so that he might not have to see his sister's restrained smile. At the door, on the way out, he blessed himself with holy water from the font. He did so out of habit, but the water was too cold for summer, like frozen rain, and it reminded him of how he'd stopped doing that a long time ago. He cursed himself under his breath, angry at the fact that some routines dwell in the subconscious. He pushed through the doors of the vestibule out into the wet August heat, full of questions:

Was his sister like him? Or was her unconscious aligned always with her outward movement? And why, he asked himself, did she want me to come?

Ulises was hurt, as if he'd been made to watch a loved one die. He wondered at Isabel's future, how the world would change—if it did change—when a person could no longer make a noise in it. He tried to recall the pitch of her last words, the vows, but all he could muster was a vague impression of forced air. She had breathed her last words.

Ulises considered the conversation he, not his sister, would have to have with Soledad. He could not imagine telling her the news over the phone—he pictured her out there in the Grand Canyon, dust under her fingernails and caking her eyelids, bedraggled and perfumed in her own dried sweat after several days under the sun. He imagined Soledad alone, hearing of her daughter's vows in the pine-smelling office of a park patrolman. Ulises saw his mother hanging up the phone and walking back out into the wilderness.

Then, for the first time, Ulises was terrified of being the messenger. When had he ever come to Soledad with good news? When had he ever brought her loving information? A stiff, happy wind in her sails? Maybe someday, maybe this coming day with this coming phone call, she would be unable to distinguish between her son and the collapse of her daughter. His voice would become synonymous with ruin.

At first, over the phone, Soledad ignored Ulises's attempts to discuss the hard facts of Isabel's vows. She spoke instead of an owl she and Henri had seen twice, across two consecutive days, stalking the riverbank for desert rats. The owl, she said, was an utterly noiseless bird; the rats made more sound drinking from the river. The owl took a snake on the second day, and I thought the creature would snap at the talons, she said, but the owl had his claws at exactly the right spot, just behind the skull and curled around the throat. I think they keep their prey alive until the final moment. They want a hot meal. I've never seen anything like it.

Your daughter, Ulises said—and the distance was necessary then—has taken a vow of silence. It's a temporary vow, I think, and so it might not last, but for now she's promised God not to say a word. She didn't tell me ahead of time, or else I would have tried to stop her.

Soledad was silent for a minute. It would have been worthless, she said. Ulises could not tell if she meant his efforts would have been too little or if she meant Isabel's will would have been too much. She didn't clarify.

We're coming back, she said.

Soledad returned to Hartford on a 747 direct from Phoenix and immediately laid siege to the Church. The first assault was an extensive letter campaign to the bishop, the archbishop, the cardinal, and eventually the Pope, each missive an indictment of the patriarchy of the institution, older authorities allowing the youth to wager their lives when they were too young to truly know any better. Soledad set her Smith Corona on a sewing table near the Sumatra plant that was Willems's first gift to her—despite Henri's insistence, Soledad had never moved the weed outside; she'd grown accustomed to the shades of green light the broad leaves cast across the living room during the day—and tested the durability of her ink ribbon. In the persistent, percussive hammering of her keystrokes, Ulises detected the same violent determination that had taken them from Cuba. Day and night she was a storm, amassing from county-courthouse testimony not only precedents for parent-guardian privilege, but also rulings against the Church in its instruction and guidance of its underage parishioners. Most impressive, she threatened to dismantle the convent itself, nun by nun, if the parish did not release her child immediately.

The bishop's response was quick: he would meet with her. But the higher echelons of the Catholic institution ignored her entirely.

Ulises watched all this alongside Willems, who seemed content to simply sidestep Soledad's whirlwind and follow closely behind with encouraging applause. They smoked cigars again in the kitchen, though now with the sound of his mother typing nearby. At first Ulises was overjoyed to see Soledad return with such gusto. It had been a little more than a year since Isabel's first confession of absolute faith, and finally Soledad was doing something about all the ensuing nonsense. However, smoking a Chico Dulce with Willems, he felt a familiar jealousy, the same envy creeping up his spine that had poked at his brain and his heart when Isabel revealed her promise to Uxbal. Here was the mother, now, devoting her life again to the daughter. Before, it had been Ulises's life as well, the ransom for escape. He recalled the story of the prodigal son. Suddenly, he wished he'd been a difficult child, a more dangerous type of human.

Ulises heard Soledad snatch another page from the Smith Corona.

For the first time in a long time, he reconsidered his position on fate. He looked at Willems, who wistfully stared through the kitchen door at Soledad. His pale face sagged, and he looked like a man who'd lost the horizon, who was adrift and hadn't touched another body in a long time. Ulises agreed finally with Isabel: he and the Dutchman were probably the same—two finless fish, helpless in his mother and sister's relentless tide.

Actually, Henri's last good lay had occurred at dusk on the morning that Soledad had first seen the owl skimming the Colorado River for rodents. They'd not been able to fuck on the train because of a cabin light that had no switch and was always on; Soledad had been embarrassed by their silhouettes against the window shade. In Phoenix, the hotel mattress had been excessive, and they'd slept so deeply, they didn't dream. On the river, their guide, a plump military vet from California, was fond of sitting by the fire all night, which meant that the game of shadows playing across the canvas walls of their tent had kept

Soledad awake and worried for her daughter; Isabel was becoming a shadow, in Soledad's mind, of some girl she once knew.

On their third night on the Colorado, however, the guide went to bed early, suffering from a bit of dehydration, and so the fire died, giving Willems and Soledad the chance to make up for lost time. They rushed through once and fell asleep, but before sunrise, which is a long, late affair at the bottom of a canyon, Soledad felt Willems behind her, and they inched slowly into each other. The air by the water was humid, and when they finished, Soledad was slick with the perspiration of two bodies and incredibly thirsty. She slid from their sleeping bag and exited the tent to drink from the portable cooler, and in the twilight before dawn she saw what she thought was a bat. She crept closer to the water. The creature was much larger than a bat and seemed not to disturb the air in the slightest bit. It was an owl! It was beautiful, and it made Soledad cry out in joy to have seen such a thing. Frightened by her sound, the bird soared back up toward the canyon's rim before disappearing into a crevasse.

She thought of nothing else the entire day. Distracted by her vision, she could not focus the following night when again the guide went to bed early and Willems rolled into her. Soledad silently pushed him aside and studied her watch until she was sure the sky was halfway black and halfway blue. She was rewarded for her diligence in the very early morning. The owl reappeared, this time to steal a snake from the river, water dripping from the tail.

The final days of the trip the guide was feeling better, and Soledad apologized for ignoring Willems. She thanked him also for taking her to the canyon, and she told him that she'd been rejuvenated by the trip. Before leaving the park, she kissed him at an overlook near the southern rim, where they could see vultures in the distance. But it was a strange kiss, because it was bare, something she was certain they both realized. Soledad had thought herself resuscitated, not emptied out. She let the notion pass as they drove back to Phoenix, which was easy, because she had the owl on her mind, the sight of the bird becoming an object of meditation as she traveled.

Back home, she made a metaphor of what she'd seen, giving weight to the empty kiss and the mute hunter. She could sense an allegory coming to life as her fingers bit at the keys of the Smith Corona: she was the captured snake, and the owl was, of course, her silent daughter. At the Grand Canyon she'd not been restored, but reborn, and if she was not careful here—if she was not vigilant—her life would be carried away by the soundless creature she'd once loved. The Grand Canyon did not give her the strength to return home but the strength for one last strike, and it had to be a good one, teeth flared and jaws open, so that her daughter might release her grip.

But this did not at all explain the empty kiss, except that maybe Soledad no longer had the strength to love Willems and her daughter all at once. He was left behind on the riverbank. It was a sad parting, she thought. She opened a new ream of paper alongside the typewriter. But it could not be helped. It was likely only temporary, and at the moment Soledad had no time for apologies. Willems could stay as long as he could stand it, but she was unidirectional, and she rattled down the warpath.

In the light of the church vestibule, Isabel struck Soledad as strange in appearance. The habit she wore was white for her preliminary phase, cupping her chin and rounding her forehead in a way that made her large brown eyes appear even larger.

Here is your daughter, the bishop said to Soledad, as if she'd forgotten the face.

Soledad handed to the bishop a thick manila envelope, which he seemed to expect and placed on a table next to a bowl of holy water.

You should familiarize yourself with the contents, Soledad said. There are a series of court dates already set for initial hearings, which

I have no doubt will lead to a trial. The district attorney has all the same materials. You may request extra copies if you'd like.

You can, of course, take her, the bishop said. But I don't think this is really necessary. The Church offers up its sacraments, and it's a person who chooses to take part in them. No one has forced these vows on her, just as no one forces the body and blood of Christ into mouths on Sunday.

Soledad felt an angry heat rise in her. According to doctrine, she said, a person dies and goes to hell if they don't cannibalize the Christ. A form of coercion, in my opinion.

The bishop nodded and then turned to Isabel. You can come back whenever you like. The doors are always open.

Soledad did not speak to her daughter, simply took her by the arm and led her to the car and then home. She'd not wanted to argue with the girl at the steps of the altar or under the influence of the cloister walls. She'd requested an office meeting solely for some semblance of neutral territory, but the bishop, not affording her even that, gave her no choice but to drag Isabel back to the house and confront her in the place she'd abandoned.

Back at the house and in the living room, Isabel remained silent. Ulises listened to his mother's urging from the kitchen, occasionally cracking the door to watch. He understood that in the girl's mind she *could not* speak, bound as she was to the Highest Being. Instead, she provided Soledad with a note she'd written beforehand, but the only words written on the tiny slip were *Please, Mother.*

How are you going to exist in the world? Soledad asked. How are you going to communicate with people? They'll think you're a mute charity case, a dumb girl because you can't speak. What about school? I don't understand how you can even pray.

But then Soledad moved into her own pain, her own guilt, holding out her hands the entire time as if the daughter could take back the failures of the mother.

Can't you speak for just a few minutes? Just long enough to explain to me why? Are you sick of talking? Were you not being heard? Did I not listen?

Isabel's large eyes widened in response to Soledad's desperation, but the girl's lips remained shut. Eventually, she tried to sign for her mother as way of explanation or, perhaps, apology.

Hot and frustrated and growing hoarse, Soledad slapped at the hands, screaming. My daughter is not an idiot mute! Slapping her once gave her permission to slap her again. Talk! Soledad shouted. Talk! She slapped Isabel on the hands until the girl put them behind her back, and then she slapped the girl twice across the face, the second time hard enough that Isabel's lip split. Finally her mouth opened, but only wide enough for her tongue to lick at the blood. Soledad stepped back, and the habit framed her violence nicely, an oval face dissolving into a rounded jaw, a red seam splitting the chin into halves.

Soledad had lost, and she knew it. She slipped to her knees, and Ulises watched as his mother begged forgiveness from his sister. Soledad cried, and Isabel ran her fingers, her delicate and expressive fingers, through her mother's hair. For Ulises, it was the final tilt of all things gone askew, the mother kneeling before the child, seeking redemption.

Isabel stayed at the house that night for the last time. She and Soledad sat quietly next to each other on the couch in the living room without talking. Eventually, Soledad handed her daughter one of her stenographer's pads. She asked questions and waited patiently for written answers, listening to the pen on the paper, a switch dragged through sand. She found herself wishing that she'd taught her children the art of shorthand when she first learned it, but she could not have imagined a need for it then.

Over the course of the night and well into dawn, Isabel satisfied her mother's curiosity: yes, the convent was a wonderful and spiritual place to live; in fact, it took only a week for silence to feel natural; no, it was not because of her mother that she'd made the vow of silence; yes, she wanted to continue her work with the deaf children of Hartford; yes, she was happy. As happy as she had ever been.

And by the time the sun rose and Ulises was searching out his boots for another day in the fields—his work hours would lessen soon, the summer almost finished, the harvests coming in, and the university reopening after Labor Day—Soledad had begun to anticipate her daughter's responses, had begun to only ask yes or no questions, attributing emotion and feeling to the nodding or shaking by paying close attention to her daughter's face. Soledad, melancholic though determined, seemed to make up for five years of unchecked freedom and thin vigilance by learning to communicate with her daughter in just one night. Words no longer clouded the space between them, and it was the closest they had ever been to understanding each other.

Reading faces became their secret language. Soledad, in the presence of her mute, holy daughter, became comfortable with silence, and Isabel learned to decipher her mother's twitching lips. They communicated constantly in the presence of the other: during Sunday dinners, during the walks Soledad and Isabel took together, often holding hands, and during the rare occasions when Isabel would sit and watch her mother sew late into Sunday night. The unnoticed consequence of their communion, however, was a melancholic haze that shrouded the whole house when Isabel was away. In between visits Soledad preferred absolute silence, creating a daily loneliness in which she could relive the unspoken conversations she'd had with her daughter.

Ulises, busy with school but not wanting to lose a grip on his field work, was not home enough to break the long spells of noiselessness. Willems was also away, traveling throughout the Caribbean and Asia, looking to replenish his stock with newer, stronger, more robust plants. By the start of October, two months after Isabel took her vows, the Encarnación household was as solemn as a funeral parlor, and its members passed through its doors as spirits between headstones.

In truth, the only outward appearance of life at the time was to be found in Ulises's body, which was undergoing another growth spurt so great, it seemed fueled by his mounting envy. He was jealous of Isabel, of the new attention his mother put upon her, and he could say nothing to his mother that would pull her fully out of the quiet in which she found refuge. So his limbs and his torso—perhaps feeling the void of love with greater sensitivity and urgency—responded with a swelling and lengthening that should have garnered the young man more notice. He wanted to be seen. Following Soledad and Isabel's reunion, he sprouted five more inches and added two more stones, bringing him to six-foot-seven and 260 pounds. He was not monstrous, but he'd started feeling cramped inside the quaint New England home. It got to the point where he could not sit comfortably at any of the rickety kitchen chairs long enough to even smoke a cigar. So, rather than lumbering about the house and disturbing the peace, he decided to dedicate his bulk to the tobacco fields.

To escape the diminishing quarters, Ulises arrived at the fields every day one minute after sunrise, worked till noon, went to the university for late-day classes, and returned to the fields to labor until dark. Consequently, he made no friends at school, but he was a local figure of interest, known not only as the brother of the Death Torch, but also by a nickname of his own. With his large head and wide mouth, he smoked tiny cigarillos, which all but disappeared between his enormous lips, such that he appeared to breath fire naturally, exhaling blue smoke like a dragon. The classics professors, who considered him an exceptional student, endearingly referred to him as the Titan.

In the fields he went about his tasks with obsessive perfectionism. In early September, he had replaced all the glass in three greenhouses by hand; a month later, he'd begun sifting rocks from the soil with a portable, handmade, grated trench bucket; and one month after that, he was rebuilding entire shading structures on his own. It was November then. Only a few men were kept on during winter's cold months—Ulises made sure one was Orozco—so he often worked in isolation.

Like his mother, Ulises became accustomed to the quiet, though the quiet was much different in a field, where one still heard the sounds of the smaller creatures, a murmur often lost under the hacking of shovels and blades. Ulises dwelled on the spirits Willems worried might be trapped in his tobacco. Though the idea frightened the Dutchman, it comforted Ulises, and he imagined a sense of camaraderie between him and the handful of ghosts he began to believe were left behind with each harvest.

Yet ghosts are of little use in the physical world, and Ulises learned this the day a shading tent collapsed on him. Walking the rows in gargantuan strides, he tapped a hammer against the corner braces of every tent he passed, listening for the hollow sound of a two-by-four gone south of sturdy or the creak of braces about to give way. Being as strong as he was, however, Ulises struck the wood of one frame much too hard and much too fast. The hammer cracked an entire plank in half, and the whole apparatus came tumbling down. Two crossbeams butted him in the head, one knocking him out, one catching his skull at such an angle as to carve an eight-inch gash into his scalp, from which he bled profusely. Ulises half awoke sometime later to a figure tugging on his arm, and he was alarmed at the sight of an angel, who, he feared, was trying to lift him from Earth and carry him toward death.

In reality it was Orozco, who wrapped Ulises's body in fallen tarps to keep it warm as he went for help. Orozco had been working in an adjacent field and saw a gap in the row of shading tents, ultimately finding Ulises unconscious in the soil. What Ulises believed were angel's wings were white canvas tarps, and the confusion produced in him a longing for his sister, an affection he'd not felt since her silencing. For all her worth as a would-be nun and possible aide to the archangel, where was she at the hour of his death? If he was to slip back into the earth, why wasn't she the one to shepherd him?

Ulises's injuries, a cranial laceration and a minor concussion, required bed rest and thirty-one stitches. But ten hours after his accident, Ulises also developed a fever, and the doctors began a series of intravenous antibiotics in case something from the soil had seeped into his blood. For the concussion, he was kept awake for the first thirty hours of his hospital stay, a time during which two nurses cut his hair and then shaved his head so that the ER surgeon might sew back together his bifurcated scalp.

When all was said and done, he appeared to have a tremendous vein snaking across his skull through which all the blood flowed into his brain. The surgeon was blunt during follow-up: You're going to have a scar, and you won't grow hair there anymore. Ulises reached up to touch his head, but the surgeon wouldn't let him.

Soledad was at his side immediately, and he shifted in and out of consciousness to find her constantly praying at the foot of his bed. She'd recently begun attending Mass again in order to see Isabel more often. They met neither before nor after the service; Soledad went only to witness the vision of her daughter, strong and Catholic, and to confirm the supposed contentment of her calling. It turned out that old habits were resurrected easily: Soledad recently had been calling out the Lord's name with greater and greater regularity. And, much as with her work at the courthouse, Soledad did nothing halfheartedly. To see her pray again was to see a blinded pianist remember all the keys by touch and rediscover the joy of Chopin. In prayer, she was as still as an icon, but the air around her vibrated as if her supplication could not exist without disturbing the world.

Ulises, under medication and not yet forty hours out of trauma, saw not his mother prostrate at the foot of his wide hospital bed, but instead hallucinated his sister sometime in the future, looking firmly into the weakness of his human form and responding with an equal force of faith and certainty, the arrogance of her prayer almost ceding his body to death, knowing it would claim something greater from the resulting dust.

It was only on the third day after the accident that Ulises regained his sense of time and place. By then, Isabel had visited him twice while he was unconscious. The first time, she startled the nurses who saw and remembered her, but they relaxed once they learned that the brother of the Death Torch was in the hospital, assuming that if she took a life, at least it would just be one and just one of her own. On this third visit, she'd brought to the hospital a small band of deaf performers. They were, apparently, Isabel's prodigies, and since October she'd converted her deaf service into deafness training, all her children being transformed from a strange, disharmonious choir into something like a military unit she dispatched throughout Hartford and across western Connecticut. Of course, they could not hear their own moaning, coughing, farting, slurping, sneezing, et cetera. What she taught them specifically was how to sign the words and lyrics of various religious plays and hymns, even some Christian operas from the eighteenth century.

More amazing, Isabel had taught her children—despite their inability to hear themselves—how to be quiet, absolutely quiet, as if in an attempt to merge the world of their deafness with the physical world around them. The effect was so striking that the children, when they visited nursing homes, high school auditoriums, hospitals, and once a prison, managed to bring audiences into their silent universe rather than entering themselves into the ruckus of life.

At the foot of Ulises's hospital bed that day, they lined up in two rows of four, a rush of noiselessness entering the room with their silent, cloudlike steps and the airy gestures of their muted hands. On a portable stereo Isabel inserted a cassette tape and pushed Play. But Ulises quickly lost track of the operatic music from *The Road to Gethsemane,* entranced as he was by the flawless synchronicity of the children's hands. When they finished, he was too astounded to clap but shouted, ¡*Gracias!* Spanish had returned to him more quickly than English. Isabel shuffled the choir back into the hallway.

Alone, his sister handed him a note. It said that her work was taking her to Guatemala, where the deaf had little public charity to support them. Because she could speak Spanish, she was going to help establish a school funded by the Church, and she was leaving within the month.

Why you? Ulises asked. You're still brand-new at teaching.

His sister removed a stenographer's pad from the large pocket at the side of her initiate's habit and began to write. *It's time for my service to take me outside the convent, but no one in the city will have me. I'm still the Death Torch to too many people here. The bishop says it takes longer to forget the moments that scare us than the experiences that enrich us. I need to go somewhere I'm not known.*

So you have to leave the country? Ulises asked. Will we ever see you again?

I don't intend to make Guatemala my home.

Have you told Ma?

She's praying on it.

You've drawn her back in. You could stay.

Isabel smiled quickly, and Ulises acknowledged to himself the weakness of his suggestion, the way in which he, too, was learning to accept her decisions without much friction or, at least, without an abundance of resentment.

Perhaps in gratitude for the brevity of his countermeasures, Isabel offered Ulises another note, this one typed out ahead of time, the sum of it confessing to her brother that her silence was a new calling, another sound she was responding to—namely, her own voice. The note described the high, painful pitch that resonated in her head every time she spoke at length. It told how during Mass Isabel eventually had had to whisper the *Our Father* just to make it through, and how the tone of her throat caused her stomach to turn if by accident she stubbed her toe and had to cry out. She said the noise was worse than the echo of her mother's moans, and only after a day of complete silence did the clatter in her brain subside.

Ulises was surprised to think his sister might fear something—

anything, really—considering her faith, and the realization softened greatly the blow of her imminent departure, which, if he understood her correctly, was not just another act of religious devotion but was also essential to her endurance. But he remained unalarmed, likely a result of the morphine, and he considered for once that the situation might truly be out of Isabel's hands, which meant he might believe in God or God's plan. But that was nonsense. The drugs are keeping me sedated, Ulises told himself, and he folded the note in his hands and looked at his sister, who scribbled something else onto her pad and held it up for him to see: *You're too tall for this bed.*

Willems arrived at the hospital by the middle of the week, and he brought with him a smattering of the seeds he'd gathered while abroad. He stormed the hospital flustered and in a sort of whirlwind, worried more so than the doctors that Ulises's fever was a precursor to death or insanity; the Dutchman's father, fearing always his own father's legacy, fretted over the spread of bacteria from one body part to the other, thinking eventually that the grandfather's mental instability had derived from migrating molecules of cholera that had somehow managed the journey from the small intestine to the brain. Willems, again unable to fully ignore the superstitions of his patriarchy, stayed at Ulises's side for two full days, asking the dazed patient to evaluate and write reports on the seeds he'd brought back from his travels. The doctors, Willems said, know diseases from textbooks, but there are simpler ways to diagnose them: decreased cognitive function was a sign of bacteria in the brain.

For forty-eight hours Willems diligently studied the curve of Ulises's penmanship and the clarity of his sentences, searching for any sign of rational decline. None came, and in addition to relief—Willems could not imagine a world in which his lover's son died because of an accident in his fields, some residual effect of his grandfather's calamity—

he felt an unexpected pleasure in the reports Ulises provided. They were beyond detailed, and they included a sensory experience of the seeds that rivaled culinary reviews he'd read in the *Hartford Courant*. Ulises's reports also drew upon his Latin training, using scientific nomenclature for certain plants and strains, which gave authority to his judgments. The accounts were also speculative at times, and these were the Dutchman's favorite parts, for Ulises would conjecture the conditions under which the seeds had been cultivated, going so far as to guess the climate of their upbringing and the particular wetness of the season in which they were formed. The guesses were part myth, part horticulture, and Willems, besides being certain that the boy's mind was sound, was also convinced he'd discovered another layer to Ulises's natural talent and passion for tobacco cultivation. In a fit of pride, he even mailed a few pages to an old acquaintance, an associate editor at the trade magazine *Leaf and Fire*.

The fever subsided not long after Willems's visit, and Ulises was sent home on the seventh day after the accident. He was told to wait two more weeks, the time remaining until Isabel's departure, before returning to school and work, and he spent those days watching Soledad finish what sewing projects she could for her daughter. Isabel was not around, having decided to fast and pray in seclusion for the remaining days leading up to her trip. Ulises couldn't be certain, but he felt again that he'd grown while asleep at the hospital, his body taking the mandatory rest as an opportunity to further expand itself, and at home he had to stoop through doorways to pass between rooms. His legs no longer fit beneath the kitchen table, and he had to take all his meals in the living room, where he could stretch out along the couch. He and Willems removed half the furniture from his bedroom—an armoire, a bedside table, and a student's desk—so that a new bed, an eight-foot-long modified king-size, could be brought in.

And because his clothes no longer fit, Ulises continued to wear the few oversize hospital gowns he'd brought home with him, which meant he never left the house and constantly nagged Soledad for specific foods (sandwich bologna, not roast beef), drinks (two-percent milk, not cream), and books (not the Edison translation of *The Eclogues* but the Rinhhauser). He was quickly a cranky, bent-over, ill-tempered convalescent, and when Soledad mentioned this to Willems—He thunders around the house like a bull, and he startles me, he's so damn big these days—the Dutchman brought to the house more seeds, and then fresh leaves, nascent stalks, and new cigars, some from the old farms, some from upstarts, for the patient to evaluate.

My friend loved the pages I sent, Willems told Ulises. A few more and he said he would publish your stuff as an article in his magazine. Something like a futures report.

Borrowing his mother's Smith Corona, Ulises spent the next twelve days emptying himself onto the page. At the hospital, writing had been a task, an effort in recall and scrutiny. Yet at home, Ulises found it fluid and unconscious. He labored at the keyboard continually, which helped him pass the days of unbearable waiting—it helped Soledad as well, the noise meaning she always knew where in the house he was—and when he went to bed at night, he had no trouble sleeping, as if his mind had run a long, winding course that afternoon and had no energy for dreams.

As he wrote closer and closer to the Monday Isabel would leave, he began to notice the same lightness of the mind he felt at night entering his limbs and muscles during the day. It was not a feeling of weakness or exhaustion, and what exactly overcame him he could not say, but the more he wrote, the less inclined he felt to return to the tobacco fields. He understood that he would, of course, go back to work in a short while, but the passion for digging trenches and carefully counting seeds was waning, and in reality that did not bother him. In the mirror he now saw a different sort of person than he'd been. He'd begun to think of himself as a man when in the hospital he found the patient's gown too small to close completely in the back, and a nurse

blushed at his walking, ass on display, to the bathroom without realizing it; she'd smothered a laugh, and he'd known why immediately
but was not ashamed. He was a man larger than expected, a bald man
because to grow out his hair looked ridiculous along the sides of the
wound, and, most strange, a man empty in the eyes. Ulises's pupils had
somehow attained a particular leanness to their black color, a thinning
of the ink toward the center that troubled and intrigued him. This,
he knew, was not an illusion, something only he could see through
his knocked skull, since sometimes Soledad would look into his face
and walk away breathless. She would say to Willems, It's like looking
into a cow's eyes, or the eyes of a fish. We should take him back to the
hospital for an MRI.

And then came the day they had all awaited: the final family dinner,
when Isabel came to the house and broke her fast. It was a Sunday
evening, and by then Ulises had written almost two hundred pages.
The articles were neither connected always nor suited for publication
as a book, but it was a magnum opus of tobacco wisdom and cigar
science that stunned Willems and, in the end, hollowed out Ulises
entirely. He wondered, after a quiet good-bye from his sister and the
sobbing of his mother, if this was what Isabel felt when she'd thought
the direction of her life had gone askew, if this feeling of knowing the
world so absolutely—he knew nothing as well as tobacco and cigars—
but without any passion was what drove her into silent pursuit of a
firmer Providence.

Meanwhile, Henri's editor friend published fifty of Ulises's pages
in *Leaf and Fire* and sent the rest to other trade magazines—*Tobacco
Connoisseur, Cigar Aficionado, A Fumar, Seed and Plant, Fuego del
Mano*. After his follow-up with the ER surgeon, Ulises still hadn't
gone back to the fields, and he stopped smoking altogether, though he

did return to school after purchasing an entirely new wardrobe. With his sister gone, his mother at work, and Willems careful not to push, Ulises spent most of his days locked in his room reading his books for class. For the fall he was enrolled in composition, introductory Greek, and two sections of Latin, one a linguistics course and the other a literature course. He ignored his science and composition texts but read, with the slow eye of a monk translating the New Testament, *Wheelock's Latin, Ancient Greek Language, Horace: A Legamus Reader, The Works of Ovid, Homeric Greek,* and Virgil's *The Aeneid.*

The surgeon had told him he was fine. He'd said the stitches would come out soon, in about three more weeks. Yet Ulises felt he'd entered a period of waiting that was not connected to his body. He was not depressed or sad or without appetite, but he was without agency. He was a stone, he felt, at the top of a hill, but there was nothing, somehow nothing, to nudge him down into the valley. So he sank into his luxurious new mattress, read his Latin texts, and waited for another life to come.

Waiting, however, was not just Ulises's plight. It was a disease Soledad also embraced, though the life she waited on was simply in another country, and all the mother wished for was Isabel's safe return; on bolder nights she even prayed for the return of her daughter's voice. But in the way a congregation of diseased people makes a colony from isolated illnesses, the Encarnación household resumed its melancholic state through the combined apprehensiveness of its inhabitants. The anticipations of mother and son, vague and indefinite, rolled into one, and the house pulsed with their uncertainties. It was as quiet as it had ever been, and nothing grew in that silence, and Willems, when visiting, often felt in the air and the woodwork a stagnancy akin to the inert soil of an overused acre. The daughter gone was like the sun dropped from the sky; but, no, it was more than that. Seeing the same listlessness in Ulises, Willems felt that something greater pressed down on the remaining Encarnacións, and, unlike the previous hush, this particular noiselessness was, perhaps, the precursor to some hellish weather rather than the denouement of a terrific, passing storm.

The letter, written in Cuban, read,

> Dear Ulises Encarnación, descendant of the island's
> east, my estranged son, and author of the article
> The Present State of Our Seeds This Season,
>
> They used to grow tobacco in the hills south of Buey Arriba,
> but the land is now a national forest and closed to agriculture.
> Still, Europeans come—Western Europeans mostly—
> because they think some plants remained untouched in
> the forest, growing in the shade, forgotten to all except the
> adventurous. There is a myth that the hills just south harbor
> the secret tobacco of Cuba that never leaves the island and
> that it is the purest and most delightful of any leaf ever
> grown. The Germans and the Dutch come most frequently,
> and it was a German carrying in his pocket a glossy magazine
> that bore your article. It was beautifully written, and I
> wonder if our Sundays at church—Do you remember that
> rickety packinghouse? It remains to this day—had some
> part in the fluidity of your language. Gospels rarely sound
> so cohesive, but your report on the recent world crop was
> enchanting. Should I take some pride in your talents for
> farming? I've been eating tomatoes since you left, which is to
> say, I miss you and your mother and your sister very much.
> The contributors' notes at the back of the magazine didn't say
> much, and what is New England? I can't imagine my family
> there, and I want to know much more than just what you are
> writing these days. Your mother let me go entirely, and I could

not keep track of you beyond Miami; did she think I would
reach up into Florida and drag you screaming back to Cuba?
The German left me your magazine in exchange for some
directions into the forest as well as a few pesetas. I bought
some fish with the money, and I spent the afternoon reading
and rereading your article while eating grouper. I'm not poor,
but I only have what I need. How did you get your hands on a
Flor de Cano up there in New England? How did you know
the draw of its smoke? Do you really find that leaf from the
Philippines as luxurious? That its vapor rises just as gingerly
as its Cuban counterpart? I can't imagine your mind. It's been
gone from here for so long, but the flavor of our dirt is stuck
on your tongue—that much I can tell. Would you write me
back? Will your mother allow? God bless you and your sister,
and God bless your pen.

—Uxbal

The letter had come from Orlando in a package from the chief editor of *Fuego del Mano,* in the third month of Isabel's absence. The
editor had received the note at his office and forwarded it, along with
other fan mail, to Willems in Hartford, and Henri eventually brought
it to the kitchen table on which Ulises read the words of his father's
hand. Besides the voice of Uxbal, which sounded musty and aching in
Ulises's head, what most surprised him was the efficacy of the Cuban
mail system and the fact that the letter had reached him at all. The
paper was still crisp, and the squat sentences seemed to have been
written just yesterday: Uxbal alive and breathing, as though he'd sent
a heartbeat through the post.

Soledad unconsciously crossed herself when she saw the letter's
signature. She'd come home from work and discovered the single
sheet on the kitchen table and Ulises alone in the living room.

He found us, she said.

He didn't, Ulises told her. One of my articles found him. Did you read the letter?

Yes, she said. It sounds just like him.

How?

Soledad sighed. He writes as though he were the mayor of Buey Arriba, as if he'd just shown a German dignitary around the town and taken him for drinks. He talks bigger than he is. That's your father. Does Henri know?

I don't think so, Ulises said, though he was the one who brought it over. In any case, you should tell him.

I will.

Did you think he was dead?

I didn't think anything.

Did you hope he was?

No, of course not, said Soledad, looking stricken.

Are you happy he is alive?

I suppose I am, she admitted. How do you feel?

Ulises looked at his mother. The same. The same as this morning. It doesn't mean anything that he's written, I don't think. Except that he's alive, I guess. For a long time I thought he was a ghost.

If you did, it was because of me.

Ulises shrugged. It doesn't matter.

Are you going to write him back?

No.

Should I throw it out?

Just leave it where it is for now.

She did, which was how Willems came to read the letter. He said it was not addressed to him, but Ulises gave him permission to read its contents when he saw Henri staring at the note while smoking in the kitchen. The letter seemed to have the greatest visible effect on the Dutchman, more so than on the mother or son, who were incapable of reacting to it, perhaps perpetuating the belief that Uxbal was gone—the vague *gone* of many possibilities: death, poverty, distance, estrangement, disinterest—by simply not handling it, not treating it as real.

The Dutchman, however, swelled in the presence of the letter, and Ulises sensed a heat blossoming inside the man. He was, after all, his mother's lover. Willems began to work furiously about the house, first warming and then condensing; he spent an afternoon trimming and repotting the absurdly tall tobacco plant in the living room and then spent the next week populating the house with smaller plants—some new tobacco leaves, a few diminutive shrubs, other flowers, everything tropical—as if trying to complement the original gift of the old Sumatra leaf with a miniature forest.

Yet as soon as all the available space in the house was colonized—every windowsill, every empty ceiling corner, every bare tabletop—Willems seemed to come to a complete halt. He went back to smoking cigars in the kitchen at night, but now with the lights off, which he claimed was soothing and reminded him of smoking in secret as a twelve-year-old on his grandfather's back porch in Haiti. Ulises joked with Soledad that her lover had been transformed into a cigar-store Indian, puffing away as silently as a wooden statue next to the black-iron range. It took Ulises some time, maybe a week, to figure out that Willems was not actually enjoying the quiet darkness but staring at the letter through the blackness—he wanted to see the thing without confronting it, without having to reread Uxbal's sturdy, palpable script. The letter, Ulises realized, was not just word from Uxbal, but proxy for Uxbal. For once, the Dutchman had to battle the presence of the husband amid his love for Soledad.

It's just a letter, you know, Ulises told him.

I know, Willems said. But I'm no different than any other man, and it's difficult not to be jealous. The man is absent for six years, but all he has to do is write a letter, and he's returned?

Time was what Henri had been wrestling with all those years. He'd thought he just had to wait for Ma to forget everything or let it go, and now, now he had to play the helpless adulterer who'd fallen in love with the cheating wife. The thought upset Ulises and forced him to understand the potency of the letter, because since when had his father been the moral standard in any equation? Since when had Henri been at fault or his mother guilty of anything but moving on? Ulises thought of removing the letter from the kitchen table, but to dispose of the sheet would have given it a past and a history—the letter was read, the letter was thrown away—and things left behind, things intentionally forgotten, he knew, had a way of coming back.

Uxbal's correspondence stayed on the kitchen table for three more months. The kitchen was susceptible to low drafts, and the fluctuating temperature of the room, due in part to the sporadic radiators—hot to cold, damp to dry—crinkled the graying fiber. The ink, a cheap, charcoal ink, began to fade. Soledad and Ulises, though always aware of the presence of the letter, had, since its arrival, taken their meals in the living room, and eventually they both managed to incorporate the missive into the general appearance of the house; it became another part of the kitchen table, which was a mainstay of the kitchen, which each could navigate with his or her eyes closed. The letter dropped entirely into the background.

But, of course, the note was never completely out of mind—there were days Ulises could not study or read inside the house, the proximity of the letter forcing him to the university library, where he could better tolerate the whispering of his peers—*There's the Titan; How did the Titan get that scar on his head?; The Titan talks to no one*—than the silent presence of his father's handwriting. In the dim basement of the library's western wing, at a table between the etymology stacks and a retired, bricked-in fireplace, Ulises engaged in a lonely study of Greek and Roman myth, though he worked in reverse, starting with the most recently published texts and articles on the subject and moving backward in time. He found a welcome distraction in the multitude of voices, in the interpretive curtain between him and the original works in Greek and Latin; more truthfully, he felt he didn't have the energy to translate, and he found solace in the number of pages he could consume when they were written in English. The ease with which he navigated this second language was, in his mind, an affirmation of his place in Hartford, evidence of a past, perhaps of a father, he'd successfully left behind. Ulises feared in secret that the letter from Uxbal was his own calling, though a silent one as opposed to Isabel's auditory warning, but it heartened him to know that he'd had to ask his mother to translate the Cuban words for *glossy* and *grouper*. The words, like the father, were foreign to him, and at a distance Ulises believed himself safe.

Yet, as Ulises moved through those classics texts, he understood only half of what he read; he had no specific knowledge of the verses referenced, and he skipped the elaborate, half-page-long footnotes entirely. The result was a glancing comprehension of the arguments and interpretations. Ancient Greece and Rome were little more than dreams or, more accurately, another man's dreams. Ulises better imagined maps of the fallen empire or vague sketches of the boundaries of the Mediterranean than he did colossal temples stacked above stone or wine-dark water. Olympus itself was more cloud than mountain, and it was the first time in Ulises's short life that he truly felt displaced and uprooted. The language of the ancient world was a field he'd plowed for years, and yet there he was, unwilling to taste the soil in his mouth.

The distance could not, did not, last, and the sensation of reading so much so fast became a rote exercise. Ulises began again to feel the weight of his family's circumstance reassert itself. Another man's thoughts were not enough; he wanted another man's story, though not just a version of the story but the original—or as close to it as he could come, and this Ulises could blame on the Dutchman, the man who'd taught him the demands of an empiricist—so that he might mill and process the raw Greek and Latin words as he saw fit. Ulises remembered Willems with his nose in the dirt; he remembered the Dutchman's dress shirts, always a copper tinge around the cuffs, the product of his hands gripping soil and leaves, the dirt and tobacco oil dyeing slowly, over time, the white cotton-polyester blend.

The impulse also reminded Ulises of his first years at St. Brendan's and the afternoon hours he'd spent translating and critiquing St. Jerome's Vulgate. He didn't understand then but understood now that he possessed an inclination toward remaking the world or, at least, reconstituting a version of the world that suited his liking. He knew in his heart that he had to attribute this, if attribution were necessary, to his father, the man still attempting, perhaps, to recast an entire island to his liking. My mother, Ulises thought, transcribes the world. She records reality. And I didn't know Willems yet. It's Uxbal who's always wanted to change things.

Ulises began with Virgil's *Georgics* and Horace's *Odes*. He then read, in a matter of three weeks, beginning to end, *The Deeds of the Divine Augustus, The Meditations* by Marcus Aurelius, Aristotle's *Categories, The History of Herodotus, Shield of Heracles* by Hesiod, Livy's *The History of Rome,* Appollonius's *The Argonautica,* and Sophocles's *Antigone.* It was Aeschylus who made Ulises cry, *The Oresteia* he could not handle. The language, of course, he found beautiful and captivating, but he couldn't reconcile either Agamemnon's original sin or the subsequent slaughter of mothers and sons. He read the trilogy all the way through in one sitting, and he wet every page with his gargantuan tears. Yet when he was done, he couldn't bring himself to read something else; he had an urge to cry further, and he decided to read the trilogy again. He cried through two more passes, and then he read until his eyes began to dry, until he could read aloud a line or two without buckling in his wooden chair.

Eventually, he sought to read the whole thing aloud, start to finish, without a single tear, as if to repeat the story to a point of literary, psychological, and expressive death. The words, he hoped, as he heard them and spoke them, would be stripped of their definitions and become something of an incantation. There were monks, he knew, who did this, who destroyed language through repetition, who estranged familiar noise for religious purposes.

Ulises was unsure of his exact purposes, but around the tenth reading he felt his mind enter a white space in which the sounds, the utterances, turned to murmur. Sitting in a wing chair in front of the bricked-in fireplace, he imagined the play he read aloud traveling in waves at the retired hearth and bouncing back, scrambled, in the direction of his ears. It was a loop or a current, and perhaps, Ulises thought, this is where the monks got lost in their prayers. This is how they escape the world. Had he needed to describe the sensation, Ulises would have said, This is what they mean by speaking in tongues, but it's not another language altogether. It's the same language, but you've forgotten what it means, which makes it a mess, and people think you're somewhere else, that a ghost has taken you over.

Catharsis, Ulises thought, but even then he knew that wasn't the right term for what was happening. He was reading Aeschylus, now for the sixth day, beyond catharsis, beyond a point of purification. Emotion had emptied out of him, but around the twenty-third reading he noticed a diminished sense of sorrow: he was performing—it was a performance after all, an out-loud reading of a dramatic narrative— *The Oresteia* to a point beyond pain. What had first moved him to tears had dissolved into that blank part of his brain, but the white background of that mental cavity eventually gave way to a stream of green and blue hues.

Is this, Ulises asked, the ecstasy? Is this where the monks end up once they stop wandering through the chant?

Ulises thought of Isabel, who claimed she could not ignore the sounds in her head, and he felt, perhaps for the first time, tremendous empathy for his twin. He could open his eyes and clearly see the oak table at which he worked or the low, square, stone ceiling of the library basement or the stunted, load-bearing Doric columns interspersed with the stacks, but he understood that he was, at the moment, in a different place, and the place had descended on him. He thought of his sister, who seemed trapped in this world or, at least, saw *his* world—the city of Hartford, the university, the tobacco fields, their quaint colonial kitchen—always through the filter of this condition, these invisible walls of sound, this state. Ulises wondered if Isabel had ever seen the world another way. He realized, then, that maybe what she feared most in life was an unencumbered view.

Ulises went on like this for thirteen days, and only twice did librarians ask him to read silently to himself. When they asked, they asked meekly, and Ulises thought it was because of his size, but really his voice—a tenor born from a mother's Cuban accent, a teenage American English, and an abundant, consistent dose of Catholic Latin—sounded so strange and carried so beautifully throughout the library basement that it seemed a shame to ask him to stop. More important, Ulises had drawn a crowd by the thirteenth day, and the audience—at first just three to four other classics students, though soon enough also a handful of sophomore dramatists as well as a modest pod of junior rhetoricians—through their presence and rapture, legitimized Ulises's performance. The crowd, which continued to grow in spurts, seated themselves at a distance from Ulises, forming a long semicircle around his wing chair.

Don't sit so close, they told one another. *It might disturb the Titan.*

Instead, they reclined comfortably against columns and dusty bookshelves, and they were as silent as the dead while listening to Ulises's passionate telling. Even on days when Ulises's voice was nearly gone, when he had to whisper-speak the drama, the audience kept its distance, which in a short time had come to exemplify a sort of reverence, something like the void between preacher and congregation, an unspoken agreement that Ulises spoke from a place of power not to be breached by onlookers. Those who stayed to the end, those who heard

The Oresteia from start to finish, suffered a sort of delirium afterward, the aftereffects of a subtle, deep drug, and when they talked about what they'd heard, they said things such as, *I was amazed, even though I couldn't understand a word,* and, *He's a natural at whatever that is.* Enrollment for spring classics courses surged.

Ulises noticed the crowd, could not possibly read without feeling some of its pulse, but their presence swelled at around the same time that Ulises began again to hear the meaning behind *The Oresteia's* beautiful words. He had passed through to the other side of the story, to the place where he could understand denotations again and could string together the tragic narrative, but the pain of doing just that was gone. He could read aloud, *But there is a cure in the house, and not outside it, no, not from others but from them, their bloody strife,* without weeping, while also understanding the exact nature of that strife, while also seeing Agamemnon's bloody robe. Ulises read the verses, *What do I call this? What fine words will do?,* and whereas, before, the lines had overwhelmed him, he now possessed them. He had read the tragedy beyond catharsis and into ownership, a power not unlike the power to name things, the power of defining a substance or an object or a person or feeling with cold, precise words. The shift occurred imperceptibly to Ulises but showed itself in his voice, which rose exponentially after the twenty-seventh day. The crowd discerned the uptick in volume and, to some degree, trembled in its wake. They cried at his reading, shaken, perhaps, by his tone, as if dislodged from an ambiguous daze. When Ulises saw their red eyes and heard their noses blowing, he thought, I've given the story to them. But then he thought longer and harder and concluded, Those were my tears last week.

Ulises cataloged all the things in his life that had been displaced— his home, his family, his sister, his language, his sense of Cuba—and he was scared that this was his only response to the world. In the semi-circle he saw his pain vicariously, some students weeping, some burying their faces in their hands, some holding each other, and he began to understand how deep his well of grief actually was. Ulises read, *My misery has been my teacher,* and it was a verse that spoke of his sister, the sounds in her head—would she say in her heart?—and the painful throbbing of her eardrums, but now it perhaps applied to him as well, as if he, Ulises, had at last been offered his own inheritance, his own sort of burdened calling. Uxbal had summoned him, a voice from the dark that was Cuba, and was that not as good as being touched by faith? Wasn't that the same question Uxbal had asked his daughter when she was just a child: will you come back to me?

For just a moment it brought Ulises a joy he could not recall experiencing, some version of fatherly love, but the letter, with Uxbal's mayorial tenor, his carefree tone—as if Soledad had taken Ulises and Isabel to a cousin's in Santiago and not to another country—was a vessel, and it had carried Ulises to the rim of a whirlpool, to a point where he could look down and see how black the tapering center was. He had forgotten, willingly, his father and home—Ulises read, *For I don't deny I did the murder*—but now he could sense the truth that Isabel, his twin, his counterpart, had perhaps always known: the heart sustains when the mind relents; the heart remembers what the mind forgets.

Soledad was herself adopting another cache of memory, though in a different basement. She had descended into the chancery of the Hartford County Courthouse, where a sprawl of fungus was rotting away, among other things, the shelved topographical maps of Hartford County. An archivist from the Connecticut Circuit Court Records Preservation Program had inspected their holdings and flatly said, There's too much mold. You have to cut out the diseased walls, maybe even the studs. You'll certainly have to evacuate. This fungus could be everywhere.

Soledad took up the project the day after Uxbal's letter arrived. After a week, Willems said, I'm waiting up nights for you.

There is mold everywhere in that basement, she said, and we can't afford to hire someone. Anyway, I don't trust anyone else to do the work.

Soledad was a proud woman, and she realized this every time she saw the Dutchman's face. She knew Henri was waiting for the moment he could watch her reading Uxbal's letter. He lurked in the dark with the hope of seeing exactly what he was up against, how badly the scribbled words had further maimed—ever since the canyon rim, the hollow kiss—what had come to seem like an eternal affair.

But rather than admit the limits of her own heart, how they were challenged first by her offspring and then by the husband of her native abandonment, Soledad moved the contents of the chancery into the courthouse attic and threw herself into buckets of bleach and piles of fetid maps.

Though it was winter and the attic was not insulated, it was the only available work space. The ceiling was extremely low, but Soledad was just short enough that she didn't have to stoop when working. She set up two space heaters to fight the cold, arranged a fan to circulate the air, and found a parka to wear while dabbing bleach onto speckled records. The fan was mostly effective, but the stench of chemicals lingered. Oddly, Soledad found she didn't mind the odor. Instead, she recognized a pleasure in the dulling of her senses, the muted nose, the tasteless tongue, eyes that stung and had to be shut. She forgot herself, forgot the scent of her hands, the feel of her teeth, the need to eat. She worked.

Soledad sponged her way through a decade of birth certificates and expired business licenses before reaching the topographical maps of Hartford County. They were beautiful: yellowed quadrangles checkered by parallels and meridians that, she quickly realized, surveyed all of Henri's leased properties. Curious, she placed the topographical maps under the translucent county tax folios, which she'd found in a separate box; she wanted to see where, exactly, in that scheme, Henri grew his tobacco. Tracing her fingers around the boundaries of his land, she immediately saw his well-contrived decision to grow Habano leaf solely on the western, cloud-gathering sides of Connecticut hillocks. She also felt the distinct possibility that Henri must have, at one point, handled maps such as these when looking for fields to lease.

Looking closer, Soledad saw that the sheer folios were marked with the faint residue of oily fingertips; they might glow if she held them up to the light. She felt, suddenly, the urge to lick the paper but didn't. Instead, she turned off the fan so that she could press her nose to them and breathe in the smell of cheap leather and citrus perfume.

The aroma, along with the milky hue of the paper and the ghostly fingerprints, brought to mind a memory of Cuban adolescence, of young men petting their groins and offering Soledad a string of pearls to wear around her neck. She had been disgusted then, but not without curiosity, and there once had been a night when she'd asked Henri to finish himself along her chest so that she could see the color of his fluid. Henri, though, had blushed and then refused, said simply, *No*, and asked her if she would turn over.

Up in the courthouse attic, Soledad still felt a little angry with Willems for that evening, a little cheated by his sheepishness. She did not know why, exactly, except for the fact of his refusal, how he'd kept some fraction of his body from her possession. Her desire, she knew, was juvenile; it spoke to the kind of love without a future, the sort of aimless sex that only happens outside marriage. Yet, surprisingly, Soledad could feel her body even now respond to the idea of Henri's semen on her skin, the vision of it streaking her brownish nipples. She understood, suddenly, that if Willems were there at her side, she would try to take him. But even that was a lie; she would take only his skin. And that made her terribly sad, terribly aware of the depth of her own selfishness. She had not thought that she could take more from him.

That night, Soledad felt incapable of leaving the courthouse, as walking home meant seeing the orange glow of Henri's cigar burning in the void of their kitchen. Instead, she worked through a moldy stack of sewer plans. At some point she began to hear mice moving in the walls, and to keep them away, she sponged bleach-infused water along the attic's baseboards. She worked for another hour before feeling the long day in her shoulders and the hours of dabbing in her wrists. Close to midnight she fell asleep at her table, the sponge not far from her face.

Sex dreams about Henri were not uncommon. Often they were sweet and vague, visually fuzzy, though reminiscent of the last place they'd had sex. Under the fog of cleaning fumes, Soledad dreamed her nipples were being rubbed as she lay inside a sweaty tent, which meant she was remembering her and Henri's riverbank fucking. The air was humid in a way uncharacteristic of the Grand Canyon, however, and there were noises outside the tent's flap that implied a flock of birds was circling their small canvas enclosure. In the dream Henri did not seem to notice, and he circled the palms of his hands around Soledad's nipples to the point of pain. Soledad did not stop him, and when they started to bleed, she pushed Henri aside and rolled on top of him. He licked her chest. She found his penis with her right hand, and she slid it into herself.

The episode lasted longer than usual, both the act and the aftermath: Soledad's orgasm was a century long in her mind, as though there was time to forget the pleasure and then remember it again; and afterward, when they were both exhausted, both covered in blood and sweat, the dream persisted. It went on long enough for Soledad to sleep within the dream, to be dream-conscious of sleeping, and to wake up again to the flocking birds. She asked Henri to go outside to see what was there—it had gotten hotter since the dream began—but Henri refused. The sound of rain had been added to the noise, as well as mosquitoes, but Soledad knew those biting pests were rare in the park. She tried to sleep, but then she smelled manure and told Henri that a mule must have shat near their tent. It's a jungle out there! she yelled. Henri grunted without waking, would not open his eyes no matter how hard Soledad slapped his arm, and eventually she peeked outside the tent herself. But when she looked, there was nothing but the black canyon, a cold breeze, and a sliver of the starry night sky just beyond the rim. Soledad felt herself shaking. She awoke in the courthouse attic, her nostrils burning, to a night janitor pinching her ear.

Henri was in bed but wide awake, and when Soledad knocked over one of the many potted plants growing in their bedroom—an orchid not doing so well, now bent like an arthritic finger from too little light—he sat straight up.

Be careful, he whispered.

I'm sorry, Soledad said. I'll clean it up in the morning.

Let me, Henri said.

He turned on a lamp near the bed and went to scoop the disturbed soil back into its pot. Soledad watched and saw immediately that he was a little drunk. He walked slowly and rigidly, and she smelled alcohol in the air. Yet she also saw how incredibly cautious Henri was with the plant; he didn't touch its roots, and he was careful to hold the orchid only at the base of its stem. The soil he patted down with his thumbs while cradling the pot between his palms.

It should be fine, he said. Soledad saw him run a finger across one of the orchid's purple-white spurs and then across a bruised labella.

I'm sorry, she repeated. She had no doubt the flower would die. I suppose if you're going to wait up for me, I can turn on the light anyway.

You could come home earlier, Henri said. It wouldn't be so dark. We could go out for a meal. You don't look well, you know? You don't look like you've been eating anything.

Is that why you're always waiting for me in the kitchen? Because you want to feed me?

Their bedroom already reeked like a garden—burst pots smelling of grass, rotted flower petals, the airy dust of pollen—but with the freshly scattered dirt, the air grew mustier. Underneath that was Henri's stinging breath—brown liquor, if Soledad had to guess—and in her mouth it all had the feel of wet chalk. Soledad looked around while Henri looked at her. She swore she could see the plants trying to breathe but not getting enough oxygen.

Could you open a window? she asked.

Henri cracked the pane nearest his side of the bed.

Wider, she said. He lifted the window higher, and the heavy air left the room. Henri began to shiver; he rubbed his chest and said, the Bird of Paradise won't last very long.

Soledad felt her nipples harden beneath her blouse, which reminded her of the dream from earlier, the agonizing eroticism.

You're not even wearing a sweater, he said, and Henri approached her slowly, took her left hand in his right hand and squeezed her knuckles with his thumb. The blood in your body is moving away from your limbs, he said. You'll get sick.

Henri pulled her against his cold chest, a place that felt foreign at the moment, but Soledad felt her thighs tense nonetheless. Henri was making excuses to touch her—a very masculine process, she thought. It was so Catholic of him. For Henri, candid desire carried a stigma. But despite the tender draw, Soledad felt the depraved want under his skin. He took her hands in his and massaged her typist's knuckles. He followed the hollows between her bones as if they would tell him how much farther apart he and Soledad could drift. He touched her as he would his tobacco, trying to see the future, trying to predict the next spring and the length of his leaves.

Henri is a beautiful man, Soledad thought.

She was certain, as he let go of her hand and found her hair, that his search was in earnest—it was not the shallow satisfaction of a craving. He genuinely was after her heart, almost as if he knew what it was worth, as if he could weigh it in his palm. He had an ego after all, bold enough to believe he was capable of loving her not just once, but twice, even after a fall, which in Soledad's mind made him godly or, at least, forgiving.

The space between them was warming now, their collective breath heating each other's neck. Soledad's nipples were still hard, but now she felt the blush of arousal, the hot collarbone. She remembered their first time, an evening spent in one of Henri's greenhouses, the same one in which Ulises would later sort seeds, and she remembered the wet heat, the humidifier installed above the entrance door that treated the incoming air, and the clean feeling of moving through a filtered mist. She remembered the dirt under his fingernails as he showed her soil samples and explained exactly what kind of mud and sand— a loamy, slow-draining mixture—he'd put into the pot of the Sumatra leaf he'd given her. In the greenhouse he had her smell it, but she refused to sprinkle it on her tongue as he did onto his. Now, in the frigid bedroom, as Henri's hands moved toward her spine, she remembered the lovely, playful thing he'd said then—Please, have a taste—as he leaned into their first kiss. It made her want to touch him again, and she did.

It was afterward, the steam of their cooling bodies fogging the glass of the open window, when Henri lazily traced the curve of Soledad's back with his middle finger. She was lying on her stomach, and Henri, rejuvenated by the sex, sat up beside her. He'd already joked about her long body, longer than his, and while Soledad contentedly buried her face in a pillow, he told her about the black swallower, a tropical fish that lives 1,500 meters below the surface of the ocean.

Poking Soledad's hip he said, It's got a belly that looks like a tumor or a pregnant gut, and it can eat a fish larger than itself. Like me, he said.

If that's your part, she said, then what kind of fish am I?

I'm not sure, but something prehistoric. The first of its kind.

I'm not that old.

You're long, like something that's been around quite a while. Something that had the space to stretch out before there were other fish to bump into.

You're still drunk, aren't you? she said.

He pinched the side of her breast, and she slapped at his hand. What do you think you're doing?

Running the ridge, he said while walking his fingers down her vertebrae from nape to buttocks.

You've done that before, Soledad said, but she could not remember when.

I'll keep doing it, Henri said. He put his hand on the small of her back, and he left it there till she fell asleep.

· · ·

For some hours, Soledad slept well and without dreaming, but she awoke in the gray light of predawn to the smell of plants and a chill in her feet. She and Henri had forgotten the open window, and the blankets on the bed had twisted around Soledad's shins, exposing her feet up to the ball joint of her ankles. Her toes were numb. She worked the blanket back down, and while upright she heard Henri's soft exhalations. He was a quiet man awake or asleep, and she had to put her hand on his chest to really know that he was breathing. Touching his naked skin—the cold did not seem to bother him—she thought of the sex they'd had hours ago and the gentle talking afterward. In retrospect their lovemaking had been satiating if not memorable, but there had been an easiness to their conversation, and it was like the beginning of a new stream, rain from a storm gathering unsurprisingly into a flow.

Henri suddenly rolled over, and there was the pale skin of his back, a colony of bronze freckles across his left shoulder blade. There was the near white skin of his armpits, the ivory of his underarms. There was the trail of his spine. Soledad remembered then the first time Henri had touched her back and said *running the ridge.* It was the night he first told everyone about his ghosts. It was the night he opened himself to the family. It was the night of *that epic fuck.*

Though she'd never shared the phrase with Henri, that was the name Soledad had given the phenomenon of their lovemaking that evening; she could not think of a physical act past or present, with Henri or Uxbal, that had had such a direct, immediate effect on her person, and she could not recall another memory that put her body in such a muted state of ecstasy by merely closing her eyes and recalling it. And despite her religious skepticism, Soledad knew *that epic fuck* was somehow biblical: it was—in the short panorama of her and Henri's love—the sacred mound, the temple on the hill, the font of their mutual faith in each other. It was the night she'd fallen from heaven to Earth for Henri Willems.

What had been epic was the conflation of two things: the feeling that Soledad had engaged a love beyond Uxbal, a proposition that had seemed, after the long path from Buey Arriba to Hartford, nearly impossible, elusive at best; and, more wondrous, the genesis of Henri as the next phase of a man she'd only ever dreamed of, the man of salvage, the man who followed the man of ruin. Henri, as Soledad had understood it that night, had looked upon his own troubled family history and said, *I'll take the weed but leave the ghosts behind.* Or, at least, he was attempting to, which was as much as she'd ever hoped for in coming to Connecticut.

Soledad bent down to Henri's still face and put her lips to his ear. She bit his lobe, and when his face moved, she said, I think you're using the same tricks on me. I think you hope our love is a Hindu nightmare. You want to play it again, Henri.

He mumbled, What are you saying? You're talking in your sleep.

The night after *that epic fuck,* Soledad recalled, she and Henri had gone on one of their evening strolls through Hartford and talked, as they sometimes did, of their pasts. In the wake of Henri's confession at dinner, Soledad had asked him about his mother and what it had been like to watch her die. Her nose close to Henri's cheek, Soledad remembered the way he had talked of his mother's smell, the manner in which the change of her scent had been the most alienating. *What did she smell like before she got sick?* Soledad had asked. *Hot laundry, dry mud, verbena, and damp cedar,* Henri had said.

In bed, Soledad still could discern traces of liquor on Henri's breath, a sour odor at the edge of his lips. He rolled in the sheets but did not wake. Seeing him turn over, seeing his pink nipples, Soledad was reminded of a question she'd never asked him: what did he do when Rute stopped smelling like Rute? She'd not asked on their walk, because the inventory of his mother's aromas had been enough to make Soledad's heart clench, but in the days that followed, she'd found herself wondering, almost hourly—and not without some awareness of her estranged husband, the estranged father of her children—what would a little boy have done under the circumstances? What does a boy do when his mother disappears? When he has so little power?

Pushing the blankets farther down, Soledad stroked Henri's abdomen.

What did you do, Henri, when your mother was nearly gone? Wake up just a little and tell me.

Do when? he said without opening his eyes.

When Rute passed.

When she died? I cried. I cried and cried.

Before she died. When her smell had changed but before she went. Did you do anything, or did you just stay away from her because she no longer smelled like your mother? Were you afraid of her?

No, Henri said slowly. He kept his eyes shut. I wasn't afraid of her, but I was afraid of her smell. I wanted to see her, but I couldn't be too close, or I would start to sob. I thought I would start smelling like her, and that maybe I would also die, even though I was already too old to think those silly things.

You were a little boy.

My fear made me irrational.

Did your father make you go to her? Soledad asked. Your poor mother must have wanted you nearby.

He did sometimes, Henri said. Mostly, he let me stand by the door and watch the two of them talk. My mother understood, and she wasn't hurt by it, I don't believe. She would put on a smile when I was watching. She wanted to coax me in.

But you wouldn't go, Soledad said. I can see your body crumpled against the doorframe. I can see you crouching by the threshold. Did you watch her die like that?

My father eventually figured out what was bothering me, so, no. Instead, he had the room filled with potted plants and flowers. He thought he could mask the smell.

Did he tell you why?

Yes and no. He didn't say it was for my sake but gave another reason. He said my mother wanted all the plants inside. He said she missed walking outdoors and in our fields and that she wanted to close her eyes and pretend she was still outside in the sun.

Do you remember the plants?

Henri rolled toward Soledad and said, Red and yellow hibiscus, flowering consolea cacti, oriental lilies, pink lotuses, purple maypops, melon cacti, two overlarge tree ferns, a handful of baby tobaccos, and at least eight white orchids.

Did he get them all at once?

No, one or two every couple of days. He picked them himself.

Soledad looked away from Willems and toward the orchid on the bedside table. The morning light was expanding, thickening, and the plant cast a long shadow on their bedroom floor. If she looked elsewhere, she could see the other flora crowding their quarters: some lilies, some bougainvillea, some irises, some yellow frangipani, some cacti, some tobaccos, some other white orchids.

Where did he get them from? Soledad asked.

From the land near our fields, Henri said.

In Gonaïves?

No, the fields were farther east, near the Petite Rivière. We grew our tobacco near the Montagnes Noires, a smaller range south of the Massif du Nord. The farms were on the western slopes.

Where they would catch the rain.

Yes, Henri said.

Like the hills here in Hartford, Soledad said, and she remembered touching the almost-waxy fibers of the lovely Connecticut survey maps.

It's a lovely idea, she said.

The scent of flowers?

No, she said. Bringing the world to her. You planted the valley in her bedroom. You resurrected a landscape.

My father did.

Naked, Soledad slipped out from the sheets. Her skin, she saw, was yellow in the orange daybreak. She rubbed her hands together and touched her neck. She left the bedside and went to a potted cactus atop the dresser. The cactus was not in bloom, because it was winter. Her fingers pressed on the thorns, but the skin was callused from her years of typing and did not break.

It's too cold to be out of bed, Henri said, sitting up. Let me get you a sweater. Or come back to this blanket.

Did it work? Soledad asked.

My father's indoor garden?

Yes. Did you go back to your mother?

No, Henri said. It brought me into her room, which smelled wonderful. It was summer and hot, and the flowers were very alive. Because we were indoors, their soil never dried out. They had the heat and the moisture, and the flowers they grew were tremendous. Our house never smelled so wild. But if I got close, if I moved within a foot of my mother's face, there again was the strange scent. It wasn't gone. It just held itself closer to her body.

What did you do?

I got as close as I could.

And then?

And then she died.

The following night Henri waited up late for Soledad in the kitchen. He found himself in the same position—despite the long night of renewed passion—he'd been in over the past two weeks, leaning against the refrigerator while eyeing Uxbal's letter and preparing for a drawn-out smoking session.

The lonely smoking was a new nightly routine, one he had unconsciously developed in the aftermath of the missive from Cuba. It required two cigarillos and a short cigar. The two cigarillos he would smoke first—they were fresher, and the leaves were not as choice as those he used in his cigars. Their flavor was brighter and lacked a depth of flavor or, rather, a depth of finish—the smoke was the same going out as it was going in—and puffing through them with abandon gave his hands something to do while his mind settled. By the time he'd smoked his way to the stogie, he could feel in his brain a gentle nicotine wash, not enough to get him fully buzzed but enough to allow his thoughts to expand instead of contract. The smoking occupied him till ten, at which time he'd end his kitchen shift and retire upstairs to read in bed.

Henri's constant occupation of the kitchen, however, was not the declaration of war Soledad had assumed it to be. It was the exact opposite; instead of rage, an exceedingly familiar sense of misery had filled Willems when he first read Uxbal's note. Somehow the letter, for Henri, was an auditory experience, and without any effort he could hear Uxbal's tenor, distinct and overglamorous and fulsome. The letter was about Ulises, but it was sent for Soledad, and Henri remembered from his own upbringing the manner in which offspring sometimes become conduits for want, another means of engaging a reluctant, distant partner.

Henri's own mother used to chew his father's tobacco behind his back. Rute was the first to give him a taste of the weed, though what she had told Henri about it was different from what she'd said to his father, Adlar. To her husband she'd say, *I am freeing spirits,* but to her son she'd say, *Don't be afraid of this. You can't be afraid of this. It's just a plant. What your grandfather did was terrible, but tell me, do you taste any blood in that leaf? Of course not. Your father is hurt, but you shouldn't be also.* Henri knew that his mother, with her thin, desperate face—she'd been a swimmer in her youth—was really saying the things to him she wished she could have said to his father. She had a tremendous wanting for Adlar's redemption, and she poured that desire into the ears of her son.

His father had been no different, especially at his mother's deathbed. A man who'd taught him the infinite depths of cautiousness, Adlar had said to Henri, the moments before Rute passed away from cholera, *When you go to kiss her good-bye, don't be afraid of the smell. It's still your mother's body, I promise you.* Her skin smelled like fish, and Henri saw the soiled sheets, what looked like rice-water staining the cotton but what he knew was her diarrhea. His father had wanted to say, *This is the terrible curse; you have to see and know it.* Henri knew that his father's greatest regret was not convincing his mother that such a thing existed and believing that it had taken her for that very reason.

But, unlike his father, Henri had not even bothered with establishing what was or wasn't real, which is to say, he'd explained the past—Rute's death, the fields in Haiti—to Soledad, but he'd made no effort to validate it. He had always presented his family's story as a nuance of his being, a quirk, a strange but mild obsession. But thinking now on Adlar's regret, Henri wondered if he'd been mistaken, if he'd brought a silent hex to his love with Soledad. Perhaps he should have warned her. Perhaps he should have looked her in the eye rather than at the toes of his steeled-toed wing tips when saying, *But my grandfather didn't listen, and all those slaves died.* Maybe then she would have said something more than *How strange and sad.* Maybe she would have pressed him a little harder, and he would have explained with more resolution how he was, indeed, afraid, and it was a fear he couldn't manage, a terror he had no means to control, so he plodded through it with abandon. He should have told her that to love him was to walk with him along a cursed tobacco row, and one might sink into black soil if one wasn't careful. But she might have also passed him off for crazy, and there would have been no love to speak of, not even a love to curse, a possibility he believed to be, in retrospect, even more depressing than their current predicament.

Staring at Uxbal's letter, Henri understood that the man's want was more visceral and bodily, more base and carnal than the abstract belief systems of Henri's parents and himself. When Willems heard the bereaved husband's voice—shot with syrupy pain, like rum—say, *I've been eating tomatoes since you left,* he saw the man alone in a dark room gingerly licking a Brandywine. In the next line, *I miss you and your mother and your sister,* the man had wedged his wife between his kids as a means to buffer his longing. But the longing was there still, and only a man like Willems, the *other* man, could see through those words to the bodily intimations. Were they vulgar? Not exactly. The tomato was, no doubt, a part of Uxbal's landscape, pedestrian to him, maybe growing in a garden by his house. Uxbal's problem was that he'd treated Soledad like native produce, a natural occurrence. He'd believed Cuban dirt and sun would keep his wife going. When it couldn't, she left.

But had Henri nourished Soledad as best he could? Even if Henri had, he still suffered the same as Uxbal: they shared the same ache for the same woman's body. Some of Uxbal's words felt exactly like his—*the flavor of our dirt is stuck on your tongue*—and Henri, thinking of his first kiss with Soledad, for a moment feared that the husband could see him there, standing in the kitchen. As if he and Soledad's transgressions were somehow apparent to the world.

All this even when he and Soledad had found each other's bodies again. He had not been exactly drunk the previous night, but on the far side of drunk, the downward slope of blurry meditation. A day later, the memory of that sex now had the feel of ambiguous sensation, as though Soledad's touches had not been focused anywhere, as if the pleasures were spread unevenly across his body. And the Dutchman remembered his performance as that of a narcoleptic, a slow but somewhat fidgety presence in the bed during which he constantly awoke to what was happening: his eyes growing wide with Soledad's breast in his mouth, a rush up his spine when her hands gripped him behind the knees, and the brief certainty that sex could cure hang-overs and drunkenness when she, on top of him, turned around and brought his penis—miraculously, inexplicably erect—inside of her. He remembered talking afterward, but still, that was like swimming in the ocean, a narcoleptic floating. Eventually, he'd said to hell with the struggle and fell asleep, slipping under. And now the memories of that night evaded him like eels in the surf, were in a manner quarantined from one another. They were a school of fish divorced, and he could not, in the end, merge them into a singular experience. Willems didn't know what to do with that.

The Dutchman wondered if Uxbal had the same troubles with his recollections of Soledad, if she was also breaking apart in his mind. He almost wished he could take Uxbal by the hand, thinking: Perhaps I should be the one to write him back.

It was at this point that Henri considered Isabel. For once, he and she had a thing in common—empathy for the madman. For a moment Henri feared he might be crazy as well, Isabel also. But, no, he still couldn't fathom Isabel's decision, the promise to her father; he had a hard enough time with her promise to the Church. And why would any father, real or saintly, ever ask for that? Henri had an image of Isabel in his mind just then, complete with the crucifix she wore around her neck. Not a cross but a miniature crucifix, with the Lord's body gone to waste and everything. Then Henri thought, If Christ taught us anything, it's that the body is carnivorous; it needs another to go on living. Henri chewed on his cigar. Maybe, though, he was just talking about men.

That was when Soledad entered the kitchen.

.   .   .

Henri fumbled for the light.

It's all right, Soledad said. You don't have to. I'm fine with the dark.

Would you like a smoke? he asked. He scoured his pockets, hoping he'd brought an extra cigarillo by chance.

Yes, that would be nice.

Henri discovered two sticks in the left breast pocket of his jacket. He lit one with a match, got it smoking, and handed it to Soledad. Their knuckles touched, and Henri remembered picking up girls as a chubby teenager with cigarettes he'd stolen from his father.

Are you afraid of me? Henri asked.

What would I be afraid of? Soledad said.

That I would go to Cuba and find him. Make some vague threats about having had his chance and blown it to shit. I'm not an American citizen. Or an exile. I could leave at any moment.

I can't imagine you doing that, she said.

Would it make a difference?

He, of course, meant something else entirely, and Soledad understood this. The dark room let him talk, and it did the same for her. She could say things as long as she didn't have to say them to his blank, open face. Soledad was struck by how tragic a situation they were in if they could not look each other in the eye. But she also knew she was capable of hurting him. What she feared now was that she might hurt him further, happily and willingly, in an attempt to see what kind of man might fight back, to test her recent theories on the state and constitution of Henri Adlar Willems.

You're afraid of the wrong thing, Soledad said.

So I do have something to be afraid of.

Not this letter, she said. Not my ex-husband.

I didn't know that you two had gotten a divorce.

Soledad took a long drag from her cigarillo, and the end lit up like an orange lightbulb. For a moment Henri could see her lips.

I could leave you in a similar fashion, she said. It would feel just as real. It would feel like I divorced you.

But that would be admitting that once in the past you loved me. You'd also be confessing to the end of our affair. Is it over?

Nothing is ever over, she said, and Soledad was imagining Uxbal walking through Henri's fields and Henri writing letters from her old house in Buey Arriba. She thought of herself in two places at once, and the barely thought-out decision she'd made a long time ago to try to love someone again. She suffered a vague but rising guilt, the painful recognition that she'd, just maybe, transposed an old love onto a new man—not just her love of Uxbal, but her love of men and what she hoped to take from them, as well as her love of Cuba, of an island, and what it meant for her to be locked to another body that was equally locked to the land. She wanted those things then, and she wanted them now, and being the same person meant she might always make the same mistakes, might always step into this sort of love with this sort of man.

Hearing his voice, measured as always, Soledad could not blame Henri without blaming herself. His cigar, which seemed mostly out, still gave off the mild stench of burnt spice and slow-burning flowers. She thought, It's the kitchen also; it's been a puff box for weeks now. The bread in the breadbox probably tastes like smoke, maybe even the ice cubes in the freezer. Soledad realized that she'd not set foot in the kitchen in just as long, because the space now had the feel of ceded ground. But she also knew she hadn't fought to keep this territory. As she looked for Henri's shape in the dark—she saw the slow movements of hands in and out of pockets, the dullest embers where his jaw should be—she considered everything she'd willingly surrendered to Henri: the notes from his courthouse appearance, the free legal advice of a district attorney, a seat at the table during Sunday dinner, of course the tiny kitchen, the windowsills, corner spaces and nightstands for his plants, her own nostalgic yet painful recollection of Cuba, time and space with her children, time and space that had once gone into their rearing, time away from her daughter, her only son who went into the Dutchman's fields, plumbed his trade, and grew the same reparative tobacco. And herself. She'd given herself to him—not in an unusual sense or a dramatic, exceptional, singular sense—but in the way that all affections are a mutual submission of wills. Soledad thought to herself, I'm guilty, too—sacrificing everything for a diseased love affair.

Do you mean to say this sort of thing will keep happening? Henri asked. More and more letters from Uxbal?

Soledad snuffed out her cigarillo in the sink. She ran the faucet and tried to watch the ash glide into the drain.

I mean that we don't have to work so hard to rebuild our lives, she said. It's all the same life.

I don't understand you.

I'm married, *and* I'm in love with you. I'm in Hartford, *and* I'm surrounded by the tropics. I have a daughter, *and* I've lost her. Soledad began to cry.

The flame on Henri's cigar had gone out entirely, and he tossed the chewed stogie into the sink. He walked up to Soledad and took her into his arms. She shook her head for a few brief moments, but then she put her chin on his crown.

Whispering into her breasts, Willems asked, What do we do about this letter? It doesn't mean anything to me if it doesn't mean anything to you. And what do we do about last night? What was last night?

A revival, Soledad said, mercifully, after some time. We noticed each other again.

Is that good or bad?

It's neither. It's the state we're in. We're seeing if the same life can be lived twice. If the same love can be felt twice.

Soledad looked up and saw the effects of her words on Henri's face. He seemed ready to collapse, and she thought to herself, We're pitiful people. We're both deceived.

Will you take me to bed? she asked. I'm tired. I want to lie down. I want to be next to you.

Yes, he said. And he took her up.

Isabel finally handled the letter during her brief return from Central America. She was home only for two weeks before leaving again, but she found the note immediately.

No one told me, she wrote on her pad, showing it to Ulises.

He thought for a moment. I don't think we knew how, he said. And there's nothing to tell. He's in the same place we left him.

Isabel wrote nothing else, and if she had a reaction to the letter, it did not register on her face or in her eyes. She appeared to Ulises to be in shock, or else undergoing a reaction beneath the surface. Ulises knew how well Isabel could be like that, a creature who experienced the external world internally. Or, he wondered, maybe for once she needs words to carry grief out of her body, but she's denied herself the privilege. Ulises winced, thinking she might yet have one more thing—he did not want to call it a cross—to bear; but then he thought, She'll go to Mass and pray about it. If she needs something more, she'll ask for it with her pad. She's not one to go without the things she needs.

But then, two months after its arrival, the letter went missing from kitchen table. The note vanished entirely, and no one said a thing.

The effect was like the wind escaping a room, leaving behind an unnatural but welcome calm. It was the silence that follows rain, a quiet that begged for noise. The kitchen was again a livable space, and when it was clear that the letter might not return—a week passed without a sighting—Ulises sat down, skeptically, cautiously, one afternoon at the kitchen table for a snack. As large he was, he'd been eating his food in his bedroom or the living room. It had become a hassle not only squeezing his broad shoulders through the narrow German door-frames of the house, but then also carrying with him a mess of plates and silverware. It had been a long day of study, and Ulises's eyes were tired from reading; he was hungry. Having cut an apple and sliced some cheddar, and having poured himself some of his mother's rum, he was about to stumble toward the blue couch in the living room. Looking through the doorway, though, he saw again the two palms abutting the sofa, saw their leaves impinging on the armrests. To hell with it, he said. He pulled a chair out and dropped his plate onto the kitchen table. He took a drink from his half-full glass, and when nothing but silence followed, he sat down and relaxed.

Ulises spent the next three evenings doing the same, and on the third evening he added a cigar to his routine, which in turn drew Willems into the kitchen. It had been some time since the two of them had smoked together at the kitchen table, and Willems, remembering with fondness Ulises's insistent questioning, asked the young man if he could join him.

Why not? Ulises said. It still smells like the two of us in here.

Ulises went to the fridge and brought Henri his own beer, and for two hours they smoked and drank in silence until Willems started speculating about the upcoming season, quoting what he'd just read in the *Farmer's Almanac* and gauging the predictions against what he hoped for his crop.

It took Soledad longer to reenter the space, two more days, than it did Henri and Ulises, but their laughter—they could crack jokes again at the kitchen table—teased her downstairs and to the kitchen door-way. Seeing her, Willems tried to coax her in with a glass of gin and some smoked salmon he'd brought home that night, but she hesitated.

Thank you but no, she said.

We'll be here, Henri said. How loyal the Dutchman was, how

endless his devotion seemed to her. He would wait forever if I let him, Soledad thought. She felt both relieved and annoyed at the possibility.

But after another day of eruptive laughter, Soledad could not stay out of the kitchen. Those were the sounds of life rattling against the refrigerator door, the cupboards, the small window above the sink. Alone upstairs, Soledad had begun to think she could hear the plants growing, so she crept out of her bedroom and sat down on the topmost stair to eavesdrop on her son and her lover.

They're talking as if nothing's happened, Soledad said to herself, and the jealousy ran from her ears into her heart, where it settled into her aorta and reshaped itself as longing and desire, the kind of want that makes one capable of poor but magnanimous decisions. She went downstairs.

Soledad entered the kitchen as Ulises and Henri were finishing a game of pinochle. The Dutchman didn't flinch when she came in but did offer her a cigarillo. Ulises got up from his chair to give it to his mother, and she and Willems had what amounted to a leisurely smoke. Ulises remained, and afterward the three of them inhabited the small space as if it were the last island on the surface of the ocean. Let's play another game, Henri eventually said. We'll make it hearts.

Isabel came by later in the night, much later, sometime near midnight, and found them halfway through a round. Henri and Soledad faced each other across the table, and Ulises knelt on the floor, because the kitchen did not have enough room for a third chair. Isabel had been too busy with preparations for her trip—heading to church early in the morning and then going right to bed when she got home at night—to have noticed that people were once again populating the kitchen. But instead of asking why they were all cramped together around a game of hearts, she laughed at how large her brother's hands were, how they dwarfed the playing cards pinched between his fingers. He was enormous, and it was impossible for Soledad or Willems to cheat, something they were both known for; Ulises's fingers, thick and long, were too large to see around. Isabel stayed and watched, some-times putting her arm on Ulises's shoulder, sometimes telling him what to do with his jacks. A subtle excitement overcame the kitchen, that of survivors finding one another post-tempest, and they silently marveled at how superstitious they'd been over the longhand of a distant rela-tive. The rest of the week was nearly pleasant, and when Isabel left again for Guatemala, no one thought of the letter.

But the letter was only the start of things. Isabel, just like the wrinkled sheet of paper, went missing not long after. She'd been back in Guate-mala only a month when the archbishop called Soledad on a Tuesday night in March to tell her that her daughter had gone to bed early one evening and had not been seen since. The phone call was a catalog of worthless findings: Isabel complained one night of stomach pains and retired to her room; she did not appear for prayer the next morning and could not be found in bed or on the school grounds; there was no note; the adjoining church was empty, though a box of Communion wafers was missing; hospitals had no record of a girl of her description seek-ing medical attention; taxicab drivers did not recognize Isabel's face in the photographs they were shown; the police learned nothing from the local riffraff; most of the ship captains in the harbor were drunks and had trouble producing passenger lists or docking records; Isabel's passport was gone, along with half her wardrobe, but the rectory had no money missing; in a church across town, an old habit was found stuffed underneath a pew; a group of Chilean immigrants claimed to have seen a vision of the Holy Mother in a nearby city water fountain.

Soledad was sick, first of the heart and second of the body. After the phone call she went directly to bed, and she remained there for three weeks. It was a bizarre quarantine in that she wanted the cur-tains always open, but no one was allowed on the second floor of the colonial when she napped. She dragged the majority of the plants in the household into the room with her, claiming that the broad green leaves breathed soothing oxygen that smelled like Isabel. Over the radiator Soledad hung all the pictures she had of her daughter, and though they wilted from the dry, rising heat, she would not allow them to be moved. She wore the same bathrobe each day, a dingy purple wrap that either Willems or Ulises would wash at night. Excused from work and school because of Isabel's absence, the two men spent the daylight hours coaxing Soledad into eating and drinking enough to, at least, survive.

I've let her get away from me, she said.

There was a fury in her voice, and it was obvious to both men that she blamed herself not only for the wrongs of the past and present, but also for whatever would come in the future. Two more weeks passed, and Soledad grew weaker still, such that even her self-loathing seemed to wane. Alarmed, Ulises and Willems brought her to the hospital against her will.

It did not take long for the doctors to diagnose Soledad with breast cancer. In the month of her bedridden anguish, she'd failed to notice the lump expanding under her right mammary gland.

I'm sorry, the doctor said.

Fair punishment, Soledad said. I lost track of one of my babies.

The doctor, perhaps accustomed to the strange responses of the diseased, nodded and ordered surgery followed by a round of chemotherapy. He said her chances of survival were fifty-fifty, and she was lucky to not have had a lump develop in her other breast, though both would be removed for safe measure.

In the meantime, updates on the search for Isabel came frequently from the church in Guatemala. Girls were sighted who matched the description of Isabel, but they often proved only to be poor or homeless or prostitutes; the general thinking became that Isabel had not been kidnapped or harmed or murdered, but that she'd simply run away. At the hospital the bishop seemed intent on convincing Soledad that

that was the case, claiming often that the situation in Guatemala was rather dire, and it would not be unheard of for destitution to drive good nuns and brave sisters away. Isabel would not surrender to the idea of futility, Soledad told the old priest, to which he responded, The devil works in mysterious ways. Soledad asked him not to return.

Once the search was expanded and made to include the possibility of Isabel's willful escape, the State Department was briefly involved, engaging as minimally as possible its satellite offices in the surrounding countries. By the time Soledad awoke in the intensive care unit eight pounds lighter, the efforts—interviews with border patrol units, coordination with local police precincts, phone calls to every Central American mortuary—had been expanded to Belize, Honduras, El Salvador, and Southern Mexico. Nothing surfaced in the other American nations, however, and within two weeks the investigation was again limited to Guatemala.

Shortly thereafter Soledad began her chemotherapy, and quickly the Encarnacions' world closed in on itself. The Dutchman devoted all his hours to Soledad, leaving Orozco in charge of operations, and Ulises formally withdrew from the university. Together, the men waited alongside Soledad for word of Isabel, but more so for the final verdict on the mother's health. They both believed, in secret and without discussing the matter with the other, they could perhaps live without Isabel if it came to that. Hadn't the girl a long time ago started leaving them? Weren't they already bracing for the moment she'd say good-bye and mean always? But a life without Soledad seemed damning. However, they also both believed that Soledad's health was tied to Isabel, and even should Soledad survive the poisons in her body, she would likely die if her daughter simply vanished into thin air.

During the period between Soledad's chemotherapy sessions, the Guatemalan authorities paid local fishermen to sweep the shallow coastal floor for clues of Isabel's disappearance. Miraculously, they discovered a smallish nun's habit, one that appeared handmade, with a single-sheet letter tucked into the pocket. Stuck also to the letter were a few pages from the King James Bible. The materials were inspected and eventually delivered to Soledad in Connecticut, where she immediately identified her own stitchwork. The letter was what she'd expected: the ghostly missive from Uxbal. The ink had run terribly, but because it had been folded up, a small portion of the signature at the bottom, the *Ux,* was still clearly legible.

It meant nothing at first, mainly because Soledad was due for another round of chemotherapy. It had been months since the mastectomy. The doctor had shown the family the most recent X-rays of Soledad's chest, and despite the majority of clean tissue they found, the physician pointed out a spot where the cancer had metastasized. They'd not seen the satellite darkness before, had not known the disease was still surviving.

It remains, the doctor said to them, looking genuinely regretful. It's a smaller clump, but, unfortunately, it remains.

It was not until the following morning, when Soledad was being rolled into the cancer ward, that she said to Ulises, It remains. The Church remains. Your sister, she said. She's gone back to Cuba. She's gone to find your father, because everything is still there. He said as much in the letter, and she heard it. Your sister is going back to him because of her promise.

Soledad took her son's hand. Ulises looked into her face—thin, taut, ashen around the eyes, a fine nose, and a beautiful chin, a regal chin—and the waiting was over then.

I was unfair to her, she said, and I think I am going to be unfair to you. Will you go find her? Soledad asked. I'm too weak.

Ulises nodded. Though he should have felt torn again from his own life by his sister's, tossed again by the weight of her existence, he did not. Despite having spent the night in the hospital lobby, he was awake. He breathed calmly, though his mother was at the brink. He squeezed her hand. All right, he said.

This, he thought, is what people call Providence, feeling capable of what you're asked to do. If this were always the case, then Ulises would suffer well the term *fate,* and even though the word was more often a phrase for the damned, he did not feel that way just then. In fact, he felt like moving, like running, when all along he had been lingering still. When all along he had been killing time. But now Ulises thought he knew: he'd been waiting for the chase.

THE SOUND

Uxbal's letter was a wave carrying with it the blue sound of Isabel's youth. It was written in the language of clay, a saltless bread on her tongue, and it filled her ear as honey poured into the chambers of a nautilus shell. It returned Isabel to Sundays at the packinghouse in Buey Arriba and to her father's wet lips, his thrilling hot breath. It put her on a bench with other young girls, their white blouses gray with sweat. It stirred an old memory and asked a familiar question.

> *My love, I hope you know how much this God has given you. Forty days he prayed and fasted in the desert, which isn't much time at all in the scope of things, but the body is a weakness, and it doesn't take that much to break it, to untangle it from its needs. Eventually, when it's hungry enough, it consumes itself. The Gospels say Christ met with the devil out in the sand, and he was tempted with food and water and power. Can you imagine food or water as a temptation? Maybe some of the tomatoes in our garden, because they're so sweet? Everywhere else in the Book the Lord commands travelers and strangers to be taken in, to be cared for, to be given food and water and a place to rest. So here the devil does the Lord's work, and it is a sin, a temptation against the master plan. God contradicts himself, doesn't he, Isabel?*
>
> *What would you have done if Christ refused you? You are in the desert, and you see him, hungry and sunburned, his face gaunt and his shoulders low. You see how red his feet*

are, the tops of them like boiled lobsters. His eyes are human eyes and nothing special. You expected to see or hear God, but here is just another man.

And you realize this: he disgusts you. The body is repulsive. It smells terribly. The skin is like wet paper that breeds disease. His breath is raspy. It rots like the guavas in the back. That's what you find if you go into the desert: human filth. But still you do what God has commanded. You serve him. Or you try to, and he tells you to go away. He won't take your water or your bread. God banishes you from him.

We think this story is about the devil tempting our faith and us. We think we're the one in the desert. We want to be the Christ; and we want to show God how we cast the devil aside. That we're stronger than our bodies, or that our faith won't crumble because of tongues and stomachs.

But we're not Christ in that story. We have no powers. We could not turn stones into bread if we wanted to. If we threw ourselves off a ledge, no angels would break our fall. We would die.

Here is the truth: we are the devil in the desert. We are the ones at the Lord's side, offering him our bread, the same bread I'm still digesting. The same bread we, a few minutes ago, called the Host. It was his body we ate, or so we think and hope and pray, but we now know that in the desert the body, even Christ's, is worthless. It becomes the thing by which we tempt Jesus.

Here's another lie: we think we want Jesus to be wholly human. We think we want him to suffer not for a single afternoon on the cross, but for a lifetime and in all the ways we have suffered. We think we want Christ to want for food and to believe God has abandoned him, not just for one day, but for weeks, for a time sufficient to cultivate lasting fear. We think we want Jesus to be as unsatisfied with this world as we all are.

The real sin of the devil in the desert is not that he offers Christ bread, but that he reminds Christ that he is God. He wants to see Jesus as God, not Jesus as man. This is us. This is you, Isabel; this me, your father; this Rosa next to you; this is Carlos, her father; this is Lupe, her mother; this is Nestor behind you; this is Zava, his wife, and Mona, his daughter; this is us. We think there is a lesson in God's suffering, something that reveals the plane of Earth we share with the Creator of all things beyond the Earth, with the Maker of stars and planets and galaxies and atoms and dust and light; the notion that we can be Christlike. But that is absurd. His suffering is a ruse; it lasts for a flash in the length of eternity, which is the time line of God. He has no sense of time. It means, in the fat scheme, nothing to him.

The sin is in the knowing. The sin Christ confronts in the desert is the knowledge that his body is useless and, dangerously, how easily he can dismiss it. He will see how tiny a thing he is doing. He will know how small he is as a human being, how little he can change the world as a lump of flesh. The moment he knows, he can and will and should let it all fall away. He will enact the right of a God on Earth; he will make food from stone. He will shake water from the clouds. He will walk into a city and take it.

So we must—are you hearing me, Isabel? Don't cry. This is the Good News—turn away from God as the Almighty. We have to burn into our hearts Christ the human, Christ the weak. We think we do this, but we don't. We make Christ strong and powerful, because we fear the hard work of a weak and human Christ. Because though it is a pathetic few hours for the Creator, three hours on a cross terrifies us. Because we are afraid of the pain and hunger, and we want to save Jesus in the desert in the selfish hope that he then does the same for us. We want to barter our way back to paradise.

People, take each other's hand. Isabel, take Gabriela's hand. Take Celia's. Hold each other. Right now I could say to you, It will be all right. Trust in the Lord. Trust in God. But I need you to be scared. I need you to understand the weight of this promise and the fear that accompanies it. You have heard me and all these men speak to the power of God. But today I wanted to say the things I have not yet said. I wanted to tell you about the fear and the pain that is coming. I hope I have been clear. I hope you feel in your chest and heart how sad a thing I am asking of you. I am asking you to feel pain, a tremendous pain, to wallow in your bodies, to dedicate your bodies to the most human purpose, the bringing of souls into this world.

I love you, Isabel, but do not do this for me. If today you make a promise, you give yourself over to a filthy, dusty Jesus. Christ was a human, so we can and should also be human. What you promise us, then, is not the birth of just another rebel, but of another human, another Christ. You give us another savior.

THE SEA

It did not bother Ulises that perhaps he'd been fated to return to Cuba. His father had never left, so going back to the island had always seemed a vague though improbable possibility. Still, bobbing in the wake of Isabel's disappearance, disoriented by the long boat journey, and traumatized by the image of his drained, flat-chested, post-surgical mother, Ulises pushed forward with an intransigent focus that allowed him to ignore what Soledad had actually asked him to do: go home. He arrived in port tired and tan and nauseated, having wanted to see the island approach from the ship's bow. After vomiting his small breakfast, Ulises hired a taxi to take him to his hotel, where he shut all the blinds in his room and slept for forty hours in a bed that was too short and too narrow for his body, waking only to drink water, order and eat room-service tomato salads, and use the toilet. In Havana, he was to do two things: visit the local order of the Sisters of the Holy Resurrection and meet with a man named Simón, a cousin of Orozco, who had agreed to help Ulises get to Buey Arriba.

When, on the third day, Ulises finally emerged from the hotel, he was greeted by an oppressive heat, which seemed to push out into the city streets all manner of people. Ulises heard German being spoken, saw girls heading to school with scarves under their collars, and thought all the beggars were dressed as itinerant farmers. Havana's population slid beneath a dull fog, and the added mixture of military vehicles and chrome-fendered limousines further unhinged him.

Ulises felt that the city existed in some sort of time warp, but it wasn't trapped in the 1950s the way those postcards with the rusted

Bel Airs might suggest. Rather, it seemed disconnected from time altogether, as if it had removed itself from Earth's revolutions so long ago
that those rusted cars were not the detritus of a better past, but the
haunting machinery of a disturbing future.

It's the sun, he told himself, which he had not forgotten in the
mind but clearly had forgotten in the skin. The light of day was overwhelming, and this was different from Hartford, where June, July, and
August were all haze, a smothering cloud. He made a joke to a passerby about the summer heat in Havana. The man laughed at him, saying, This is the *only* season, which made Ulises feel like a foreigner,
the blood in his heart not his own.

He hailed a taxi, which took him to the Church of Christ the Savior. He discovered that the church was a sort of tourist attraction—
a horde of Italians were taking pictures—because of a minor miracle
supposed to have taken place on its steps sometime in the seventies: a
deaf child had fainted near the doors, and when he awoke in the hospital later, he could make out sound in his right ear. At the entrance,
Ulises approached a small man collecting donations for the site and
asked to see the Mother Superior. My sister is missing, he said. The
man went to fetch the nun.

Ulises waited at the door, and people began to confuse him for
the foyer attendant, so he found a pew and sat down. But he felt out
of place among the handful of supplicants, and he lowered a kneeler
to the floor as gently as he could. The church was a castle compared
to the packinghouse in Buey Arriba, the only place in Cuba he had
ever prayed. Still, his legs were too long for the space beneath the
bench; they knocked against the kneeler behind him, so he turned at
an angle, facing not the altar but the tabernacle situated in the eastern
transept, a small nook flooded with reddish light.

He thought of the Eucharist inside, which he'd not tasted in years,
and he imagined a severed leg instead of a wafer of bread. It was a game
he used to play at morning Mass when he was younger, imagining all

the body parts of Christ the other children were eating. It reminded him of Tantalus's stew, and Cronus, and all the men or gods who ate other men. Debts being paid, Ulises thought, and he saw then his mother's breasts in the tabernacle. He felt the need to cry, but instead he began to recite Latin exercises under his breath. Eventually, he found it easier to simply speak in Latin, which had been the language of school services, of Mass at St. Brendan's, which is how Ulises got to praying. And though he started with the Lord's Prayer, he quickly slid into more specific supplication: Ulises asked the Lord to stop disturbing his sister, to perhaps grant a pardon on her faith and then, if there was time, to keep his mother alive that Soledad might see her daughter again before passing away. The invocation seemed to admit the death of his mother or, at least, that things looked bad, which, of course, they did, so Ulises started over, praying for good weather in Hartford and for kind doctors to attend to his mother. But in doing so, his skepticism returned, and he realized that to keep amending his wants, if he kept asking for less and less, he eventually would ask for nothing and never be disappointed. This, maybe, was the real difference between him and his sister: Isabel could be disappointed by God, but Ulises could not. It made him feel small and young again, a child in a space suddenly monstrous. It was in that state that the Mother Superior, a broad woman who introduced herself as Sister Espinosa, came upon him.

Your sister stayed here two nights, she said. One to rest and one to pray.

What condition was she in? Ulises asked.

Troubled, maybe, or just tired. She was at our door very early in the morning, and she hadn't eaten in a while. We fed her, and then she slept for most of the first day. She smelled terrible, and we had to convince her to shower. It took us half a day to realize she was mute and to give her a pencil and some paper.

A vow of silence.

She didn't mention it, Sister Espinosa said. She eventually told us she was a novitiate elsewhere. We offered her a new habit and some of our clothes, but she wouldn't take them. Your sister is not an easy woman to reason with.

She has her own faith, he said. It looks like yours but is something else altogether.

It's stronger, she said. On the second day we had no services, because no one would enter the church while she was praying.

Why not? Ulises asked.

She seemed possessed, the nun said. Well, not exactly possessed. Shaking possession. But people saw her from the door, and something made them stop. They congregated at the entrance, and when they realized she wasn't going to finish praying anytime soon, they gave up on Mass for the day.

Did she tell you where she was going? he asked.

She didn't even tell us she was going until right before she left, Sister Espinosa said. I thought she might stay longer. I thought she was purging herself of something.

Ulises wondered if this had been the place where Isabel's faith was tested, whatever that meant, against the loss of himself and his mother. He realized he wanted it to have been a struggle for her to go. Or because he had never been able to demand much of Isabel, he wanted the church to be a place where she had, at least, considered them, if only briefly.

We did give her a backpack, Sister Espinosa said. She asked for one.

What did she take with her? he asked.

Mostly food, but also a sweater, a shirt, and a bar of soap. We gave her some boots as well, and she left us her slippers.

She was leaving the city, Ulises said. She was heading east to Buey Arriba.

I think she was heading into the woods, Sister Espinosa said. No one wears boots in the city. Miraculously, we had a pair to give her.

What kind of boots were they?

The kind for cane cutters. Thick soles and an ample toe. Your sister was desperate for them. She reminded me of the campesinos south of Camaguey or northwest of Santiago, the ones along the coast right after the revolution. When they heard that Batista had fled to Miami, they cheered, and then they started asking for things. Sister Espinosa put her hands together. She said, I am very old to remember that era.

She crossed herself once and kissed her fingers.

There are two Cubas, she said, the one in the city and the one in the country. Your sister seemed to want the latter. The cities are cramped, and there's only room for one kind of Catholicism, but there's more room and fewer churches out east and away from the highways. Out there no one is going to tell you how to pray. That's how your sister prayed, as if she were on her own with God.

So the faith falls apart the farther east I go, Ulises said.

It fans out like a wave and runs over everything, but only enough to wet them, to give them a taste of God. They substitute the rest with what's around, chapels or not.

Leaving, Ulises put another donation for the church in the box at the entrance, and the man by the door tried to shake his hand. It was bright outside, sometime after lunch, and the city was napping. Despite the efforts of a cabdriver, it was difficult to find an open restaurant. The driver said it would be at least another hour before the gears began to grind again and to maybe order something from room service at the hotel.

At the front desk there was a message from Simón: a hurricane was coming, and though he would be late to Havana, he would meet Ulises at the Blue Dolphin for lunch the next day. Ulises asked the hotel desk attendant about the hurricane, and the man politely said, yes, there was often a hurricane coming, but the hotel had only to close its shutters and lock its doors in preparation. Only when the winds blew over one hundred kilometers per hour did anyone really take notice.

Not tired, Ulises ordered two sandwiches from the hotel kitchen and took them on a walk down to the harbor. This was not the harbor through which he'd left Cuba, though of that moment in time Ulises only remembered the throng of escapees. They carried with them lumpy pillowcases, packed in a hurry and spilling clothes, money, papers, and photographs. There was one man who'd written prayers on his body. Aboard the boat, he took his shirt off in the sun, and Ulises could read across his chest incantations to the Holy Mother, his begging for calm waters. He remembered also the lighthouse in Mariel, set on the western side of the harbor. In Havana, the lighthouse was part of an old Spanish fort, and it guarded the eastern bank.

By midafternoon, a mixture of tourists and natives populated the white sidewalks and the lovely paths along the seawall. Ulises stopped at a street vendor and bought a pair of sunglasses before finding a café. He ordered rum and Coke, as well as some paper and a pencil, and wrote a letter to his mother and Willems while sipping his drink in the shade. He would call them later, but he'd been told phone calls to the U.S. were not affordable and the connections often failed. The clerk at the hotel told him the mail was more reliable despite its sluggishness.

In his letter Ulises recounted his safe journey to Cuba and even noted for Soledad the strange awareness he'd felt when he approached Havana by boat. He left out his seasickness but detailed his conversation with Sister Espinosa, though he did not mention the boots. As Ulises pictured his mother in his head, Soledad grew weaker by the second. She aged with every imaginative act, and he felt himself attempting to take the burden of Isabel from his mother's shoulders completely. He believed it would not be wholly unacceptable for her to die—when had he come to this conclusion?—with the belief, no matter how improbable, that her daughter could be brought back. Ulises ordered two more rum and Cokes as he finished his letter on a bright note, mentioning Simón's message at the hotel and stressing the fact that Sister Espinosa had known exactly who Isabel was.

The rum came, and this time the waiter left the bottle of Havana Club on the table, and when Ulises asked him if he could purchase an envelope nearby, the young man returned with one for free. Ulises, feeling a bit drunk but pleasant in the shade, watched a weather vane atop the Castillo de la Real Fuerza. The weather vane was in the shape of a woman, a flag in one hand, some sort of branch in the other. Curious, he leaned over to disturb the two women at the table next to him, one a thin brunette in a long skirt, the other tall and pale despite the sun.

What's the meaning of that weather vane up there? he asked, pointing.

They told him the statue commemorated the wife of the explorer Hernando de Soto, who was also the seventh governor of Cuba. When de Soto went to explore North America, his wife had supposedly waited for his return by walking along the harbor wall every day for four years, and when she heard he'd died of a fever along the Mississippi River, she died four days later.

One of the women said, She was faithful, you know?

The women explained how the weather vane was a replica. The original had been blown down in a storm and was now on display at the Palacio de los Capitanes Generales, home to the Museum of the City of Havana. Before the waiter collected Ulises's rum bottle—now empty—one of the women grabbed it and tapped its label. Ulises saw that the rum's logo was the same figure.

What was her name? Ulises asked.

Isabel de Bobadilla, she said.

At the museum, crowds of tourists shuffled about the courtyard, and Ulises watched as bookish guides directed whispering pods through the arcade and into various rooms. He saw that the second story had a beautiful limestone façade, and embedded in the limestone were any number of marine fossils, which made Ulises think—though this likely had something to do with the rum—that Cuba was a bandage on the ocean, a floating scrap. I am on a ship, Ulises said to himself, and as if by command his legs wobbled at the knees. He stumbled slightly and made his way to one of the pillars that upheld the arches of the arcade, and he leaned against the column.

A hand touched his shoulder, and a woman asked, Mister, are you all right? Would you like some water?

The woman appeared young at first but was maybe even older than he. But I *look* much older, Ulises thought, and he touched his head and found sprouts of hair there. He'd cut it back before he'd left, but it had been days, and the patches that still grew out, the little forest surrounding the ridge that was his scar, were taking root. The skin was also hot. Ulises pressed a finger into his scalp, and he felt a tingle. How long had he been walking around outside? How long had he been burning under the sun? He patted his pockets and found his wallet, but his new pair of sunglasses was missing. The girl waited for his answer. She wore a yellow blouse, a red handkerchief, and a long skirt. She had pretty dimples and green eyes, and Ulises wanted to think she looked like Isabel, but that was entirely untrue. She was rounder than his sister, not really plump, but the shape of girl who ate regularly and slept well.

Are you a guide? Ulises asked.

I can be your guide, she said. Would you like a tour of the Palacio?

Some water first, if that's all right.

Around the girl's shoulder was what seemed like a small purse, and from it she took a thin plastic bottle. It reminded Ulises of a flask, and he drank from it.

How much for the tour? he asked.

Depends on how long we walk together, the girl said.

Can we settle at the end? See how far we go?

The young woman said, Sure, but I will need at least fifty. Ulises agreed. Where would you like to start? she asked.

The statue of the woman, Ulises said. The woman who is the weather vane.

She's beautiful, the girl said. I'm Inez.

Inez took Ulises by the arm and led him inside the Palacio. She brought him to the foot of the stairs that led up to the mezzanine, and there was the statue of Isabel de Bobadilla.

It's named *La Giraldilla,* the girl said. She stepped back from Ulises and pushed gently on his back. She said, You can touch it if you like. It's good luck for travelers.

The statue was four feet tall and had the green hue of old copper, but the torso of the figure looked more like a man's than a woman's. One of the knees pushed outward from beneath the skirt, however, and the exposed thigh—plump and curving, dimpling as it dissolved into the knee—was without doubt that of a woman.

Did she really walk the seawalls?

Just a myth. When Isabel learned that de Soto was dead, she sold all their lands, abandoned Cuba, and returned to Spain. I'm sure she died comfortably in Madrid. But that doesn't mean she wasn't faithful.

Inez asked Ulises what else he'd like to see, and he told her to show him whatever was best and nothing very political. She told him that was nearly impossible. She spoke of the Culture Department and pointed out that even the Palacio they were currently touring had been the governor's mansion during the island's colonial period.

You don't sound very fond of the city, Ulises said.

I'm not from here, Inez told him. I'm going to university. I study Caribbean art history.

You seem to know everything.

Ulises was immediately embarrassed, because he found her attractive, but what he'd said was condescending and empty. Had he not

been so sunburned, he thought she would have clearly seen him blushing, but all she said was thank you.

What else? he asked.

Inez took him to the Plaza de Armas, La Habana Vieja, and even
the Catedral de San Cristóbal. Ulises had no interest in the Cemen-
terio de Colón or the forts guarding the harbor entrance. They walked
between squares and avenues, briefly flirting with a length of the
Malecón seawall, but then decided to head inward toward the city's
center, where Ulises said the surroundings seemed more recognizable.
He even began to think there was a chance he would remember something of his last brief visit.

But though the streets were rife with statues and small shops and
memorial plaques, Inez told him every inch of concrete was crumbling. Every day, she told him, another building collapsed. The mu-
nicipal workers, the contractors, the laborers, could not keep up with
the decay. She pointed to a fresh apartment complex abutting a dilapidated church. There, Ulises saw that the sacred walls were caving in.

Two days before his departure, Ulises had hugged Soledad to the point
of pain, as if he could not get close enough. There was air between
them, the physical space where her breasts once were, and she knew
he sensed that absence.

She said to him then, It's all right. I've already forgotten them.

Bullshit, he answered.

She shook her head. It could have been worse, she told him. It
could have grown somewhere hard to reach, like my spine. Or it could
have been stomach cancer. It could have been in my face, and you
might not have recognized me after surgery. I could have lost an eye or
maybe my throat from smoking with Henri. I'm lucky.

But despite those rationalizations, and with her son about to leave,
Soledad began to feel more desperately her mounting losses. A son in

Connecticut, she knew, was probably worth two children in Cuba. But she also knew from being a courthouse auditor that the world was plump with routine loss, and rarely was it the stolen-from who pled a case; lawyers and counsel—surrogates—were always speaking for the aggrieved. The Bible said as much, and this Soledad couldn't ignore, because the pages recovered alongside Uxbal's letter, a few sections from Judges, remained in a plastic bag atop her nightstand. She read them every night before falling asleep: *Now after the death of Joshua it came to pass, that the children of Israel asked the LORD, saying, Who shall go up for us against the Canaanites first, to fight against them? And the LORD said, Judah shall go up: behold, I have delivered the land into his hand.*

Soledad wondered if her daughter had memorized the verses, if she read them inside her head—maybe while sleeping on a boat between Central America and Havana? Maybe while walking through a hot city she hadn't seen since she was a child? Maybe when spotting the green hills behind the whitewashed house?—and if they gave her strength. Soledad closed her eyes and saw their home in Buey Arriba, the green countryside replete with cattle. Her vision wasn't nostalgic but primitive. It's an old, old place, she thought, and she remembered the weather of Oriente, the steady climate, the thermometer mercury peaking almost always around twenty-six degrees Celsius. But she knew that Cuba had only the illusion of constancy, and Soledad could not see her daughter entering that space again with ease. A person can't go back to paradise, she thought.

Yet Soledad also remembered the heat rising off the black backs of wandering cows, an appealing warmth when compared to the always-tepid air of St. Anthony's chemo ward. There, in a slick vinyl chair, pale beige machines pumped her full of chemicals. They whirred next to her ears as she suffered for hours the journey of poison through her veins, and they put her in a state of disgust for the modern era. And though anyone would prefer the hot grass of Buey Arriba to an angiocatheter, Soledad, for a brief moment, felt her heart cut in two, one half troubled with regret, the other grateful to discern maybe the same draw homeward, the same current, that Isabel swam in. It felt like commiserating.

Soledad was grateful, though, to have something of her daughter's, maybe even the girl's last prayers before going home, and she got into the habit of delivering verses to the plants in her house when Willems was not around. While Henri was out running errands or talking to doctors or even napping because the night before she'd kept him up with her vomiting, Soledad recited Bible lines emptily, not wanting to understand their meaning but to pretend her voice was Isabel's. *March on, my soul, with might!* But because of the chemotherapy, Soledad's throat was often sore, her voice weak, and what she heard when she spoke was more noise than song.

When she couldn't sing, Soledad found herself touching the places where her nipples used to be. Slipping her hands beneath her blouse, she'd trace her thumbs across the fresh equator of her chest. She'd pull the fabric away from her collarbone and squint, briefly imagining mammary glands, two sumptuous hills, eight more pounds of flesh.

Hands pressed to her scars, Soledad was learning how to miss Ulises as well as Isabel, a doubled longing that mocked the stitched-together plain of winter-yellow skin that now blanketed her sternum. She often reminded herself that though she could have sent Henri— a traveler, a free wanderer, a Haitian citizen, a devoted man, a relent- less man—she chose Ulises for his eyes, which were her own. She wanted their glinting familiarity to draw Isabel out of her foggy, ab- stract faith and back to the skin and bones of her family.

But, truthfully, Soledad couldn't bear to ask another thing from Henri. She should have, before the cancer, before Isabel's disappear- ance, set him loose. She should have told him to go. She should have told him to save himself. But Henri had more resolve than most peo- ple figured—here Soledad remembered the farmers and their lawsuit against the Dutchman—and the cancer was like a promise to him, an opportunity. Where the sex had failed to ignite, they now had the cool, intimate relationship of a caregiver and his charge: Henri helped Soledad to and from her therapies, he washed their bedsheets, and in the shower he helped her reach the nether-regions of her long, luxurious back. He even dried her hair, slowly, with a thick towel instead of the cranky blow dryer, patting at her gray and black strands and not saying a word when they came away with the cotton.

At the same time, Soledad couldn't ignore the fact that she wanted him at her side. Her actions were gutless; she was in need, and he would allow himself to be abused. But, oddly, her demands on his day—nearly all of his work hours, save a few phone calls to his office and his greenhouses—were also something of an apology. Soledad was offering Henri, the more and more she worried about it, the last pathetic minutes of her life. To have asked him to go to Cuba would have been a passive sort of dismissal, the same as whispering, *This is the start of your going away from me.*

The aftermath of that decision, the choice to cling to the Dutchman, however, fostered a restless guilt in Soledad's body, and this she could somehow discern from the whole host of side effects—cracked fingernails, swollen toes and knuckles, constipation, memory loss— she suffered from the chemotherapy. The guilt was perhaps the only thriving element under her skin, and it flared like an itch at her elbows and behind her knees, sometimes in her shoulders and ankles. And despite her fatigue, Soledad felt the urge to pace around her room during the day, an impulse to lift plants off windowsills just to release the brief but sharp flashes of anxious energy somehow expressing itself in her joints.

More important, the doctor had told her that her sexual appetite— something that had already seemed lost, absent as her draw to Willems—would disappear for a while, but it had, in fact, resurfaced. Amazingly, she felt it reemerge in the empty space where her breasts should have been, as though she were experiencing phantom limbs. Sometimes she was certain she could even feel the tips of phantom nipples. Her long periods of rest became punctuated with brief moments of inexplicable physical ecstasy. She would wake from a nap, sit up in bed with her eyes shut, and as long as they were shut, she could believe without a doubt that she felt the weight of a woman's chest bearing down on her torso, pulling forward slightly her shoulders as her breasts once did. She'd not dare touch herself but waited, instead, sometimes for an hour, for the sensation to fade.

Drenched in her own excited sweat, she'd say to herself, They're hallucinations, really wonderful hallucinations.

But she didn't ask her doctor about them, and she didn't tell anyone, neither Henri nor Ulises, about the episodes. She wouldn't admit they were anything but the natural expressions of a body losing itself, the sane, expected motions of a system in shock. She told herself repeatedly, The dreams will fade. This phase will pass.

Yet Soledad found she could not keep her resurrected libido a secret from Henri. In bed and despite how upside-down she felt from the second round of chemotherapy, she turned her desires onto the Dutchman. Her hands were relentless in the dark, and they found not only the Dutchman's penis, but also his armpits, his anus, his earlobes, and *his* nipples. Soledad discovered an extreme pleasure in twisting the Dutchman's areolas with her thumb and middle finger as a way to rouse him in the middle of the night, and grasping at his chest while suffering blindly the phantom weight of her absent breasts was satiating in a way that Soledad could not understand. If she believed in religion still, she might have called it a religious experience, though the joy of it was too consistent, too regular, for anything she would ever attribute to God.

Sometimes Henri shot up in pain, and once, just once, he'd instinctively punched her in the side of the head—he was only half awake and had no idea what he was doing. This somehow encouraged rather than deterred Soledad, and she found she welcomed the pain, the throbbing consequence. As a result, she made it her mission to provoke the Dutchman whenever she wanted his skin, to not only get him hard, but to bear down on him like a hurricane. The trials of her body, its aches and weaknesses, were, as a result, sacrificed to the gust of pleasure the memory of her chest had blown. Each midnight romp became a mixture of pain and suffering and undeniable, utterly unpredictable satisfaction.

For Henri, it was as if the Holy Ghost was entering the bedroom in the middle of the night to abuse his whole being. It was as if he was being burned alive by a strange faith, and under the sheets he whispered or shouted, Jesus God! Regardless, he let Soledad do whatever it was she wanted, and often enough he was aroused; feeling isolated for so long from her, he was eager to oblige.

But Henri found that Soledad wanted not only to make him hard, but for him to then turn on her, to take over the act. She might slap his erect penis and then moan when he was rough with her neck or pinched her clitoris. It was cruel, Willems thought, and not to her but to him; their lovemaking had turned into a reciprocating submission of the will, and this was not the equitable love he'd grown accustomed to. He could only imagine—and this from remembering the slow death of his own mother—that in the darkness of life giving out, that one wants more than anything to be taken over, to be overwhelmed. It was a way of letting go, and if something, God or belief or ghosts, swept in to carry you off, then there was another life to go to. It was a test of faith, and Soledad's faith, Willems believed, was so fierce and violent because of how long she'd kept it submerged. In the absence of Isabel and Ulises, Henri thought it had awoken, and it seemed to want to make an offering of both her body and his. The Dutchman had not forgotten the quiet, unresolved disturbance between them, but he was also amazed by the limitlessness of their consensual torture. They had come to an implicit agreement in bed, in the wet, earthy air of their plant-ridden bedroom: the body could not last, it would not last, and therefore it was ripe for sacrifice.

Willems mentioned this to Soledad's doctor. He was afraid Soledad might wear herself out, that she was busy fucking when she should have been convalescing. He was also afraid of himself. A few nights past he had not only turned Soledad over in bed but had reached around her side and grabbed, with not a little force, the scar tissue of her chest. He'd never done this before, and it made Soledad heave. She'd cried out, but when he let go, she took his hand and pressed it harder into the scar. She'd liked it, and so had Willems, but the gesture had opened a door, and before the night was over, he'd pulled out a tuft of her hair, grasped her neck hard enough to bruise the skin, and bit her in the ass; they had not known it till the morning, but he'd broken the skin, and the sheets were streaked with Soledad's blood. Willems was terrified. He felt as though *his* body were succumbing in some way to the cancer. Soledad's form was retreating before his eyes, and with her permission he'd gone about reclaiming it. Willems had never felt so powerful. He'd also never felt so shamed, so childish, trying to hold on to something that was clearly in the early stages of decay, as if he could hold Soledad back from the pit of death.

The doctor said, You love her. This is strange but not unnatural. You want to keep her.

She's not mine to keep, Willems said. She's not a possession.

Our bodies, the doctor said, are not the people we love. And it seems she wants you to keep at it. If it makes her feel better, I'd keep doing it.

Willems shook his head.

Maybe also schedule a few sessions with a counselor, the doctor suggested. It doesn't sound like she says much about it, and sometimes it's helpful to just talk about these things with no real goal in mind. Just describe the circumstances, characterize it, define it, and whatnot. Perhaps schedule a few sessions for yourself as well. These situations are often harder on the family. They're the ones left behind.

A week later and in a psych-ward office smelling faintly of sawdust, a psychologist asked Soledad how she was feeling lately.

I miss my children, she said. The chemo is fine. I know what to expect this second time around, but I miss my son and my daughter. They're twins. That's from their father's side; their father's mother had a twin sister. Mr. Willems is not their father. That man is in Cuba still. Ulises was born a few minutes before Isabel, but you'd think she was the older one. I don't know whether birth order really means anything, though perhaps it's different when twins are involved. The house was quiet before they left. One of them, my daughter, doesn't speak. She can but chooses not to. I wish sometimes that the difference between them being home and away was more obvious. I keep expecting to walk through the kitchen and see one of them. I can't believe the silence means what it means. Does that make sense? It sounds like nonsense when I say it aloud.

The psychologist asked about the condition of Soledad's body: did she notice any difference in reaction to the second round of chemo compared to the first?

Yes, I do, Soledad said. I am awake at night constantly. The first time through I slept like I was already dead. My body, I think, was in a state of shock from all the drugs, and it just wanted to shut down completely between sessions. Sitting up for hours for the treatment nearly emptied me. As soon as it was over, though, I started to feel re-markably better. The tumor hadn't left, but my body was acting like it had. They originally thought I'd only be strong enough for one round. But here I am, and this second round is a different world.

The psychologist wondered what Soledad thought about all night when she was awake.

My body. I've never been so aware of what my body feels like as I am now that I'm stuck in bed. Before when I slept, I had favorite positions, places I liked to put my arms and legs. But now that I've been altered, I can't find the same spots. My arms lie differently without breasts. Sleeping on my chest isn't painful but it is odd. And I don't like sleeping on my back at all.

The psychologist got to the point: new appetites?

I just want to be tired again, Soledad said. Our sex used to be wonderful, but it didn't ever exhaust me.

We could try sleeping pills, the psychologist suggested.

I suppose. But that won't really make me tired, will they? They'll just shut down my brain, put a fog over it. My body will still feel the same. I take enough pills as it is.

Do you think, the psychologist said, that this is something you should share with Mr. Willems?

I don't see how Henri would benefit from knowing this, she said. To be frank, he hasn't stopped himself from being rough with me. Even if it does disturb him, it doesn't stop him. But if he knew what it was I was after, I'm sure he'd suggest something else. Taking up a sport or longer walks or something without any adrenaline.

What was the sex like before?

Loving. Or passionate. It was heated, but nothing like this. This feels necessary or, at least, necessary if I want to stay sane. Before it was mostly pleasure, mostly another way to enjoy each other's skin.

Do you still find Mr. Willems attractive?

Yes, she said, though to be frank, I am more interested in what he's capable of doing to me than I am in exploring his flesh. It sounds like I'm testing him, doesn't it? To see what he'll eventually do.

Do you think, the psychologist wondered, he could really, truly hurt you? In a matter that goes beyond play?

Soledad thought for a moment. Only if I asked him to.

It's exciting, the psychologist said.

What is? she asked.

You smiled just now, he said. You said *if I asked him to,* and you smiled just a little bit.

Now I feel myself blushing, Soledad said.

What's thrilling about it?

Soledad paused a moment. Throwing away my body, she said.

Doing what you want with it, the psychologist said.

She said, Maybe that's too simple.

Of course it is, but you haven't yet told me how.

Willems also visited a counselor, but not the same one as Soledad, a distinction his counselor pointed out right away.

It didn't seem like a good idea, Willems said. I thought it might make it harder for Soledad if she knew I was talking to the same person. Like I was telling our secrets, confessions a therapist could use against her.

Has she done something wrong? the counselor asked.

No, of course not. She's ill. I just mean it would seem unfair. If her counselor knew things ahead of time, I feel like he or she might come to certain conclusions. Then it might not matter what Soledad is saying. Maybe a diagnosis would already be under way.

Did you tell her counselor anything before their session? Did you write anything down on the intake sheets?

Yes, I think so.

What did you write? the counselor asked.

That our situation feels different now, Willems said. That we don't interact the same way. It feels like our connection is askew.

Anything else?

I mentioned our lovemaking has changed.

I saw that. Very different, it seems. Do you feel that was a betrayal somehow?

I had not considered it one.

But, the counselor said, you didn't want to share the same counselor.

No, that didn't seem like it would be helpful.

So really you didn't want to betray her trust more than you already had, the counselor said.

I know that's not an accusation, but it feels like one. But I see your point. Yes, talking about our problems to the same person would have felt wrong. My version might have skewed the truth. This is her illness, not mine.

So she can talk freely? the counselor said. She's allowed to betray your trust because she's the one who's ill?

Am I afraid she's telling our secrets? I hope she is. I hope she's talking about everything she needs to.

What do you think it would be like if you were talking to her psychologist right now instead of me? What if your session came right after hers?

I believe I'd have a hard time with that, Willems said. I'd feel as though the psychologist would know too much about me, or that he'd know the same things I did, which might be unsettling.

How come?

I don't know. Actually, isn't it obvious? No man likes the idea of another man having intimate access to his wife.

But you two aren't married.

Maybe I've come to think of us that way, Willems said.

You think you've earned that distinction, the counselor said.

We have been through a great deal of pain together, and I can't imagine leaving her.

Is that love or marriage, though? You seem to love her very much, but marriage, if I am being overly simplistic, is someone accepting that love completely. Do you feel completely accepted by Soledad?

I don't think she would do the things she does with me with someone she does not accept. I think that our strange behavior is possible because of our closeness.

And before? Before the new kind of lovemaking, did she accept you then? Or is this now the moment you feel brought in entirely?

I don't know. There wasn't a time stamp on our relationship before. She wasn't dying yet, and we were happy. She does seem to be letting go of herself. But I can't say if she's giving up or giving herself to me. I'm not sure she knows what's happening, which is why we're here.

This, for you, is maybe about commitment then. You are asking yourself if this is her proposal to you.

Maybe, Willems said.

Do you worry about her past, then? The manner in which she left her legal husband?

No.

Have you ever met her husband? the counselor asked.

No, never spoken with or seen the man. The closest I've come is a letter he wrote to his son.

The counselor asked what Willems thought of Uxbal.

Nothing really, Willems said. I can't picture him in my mind. I've hung around his son enough that you'd think I'd be able to extrapolate something, but I haven't. At best, he is the man who gave Soledad children. At worst, he is the man who hurt her.

Who are you in all of this?

The man who deals with her pain.

Do you think about the letter often? the counselor asked.

I think about it the mornings after sex.

The rough sex?

Yes, Willems said. After the rough sex. I think to myself, there is a man shouting out into the void. There is a man who knows things about the woman I am with that I do not. Soledad has said before that her husband and I are not too dissimilar in some cases. Our best parts, she's said, often line up.

The counselor said, You have all these years together now that her husband doesn't. Don't you think you know some things he does not?

Yes, yes.

I don't mean to be crass, the counselor said, but do you think he's ever bitten her on the ass?

Willems said, You're right, of course. Unless this is some older version of Soledad. Unless this is who she used to be when she was with him. Which means I'm the one still learning how to touch her. I feel like she is leading me on, sometimes, but I can't figure out why. She used to want me, but now she wants *something* from me. It's like we've started all over again. As if we're just now at the beginning.

On the streets of Havana, Inez kept touching Ulises's elbow as she guided him. Inez also touched him when they changed directions, when she read from the plaques they came upon, when they slid between parked cars. She slipped her arm into Ulises's, and he thought this was a custom of the city. At one point a truck rushed by, nearly nicking their heels as they passed an alley, and Inez put her hand on Ulises's chest. She touched him enough that Ulises forgot that he was on a tour and acted as though they'd stumbled upon one another as old friends do sometimes. Yet this was a friendship of a different sort, more like an old devotion resurrected, as if Ulises had pined after Inez in childhood. Her fingers—mariposa stems compared to his thumbs, thick as mangrove roots—kept finding his knuckles or palms or shoulders. They put him at ease, and by nightfall he asked her questions he'd not ever thought to ask a woman.

You told me you're not from here, Ulises said.

I'm from the east, Inez said. Near Palma Soriano.

The country? he asked.

A bit like the country, she said, but not entirely. On the edge of the wilderness, maybe.

That's where my family is from, Ulises told her. He told her Buey Arriba was also on the edge of rough country, but he realized he was only guessing. He said, Anyway, there are mountains just to the south, and I've known people to get lost in them.

I didn't think you were a native, she said. You have an odd accent, and you don't seem like you grew up here. You're too big for this city. You take up the entire sidewalk. Is this your first time here?

It's my second time to Havana, he said, but I don't remember much of the first. I was young. I'm looking for my sister. She's left our family, and we think she came through Havana. We think she's gone back to Buey Arriba.

I'm sure you'll find her, Inez said. The towns out east are much smaller. There are fewer people, and they all know one another. A different sort of place than Havana.

I was told that, Ulises said. He asked, Why did you leave?

For school and work, she said.

There are no museums in Palma Soriano? he asked.

There are more here.

And your family?

Still there, she said.

Do you make it back?

I don't, she said.

Inez took Ulises by the forearm and asked him if he was hungry. The rum had long since worn off, and he said yes. She took him to a barrio just east of the fading Chinatown, and they slipped quietly into a restaurant serving tuna wontons, ham sandwiches, greasy noodles, mangoes, glazed herring, and plantains. Inez did not eat nearly as much as Ulises, but she sat as close to him as possible, and once or twice she touched his leg, though when Ulises looked up at her, she'd turn away. She seemed to be making a decision about something that did not concern him, and he found himself jealous of whatever thought kept her attention from him. He wondered if he'd somehow offended her. There, perhaps, was another reason for her migration to Havana, a troubling background his questions had evoked, but the notion only intensified Ulises's attraction to Inez, the possibility that she too had left her home without much choice. He felt his thumbs throb and his lips sweat, and he could not keep himself from looking at the shape of Inez's neck or smelling the gasoline musk she'd acquired from their long afternoon of walking the city and dodging ancient diesel pickups.

I miss my women, Ulises thought. He knew the sentiment was a little perverse. Inez's presence was not the same as his mother's or sister's. He also knew, however, that he'd spent his entire life between those two women, one far ahead of him and one just behind, and there was no separating their DNA from his, no way to extract genes from the skin or memories from the mind. Reflected at the bottom of his empty glass were his face and his eyes, both offshoots of his sister's, both products of his mother. He began to understand his family, the Encarnacíons, in the same way he was beginning to understand his mother's body: short on time. He felt an urge for Inez, but in that urge was the strange, regenerative force of procreation, and Ulises thought of a future when he had daughters who looked like Soledad and Isabel. But he could not parse exactly between the want of his body and the longing he had for his family. I'm fucked, Ulises concluded, and he ordered another beer.

But then Ulises considered that it might just be the heat and the city, the excitement of being a solitary man for the first time in his life. Havana was an aphrodisiac inasmuch as the weather, the low-hanging moisture, kept shirts loosely buttoned and feet mostly bare. He remembered his steel-toed boots back home and how tight he would tie them in February to trap the heat. Beneath the table he could see Inez's toes wiggling, and though Hartford summers were damp, they had an end. Willems had once told Ulises that on the hottest days in Cuba the laborers drank steaming coffee from the moment they woke straight through to the end of their shifts to keep their sweat up. One was cooler if one was a little clammy, and it occurred to Ulises that the only way to sleep at night in Havana, besides vomiting oneself to exhaustion, was to find another body and sweat it out together. And where Ulises had expected the city to dull a little in the evening, to rest quietly in the welcome dark, the streets were, instead, filled with the humming of a thousand electric fans all spinning at once. His hotel room, he recalled, had two fans, and the restaurant they were in had six. On their walk he'd seen a twirling blade atop almost every windowsill, as if Havana planned to take a large, collective breath as soon as the sun set. The sea breeze, he imagined, was wonderful at night, and it took a mechanical effort to bring that moving air into houses and bedrooms.

The waiter brought Ulises another wet glass of pale beer, but before Ulises could take it from the man, Inez asked, May I? I'm not thirsty enough for my own, but a sip would be wonderful.

Ulises watched as Inez drank from the glass, and he saw some of the grease from her lips smudge the rim. She picked up a napkin, and he thought she would wipe away the stain, but, instead, she used the cloth to soak up the condensation. With the damp rag she wiped her forehead.

Like living in a rain cloud, she said, and she laughed a little at her own joke.

She swiped the napkin across her cheeks, and then she pressed it against her chest. Ulises watched as the smallest trickle of water ran down her sternum and into her blouse. Ulises wondered at the effort it would take to bring Inez back to his room, but then he realized he had no idea where they were anymore, and she, perhaps fortunately for Ulises, would have to walk him home. He had never been alone with a woman who wasn't his mother or sister, and this he knew was partly due to his size and appearance. The scar on his head was magnified by his bulk, and the two together afforded him as much solitude as he could want, a condition he'd grown so accustomed to that he'd barely ever noticed the few women who populated his introductory classics courses at the university.

Moreover, his earliest memories of sex were filled with his mother and Willems's moaning, and alongside such noise he had endured the distinct and overwhelming asexual silence of his sister. Yet drinking his beer and looking at Inez, Ulises saw how unafraid of him she was; she might have been even arrogant in front of him, speaking knowl-edgeably about Havana, sometimes, as if he was a younger man or a cousin of hers. At the same time, she was flirtatious, though Ulises couldn't tell if this was intentional or accidental. He couldn't classify the difference between their erratic arm-locking and the dictatorial manner in which she sometimes pointed out landmarks or told him where to turn. But above all that, she didn't shy away from him or his body, and though that was a far cry from attraction, it was still fresh territory for Ulises, a place in which he could talk to a woman—and it felt like he was meeting a woman for the first time, unfair as that was to his mother or sister—as though he had no body, or as though his body was no longer a wall between him and routine conversation. And when Inez did seem to flirt, when she touched him for no rea-son, all of a sudden Ulises *was* a man—again, as though for the first time—because he was wanted. He began to think, as the girl stole yet another sip from his lemon-colored beer, that sexuality was a gift given from one person to another, that desire begat desire in a way that was both more subtle and permanent than he'd ever imagined.

After Ulises paid for dinner, Inez did lead him back to his hotel. Outside, clouds had gathered in the sky above the harbor, and on their walk it rained in little spurts. The air smelled of salt and fish, and just enough precipitation fell to wet their clothes for Ulises to offer Inez a towel from his bathroom. He told her he could also ask the front desk for an umbrella if she'd prefer. Inez refused the umbrella but accom-panied Ulises upstairs.

A hurricane is coming, Inez said to him once they were alone— sitting on the edge of his hotel bed. The room was cool compared to the air outside, and someone—a maid, perhaps—had come in while Ulises was gone to turn on his two fans.

You're the second person to tell me a storm is coming, Ulises said, but no one else seems to know. The clerk at the desk knew nothing when I asked him.

The showers we walked through are the outer rain bands, she said. They stutter like that before a storm hits. There was some time between them, so maybe two days until it's here.

Inez's shoulders were wet, and her shirtsleeves clung to her elbows as she spoke. Sitting close to her and with the lights on, Ulises could see that her face, which he had first thought was rounded and full, was really just square. The jaw, which maybe in another kind of light seemed to curve, possessed a sharper line, and it stretched beautifully when she spoke.

What happens here during a hurricane? Ulises asked.

Nothing, except most folks get a day off from work, she said. If the water rises too much, they'll evacuate the city.

It doesn't seem like they have plans for an evacuation.

It's too soon to tell.

Where do you go when they evacuate you?

They send people inland to the sugar plantations, where they set up makeshift dormitories, Inez said. Men in one dorm, women and children in the other if there's time.

It seems odd that they would separate families.

It was odd to me at first, but it's to protect the young women.

Have you ever lost your place? Ulises asked.

No, she said. I have an apartment not far from here. It's in a newer building and on the seventh floor. It's usually safe. Sometimes I don't evacuate. I'll probably stay there for this storm as well. The rain was not so bad.

Will you stay there tonight? Ulises asked, and he realized as he asked this, a question about where Inez would sleep, that he could be no worse a coward. He wished that instead of speaking he'd touched her neck and gambled for something more than the curt *no* he was hoping for.

You haven't paid me yet, she said.

For the tour?

For the evening, Inez said. She blinked and added, They'll charge you more if I stay the night.

He said, It's all one rate, isn't it?

For couples, yes, Inez answered, but not for hookers.

You told me you were a history student.

I am, she said, but books aren't free. If you're worried, I visit the doctor once a month. You don't want to pay for it?

I feel tricked, he told her. Take whatever you want out of my wallet.

She said, I'll take seventy, but I deserve more. The money is for what we're going to do, not for the dinner or the walking together.

I don't know what to make of that, Ulises said. One led to the other, but you're telling me you were a separate person for each. Would you have slept with me without being paid?

Of course not, she said. You're a traveler passing through. Why bother when we talked first about your going east and second about my spending the night?

You worked me, he said.

I could have lied to you, Inez said. I could have slept with you and then left in the middle of the night, taken whatever I wanted out of your wallet. I could have propositioned you from the start. You *were* nearly passed out, and I would have had every right to drag you straight back to this hotel room, nurse you with more beer, and then take off your pants. Do you think, she asked, that when I work, I sleep with only one man a day? That I walk the streets with every man before I bed him?

Inez stood up at the side of the bed and placed a hand on her hip.

She was waiting for him, and Ulises, seeing the rigidity of her pose, was reminded of the *Giraldilla* weather vane. The severe figure supposedly awaited her husband, but the fleshy, exposed right leg—Inez's right leg held beneath her skirt, though Ulises could see the faint outline of her thigh pressing through the damp fabric—seemed to call for any man. It lacked modesty, but Ulises would hardly call it vulgar; instead, the iron thigh exhibited the same bravado that Inez displayed. They shared clarity of intentions. But as Ulises thought about it, the truth of the matter—whether or not their walking together had been a scheme or an unexpected joy—became less and less important. He wanted to consider their meal together a brief romance, and the possibility was enticing enough. She had already confessed some affection, and Ulises didn't know if it was fair to ask her to abandon her role entirely, to ask her to live beyond what were her normal means.

Inez asked, Do you want me to touch you or not? Do you want to sleep alone tonight? There's still time for me to find another passerby, but I'd rather stay with you.

She approached Ulises and placed her hands around his collar. She pressed her palms into his skin, and then she slid her fingers into the gaps between the buttons on his shirt. Ulises had not worn an undershirt, and he could feel Inez's hard nails tap against his perspiring skin.

She asked, Do you want me to take this off?

Please.

The sex was painfully slow for Ulises, who, once he was naked, was more adventurous and forthcoming but clumsy. He did not know when to move his lips from the neck to the collarbone or to anywhere else. He did not know where his lips were welcome. He stalled for long seconds, like a plane headed straight for the sun, until Inez became the timekeeper and the pacesetter: she eventually made him undress her one article of clothing at a time, and she asked that each bit of fabric be placed on the chair near the room's desk instead of being tossed onto the floor.

I don't have so many pretty skirts and blouses, Inez said, and when Ulises made to bite at her neck, she bit him first on the ear and whispered, You can't leave any marks.

He came to a standstill when she took his penis first in her hand, then in her mouth, and she seemed to know when to slow down or stop altogether so that the act might last a little longer. He wasn't sure if he should kiss her when she stood, but he did, and he was glad he did, because she pushed him then onto the bed and slid her hips over his crotch. Her hands were in his stubbled hair, and miraculously he was inside her. Gusts of wind knocked at the fan on the windowsill, and their two bodies rocked like icebergs in the night, which was a soothing image under a full moon but a dangerous thought for a sailor in the dark.

Ulises came quickly but was atop Inez when he did, and he felt both a masculine pride he associated with Cuban machismo as well as a lingering Catholic guilt despite his agnosticism. The hazy duality reminded him of his mother and sister; for as long as he could tell, a woman was reason enough to leave a place behind—his mother, Cuba, his sister, the United States—but he decided, while catching his breath, that a woman was also reason enough to stay. He knew he was drunk on sex, but seeing Inez's naked body, the way she pushed the black hair out of her eyes and, reaching down to her crotch, the way she readjusted the folds of her labia, he thought stupidly that lost things could be replaced.

Dreaming in this fashion, he worried about Inez, who sat next to him drinking a glass of water. He thought of leaving her, which he would do in the morning with Simón, and he wondered if they might have sex again, which caused his flaccid penis to rise a little, though it still ached. He touched his foreskin, which was wet, and saw a milky drop of semen pool at the tip.

He said to Inez, I'm sorry.

For what? she asked.

I didn't think of getting you pregnant.

Inez handed him the glass of water and said, I'm infertile.

I assumed otherwise, he said. I'm sorry.

Would you have behaved differently?

No.

Inez got up from the bed and went to use the bathroom. When she returned, she began to dress.

Is this why you never go home? Ulises asked. Because they know what you do here?

I don't go home, Inez said, because a man I was married to still lives there. He divorced me to marry a woman who can have children. I don't go home because I don't want hear about the man's children growing up down the street. My mother knows that I support myself and that I attend the university. She knows that I don't plan on ever going home.

We all have to at some point, Ulises said without thinking, though he knew immediately the idea had grown out of his own guilt. He sensed the unspoken promise he'd made to himself a long time ago to never go home, mostly because of his father's offenses but more likely due to his fear of finding Buey Arriba a sham and a mess: rotten tomatoes, a dilapidated town, a meek and ruined father, an enemy without power despite what he'd convinced himself was actually there.

He asked Inez, Do you know for sure that your ex-husband has children?

No.

Then how can you be so certain he's happy? That he has a growing family?

Inez shrugged.

The longer you stay away, he said, the larger his family grows.

Don't preach to me about going home, she said. Your sister is still missing, and here you are in Havana, sleeping with a hooker.

I leave tomorrow afternoon, he said.

Inez faced the window. Most likely sooner, she said. The wind is picking up.

Ulises looked out the glass and saw a clothesline across the street struggling to remain attached to a wrought-iron balcony. Two dresses hung from the rope, and as Ulises watched the line swing in the intermittent gusts of wind, one of the dresses was blown away. Then the line snapped altogether, and it began to rain.

Are you going to stay in the city? Ulises asked.

Yes, Inez said. I doubt they'll evacuate us now. It's too late.

The windowpanes shook against the moving air outside, which seemed to be gathering strength, but then it stopped, and even the rain ceased.

There will be sirens in a moment, Inez said.

Is it that close? Ulises asked.

No, they just mean to turn on your radio.

There was a small radio on the bedside table, and before Inez reached it, Ulises could hear the sirens calling, a series of long, low wails. Inez tuned the dial, but all Ulises heard was static. They waited a minute, and then the static was cut off by an echoing voice. The voice said that local brigades were preparing for evacuation and that people should make their way along designated evacuation routes to designated evacuation sites. The city would flood, but there was time to safely and methodically exit. But first prepare yourselves. Do not forget water bottles, and pack extra medicine of any sort if you have it. There will be food and cots. There will be heat if it gets cold. The inhabitants of Havana will be cared for. Wait for further instructions.

Who's speaking? Ulises asked.

That's Castro, Inez said. If we had a television, we could watch him predict the pattern of the storm. He likes talking in front of maps. He refers to hurricanes as a bad bit of weather.

You seem to treat it as such, Ulises said.

Inez looked at him and said, I should go. I have to get food and water before the flooding starts.

How long do you think the city will be underwater? he asked.

Three days. It should be two, but the city sewers are old and drain slowly.

You'll be alone for three days in an apartment, Ulises said. I'd get lonely, or claustrophobic, if I had to stay inside for that long.

Ulises got out of bed and put on his pants, but when Inez said she did not need him to walk her out, he left his shirt on the floor. Moving around the room, he felt very hot, and when Inez touched him before leaving, she said, You're badly sunburned. You should cover your head in damp towels. It's going to hurt tomorrow. Your skin feels about to burst.

Ulises touched his scalp and winced. The skin had tightened, and he could feel the same effect on the back of his neck.

I didn't notice it until just now, he said.

You were preoccupied, she said.

She let him kiss her before she departed, for free this time, since he'd already paid her, and she was careful not to press her fingers too roughly into the side of his face, though Ulises felt an ache in the fingertips and thought, I'm sick with women. But then Inez left, and Ulises went to the bathroom, where he soaked the two washcloths hanging on the rack. He lay down again on the disheveled bed, made a mask of the wet towels over his chin, cheeks, forehead, and scalp, and after a while he managed to sleep.

Isabel awoke with a sudden need to vomit. She had been dreaming of God making promises to Sarah. Outside her wooden lean-to the forest was loud and black, and the mosquitoes bit at her ankles and ears. She retched as quietly as she could, trying to muffle the odd sound of her hiccupping, and she spat and wiped her greasy lips.

She considered Sarah in the tent laughing at God, disbelieving the child he'd promised Abraham. For months now, the matriarch's story had crept into Isabel's thoughts. She had been hearing His sound slipping through the canvas flap in response to the old woman's amusement, the voice an angry rush of floodwater.

It was night in the rebel camp, and one couldn't see the ragged shacks circling the brief clearing between a bamboo grove and a wall of sabicu trees. Isabel closed her eyes and saw the faces of two men, two rebels. One had a scar above his right eye and a long, blunt nose. The other had eyes of different colors, a brown iris and a black iris, and a small mouth missing three bottom teeth. Just days ago, Isabel had gone to bed with each of them, despite their filthy skins and body hairs thick with grime. *The Lord visited Sarah as He had said, and the Lord did to Sarah as He had promised.*

Isabel tried again to keep from retching. She remembered their breathing, their heaves as they were astride her. It was miraculous that either of them had finished, had come inside her, so starved were their bodies. The rebel camp—populated by four other men, six women, and a handful of children—was a wasteland where food was scarce. Exhaustion was a state of being, and Isabel had been nervous to touch the two men with any sort of force. They had both floated above her, working their hips and scraping their knees toward an uncertain climax, and Isabel had tried not to look too long into their wild eyes, pupils dilating as though they were remembering past miracles. Rather, she'd focused on their rib cages, flexed against their thin, pale skin, threatening to tear their chests apart, to spill the contents of their abdomens. With both men she'd thought, Not a bone to spare, and she'd worried their intercourse would be for nothing. That she'd not be as blessed as Sarah.

But when Isabel was certain something had passed from their bodies and into hers, she'd turned quiet and grateful. The hot air of their lungs escaped them in a rush of acrid breath on her face, on her neck, and the men held themselves like statues. It was, she'd decided, the presence of God, the same stillness He had brought inside the tent with Sarah. Afterward the men shivered with cold, but Isabel sat still, listening to the quiet between their gasps, believing, out of faith rather than evidence, that miracles were born from dire circumstance, from under duress: Sarah the aging mother and Eve the cribbed offspring of a diminished, anesthetized Adam.

A wind came through the encampment, and Isabel opened her eyes. The nausea subsided. She still could see mostly nothing, but she knew which direction to walk if she wanted to find either one of those two rebels, which shacks were theirs and where on the floor of each they slept. The first one she'd gone to, the one with the scar, was probably the younger. His name was Efraín. He'd groaned at the very start and was unable to control the volume of his panting. He had clearly never slept with a woman before, and he'd barely kissed Isabel before pulling off her boots. It had rained that day, and Isabel had hoped the running water would hide their noise. But Efraín couldn't contain himself. He shouted as he entered her, as he finished, and Isabel realized that the young man didn't have the strength to have sex and temper his voice at the same time.

She slept with these men while Uxbal lay sickly, holed up alone in a bamboo hut like a waning emperor. What are you doing? he asked her the night following her tryst with Efraín. Everyone heard that racket.

She'd said nothing.

Speak to me, he'd begged her, but she wouldn't.

Isabel had been at the camp for over a month by then, and she hadn't said a word to anyone—not even to Uxbal when he cried at seeing her thin, dehydrated face coming out from the forest that first time at the twilight hour. She'd not expected to remain silent. She'd thought her voice would come charging back from its hibernation the moment she saw her father. He'd said to her, You've come like a vision. She took his hand and kissed it.

He was weak then, walking with a stick, and he was even weaker now, in bed most of the time. His breath and body shared the same rancid odor, as though his skin were fermenting. His canvas cot smelled like sugar-water gone sour, and he'd lost all his molars. He told her he was not well but had suffered worse, though soon he was begging her to speak, claiming that to hear her voice would give him strength. In response, Isabel could only shake her head. In the dirt of his shack she wrote, *I took a vow.*

Why? he asked her. Why? You're torturing me. I haven't seen you in years, and finally I can touch your arm and look at your eyes. But I can't believe my senses if you don't talk. I don't know if it's really you if I can't hear your voice.

Isabel wrote him notes but ran out of paper fast, filling up in just a matter of weeks the five stenographer's notebooks she'd brought. She wrote incredibly small letters on the page, but some were so tiny, Uxbal could not read them. His eyes were going too. On the cardboard flap of one notebook she scribbled, Why are you ill? What have you got?

I'm old, Uxbal said. I don't know. It could be just a cold. It could be something else.

Isabel knew he was worse than that.

Uxbal asked her a thousand questions, and she responded to each one, writing twenty notebook pages on her time in the United States, her brother, her mother, and the Dutchman. She wrote extensively about her work with children. She wrote about God. Gathering the pages, Uxbal rolled them into a tube and tied them together with a string. He hung them from the roof of his shack so they wouldn't get wet and fall apart. He read them every evening before the sun set, and then he and Isabel would sit next to each other, holding hands. She would pray, and Uxbal would stare at his daughter's fingers and say, They look like your mother's. But your arms are long like mine.

She wanted to say something back, but she felt she didn't have the words with which to break her vow. At times she wasn't sure she had a voice anymore, and she prayed to St. Paul, whom God had told to preach: *Be not afraid, but speak.*

Isabel didn't know what she was afraid of. Sarah, she decided, had been afraid of dying. She'd been an old woman, and it was dangerous, what God had promised her. It might have killed her. It might have broken her open and left Abraham with a son but no wife to nurse him. Miracles are dangerous, Isabel thought, and she'd always considered her vows minor miracles, the incredible effort necessary to stay hushed in such a loud world. It would be another sort of miracle for her to break the silence. She wasn't sure Uxbal understood what it was he was asking of her when he said, Speak!

Of course, Isabel could see that it pained him; he called out to her relentlessly, and she saw that he was made weaker by the effort. His body was a testament to frailty: it farted when he napped after meals, it stank when he sweated, which was all the time, and it refused to digest enough food to nourish him completely. When he was short of breath, Uxbal would reach for his cane and push himself up against the wall nearest his cot, coughing gray phlegm into his hands. Often he would struggle, and those were the moments Isabel drew closest to him; she would slide her long arms under his sticky pits, her chin dipping behind his damp clavicle, and lift him with a delicacy she'd acquired as a hospital volunteer. Sometimes she would even press her palm into the small of Uxbal's back, forcing the old man to push his chest out and make more room for his gasping lungs.

In most ways he reminded Isabel of the lost causes of St. Anthony's and Jude the Apostle, the nearly gone bodies she'd visited by candle-light. His shack was as spare as a hospital bedroom, and even the cot with its aluminum frame echoed the steel bedrails of a gurney.

In truth, Isabel did not speak because she feared she had returned to the land of the dying. It was the familiar, quiet terrain between the here and the hereafter, a place that, through her years of service, had become a language-less region. Isabel thought she could feel a similar desolation around Uxbal's diminishing form. It was not a silence, for all her belief and devotion, she was prepared to test the magnitude of. Was it gathering still? Was it close to consuming him? Or was there time yet? Only once in her long career as a volunteer had Isabel ever disturbed the air of the suffering with her own clean breath, with the echoes of life. Only once in all her 944 hours had she cruelly brought a person back into the world with her careless tongue.

It happened when Isabel was a junior nurses' aide, before she became the Death Torch, when she had signed up for the dark hours of the early morning that no other volunteer could stand. She walked the hall-ways of the hospital and hospice center between two and six, encoun-tering respirators, soiled bedpans, moaning newborns, and exhausted residents. But she was diligent and fearless, and she was freshly pos-sessed by the image of the blue-lipped boy she'd held at Opal's Lake. It was her devotion that eventually led her, one day, into Room Three of the hospital's southern wing, the children's cancer ward. There, Isabel intruded on a young girl who was wide awake at four in the morning and staring blankly into the half-light with an amber cat's eye. Some disease had colored her iris a thin, gorgeous shade of honey.

Started by a stranger's entrance, by Isabel's quiet gasp, the girl cried out. But then, seeing Isabel's face, the girl said, It's not killing me, just making me go blind. The leukemia is what's killing me.

She was bald, and she sat straight up in bed as though she'd been expecting a visitor. Her hands were busily rubbing her kneecaps beneath the purple hospital blanket. Behind her, the orange glow of a streetlamp slipped through the blinds covering the window.

I'm not scared anymore, the girl said.

Isabel wondered if, when you are dying, do people stop asking you questions like *How do you feel?* or *Are you scared?* The answers are short-lived. She said nothing but walked up to the bed and offered her hand. As the girl took it, she blinked, and Isabel saw again the golden eye.

You startled me when you came in, the girl said. I thought you were one of the night nurses. They come barging in like it's the daytime, like we're not trying to sleep in here.

I'm sorry, Isabel said. I didn't mean to scare you.

The girl, still holding on to Isabel's hand, lay down and closed her eyes. I thought someone had come to my room because I had died, she said. I thought I was watching myself from above.

An hour later, her heart monitor began to chirp. Where is her family? Isabel wondered. The girl's breath stopped. Another minute and the monitor's alarm gave out, some fault in the wiring, and even the baseline hum of the girl's pulselessness was gone. The sun came up, and the room yellowed. The ceiling fan stopped turning. It took a long time for the nursing staff to arrive, and when they did, they entered the room with tired, dipping chins but also bright, shifty eyes. Isabel realized they were grateful the girl had passed; she understood they had been waiting a long time for this.

After the body was taken away, Isabel went and asked a nurse at the desk where the girl's parents were.

They died the year before in a car accident on a highway, said the nurse. An aunt adopted the girl, but she's unmarried and works long hours. She came every night at 6:10 and watched TV with her niece, but the girl was most often by herself.

The nurse was called away, leaving Isabel alone at the desk.

Isabel then did something she shouldn't have: she went behind the nurses' station and peeked into the girl's chart. In the myriad handwritten doctors' notes, she saw the patient's date of birth, the record of her diminishing weight, her fluctuating body temperatures, and the progress of the cancer. She read the shaky, partial prognostications of chemotherapists, of the resident oncologist, of the surgeon who'd cut a growth from the girl's leg. She saw the girl's name: Daphne Bergmann. Tucking the chart under her arm, Isabel retreated down the cold corridor.

Back in the room, Isabel noticed for the first time how empty it had been all along, how devoid of toys or books or even a child's teddy bear. As if all evidence of the world had been consciously removed, possessions somehow a distraction in the final hour. Isabel spent an hour tidying Room Three. She changed the linens on the bed, emptied the trash cans, and dusted the room's surfaces most often overlooked by the cleaning staff: the top of the window frame, the blinds, the space between the headboard and the wall, the inside of the nightstand drawer, and the protruding back of the mounted TV set, which was something like a bulbous gray tumor.

When Isabel was finished, she went to the hospital chapel, a small room in the eastern wing decorated with only a white cross on the northern wall, a vase overflowing with daffodils, and six rows of gray folding chairs. Isabel was surprised to see no specifically Catholic ornaments. In the front row and with Daphne Bergmann's chart at her side, Isabel sat down to pray for the girl and her deceased parents. She said her prayers aloud, because the nuns had taught her to always recite with conviction; there was no shame in asking if what you asked for could be asked aloud.

Because Daphne Bergmann had been young and motherless, Isabel spoke directly to the Holy Mother. She began at first with a Hail Mary but soon realized she didn't have a rosary on hand. Isabel considered a lengthy incantation to God's inscrutability; but the girl had died instead of being resurrected, so Isabel chose against the Sorrowful Mysteries, which gave meaning to death by pulling death itself from the void.

Instead, Isabel settled on a private novena for Daphne Bergmann, one that would last nine hours instead of nine days. She glanced around the quiet room. A novena demanded replication from a printed text. At St. Brendan's, there had often been a Bible passage or a chosen hymnal printed on a pamphlet from which the congregation would read. When one of the teachers had died, they'd used hand-size, blood-red leaflets. But the chapel was empty.

There was Daphne Bergmann's chart, however. It lay closed on her lap. With careful fingers, Isabel opened it and began to read: Name, Daphne Bergmann, Date of Birth, August 17, 1973, Height, 5 feet, 1 inch, Weight, 95 pounds, Address, 3486 Copper River Road . . . red and irritated eyes, early signs of glaucoma, deteriorating vision across long distances, increased squinting . . . pain in the left leg surrounding the femur, trouble walking, limps slightly according to the aunt . . . osteosarcoma as a result of metastasized retinoblastoma . . . chemotherapy dependent upon patient's postoperative condition . . . hospitalization and monitoring . . . cisplatin, doxorubicin, high-dose methotrexate . . . ineffective drug therapy, referral to Boston Children's . . .

Reading the chart both illuminated and muddled Isabel's vision of Daphne. The records were meticulous, and something told Isabel that children's records were more deliberately maintained than adults', that their smaller faces inspired in doctors greater diligence. It noted coolly all the weaknesses of the girl's ailing body: how the cancer had spread but also how it had strengthened and divided, how it had sought fresh parts of Daphne Bergmann to consume. But it said nothing of Daphne's background, noting only that her parents were deceased. The chart's main figure was the aunt, who came across as an observant caretaker, offering surgeons and oncologists an active portrait of her dying niece: *she limps and complains of not being able to see the TV, at night her bad eye disturbs her in the wrong light; she cries when I touch her thigh; she's just weak more often than she's strong.*

After an hour of reading aloud, Isabel detected a shift in the woman's tone as she tracked her niece's deterioration. Through the scrupulous notes, Isabel could sense the aunt's palpable fear, but as Daphne's illness progressed, the girl was eventually transformed into a foreign body. For all the time the aunt spent watching and caring for the niece, she seemed, in the end, incapable of knowing Daphne beyond her skin. *She feels better if she drinks three glasses of water at 7 each night; she needs a pillow under her left leg in the mornings from 8 to 10:30.* The aunt's precise observations implied a mechanical distance and a sad truth; Daphne, at some point, had become her illness, was no more than her body and its failings. Isabel cried at this, though she kept reading, and her tears wet the doctors' dictations and the stiff X-ray sheets, black and now leaking thick, inky carbon onto Isabel's fingers.

By the fourth hour of recitation, Isabel's lips were dry and her throat was sore. She had to whisper to keep going, which was actually a blessing, because the sound of her own voice had given her a headache. A severe pain had lodged itself behind her eyeballs, producing bright flashes of blue light if she spoke too loudly. The softer she spoke, the more bearable the prayers became, and eventually she spoke only on the exhale, only when air needed absolutely to leave her lungs. She was beginning to memorize parts of the girl's chart, and she could, by the fifth hour, anticipate the single instance in the chronology of Daphne Bergmann when the cancerous cells seemed to be moving into remission, a lone, optimistic mark by the sloppy hand of a doctor looking for hope: *recent therapy showing somewhat positive shifts in disease management.* But that was the only deviation in a long decline, and eventually Isabel felt herself going the way of the aunt, losing the brief, though startling, image of Daphne in her mind she'd only just recently acquired: the cat's eye. The orange glare was fading, and Isabel felt the young child dissolve first into a body, second into a vaporous plague, a malicious biology, and finally into nothing but noise.

By the seventh hour Daphne was little more than a name, a sound Isabel could barely utter.

Yet the girl had been Isabel's first patient, the first dying person she'd sought out and spent the night with, or, at least, some moments, escorting her across the darkness. Isabel felt she'd at last begun to enact her revelation at Opal's Lake, but right then she could barely recall Daphne's face. And now, after the fact, following the transcendent moment, she felt no different. There was no blush in her neck, no heat rising in her chest.

Isabel recalled Daphne's throaty voice. *You startled me,* the girl had said. And she had looked to be in a trance just before she died, fixated on something Isabel couldn't quite see.

She was shaken loose by my voice, Isabel realized. She was awoken.

Had she been late? Was Daphne already on her way when Isabel pulled her back? Maybe returning to the world is more frightening than moving into the next, Isabel thought. Maybe I shouldn't have made a sound.

In the ninth hour Isabel did something she'd never done before: she spoke directly to God as though he were a man at her side. She closed her eyes and asked, Where did that girl go? Did I take her somewhere, or did you take her through me? Why doesn't this feel like that afternoon with the boy on the frozen pond? Why does my skull ache?

Isabel opened her eyes. She stared at the floor. Then, to her right in the folding chair nearest the wall, she saw a pair of brown shoes and a pair of legs in dusty blue pants and a pair of thighs making a lap upon which rested a pair of hands folded one atop the other.

Startled, her whole body tensed. Her scared hands bent Daphne Bergmann's file at the edges, and her knuckles blanched. Her breath, which had been steady, was suddenly lost, as if she were drowning.

Too frightened to cry out, Isabel waited for the body to move or for an unseen mouth to talk. Eventually, she noticed the hands, which were stunning and beautiful, the fingers long and the nails pink, the cuticles clean and trimmed, the knuckles hairless, and the backs clear and brown. The thumbs seemed especially prominent, capable of circling the palms entirely, and all the digits together reminded Isabel of tarantulas, of spiders crawling in many directions. She knew then that the man was a surgeon, and she found herself envisioning his practitioner's hands slipping, ghostly, into the abdominal cavity of an anesthetized patient.

I'm insane, she said, and her own voice was like a needle in her heart, an electric shock to the base of her skull. This is a delusion.

Another pang at her temple. She closed and opened her eyes, but still the hands and legs were there, still his pants cuffs were dingy with gray dust, as if he'd walked through a field of ash. For the first time in her short life, she doubted herself. She thought, The man is a surgeon because I've made him that way. I chose to witness a young girl die, and nothing happened. The nurses came and cleared the room. I washed the television set. I washed the windowsills. Nothing has happened except for this headache. I am seeing a false god to make up for these things. He's a surgeon because surgeons heal the sick. I want to believe God is a surgeon, that he took Daphne somewhere else to cut the cancer from her body.

Isabel remembered the afternoon on the pond and the eyes of the dying boy, the layer of ice she thought was freezing over his pupils. She remembered the blue tips of his fingers, and eventually she recalled things that she had forgotten: her own purple fingertips, the way her cold, dry lips had stuck together, the sensation that her body might give out, the heated blood in her veins popping through her capillaries and arteries. Why was there no counterpart here and now? Where was the confirmation of her work? Why did her veins shrink into themselves? Why were her arms cold, and why did her own voice send waves of guilt and pain down her spine?

Because she could not help herself, she asked the man, Do you normally make the work so mysterious?

Isabel tabulated a handful of God's mouthpieces: Abraham, Isaac, Moses, Sarah, Aaron, Amos, Isaiah, Jeremiah, Esther . . . and not one of them had moved along a straight path; even the first two had been a complicated mess of indecision, the father told to kill the son, who then becomes another prophet.

Isabel asked a better question: Can you tell me why my voice is poison?

And because she asked this question in earnest, Isabel couldn't help but look up. She was ready to see the man's face. But, looking, she found the face hidden beneath a surgeon's mask, and the man also wore a surgeon's cap on his head hung so low that Isabel could not make out his eyes. What she gained was a view of two beautiful arms emerging from a surgeon's pale green scrub shirt, both appendages long and coffee-colored. The face stared back at Isabel, and she saw the mask pucker and flatten. For a moment she thought it was the surgeon's breathing, but then she decided his lips were moving beneath the sterilized cloth. He was speaking something to her or, at least, mouthing some words.

Isabel felt her voice gurgling up in her throat, but she clamped her jaw shut. She slid toward the stranger. Her white hospital shoes, dragging across the carpet, did not make a sound. Isabel listened for the air ducts, then for her own breathing, but heard nothing.

The world has gone away, she thought. Or I've gone deaf.

Isabel saw the man's feet shift, and she faced him, looking to see if his lips still moved. The surgeon's mask fluttered like the wing of a moth, and Isabel felt an ache in her ears, a reaction to the silence, a craving for sound. She leaned toward the stranger and put her ear next to his mouth. She held her breath. Her cheek was nearly pressed to the man's chin, and though she could not describe, either then or afterward, the quiet she experienced next to his mouth—overwhelming, drowning, submerging, swallowing—she would remember always how cold the skin of her face became. There was a slim pocket of air between her body and his, but the air didn't seem to move, was as frozen as water in space, and it cooled her cheek to the point of pain.

This, Isabel thought, cannot be the God of my making. I'd make him speak.

Isabel began to sob. As she wept, she heard footsteps outside the chapel in the hallway. She heard them approach and then pass the shut door. She heard a clicking in the air ducts, the sound of air moving again though the floor vents. A fluorescent bulb above her flickered and buzzed, and then went out. The room somehow grew brighter. Isabel blinked, and the surgeon was gone.

In the hallway Isabel once again encountered the world of sound. She covered her ears with her hands and retreated to the doorway of the chapel but stopped short of reentering the room. She heard the grating whine of gurney wheels somewhere in the next ward; she heard the scratching of pens on charts and the shushing of air from ventilators. She took a deep breath and crossed the hallway, slipping into a janitor's closet.

There, among the bottles of bleach, dirty mop heads, and boxes of latex gloves, Isabel was able to take her hands from her head. On her chest lay the brass crucifix necklace; she found it with her quivering fingers and discovered that the metal was ice-cold. She breathed hot air onto it. When it didn't warm, she took the chain from her neck and examined the face of Christ. She remembered the face, or lack of face, of the stranger in the chapel, and she shuddered. She hung the crucifix on a hook on the back of the door and rummaged around in the closet, eventually finding a box of matches.

Isabel lit a match and held the burning end to the brass face of the figurine. The flame burned down to the tips of her fingers, and then she lit another match, holding it also beneath the Christ's chin. After the fourth stick she pressed her thumb into the metal; it was hot but solid. Isabel spent the remaining matches, hoping the brass would soften, and when the matchbook was empty, Isabel gripped the crucifix and slammed its face against the metal knob of the closet door. She struck the handle seven times until the icon's nose was mangled and its eyes were shut, until its mouth was also gone. Standing, she drew the chain over her head, but the brass was still hot, and it seared her neck. The heat startled her, and she put her hand to the faceless icon and pressed it deeper into her skin.

Isabel opened the closet door, afraid again of the noise that waited on the other side, but the sound of the world was tolerable again. She could hear her heartbeat echo against her eardrums, but it was not agonizing. Stepping into the hallway, she realized it was nighttime. The ceiling lights were turned down low, and only the lamps above the nurses' station were fully lit. The nurses' station was empty. The phone atop the counter blinked mutedly with incoming calls. This was the floor bodies were taken to if they survived the ICU. All the doors in the hallway, save one just beyond the station, were shut. The open door, Isabel could see, was that of a patient's room. And though Isabel saw nothing besides a blue light escaping the suite, she knew there was a human being lying awake in a bed in that room. Shutting the door to the janitor's closet, Isabel grasped her crucifix. The hallway was quiet and peaceful, if a little cold, and there was a person waiting, perhaps an old man who was himself quiet, who was starting to feel the particular space between life and death. She went to him.

Yet Isabel, for all her Providence, had not anticipated the brokenness of Uxbal's mind and body. Her first weeks at the camp she'd sat by her father's bed day and night, wanting to be near him because she barely recognized him—his voice had proven as foreign to her ears as her silence must have to his. Eventually, he told her of his rebellion during their time apart, but those stories were, in Isabel's mind, passing political history. They did little to explain how Uxbal had come to such ruin. Instead, Isabel found herself scribbling desperate questions onto scraps of paper.

Why did you send Ulises a letter instead of me? she asked one night.

I didn't know if you and your brother were together still, Uxbal said. I didn't have a sense of what had become of you. His article came to me in the way I said it did, carried in the pocket of a tourist by stupid luck. I could write the magazine on his behalf, hoping the letter might reach you too. The censors would see the address and think, maybe, here is a man writing about Cuban cigars. If they opened it, they would read my nostalgia for a family I'd lost, and they'd let it go. They'd assume the magazine, should the letter make it that far, would pitch the letter aside as the workings of a senile father whose family had had the good sense to abandon him. Had I written you, I wouldn't have been able to hold myself back. Who knows what I would have given away about this place and myself? Putting that on a sheet is like building a paper bomb, and you don't know when it will go off.

Isabel watched as her father drew a long breath—as if he'd been holding air the entire time it took to explain himself—exhaled, and closed his eyes to sleep. She moved to his side, closed the unbuttoned gap of his dirty green cotton shirt, and kissed him on his dry lips. She touched his clammy chest and found it faintly rising. She put her fingers to his mouth, above the lips she'd just tasted, and felt a cool air. Isabel watched Uxbal for an hour, until he no longer looked like a man or her father, until he was simply a quiet, ailing body.

A breeze came into the shack, and parts of the walls shook. The scroll above Uxbal's head turned in the wind, and the old shoelace holding it to the ceiling coiled and looked ready to tear. Almost every day she wrote to him on these scrolls, asking, Where do you hurt? and almost every day Uxbal said back to her, I am fine. Touch my forehead. It's cool. I am fine. Feel my dry, happy palms.

Uxbal coughed suddenly, but he didn't wake, and a minute later his face was so still that his sagging skin was like a mask. It reminded Isabel of the cloth covering the stranger's mouth in the chapel and of the chapel's overwhelming silence. It was then that Isabel realized the Lord would take her father from the mountaintop; she had returned there to see Uxbal die, and his lips, his nose, his shut eyelids, his chin and beard—they made the face of God.

Uxbal began to snore, his whitish lips slipping back to show his yellow-gray teeth, the soft palate of his throat trapping air. This was Uxbal after years in the desert. That skin, those bloodshot eyes, and those thinned-out limbs: they were her father's remains. But unlike Christ, Uxbal, after death, would not be reborn. His skin would not heal itself. He would not regenerate into a Second Coming. The desert, Isabel saw, is for men and women—and she thought now of the other rebels in the camp crawling toward the same undignified end—a place to let the body go. It is a place where the elements, the sand and sun and dryness, are as stark as the breath of God, as overwhelming as His silence, the underlying question being, always, When, when, when?

Isabel waited till the following morning after he'd slept, when he was his freshest and his eyes stayed open for the longest stretches, to write in the dirt, How often do you pray?

Not ever, Uxbal said. But my life is a sort of prayer. I keep going even though I don't feel like it. His voice was as loud as it had been since her arrival, perhaps louder: this neglect was the thing he was most certain of.

Isabel suddenly craved the air outside. She moved to the opening of Uxbal's shack and saw the sunlight through the canopy, but it was still early, and the forest floor was dark and blue. She could feel moisture budding on leaves and a mist trying to rise. She wondered whether her father was awake now because he had finally slept enough, or because this was the time of day that most reflected his condition. She wondered if it put him at ease to see the world hushed.

Uxbal moved in his cot, and Isabel heard his stomach churn. His body released some gas, and it seemed to Isabel that his bulk of flesh was doing exactly what it was supposed to: it persisted in the world or, at least, attempted to; it survived. Isabel thought, This is the world of sound. His . . . His is not. She wrote another question in the dirt: What about the men and women?

I think some of them still believe, Uxbal said, but I can't tell. For a while we thought we were being searched for. That the CDR was coming for us. For a month, maybe a year or two ago, the same helicopter would pass over the range three times a day, each day at the same hours. Five in the morning, then one in the afternoon, and the last time at six in the evening. Sometimes the evening flight would come later, when it was dark. They had a spotlight, but its trail was always a straight line. I don't know if they were sweeping the land or just following the peak. It might have been a tour of the hills, but then again it might have been the military. We took a vow of silence.

Who did? Isabel wrote.

The whole lot of us, Uxbal said. It was practical. If there was a helicopter, why not a scout? Why not a forest ranger? Why not a troop sweeping just for the sake of sweeping, just for practice?

Was this your idea?

Yes, he said. I am the leader. He closed his eyes, then opened them, and said, We didn't speak to one another for a year. We made up signals with our hands. Didn't I tell you this? I thought we'd already talked about someone's hands. Maybe yours. Maybe I was teaching you our signals. They're not afraid of you, the others. They are just being quiet. They might talk to you if you press them, if you want. They keep their distance because I'm sick, because I told them to. You've seen their forms. They're no better off than I, except that they aren't ill. I don't want to infect them all. I told them not to touch me. I might have told them to not even touch one another. Silence and abstinence go hand in hand in this camp.

How do they worship? Isabel asked.

If they pray, he said, they do it in silence. My guess is that they do it alone. I never got around to making signals for prayer. I always said them in my head until I didn't. I haven't taken Communion since I've been up here, though that has more to do with a lack of bread than with faith. Truthfully, I've forgotten the prayers myself. They seem now like words for another time. Don't write them out, if that's what you're thinking. I won't say them even if you remind me. It would feel like begging God.

She wrote, Are you afraid to ask for something?

I know the answer, her father said.

Isabel thought, This forest is a spiritual wilderness. This is not my sermonizing father. I have maybe met the devil out here.

She watched Uxbal curl his toes.

Or, she thought, I waited too long. I have just missed him.

Uxbal seemed ready to sleep again. He said, Hand me those papers, will you? I want to read them some more. Maybe I will finish them today.

Isabel untied the hanging scroll and placed it in her father's shaking hands. He was gentle with the stack and counted the pages before reading them. Despite having been hung, the sheets were damp and the paper stuck together. But Uxbal was patient, as though time did not exist, and his eyes widened as he realized how many pages he held, how full the sheets were of Isabel's writing.

His lips moved as he read, and his eyelids slid halfway down his eyeballs. There was so little light in the shack that Isabel didn't know how her father could read her minuscule script, but as she watched, the answer was slowly—perhaps letter by delicate letter. A pair of flies entered, one pestering Isabel, the other Uxbal. When the one circling his face landed on his ear, he didn't flinch, and Isabel understood where her solipsistic focus came from, the way of thinking she had that obliterated the world. It reminded her of the prayers she'd said for Daphne Bergmann, and then Isabel wondered if her father's patient reading was a novena for his own death. They were cruel thoughts, and they made Isabel shake. She had to bite her tongue to stop her trembling, which might lead to sobbing, which threatened to lead to woeful speaking.

Since that night and every day after, Isabel wanted to beg God for her father's life, but she knew then that the most merciful thing to ask for was his death, and that she wasn't prepared to speak aloud, certainly not as the first words to break her silence with. Uxbal had forgotten that God on Earth passed between the mouths of people, through prayers and hymns, through the eating of the flesh, through singing and saying the Lord's name; yet that was what she'd surrendered in order to see him again. Mostly, Isabel felt betrayed; she'd been keeping God since she was young, been one of the virgins with the flames, and she'd fed that flame all her oil, every glistening drop, only to find Uxbal living in darkness and herself incapable of calling for salvation.

The vomiting had made Isabel's mouth dry, and she left the camp to walk west toward a nearby brook that, swollen from the runoff of morning condensation, tumbled into miniature waterfalls. Alone at the stream, she was reminded how little anyone else in the camp, not just her father, moved. She knew that the others, the men and women and children, were equally hungry, and she knew that her father's state, his apathy, might have as much to do with a lack of food as it did a lack of spirit. Her father's body was evidence enough of atrophy, but Isabel also knew that, without nutrients, one's sensation of hunger began to wane, meaning that a person couldn't tell anymore if he or she was dying. It was unimaginable how long Uxbal and his rebels had managed to exist, especially when all manner of things could wipe them out in an instant: a hurricane, a landslide, a wayward hiker, a convoy of soldiers, one soldier, a deeper famine, an infestation of mosquitoes, a heat wave, Uxbal's illness, a second illness, a fatal flu carried into the clearing on the feathers of a bird.

Isabel knelt on the ground and scooped a handful of water into her mouth. As she drank, she tasted algae and limestone. She was thirstier than she'd first realized. She drank until her stomach was full and began to ache. The stretching of her abdomen seemed suddenly effortless, as if this were a world where everything was easily given over.

The bloat brought to mind Efraín, the rebel with a scarred brow, and she remembered with amazement how she'd made a sacrament of his body. She hadn't asked him in advance if he'd like to touch her, and she had not attempted anything close to seduction. Instead, she did as she had always done and simply took what she wanted.

She'd found Efraín by the very same mountain stream, the source of all the camp's water, and—silently, of course—she slipped her hand into his as softly as she could. She led him back to the circle of shacks, to a deserted shack, and there she hung a dirty blanket across the doorway behind them.

Uxbal had said to Isabel from his death cot, *I know the answer,* which was the same as saying, *Forget your promises; He won't hear us.* The act that was Isabel's Providence became, then, not the apex of her faith, but a new question against it: would her faith die with her father?

Quickly, though, as quick as a swelling vein, as quick as a gasping lung, as fleeting as the first sensation of skin inside skin, the act also became the answer. A child, a speculative infant—and maybe it had now begun; maybe Efraín, as his sweat mixed with the dust in the air, as his penis stiffened against Isabel's agitating thigh, was not entirely empty—could now be a renunciation of the past. If Uxbal was without God, he was not fit to be her father. His parenthood would be replaced by her own. She might break all her vows, but not the first.

And that was how Isabel eventually began to speak again, not because of Efraín but because of his naïveté. Their sex was rough and unpleasant; he was afraid to touch her, so she had to grasp at him, and they struggled through the awkwardness of losing one's virginity. He couldn't read her hands and made no effort to read her face, so he stumbled and went too fast, and he hurt her without understanding how.

I am Christ in the desert, Isabel told herself, and I am not forgetting my body, which makes me human. I'm not forgetting my own wet skin.

Efraín's skin tasted like mushrooms, and there was a layer of oil atop of it that made holding him difficult. His black hair was long and covered his dull brown eyes, and his beard, somehow hard and brittle, scratched her neck. The cross she wore slipped behind her back when Efraín, finally alive enough to utilize his hands, pushed Isabel down. As he spent the last of his strength slipping inside her, she felt the blunted crucifix dig into the soft spot between her shoulder blades. By the end, Isabel decided that she'd not sleep with him ever again, no matter how badly she wanted a child.

What Isabel truly began to fashion beneath Efraín's thin frame was a calling for the brokenhearted, and as soon as she realized this—sometime after Efraín but before Guillermo—she felt she could see into the future, which was dark. She was not entering a dark night but a dark century, at the very least some ill-defined set of dark years. The child, when it came, would be a living scar, a private Christ, and if she followed it through the length of decades—away from the mountaintop, away from Uxbal, away from his failed path—then, she hoped, she might find God again, who, she was beginning to think, had rightly forgotten her father.

It was a prodigal path and an exceptional trial, but Isabel felt, for the first time, something like a finite person, because she understood she could not love God again—not after the cold years in Connecticut, not after these days with a decaying father, not after the degradation of all her oaths—without first abandoning Him. Faith, she thought perhaps at last, was the space between broken promises and the will to return, and there was nothing more Isabel wanted in the world than the desire—physical, sensual, sexual, atomic—to eventually return to God.

So, wanting nothing more from Efraín, she took Guillermo. Because he was older, he was rougher. He seemed to know what he was doing but didn't care, as if she'd offered him a body without a soul, a human doll, and what first was a rush of excitement—Guillermo's hands around her ass, then suddenly at her anus—became a violation, a probing that didn't respond to her clenching buttocks. Isabel struck his face. He scowled and asked her if she'd brought him to the shack just to fight.

Breaking the highest of her vows, she said to him, I want a child. I don't want you to throw me around.

Her voice disturbed Guillermo, who, like the rest of the camp, had thought she was a mute. She surprised herself as well; her sound was deeper than she remembered and low, and the words came slowly but clearly from her throat.

Do what I tell you, she said.

Guillermo, frightened at the depth of Isabel's voice, nodded, and from then on she placed his body where she wanted it, told him what rhythm to keep, and positioned his hands where they felt the most natural to her. When she spoke, his body responded; his shoulders moved, his lips parted, and his legs flexed. She made him shudder, and then she herself found some pleasure in the sex.

Ulises awoke to a pounding at the door. He assumed it was a bellhop coming to tell him that the evacuation had begun. Instead, it was Simón, Orozco's cousin, who'd bribed the front desk for Ulises's room number so that the two of them might catch the last train leaving the city that morning. Simón looked very much like Orozco: short and broad, tan and dried out. He told Ulises to get dressed and to pack the smallest bag he had with money, two shirts, and all his papers. The rest they would have to leave behind.

Have you ever seen a city after a flood? Simón asked.

Ulises told him no.

It's a sloppy circus, he said. When we come back, the animals we forgot are desperate and loud. The streets sound like a domesticated jungle.

Thank you for coming, Ulises said.

Orozco is fond of you. But what's wrong with your face?

Sunburn. I got drunk and fell asleep.

Simón leaned closer to Ulises. I think in a short while you're going to be in a lot of pain.

The passenger car was choked with standing evacuees. Fighting their way through the crowd, Ulises and Simón found their bench between an older white couple—tourists—and a black mother with a young boy. Ulises watched as the mother calmed the child by gathering his small body into her arms and forcing the boy's face into her neck. Ulises remembered Soledad's scent as a mixture of cologne and hair spray. Her neck, the last time he had seen it, was gaunt, ravaged by chemotherapy.

What happens to the telephone lines when a hurricane hits? Ulises asked. My mother will think I'm dead.

The connections are worse than ever, Simón said.

She'll pass away, Ulises said. She has cancer. She could die, and I wouldn't know it.

Orozco told me your mother is strong. She'll hold on to the last. She won't go before she knows at least one of you is coming home from Cuba.

What can we do?

We'll see about a mail boat out west. We can send something to the Dominican Republic and from there, up north. How is your face?

It feels like a canvas sack, Ulises said.

Later, as the train lurched past the city limits, Ulises's stomach began to ache.

I have to throw up, he said.

People moved out of Ulises's way, and a ticket checker opened the door for him with a look of sympathy. On the platform Ulises tried to expel whatever was left in his stomach from dinner the night before, but he only managed to spit up a yellow sauce. The sun was rising, and a mist carpeted the rails. Ulises saw that they were nearing swampland, and in the distance he could see the high grass give way to wetter ground, turning into a river. He breathed deeply, and the sickness subsided, though his knees wobbled as he returned to the car.

My sister doesn't know anything about our mother's cancer, Ulises said to Simón. She's disappeared for more than half a year.

You'll tell her?

I hope to, but I'm afraid she might not care. I think she's been forgetting us for a long time now. I don't know if she's capable of hearing what I have to say.

Simón said, Orozco's mother lives with mine in a house in Ingla

Solsta. He only visits once a year. His mother is shrinking—dying, really—but it's impossible for him to know how fast. He hugs her the moment he arrives, but he can't remember exactly how much she weighed the last time he was there. He can see that she's smaller, but the degree of which he has no clue.

That's terrible, Ulises said.

I have to tell him eventually, but I'm not sure he'll believe me. That's not something a person wants to know.

Ulises struggled to imagine the moment he'd tell Isabel why he'd come. He could hear her say, *I will pray for her,* and that was the same as, *Lord, take this from my hands.*

The train rolled directly into the morning light as it headed east. Packed with bodies, the railcar was already hot, but soon the metal roofs were baking, and the cars filled with steam. Ulises began to sweat, the few hairs left on his head curling, his sunburn swelling. He felt a throbbing in his scalp and was certain he'd burned his scar even uglier. The throb became a tapping, and Ulises realized it was not the sunburn but a small finger poking the tissue. He turned and saw the little black boy who'd been asleep in his mother's arms, now standing on the seat. The woman slept. The boy seemed to want to smile, to see if perhaps Ulises would play a game with him. Ulises touched his scar, and it was tender, as though it were still an open wound.

The boy said, *Quemado*—burnt.

Ulises told him yes and no. He said the sun made his scalp so red, but it was an accident that first cut him. The boy's hand wavered, and Ulises nodded. The boy put his thumb on the scar and turned it in circles.

Be gentle, Ulises said. But the boy pressed his finger into the scar, which made Ulises yell. The mother woke and grabbed at her son. She spoke too fast for Ulises, and Simón turned to help, but before he could explain, the mother and her son were pushing toward the rear of the car. Ulises called out his apologies.

What were you doing? Simón asked.

The kid wanted to touch my head, Ulises said. It seemed harmless. Do you think she's going to stand the rest of the way?

Her choice, Simón said.

Ulises stood and tried to find the faces of the mother and son in the mass of upright passengers, but he could not. I didn't imagine them, Ulises said.

Sit down, Simón said. You're going to make people nervous.

I remember that boy from somewhere, Ulises said.

Impossible.

Suddenly, the train was slowing. It came to a stop, and a conductor walked through the cars, instructing the passengers to disembark. The train, he said, was headed back to Havana for another shipment of supplies before the storm hit.

Out on the platform, Ulises and Simón discovered they'd only made it as far as Santa Clara. Simón asked around, and miraculously he found a squad of soldiers headed as far east as Las Tunas. He and Ulises could join them if they didn't mind a hot, bumpy ride in the back of a transport truck.

In the cargo hold a soldier brought out a guitar and began to play while the rest of the men smoked cigarettes and chatted as best they could over the grinding engine. Some soldiers requested songs, and the musician asked Ulises and Simón if he could play something for them, but Ulises's stomach churned, and he shut his eyes after saying no thanks. A young soldier slid over to Ulises's side and pushed a cigarette into his hand.

The nicotine is good for the nausea, the young soldier said. He asked Ulises what he and Simón were doing that they had to travel during a hurricane.

Visiting family out east, Ulises said.

A visit? the soldier asked. Come on, man. I'm not the CDR. I'm just talking.

The CDR, Ulises said. I remember them. Neighborhood watch?

And I thought you were a tourist, the soldier said. I should have guessed otherwise since your Cuban is so good. Yes, neighborhood watch, or something like that. Mostly they tell on you when you say shit about the government. Committee to Defend the Glorious Revolution and whatnot.

My sister is missing, Ulises said. We think she's in Buey Arriba. I've come to take her home.

What's his name? the soldier asked.

Whose? Ulises asked.

The guy your sister ran off with. The macho who thinks he's got her away from you.

Our father, Ulises told him.

Fuck, the soldier said.

It's not like that.

Still, the young man said. My Nicanora, she's older than me, but she tried scooting off to Jaronu with this black guy who's about thirty kilos bigger than me. What could I do? I joined the army. Four weeks' training, then I was assigned. First break, and I got my whole platoon to go to Jaronu. We beat the crap out of the guy and then took a nice dip in the ocean. Brought my sister with us to Playa Santa Lucia. Beautiful beaches. Then she fucked one of my buddies there. I told them to get married, and they did. Three kids, and they're all right, because he made sergeant. You got an army with you or just that guy?

Just me, Ulises said.

I hope your papa's ill, the soldier said. Girls love their daddies.

He stopped talking to light himself a cigarette, and Ulises watched how he held the stick in the corner of his mouth, just like Willems, who could buoy a cigar with just his bottom lip.

What did you do before the army? Ulises asked.

Cut cane.

Do you like it?

Cutting cane?

No, riding in these trucks and building barracks and wearing fatigues, Ulises said.

It's all right, the soldier said. We have more time off than most. I meet a lot of women around the island. A lot of cheap smokes.

I grow tobacco in the States, Ulises said.

No shit, the soldier said. How do you like our cigarettes?

You don't toast the leaves long enough. They're chalky because of it. Ulises looked at his cigarette, which had gone out, and then he asked, What did you say to your sister? To get her home?

Nothing, the soldier said. I told you, we beat the shit out of that black *coño*. You don't ask the girl; you just take away all her reasons for staying.

I'm not going to beat up my old man, Ulises said, but he was quiet then, because he'd not called Uxbal his old man in a long time, not since he was a boy on the island and there were other friends he ran with who had their own old men to watch out for. I haven't seen him in years, he said.

The soldier could barely pinch what was left of his cigarette.

Better for you, he said. No love lost. You just go and tell him straight up. He's probably got some gray on him now. A man starts to weaken after thirty-five, so you've got him there. They teach you that in the army to remind you how few years you've got to be a strong soldier. They'd prefer it if we were smart soldiers, but who's going to listen to that when they're eighteen and feeling fine?

How old are you? Ulises asked.

Twenty-three. The soldier laughed but then stopped and said, You've got to do the talking, man. Don't let your father start. Fathers know.

Know what?

They know all the mistakes you've ever made, because they made them first.

My father used to be a rebel, Ulises said. But that was years ago.

Rebel for what?

I'm not sure. He didn't love the revolution. I think he thought the island would turn out differently. Can I have another smoke?

The soldier gave Ulises another cigarette and then lit one for himself. The two of them watched the road from out of the back of the truck. It was wet. The soldier said it was supposed to be a highway, but this stretch no one had ever finished. It had rained that morning, and so the dirt was mud, and the tires spun out every hundred feet or so as the driver tried to pick up speed. The sun was way up high, and though the morning steam had burned off, it was replaced with the sweat from the soldiers and the Caribbean humidity that never went away despite the winds coming from the gulf.

Are there rebels still? Ulises asked.

Some, the soldier said. But they're crazies. They live alone and steal food. They don't talk to nobody. Mostly they think the army is going to revolt against the *Líder,* and they'll join when it happens. Bunch of stupids waiting for something to come that already came. Missed the boat, you know?

My mother said the army used to raid the hills once a month. Like checking for mice in the walls. They'd set some fires and smoke out the rebels. She said it was how they cleared the cane fields of snakes.

Not anymore, the soldier said. The CDR finds rebels, if there are rebels to be found, then they call us, and we pick them up. We don't go hunting for them anymore.

If my father is still a rebel, I could turn him in, Ulises said.

The soldier threw his butt out the back of the truck and shook his head.

That would be bad, man.

What happens to rebels? Ulises asked.

They go to rehabilitation camps for two years. Then they go to work in the cane fields. Between cuttings they build roads.

My father grew tomatoes when we were young, Ulises said. He could work in a field.

The soldier shook his head. After five years they would execute him. They would wait five years to try him in court, and when he was beaten down and done, then they'd put him in front of a judge. He would confess on paper, if you know what I mean, and then they'd take him out back of somewhere and shoot him. You don't want that for your papi. You'd go crazy yourself knowing what you did, maybe kill yourself after a while. Or you'd get some dumb idea in your head that you could make up for what you did. You could start your own revolution in your father's name. Then you're just another *coño* waiting to be picked up by the CDR. Then you're just as bad as your pops.

The day after Isabel took Guillermo, Uxbal denounced his daughter during his bath.

Those men are disgusting and probably sick, he said. You shouldn't touch them. Who knows what diseases?

Upright on his cot, he smelled not only of body odor, but also of weeds, an aroma Isabel was never able to wash completely from his skin. She was kneeling at his side and scrubbing the rough gray surface of his kneecaps when he started chastising her. His tone was suddenly like that of his preaching days: caustic, sharp, arrogant, and bullying. It put a fire on her tongue.

Is anyone among you sick? Isabel asked. *Let him call for the elders of the church, and let them pray over him, anointing him with oil in the name of the Lord.*

Uxbal didn't answer, but he reached out and gripped the hand in which she held the washcloth.

Your voice, he said, and he closed his eyes. He could not look at her and hear her at the same time. He shook, but Isabel thought it was only the cold water on his knees. She took her hand out of his and let Uxbal slump back onto his bed, half-washed, half-covered in soap.

Why did you put me up on a crate when I was a kid? Isabel asked. Were you really interested in the future of Cuba? Or were you scared that Ma was already leaving you? Were you scared of being alone, so you asked me to do something that might bring me back? Aren't these the things you asked for?

Is this where you want to have a child? Uxbal asked.

Answer me. Was it all just shit?

I remember believing.

I think that you were happy to see me because you were alone and because I was so different. You were happy because you thought the girl you'd taken to church hadn't come back, and you wouldn't have to deal with her promise.

Uxbal opened his eyes. That's all finished now, he said.

The vow was mine, not yours. And I've only just arrived.

Uxbal seemed to shrink then, into an even smaller man. His head sank farther into his shoulders, his neck shriveling like a worm in the sun.

It was then that Isabel understood she couldn't remain this close to her father. She had been giving herself away to him her whole life, and his voice was the sound *she'd* waited in silence for. But he spat condescension at her as she gently scrubbed the scent of excrement from behind his knees. That his words could shake her still deeply frightened her.

And despite having broken almost all her vows, Isabel wanted desperately then her Catholic God. Uxbal spoke as though his daughter was bored—which to Isabel meant purposeless—and wanted, on a strange mountain range on an island she'd long since nearly forgotten, another kind of new terrain: fleshy, alive, pulsing, unclean. As if this were the place, because it was itself already ruined, to reach out in all directions and experiment unabashedly with filthy otherness. As if she were done with the sharp, righteous spirit she'd been honing her entire life.

The bath unfinished, Isabel abandoned Uxbal and wandered the decrepit camp. Ants canvassed the mountaintop, marching in black veins up and down the walls of every shack. The bugs dripped through the wood and into the damp spaces where she knew humans waited in silence for nothing. She heard, faintly, hands slapping at the flies that lazily came and went from hut to hut to feast on dead skin and earwax and dried snot and the oils of an unwashed beard. All around her the settlement was decaying back into the forest: the woolly undergrowth threatened in all directions; a whitish cloud circled perpetually around the peak; lyonia overran the small clearing between the shacks, the rebels' footsteps not enough to wear the ground down to dirt.

Of the vacant shacks, Isabel chose the one with the fewest bugs, the sturdiest frame, and the most light when the door was open. The space inside was not large, perhaps the size of a priest's vestry, and the roof sagged toward the back. But the floor was even, and the rear wall had been nailed to a wide royal palm, which meant it could survive a passing storm. Clearing out old clothes, a broken chair, a fabric-less cot, and a scattering of beetle husks, Isabel went about making a chapel in which to pray, a place for God in a place He seemed unconcerned with.

Days passed, and Isabel began to worry that someone had died in the shack, because when she was inside and working—plugging holes in the walls with clay she dug from the mountain streams, lashing fresh palm fronds to the underside of the roof—shadows flickered noiselessly across the open door. She'd look up and see nothing, hear nothing. To ease her superstitions, she began to sing as she worked. She found she loved the tenor of her voice. The cords in her throat shook evenly. They had been resting for so long, they seemed to have an uncommon strength. And perhaps it was the years spent listening so attentively to hymns in church, but somehow Isabel could carry a tune.

Isabel was not being haunted, however; she was being watched by two of the rebel children, a boy and a girl. They'd heard her songs and were enchanted. While the adults of the camp, Uxbal included, shied away from Isabel's voice, the two children, the youngest among the group, could not help themselves and pressed their bodies against the outer clapboards of the chapel-in-progress. They sought out the wood's cracks and hollow spots so that they might hear more clearly the unnatural and bewitching sound of the outsider.

Isabel discovered them on a day when the girl tripped on a root outside the shack and, being a child, began to cry. The boy abandoned her and ran off. Isabel, finding the girl outside and bleeding from her big toe, picked her up and brought her inside. There was a post at the door that Isabel had hacked away at with a rock and into which she'd wedged a scooped piece of bark. She'd poured water into the bowl and in the mornings blessed herself with it, making the sign of the cross. Cradling the girl's heel, Isabel dipped the bleeding toe into the makeshift font and washed away the soil and grass. She examined the toe for the depth of the cut and saw that it was only a nick. Using the underside of her shirt, she put pressure on the bleeding skin and stanched the blood. The girl looked up at her, and Isabel was caught off guard by the blankness of her eyes, as if she'd not been taught how to be held, how to be so close to a larger body, or how to be close to another face without disturbing it.

This is the weight of a child once she's left your body, Isabel thought. This is what my daughter will feel like.

Isabel did not know why she assumed her baby—if she was pregnant, though she could not know just yet—would be a girl. But it seemed logical as she held the rebel child in her arms, her presence a natal omen of sorts. The girl reached up and put her dirty fingers on

Isabel's lips. She pinched the lower lip, and Isabel drew back her face, telling the girl, Don't do that.

The girl stopped immediately, and this Isabel was familiar with, children who could understand what you meant when it was said straight at them but who couldn't say anything back. The girl reached again, but this time her hand found the throat, and the grubby fingers caused Isabel to cough. The girl was startled, and her vacant expression gave way to wide eyes, as if she'd understood something, and she pressed her palm against Isabel's windpipe.

Sing, Isabel thought, and she sang about the Blessed Mother.

The girl stayed near Isabel all afternoon. She sat on the dirt near the back of the chapel where Isabel was busy lashing together a cross from two pine branches. Isabel sang everything she remembered, and, watching the girl intermittently, she saw that the child preferred slower songs with drawn-out vowels and simple harmonies. The girl is drawn to time, Isabel thought, sound spread out over seconds. Isabel remembered Uxbal's mandated silence, and she thought the girl was craving somebody's words again. *And the Word became flesh and dwelt among us.* People were not people, Isabel thought, unless they communicated.

The girl watched her as well as listened, and she seemed to know what Isabel was going to do before she did it. She could read bodies, see the future in a bending knee or predict the action of the hand in a single twitching thumb. But watching a body is not the same as feeling it. Isabel recalled the deaf children at the convent who listened to pop songs by pressing their palms onto the stereo speakers in the rec room. They felt the music. The rebel girl's mouth hung open as she listened, and she maybe wondered if her own throat might be capable of such noise. It was clear that it been a long time since she had been spoken to. After a few hours the girl seemed tired, and eventually she lay down, closing her eyes. Isabel stopped singing, but the girl sat back up, and Isabel had to go on.

Isabel made only slow progress on the chapel. Using an old cot, discarded nails, and a few boards from another collapsed hut, she fashioned an altar. For kneelers, she stuffed grass into the old T-shirts she'd found and tied off their ends. Stumps and rotting planks would do for pews, though there was only room for three benches in the entire shack.

Throughout all this, the girl—once the novelty of Isabel's voice waned—helped as best she could, though she was small, couldn't lift much, and walked with a limp. She, like Uxbal, was clearly mal-nourished. Isabel continued to sing but also began to teach the girl things. She taught her how to bless herself when entering the chapel, how to kneel before the cross, and how to hold her hands in prayer. She tried to teach prayer in the general sense, but the girl's expression remained blank throughout the explanation. The child still couldn't or wouldn't speak.

One day the boy came to the chapel with the girl, and he knew how to cross himself, kneel, and hold his hands in prayer. The girl had taught him, or maybe he'd asked what went on inside the shack with the singing woman. When Isabel sang, he listened just as intently, and sometimes he would rock in place. His hazel eyes were more expres-sive than the girl's, and whereas she fell into a trance at each song, he seemed to experience brief states of ecstasy.

Isabel didn't know what to call them. When it had been just she and the girl, she could speak, and it was obvious to whom she spoke. The boy confused things. Eventually, Isabel went to Uxbal. She still didn't want to see him, but she had, very quickly, grown attached to the children. Their presence was restorative, and Isabel, wanting to feel again like her old holy self, found interactions with the boy and girl reminiscent of her work with the deaf in Hartford. In their presence she was suddenly an authority again, a force for change in their lives. Uxbal was, of course, still festering in his shack, and though he had managed to finish washing himself, his feet, knees, and hands were dirty again, which led Isabel to think her father had since fallen out of bed once or twice. It pained her, but she didn't ask him about his health and instead demanded the children's identities.

What are their names?

The girl, he said, is Adelina. The boy, Augusto.

Who are their parents?

I don't know, Uxbal said. They might not be here anymore.

Who feeds them? Isabel asked. Who takes care of them?

It seems you do.

She went to Efraín, who thought she'd come to sleep with him again, and he had his shirt off before Isabel could get a word out.

No, she said, and her voice, as with Guillermo, frightened him. He sat on a cot in the shack he shared with three of the other men and shrank into himself.

Whom do Adelina and Augusto belong to? Isabel asked.

Efraín shook his head and shrugged.

You can talk, Isabel said, so talk.

But he didn't. Terrified of her, he curled into a ball on his cot and covered his ears. She tried Guillermo as well, but he just whispered, I don't know, and he walked away.

Adelina and Augusto loved the sound of their names, and Isabel worked them into songs. She was aware that doing so turned them into sheep and that they would follow her blindly when she called them. But she abused her power only to teach them things, namely the sign language she still knew. Because they could read bodies, they could very quickly read hands, and as soon as they grasped the language, the basic motions and elementary symbols, they could talk to each other even from distance, something they did constantly. Isabel understood that they were like infants, though they were probably four and five. Having learned a new way to disturb the world, they could not stop.

There was another consequence to this education: they began to ask questions, and sometimes Isabel could not sign and speak to them fast enough.

Adelina asked, Can we have more food? Where did you come from? Why does your Spanish sound that way? How come you don't talk to the old man anymore? What is prayer? Why do we wave our hands around when we enter the chapel? What does that sign mean? Why are hummingbirds so small?

Augusto asked, Why did you come here? Do you have children? How did you learn to speak? Do the other adults know how to sign? Why won't they sign with us? How do you know the old man? Is he dying? Did you come here to build this chapel? What happens when you pray? What is God? Can I have a new shirt? Will you teach me to sing?

The both of them asked, Are you our mother?

Isabel told them, I'm sorry. I'm not. I don't know who is.

It was the first answer she could not give them, and she saw on their faces that speaking, through one's hands or mouths, did not really mean one knew anything more, that it wasn't really knowledge. It was the first time she'd disappointed them. She sang them to sleep that night—they shared a shack with two bedrolls instead of cots—but as they listened, they stared at the roof, and they shared the same blank expression, meaning they were, without a doubt, siblings, something Isabel offered them in exchange for parents.

He is your brother, I think, and she is your sister, Isabel said. You look too much alike not to be related. But it was nothing they hadn't already sensed, and Isabel had to leave them that night with the same hunger she'd suffered all her life: a desire to understand where they were from and why.

Alone, Isabel went to the chapel. She did not feel tired, only guilty for what she'd done to the children, which was give them a voice through which they could discover that they were hungry and lacking.

She felt slightly ill and imagined it was morning sickness. She thought about the new cells possibly multiplying inside her, breaking apart in order to propagate, dividing and making space for bones and veins, layering like mud. Her sense of gestation, she knew, was more biblical than biological, but still she reveled in the idea of the Lord working his hands into her womb, perhaps in the same fashion he had with Sarah or Mary, and molding from her own flesh a new human. Yet, where before she had been righteous of God, she now, with the smell of the rebel children lingering in her nose, felt dangerously culpable for the hypothetical baby. Her decision had not been exactly rash, but the cost of her new calling had become a human life.

She wondered if Sarah knew what the Lord wanted of Isaac so many years down the road. Isaac, Isabel remembered, meant *laughing one*, but Abraham, not Sarah, named his son. Perhaps he thought it was a joke as well: Abraham a hundred years old and having a newborn boy. What could an old man teach a boy that young? Descendants as many as the stars, but on whose back would that universe be built? Until the final moment, until the angel intervenes, on Isaac's back or, at least, on his chest. His blood flowing from the wound God told Abraham to inflict. The children like lambs. Hypocrisy and lunacy all at once. Isabel thought, I am a part of this.

Isabel pushed her palm into her stomach to see if she might feel something, though she knew she wouldn't. Like Adelina and Augusto talking through their hands, begging for answers—Who are our parents?—and not finding any. Feeling nothing, it struck Isabel that her child, the girl, when she was older might want to know who her father was. She might want to seek him out one day. She would have the same questions as the mute rebel offspring, and Isabel couldn't stop her from asking. The righteous anger came back then, because Isabel saw Uxbal in bed, heard him telling her what to do, even after she'd come back to him and he'd abandoned his faith. Isaac like a lamb, Isabel as dumb as a sheep, Abraham as obedient as a blind cow.

What could she tell her little girl that would put an end to the searching? What could she say to a young woman that would keep her from looking? A man could be found. She, of course, knew this.

Six men, however, might not be found. Six men, like seeds cast into the wind, might spread so far apart that it would be nearly impossible to track them down. Especially six men who did not want to be found. Who were accustomed to their isolation, who would not see their face in a child even if God whispered the truth into their ears. Six rebels, Isabel thought, are better than two. I would not know. I could not know. When she asks, I could just say, I'm sorry. I don't know. It's impossible to know. You don't really have a father. Not in the way most people do. But you have a mother, and she loves you to death.

It was nearly dusk when the truck pulled into Las Tunas. Ulises and Simón, as payment for the ride, helped the soldiers transfer cargo, loading a hundred boxes of gauze bandages onto the trailer. Ulises asked where the soldiers would sit on the ride back to Santa Clara, and the young one said they would stand at the rear. They would make a game of it and try to shove each other out the back.

The young soldier invited Ulises and Simón to a bar where the food was cheap and there was a jukebox. It was dark and windy out, and the soldiers said it would rain overnight as the hurricane slammed Havana. One of the men said a prayer at this and crossed himself. He had been the one playing the guitar on the truck, and Ulises real- ized that the songs he'd heard on the ride were religious tunes, string variations of Catholic hymns.

Inside the bar, the musician said grace over his food, and when the young soldier, the jealous brother, noticed Ulises studying the guitarist, he said, Paulo wanted to be a priest, but he was too dumb. He couldn't keep track of all the saints' names or the dates of their deaths. Doesn't have a mind for books.

St. Cecilia's got him, Simón said.

She did, because Paulo, after only a few bites, had gone over to the jukebox to study the record list. Ulises thought the man must have had a song already going in his head, because he tapped out a beat on the floor, but the song he paid for was a leisurely ballad between two lovers living on the opposite sides of a bay who sang to each other across the water.

Paulo thinks all ballads are really about God, the young soldier said. He says to read Song of Songs.

The food was passable, and Ulises ate in silence. Simón spoke to the bartender about a ride farther east, but the barkeep couldn't help, though he did have an aloe plant growing behind the building, and he offered a branch to Ulises for his sunburn. The soldiers drank slowly but steadily, such that hours passed but no one really got drunk. Some girls came in later in the evening and danced alone between a pair of tables. A few of the soldiers approached them. The girls looked very young, but their makeup was pretty, and one of them had a blond dye-job that wasn't terrible.

At one point the girls stopped dancing and started singing. They surrounded the jukebox and crooned about a *campesina* who grew peppers in her yard and whose husband died one day in a burning field of sugarcane. The widow cut stalks from the burnt crop and pressed her own juice, stewing it with her peppers. She gave the peppers to men she knew were not faithful, and they returned home to their wives. The blond girl sang the loudest. Like her hair, her voice was not terrible. The other patrons in the bar had quieted, and Ulises saw that even Paolo seemed impressed, so much so that at the next song he asked her to dance.

The other reason why Paolo could never be a priest, the young soldier said: a girl with a decent voice makes his dick hard. You imagine that in church? The priest's robes with a little pop at the crotch?

She looks too young, Simón said.

Country whores, the young soldier said.

Paolo was pulling the blonde closer to him, but the song was too fast, and she kept dancing away.

Kids playing dress up, Simón said. She's going to slap him if he doesn't give up.

Paolo left the girl after the song ended, but a couple of numbers later he went and touched her on the shoulder, which made her jump.

She looked scared, and Paolo smiled as best he could, but then she said something, and he grabbed her by the arm. The blonde's friends started yelling. The bartender told the young soldier to do something. The young soldier shook his head but didn't move.

What if that was your sister? Ulises asked.

Fuck you, the young soldier said, but he got up from his stool.

He went over to Paolo and took him by the arm, which prompted Paolo to swing for the young soldier's face, which led to more blows. Together they knocked over some chairs, but in the end they fell to the ground, the young soldier—the bigger of the two—atop Paolo, and they seemed drunk at last. Finally standing, Paolo wrapped his arm around his friend and mumbled apologies. The girls were long gone.

Dragging Paolo out the door, the young soldier called out to the bartender, Smokes, water, whiskey!

The bartender put the drinks and half a pack of cigarettes in front of Ulises and said, They can smoke in here if they like.

Outside, the young soldier took the shots from Ulises and gave both the waters to Paolo.

That wasn't my sister, he said.

Have a smoke, Ulises said. He pulled a stick from the pack and tapped it against the box, lit it, and passed it along.

He did the same for Paolo, who instead of thanking him said, We were talking while we danced. She kept asking me where we were going, what we were doing, which cities I'd been to. She asked if I could take her in the truck with us, and I said, of course not. One girl and twelve men? I asked her what she thought that would be like, and she said fantastic. I told her that we couldn't take her, but she wasn't having it.

I'm sorry about your face, the young soldier said. Your nose looks like shit.

Paolo waved his hand in front of his face to clear the smoke, which hung like a mist because the night was so humid.

He said, They think you're out having fun all the time. They don't know how sore your ass gets on that bench in the back of the truck. It's a miracle we can walk after driving around all day. You just want to stay somewhere for a little bit, not keep running around, and they want to start a fucking voyage across the island.

Ulises recognized boredom in Paolo's face, the appearance of having done the same thing over and over again until it was reflex.

You get in a lot of fights? Ulises asked.

Some, he said, but this guy always takes me down. He's not the first subofficer, but he leads. He kept Salvo out of jail once for hitting a girl.

Same story, different asshole, the young soldier said.

Do you get tired of it?

It's my lot.

The infantrymen slept in the truck, but Simón got a room for Ulises and himself just above the bar. It was the bartender's apartment, but because he worked all night, the space was free until the morning. There was a bed and a cot, and Ulises pleaded with Simón to take the bed. He eventually did, and Ulises climbed into the cot, his limbs hanging over the edges, and turned out the light.

Soldiers are a boring bunch, said Simón.

They were drunk, Ulises said.

They're bored, so they pick fights.

The young one seemed sincere. We're probably around the same age.

He was the worst, Simón said. Some romantic ass. Poets and warriors, equally annoying. They go looking for trouble, and then they whine about it.

Ulises said, That's not new: *Arms, and the man I sing, who, forc'd by fate* . . .

What's that? Simón asked.

The first line of *The Aeneid*.

Isn't that about a soldier who abandons his city?

Yes. But then he starts Rome.

And then Rome burns, Simón said. I'm old-fashioned, but people belong in the fields. The plants are supposed to die, so they can come back. Bananas are perennials. They die ever year, and you get used to it. You don't worry about things going away.

That soldier was worried about his sister going away, Ulises said.

A generation goes, and a generation comes, but the earth remains forever, Simón quoted.

I didn't think you went to church, Ulises said.

Only when I visit my mother, though sometimes the Bible comes back like this. When I'm with her, I can't forget it. In Mexico, I could recite the whole book.

Isabel reminds me of Cuba, Ulises said. When I see her, I see our father. I remember our old house. When she's gone, it's harder to picture the place. I could draw pictures of my father's tomato vines if Isabel were at my side.

You won't need her in a day or two, Simón said. You're going to see it all again.

In the morning Simón left Ulises halfway through breakfast to see about a bus. There were rumors that the hurricane had turned north toward Florida, so the island was coming out of its hole. No one knew for certain, however, because the TV and radio signals were still a jumble of white noise. When Simón returned to the bar, he came with a horse. The buses were coming, supposedly, but not a soul knew when, and the distance to Bayamo was only ninety kilometers. They would be there in a day and half, and Buey Arriba was only forty kilometers from there.

Where did the horse come from? Ulises asked.

There's a lot in town for loose animals. Because of the hurricane.

The storm hasn't landed here, Ulises said.

The animals run ahead of the weather, from west to east. And no one's going to chase a horse across the island.

The horse had no saddle, but Simón said they would go to town and purchase some blankets, and they only had to suffer for a day and a half anyway. In town they also bought Ulises a baseball cap, a new pair of sunglasses, and a bottle of sunblock. Simón told Ulises to tie his glasses around his neck with a string, both because the horseback ride would be bumpy and because sunglasses were easy to pickpocket.

On the road to Bayamo Ulises saw many things. He saw herds of Siboney cows crossing weedy fields between irrigation ditches. He saw abandoned silver mines, the pits often not twenty meters from the road with shallow, green-tinted rainwater collected into ponds at the bottom. He saw what Simón told him were *palenques,* or crumbling, walled-off villages built by escaped slaves three hundred years ago. At crossroads he saw roadblocks stacked along the highway's shoulders, and Simón said they were used to guard the coffee harvest as it was transported east. To keep the caravans from being pillaged, raided for the black market, the military cordoned off the highway and made a road with walls on either side. Ulises saw children carrying sacks of what he thought were stolen beans. On the second day he saw a great lizard cuckoo flitting about at dusk, chasing moths, and when, finally, they were within sight of Bayamo, they were also in sight of the Sierra Maestra, and Ulises saw the hills he'd known as a boy.

There, he and Simón rented a room at the only hotel for miles around—really a hostel, really the second floor of a bakery with a few storage rooms given windows. From their window Ulises saw, in the moonlight, smoke rising from the east, though he saw no fire. Later, from his bed, he saw a painting of Che Guevara on the western half of the ceiling. He closed his eyes, and in that darkness he saw his mother, and he missed her. He saw his sister, and he was angry. He saw his father and did not know what to feel.

. . .

Ulises awoke while the morning was still gray, and he awoke not because he'd had enough sleep, but because he smelled calcium hydroxide in the air. He knew the odor from his childhood, from the sugar refinery just east of Buey Arriba. The compound was used to purify the crystals, and it made the air drifting into Buey Arriba heavier. Ulises remembered walking outside on summer days when the wind was barely there and feeling as though to breathe was to lick the earth.

Getting up from his hotel bed, he went to the window, and he saw the same smoke from the night before. There was a refinery nearby, and that fact made Ulises restless. He wanted to hurry and get to Buey Arriba. It was the first time he'd been eager to arrive. He was sick of the journey, and everything he saw or smelled now would have a similar effect on him, reminding him of home, though he wasn't there yet. When Simón finally awoke, he told Ulises to be patient.

We have to find a phone line, Simón said. Or, at least, a messenger, remember? Your mother needs to know you're alive.

They found neither in Bayamo. The phone lines were still down across the country. The hurricane had turned toward Florida, but it first had ravaged Havana and the northern Cuban coast. No one in Bayamo was worried, though. The city would suffer only heavy rains. Still, people sat outside on their porches, and most businesses were shut down, as though the storm was inevitable. At the post office, which was open but nearly empty, an older worker told Ulises and Simón to go to Santiago if it was urgent. They could send word by boat to Port-de-Paix in Haiti, where there were American hotels.

Ulises said to Simón, I'm going to Buey Arriba.

Take the horse, Simón said. I'll find a ride.

I have a much shorter way to go. You take the horse and go to Santiago. Then you can come back more quickly.

Simón gave Ulises some of his money and another shirt to put in his sack. He said, Take care, and Ulises thought then he sounded just like Orozco, low and informal, as if they were parting at the end of a workday. Or Simón was the shadow of Orozco, the part Orozco was forgetting each day he was away from Mexico and his mother.

The forty kilometers to Buey Arriba were not hard to walk, as Ulises had been sitting for what seemed like weeks. His legs felt good, and with his hat, sunglasses, and sunblock he could manage the heat. It was afternoon when the road, populated by a few stray farmhands on pony-driven carriages, brought him to the lake outside Buey Arriba. The body of water, a reservoir, if Ulises remembered right, had no name, and it was the mountain runoff of the rains that broke across the northern face of the Sierra Maestra. Ulises stopped to eat some of the bread he had purchased in Bayamo, and he cooled his feet in the lake water, as they were swollen from the long walk. The river that fed the lake began in the mountains, somewhere near Pico Turquino, which had on its peak a bust of the national hero José Martí. Uxbal had taken Isabel and him up the mountain once. They had hiked along a narrow, one-way road halfway up the range before scrambling to the top.

Uxbal had said, That's José Martí.

The bust, however, had been installed out in the open, and the face, after so many years, had been worn away except for the eyes, which were deep set because Martí had been small and gaunt. Uxbal had let neither Ulises nor Isabel touch the bust, but he'd made them cross themselves and kneel in front of the figure before they turned and headed back down.

From its border, the town seemed no bigger than Ulises remembered, but it was louder. There was an abundance of Russian trucks, and the ones that passed nearby had cargo holds full of dirt or manure. For a moment Ulises thought he'd made a mistake, but he looked in all directions and remembered quite clearly the warehouse being the last building out of town and the river not far off; it was where the workers would eat their lunches. The residents of Buey Arriba raised cattle, which could be heard lowing in all directions, and Ulises remembered cows outside of Sunday service. He saw a band of oxen in a small field beyond the packinghouse and remembered how loudly they chewed their grass. It was never quiet in Buey Arriba, Ulises heard his mother saying, because the cows are always hungry, which was why the tomatoes grown locally were called oxhearts instead of tomatoes, their shape something like an overgrown strawberry.

Making for the town center, Ulises passed by the shell of the old packinghouse his father used to work at, but it was empty, and all the window glass had been knocked out or, more likely, stolen. Nothing remained, but Ulises was compelled to make a tour of the hollow structure.

The interior, which had the appearance of a factory cleared out by a flash flood, smelled of cat urine, and the floor was stained a greenish pink from the thousands of broken guavas spilled over the years. The light pouring in through the open windows illuminated the dust Ulises's boots kicked up, and behind him he left a trail of faint footprints. Because there were no chairs or tables or even a front desk—hadn't there been a desk with an old man once who checked you into work?—Ulises had trouble remembering the orientation of the room. He couldn't tell which end of the building he was at, whether he walked through the loading zone of jam-packed guava crates or whether he was near the spot of the old picnic benches, the three splintered tables the congregation would slide against the walls to make room for Sunday Mass.

But then Ulises saw the wide trucking doors in front of him, where the guavas were stacked on pallets strung together with fresh twine before being trucked out east or down south. Behind him, then, was the area for prayer, and Ulises, walking to the other end of the structure, thought maybe he saw the scratches on the northern wall where his father or someone else's father or someone else entirely would hang their homemade cross on Friday afternoons after work let out. It would stay there until Monday morning, when the first man to work would take it down and the cavernous building was transformed again into a place for monotonous labor.

This was the first place in which Ulises had ever heard the Bible read aloud. The congregation had used a French translation, and there had been a celebration when someone stole—from a tourist? a missionary? a traveling horde of nuns?—a copy of the King James. Though the workers weren't fluent in English, they, at least, knew more of it than French, and the first Sunday they read aloud the English text, the packinghouse had never been quieter, all ears open, all mouths shut. It was hot because it was always hot, but some force arrested the air that day, and the only wind came from the mouth of the man—it wasn't Uxbal, maybe a foreman, maybe another shift leader—slowly making his way through the Gospel According to John. Uxbal had sat on a bench, a wooden plank across several crates, leaning against the eastern wall. Overwhelmed by the reading, he had rocked on his ass, his head dipping in agreement every few words or so.

Ulises thought, This is what Simón was talking about.

But, strangely, his sister wasn't present in the memory, and he wondered, Did she have a fever that day? Had the last of the tomatoes needed picking, else they would have gone bad? Had she disobeyed Uxbal on some issue? Had Uxbal wanted only his son that Sunday morning? The last guess was, of course, the least likely, and there existed suddenly the possibility that the righteousness Ulises had wedged between his sister and himself had corrupted his memories of Cuba.

He approached the northeastern corner of the packinghouse. The walls were made of corrugated sheet metal, now rusted and flaking. Gently, Ulises traced a thumb along one of the raised spines, and he noticed a series of hash marks near the ceiling. The markings, he then remembered, had been the congregation's Holy Calendar. The nicks in the metal tracked the seasons of the liturgical year—Ordinary Time, Advent, Lent, the Triduum, Easter—and each scratch had a hole at its end where a tack had been plugged to mark the day. At his feet Ulises saw a scattered handful of tiny black nails.

Simón had said to Ulises, *You won't need her,* and now Ulises thought he really understood: he could stop seeing this place through Isabel's relentless wanting.

I could just let her go, he whispered.

He exited the packinghouse to find the sun low in the sky and the cattle settling into evening meals of grass and weed. Looking toward the Sierra Maestra, he thought of his childhood home and its orange roof, and he decided it would be the only place in Buey Arriba his sister might go. The house was on the south side of the town, as close to the edge of the national forest as possible. Ulises walked in that direction.

The property was beautiful, and Ulises was inexplicably certain it had always been that way. In his childhood, the house had been walled in year-round by a series of trellises straining against a singular but seemingly perpetual tomato vine. The trellises somehow remained, sagging with oxhearts. The house itself, which he'd assumed would be cracked and falling apart, appeared freshly whitewashed. Hungry, Ulises plucked a tomato from the vine and bit into it. It was delicious, though a little underripe, and he took another bite. He turned the fruit over in his hand. Half the inside was still yellow. He wished to God he had some salt or basil.

He ate the rest of the tomato, plucked another, and ate it as well. He sat on the ground and was tired, because the taste was so delicious and familiar. He recalled how impossibly thin Uxbal could slice a tomato, so that the cuts were translucent and Ulises could put them over his eyes and they would turn the sky a rosy hue something like a Caribbean sunset. He recalled how his mother ate tomatoes as though they were apples, the juice on her chin, and how she would spit out the seeds. It felt as though he'd forgotten everything. Then he heard a strange voice, the voice of an old woman calling to him, and he looked up. The sound came from a body shuffling in his direction, and it called out to him, Uxbal! Uxbal!

In Hartford, Willems bought Soledad a television set. They put it in the bedroom so Soledad, who had never been in the habit of going to the movies, let alone watching TV, could do something between sleeping, medicating, therapy, and sex. Up until that point newspapers had sufficed, but now she found she couldn't concentrate long enough to read an entire article anymore. The stories, always so political, always so objective and distant, were about as distracting of her pain as watching tobacco grow in August. After seeing a few episodes of *As the World Turns* during a chemo session in the hospital's treatment clinic, she was hooked, and she asked Willems if they could get a set.

At first she and Henri watched shows together, mainly in the afternoon after long, violent sessions of lovemaking that left them both bruised and not a little dazed. The silence that followed, which previously had been pregnant with their doubt—what has become of us?—now was interrupted by the intersecting lives of Nancy Hughes, Lisa Grimaldi, Barbara Coleman, Holden Snyder, Lucinda Walsh, et alia. Willems fell asleep to fitful dreams more often than he caught whole shows, but Soledad could not take her eyes from the screen. Her watching developed into an obsession, and one afternoon she started scribbling furious notes into her stenographer's pads. While Henri napped beside her, she categorized all the players in the drama, recording with unnecessary detail their loves, losses, and reincarnations. This became her daily routine.

Willems, when he realized what she was doing, took her cataloging as a positive turn. He thought maybe she was reaching for her old life, the one in which she codified the world with shorthand and loved him. Half-awake, he asked her to show him what she'd written, but she told him to wait for a commercial.

When the episode ended, Henri said, I almost forgot how your notes look. These might as well be hieroglyphics.

I don't want to miss anything, Soledad said.

It all seems a bit tedious, he said. I wonder what you're getting from this. Maybe you're thinking of going back to work?

I'm not.

You seemed to have found some of your old energy.

It doesn't take anything for me to scribble on a pad. What are you worried about?

I'm worried that you're not getting enough rest.

I don't believe you. But if you're serious, you could fuck me harder, and then I'd be more tired at the end and could nap with you.

Henri got up from the bed and put on his pants.

He said, That's a cruel thing to say.

Soledad slipped back under the covers. She felt hot. She felt the urge to touch herself, and she did.

I'm sorry, she said. That *was* mean. What are you really saying? Come back to bed and tell me. Or, better, come here and kiss me again.

We were sharing this, together, you and I, Henri said.

Sharing what?

Your dying.

We're the only ones here, Henri. You're the only one watching me die.

Soledad took her hand from her crotch. She pushed her hair back, and when her hand passed by her face, she could smell herself.

You think I'm finally dying? she asked.

I worry that's what this means. You're acting like those notes are private. So maybe you're retreating from our life together, or from life altogether, in anticipation of going. Do you want to be alone right now?

I want you here, Soledad said. Note-taking is an old habit. You're asleep, and I'm awake, and I'm a little less alone with the TV on, but my fingers can't sit still. All it means is that I'm awake. I'm not nearly as far away as you fear I am. I'm just at the edge of the bed, waiting for you to wake up.

Yet soon enough Soledad was watching two episodes in a row, both the current day's installment and the rerun of the show from the day before. Watching the rerun, she would fact-check yesterday's shorthand. Rarely would she find an error, but she did find some joy in adding to the basic who, what, where, and when potential whys and hows. She began to keep exhaustive lists of characters, not only of their roles and the telling details of their faces (hooked nose, chinless jaw, angled eyebrows, soft shoulders), but also any inferences she felt comfortable making (sleeps late in the day, avoids heavy foods, prefers taller men, never exercises for more than thirty minutes, has trouble sharing). On weekends, when *As the World Turns* didn't run, she transcribed her notes, which she realized were becoming unwieldy family trees overripe with exorbitant personality sketches.

It did not take long for the soap opera to infringe upon the sex. More and more frequently, Soledad would stop in the middle of prodding and biting and pinching and roughhousing and say, It's one o'clock. A greater distance emerged between her and Willems then, as Soledad seemed to be fucking Henri simply because she thought he'd come to expect it. But every day when the magic hour struck, she'd unceremoniously unfold herself from whatever position they were in, crawl to the edge of the bed, and turn on the television set. There she'd sit entranced, notepad and pencil in hand, the volume turned up needlessly high.

One day, when again *As the World Turns* loomed but their fucking wasn't finished, Willems considered hitting Soledad, and not in the passionate though moderately painful way in which they'd struck each other up until this point. Briefly he thought he might actually strike her face and leave a mark, a black eye perhaps, just to test the adrenaline, to see if he was boring her, or to see if she wanted him to have her at all, if that meant anything anymore.

Willems did not hit Soledad, but as she pulled away from him, he said, Tell me who your favorite is.

Favorite what?

Leading man, he said.

I don't have one.

I've seen you touching yourself sometimes during the show. Seth? Holden? Dusty?

Have you been reading my notes? Are you pretending to sleep? And I don't touch myself. That's probably what's going on in those dreams of yours. You shake unbelievably sometimes when you're napping. I can barely write in a straight line.

Let me guess, he said. It's Holden.

Soledad went to the bureau to retrieve her pencil and stenographer's pad.

You sound jealous, she said.

Sometimes I'd like to forget what we do to each other in bed, Henri confessed.

We don't have to have sex if you don't want to, she said.

She approached the television set but didn't turn it on.

I want to, but I'm not sure I can keep going this way. I feel cut up, like you're pulling my body apart piece by piece, until you've used everything from my eyes to my asshole.

You don't push me away when we're under the covers.

I'm trying to understand what it is you want.

I want to touch you. I want to watch TV. I want my children to come home.

No, I want to know what it is you *will* want, Henri said. I'm trying to understand what happens if you wake up one day feeling healthy, free of pain, the cancer disappeared into remission. What are you going to say to me then?

I won't imagine that place, Soledad said. Honestly, it's too fragile. I don't want to dream about it, only to never see it come to pass.

Then where are you now? he asked. Where's your head, if not in the future? If it's not looking past the day Ulises and Isabel come home?

It's here, only ever here. I'm having sex with you, every day at the same time. I'm watching my show, every day at the same time. I'm watching these people come, go, and return to the same place. I can't handle anything more than *right now*.

You're saying you're stuck? Henri asked. We're stuck in the moment right before you die?

Soledad put down her notes. She returned to the bed, where Henri was still naked, where a fold of blanket hung loosely over his crotch. Where his hands trembled in his lap.

I'm sorry, love, she said. I'm sorry you're sick of this. You should be. It must be exhausting. You're my cook, cleaner, bather, gardener, lover. You offered yourself to me, and I'm afraid I took you. All of you. But I've got nothing to give back. I should have said this already, before the cancer happened, but you should desert me. You can't keep pouring yourself into me without feeling the loss.

We haven't tried everything, have we? Henri asked.

Soledad said, Look at me. I'm not a body that can be replenished anymore.

Willems told the counselor everything. He told her about the soap operas and the notebooks. He told her all the things Soledad had said, and he even told her about his violent urges, fleeting as they were.

How close have you come to hitting her? the counselor asked. In order to hurt her, I mean.

Not very, Willems said.

Are you certain, Henri? There's no going back from that. I have to make sure you don't leave this office with the intent to abuse.

Do you think I'm capable of that?

I think you're angry about this issue with the TV, and I don't think you know whom you're angry with. If it's Soledad, then tell her again, and if she doesn't hear you out, then you have the option of leaving her, which she seems to expect on some level or, at least, would understand. Cancer is not a reason to mistreat another human being, and you present yourself as mistreated to the point of violence. If it's not Soledad, then we have to figure that out.

Should I leave her? Willems asked.

Let's not start there. First, tell me: What's its like watching Soledad watch TV? Do you really pretend to sleep, as she claims?

I don't pretend to do anything. I'm awake, and I watch her. She gets into her trance at the end of the bed, and there's no need to sneak around, because she's so far gone.

How long does she watch TV for? the counselor asked.

Two hours a day, Willems said.

Do you feel like that's too much?

She usually spends another hour organizing her notes, and several hours on the weekend writing them out in longhand.

Do you have intercourse on the weekends?

Yes, but it lacks the same power as it has during the week.

The sex is gentler?

No, not exactly. It's still rough. What I'm saying is, she can pull herself out of it. It doesn't overwhelm her like it first did. Even when we're fucking, I feel her absence.

Forgive me, Henri, but have you come to enjoy the rough play? I'm not trying to be funny, but it almost sounds as though you're nostalgic for it.

It's stupid, I know. Wanting something that I didn't like just because I had it before.

The way you describe it, you could barely keep up.

It was the last thing she was giving me.

And now she's not offering it anymore.

It's childish, isn't it? A grown man wanting to hit a woman because she won't give him what he wants? She's dying, and I'm still trying to take things from her.

It's difficult watching someone we love pass away, the counselor said. Or I should say, complex.

I know, Willems said. I watched my mother die.

What was that like?

Willems told the counselor about the color of Rute's skin, which went from sandy brown to yellow to cream and then to blue right before she went. He paused at the thought of his mother's blue skin, but then he went on to list the other facts of her going: the fluctuating body temperature, the diarrhea, the kinds of fluids they fed her, the number of days in bed, the hour of her death, the color of her bedsheets, the weather patterns of that week, the meals he ate that she could not, the feel of her skin as it dried out, the names of all the nurses who nursed her, and the number of minutes between her passing and his father's touching of her body, his closing of her eyes. He mentioned last Rute's mysterious smell.

How awful, the counselor said.

It was, Willems said. She was like another person. I even started hating her for it.

Really?

Isn't that terrible? I think that's worst part. At first, I was afraid of the new smell, but eventually I was just angry about it.

You were mad that it was so different?

I was mad at my mother. I started to think she'd changed her smell on purpose, like switching a perfume. I started thinking she wanted to leave us and that she didn't want me around at the end. Right before she died, I refused to see her, and I wouldn't tell her why.

Why do you think you did that?

I'm sure I was feeling the sort of abandonment any child does when they have to watch a parent die. It was easier being mad at her for going than becoming sad about her being gone.

Is there a chance this is where your reluctance with Soledad comes from?

That's a stretch, in my mind.

Have you ever shared any of this with Soledad?

Yes, some of it.

Which parts?

I've told her about my mother's changing smell, but not about my hating her for it.

Why not?

It's embarrassing.

You were a child.

Willems closed his eyes. He thought of the smell of Soledad's skin—metallic and sterile—when she returned from chemotherapy. He heard the counselor shift in her seat, and he opened his eyes.

Where did you go just now? the counselor asked.

Henri, who'd spent the majority of these sessions staring at his knees, studied the woman across from him. She was in her fifties, she wore a brown dress, and her hair was pulled back in a ponytail. Her mouth was set into a line, and her cheekbones were nonexistent, as if her face were a plane. It gave him the impression that he spoke to a painting.

I was thinking about the women I've lost, Henri said.

The women you've lost, the counselor repeated.

Yes.

Is Soledad a part of that group?

Willems paused. He said, I suppose I'm also counting her.

Why?

I seem to keep things from the women I love when they're about to die.

The things we talk about here?

Yes, and other things.

Such as?

Willems said, Sometimes I have dreams.

What kind?

The kind where I see Soledad after a beating.

Describe one.

In the dream Soledad has a bruised eye and a swollen nose. The nose might be broken. It's bloody around the nostrils. I can feel my fists. My knuckles throb. I can hear Soledad breathing through her mouth.

The counselor asked, Are you aroused?

No, Willems said. I'm not. I don't think I am.

The two of you are alone, the counselor said. You stand across from each other and look into each other's faces.

Yes and no.

Explain.

There's another man in the room. I can't see him. He's behind me. Soledad can see him, and she looks at both of us. She looks over my shoulder to look at him. He looks over my shoulder to look at her. He wants to see her. He's confused, because Soledad's face is her own, but it's not. It's misshapen, because I've hit her.

The counselor asked, Who is he?

Uxbal.

For the first time during one of their meetings, the counselor got up from her chair. She brought a pitcher of water from across the room and poured Henri a glass, then sat down next to him. So close to her, Willems was suddenly afraid.

Are you showing Uxbal what you've done to his wife? the counselor asked.

I don't know.

Do you hit her in the dream, or is she bruised when the dream begins?

I have to hit her.

How does she look before you hit her? Is she happy? Depressed? Is she asking you to strike her?

No, she doesn't ask, but I hit her twice with an open palm.

And then she changes.

Yes and no. Her form is different from the start.

Her form? the counselor asked. How?

In the dream, she doesn't have cancer. She hasn't had surgery. In the dream her breasts are still there. I can see them under her shirt.

In your dream she is healthy.

Until I hit her.

How do you feel, the counselor asked, once you've hurt her?

I want to take her in my arms, Willems said.

Does she fall into your arms?

She doesn't.

Why not?

Because I'm the one who hurt her.

Uxbal does nothing?

He's quiet. He stays behind me like a shadow.

Do you say anything to Soledad?

I tell her I'm sorry. I tell her I love her. I tell her that she is beautiful.

Is she?

Incredibly so.

Even after you've struck her? Even with her bruised eye?

Always.

In the house the old woman served Ulises a plate of chilled cherry tomatoes sliced and mixed with olives and pimento. On the table she also placed grapefruit and fried plantains, which she'd been warming under the sun on the windowsill, and she told Ulises to eat, eat, but he could barely understand her. She spoke with what Ulises assumed was a distant countryside Spanish, though, unlike the Cuban slang he remembered from his childhood, her words did not run together. She made sounds that were close to words he knew, but it was as if she'd not had a lengthy conversation with anyone in a long, long time. Her clothes made him think the same. She wore a loose floral blouse and a canvas skirt, the kind made for farmers' daughters, but underneath her skirt she wore pants as well, fatigues the hunter green of a soldier's uniform. Ulises wondered how she didn't faint in the heat.

And she kept calling him Uxbal. He tried to correct her, but she waved her hands at him and pushed more food onto the table, some peaches and the thinnest pork chop he'd ever seen. She poured him a glass of what looked like water but was, when he drank it, clearly liquor. He thanked her and pecked at the food, but she kept waving at his plate, so he traded bites for answers. After an hour he knew that he should call her Granma, that Uxbal had not been to the house for some time, and that she couldn't see well at all.

You find everything in this kitchen with ease, Ulises said.

A map in my brain, Granma said.

How is it you know Uxbal? Ulises asked, but the woman laughed as though it were a joke. Are you feeling well? he said.

The same as always, Granma told him. Old and older.

How old?

She clucked at him. The food gets cold, she said.

It was an exhausting way to talk, so Ulises just kept eating. By the time he finished the meal, he'd made a mess of the kitchen. He'd been covered in dust from walking the road from Bayamo, and when he moved, it shook from his body onto the floor and made a ring of filth around his chair.

Clearing his plate, Granma noticed this too, rubbing one bare foot on the tile. She ushered him out of the kitchen, through a bedroom, and into the house's only bathroom, where there was a wide tin tub, nearly twice as wide as ordinary tubs, with a wooden chair inside it.

The old woman probably couldn't stand in the shower without it being a danger anymore, Ulises thought.

Granma left him alone to bathe. As the water ran, he watched the dust from his walk turn to silt at the base of the tub, and he worked it with his feet into the slow drain. When he was done, he went back into the bedroom and found clean clothes laid out for him: a denim shirt—the kind his father had worn—a green canvas belt, and a pair of dungarees. His sunglasses and hat were also on the bed.

Ulises was tired from the food and thought he should nap before trying to talk to the old woman again, but when Granma saw that he was bathed, she put him to work. She took him around the house and pointed out small, waiting repairs: three trellises had cracked from the weight of the tomato vine, a flower bed was in desperate need of weeding, a pipe under the kitchen sink dripped, the kitchen door would not close all the way, and the legs of an end table in the small living room were rickety. On the kitchen table Granma had placed a toolbox. She took Ulises there last, pointed to the tools, and went into her bedroom, perhaps to take the nap he had wanted.

Ulises moved first through the house—the kitchen door, the pipe, the table legs—and then outside. Of the weeding he made steady work, but for the broken trellises he had to scrounge for scrap wood. In the end he found some old window parts in a closet that would do. He found some rocks as well, and he buried them at the base of the trellis for more support. The whole time he fought what he thought were bees or, at least, extraordinary Caribbean flying insects. They hummed as they zipped past his ears, but he couldn't catch sight of them.

The work was light compared to what he'd done for Willems. He fell into an old pattern easily, tuning out the world and focusing his efforts on one task at a time. Consequently he didn't notice the light rain that passed over the house, wondered how his shirt had gotten so wet, and had it not been for the squawk of a cuckoo, he wouldn't have looked up to notice a boy watching him labor. The kid sat atop a gray bicycle that was too small for him and rubbed his arm while he watched. Ulises waved, but the boy did not wave back. Ulises stood up, which caused the kid to grab his handlebars, and when Ulises offered him some tomatoes to take home, the boy rode off.

In the house, Granma was waiting for him, though she'd changed her clothes and now wore an impossibly thin linen robe, which did little to preserve her modesty. She didn't seem to mind, however, and she took Ulises by the arm and led him back into the bathroom, where she'd drawn a fresh bath. Ulises stood by as Granma disrobed, and when he made to leave, she grabbed his arm and motioned for him to help her. She smelled terrible, and Ulises wondered how he hadn't noticed that before. Perhaps he'd had his own stench from traveling. He'd not showered in the bartender's apartment in Las Tunas, and the hostel in Bayamo hadn't had a bathroom. But Granma somehow kept her musk pent up in her clothes, beneath the skirt and the hunter green pants. She seemed to think it might drive him off, because she held fast to his arm even after sitting down in the wooden chair.

Ulises realized he was to bathe her. Strange as this seemed, she had fed and clothed him. If she needed this help, this might be her only wash for a long time. Touching Granma's arm, Ulises smiled at the old woman till she let him go. Into the bath he poured some shampoo, and when there was a good lather, he began with the woman's hair, going slowly. Granma's face relaxed, and her body leaned against his. He went slower, and now when she spoke, she spoke slowly, and Ulises could understand much more, though still not all, of what she said.

How long do you stay?

Ulises understood the old woman's eyes were still seeing Uxbal, and Ulises decided not to correct her anymore.

I'm just passing through, he said. I am looking for someone.

When you were last here, she said, I can't remember. You've wasted tomatoes.

Am I supposed to come get them? Ulises asked.

Someone gets them, she said. But not for a long time. A year? I don't know. No clocks. Do the back.

It's been a long time since I was here, Ulises said. Have you changed the house much?

Cleaner, she said. You never kept it clean. The walls aren't accidentally white. Your clothes are together. Same closet. I think you'll leave tomorrow.

Why do you think that? he asked. And where would I go?

The mountains. You have *guaro* here. Take it with you. I can't drink it. My heart jumps. You'll take it?

Is that what you served me at lunch? he asked.

She nodded.

All right, he said. I'll take it. Am I the only one who visits you?

Barely, Granma said.

Have you seen my daughter? Did she come through here ahead of me?

I met a young woman, and she took our tomatoes, Granma said. Don't scold me: I told her to. She was beautiful. She was like a filthy saint. I fell asleep. When I woke, she wasn't here. I'm old. I dream a lot.

I don't think it was a dream, Ulises said.

Don't say that. You look like a dream. Your arms are not real. You've gotten stronger now, bigger too, but you should be older and thinner.

Granma reached out of the tub and touched Ulises's face. She ran a hand over his cheekbones and across his forehead. Her hand went higher, and when she discovered his scar, she asked, What did they do to you?

Who? Ulises asked.

Granma pulled away. The water is cold, she said. Help me out.

Ulises lifted her from the tin tub, and she hurried to wrap her body in the robe, which stuck to her wet sides, and suddenly she was bashful, as if a stranger had walked into the room.

She said, I miss you, but I want you to go in the morning. The girl looked like your wife, but a thousand years ago. You look like yourself, but a thousand years ago. I must be dying.

Granma took a towel, walked into her bedroom, and locked the door.

Ulises did not know what to say, so he cleaned the tub and dried the water off the floor. He went into the kitchen and poured himself some of the *guaro,* and he sat there thinking how strange the woman was and wondering how she knew his father and his family. And though she was not far away, just locked away in another room, he missed her presence. She'd smelled like lemons coming out of the bath, and Ulises thought of the women in his house, not as they were at that moment but when they were both healthy and sane, and how pleasant they always smelled. He missed their talking and the quiet way they moved.

This house was also a pleasant place, quiet and undisturbed. He'd wanted to ask the boy on the bicycle about life here, who the woman was and for how long she'd owned his childhood home. He wanted to know enough to ask the woman to stay, to feel comfortable staying. He had been moving for days now, and it seemed like the time to rest. He wanted to wake up in the second bedroom and plan the next day around the ripe oxhearts that needed picking and the flower beds that needed weeding.

He wanted to be touched again on the head by the old woman, and he could see her kissing him on the cheek, cooking vegetables, and washing his clothes. The house was a tiny castle, a little kingdom.

In the morning Granma emerged from her room in a clean blue dress and with her hair done. Ulises thought she looked like someone he should have known. Granma wore a perfume different than the bath soaps, and the house filled with the scent of lavender. Ulises decided he was aching for Soledad at home before she went to work. At the courthouse his mother wore polyester dresses and put her hair up. She was well gathered, Willems used to say. Granma made Ulises breakfast, bread and guava paste, some fried tomatoes, a banana, and some coffee, which was exceptional. The old woman walked around Ulises, and he noticed how careful she was to not brush up against him, and this, he figured, was how he would act if a ghost came to live in his home.

Where did you get the coffee? he asked. It's wonderful.

You brought it, she said. From the hills.

The old woman shook her head, and Ulises felt sorry for her. He could not imagine the terror of being near blind and finding yourself either in the presence of the past or never having left it but having grown old. Or maybe she thought that she'd grown old faster than everyone around her. More likely she realized she was entertaining a stranger and was terrified that he'd given her a bath.

Do you know I've forgotten? Ulises said. I don't even know which hills you're talking about.

The old woman shook her head again, and Ulises knew he was being cruel, but he had no idea where he was going after breakfast, and he couldn't imagine his father hiking into the hills just for some wild coffee beans. Granma looked at Ulises and blinked twice.

I meet you at the river, she said. Or, I did. Now my hip. It's too far to walk.

Of course, Ulises said. He thought she was speaking of the same river behind the packinghouse, the one that fed the nameless lake and came down from the mountains. I remember, he said, and this seemed to cheer the old woman up, because she smiled for a moment.

Can I take some food with me? Ulises asked.

Granma came over to him and touched his shoulder. A moment later she kissed him on the face, and Ulises knew this was what happened when Uxbal came—he stayed the night and left the next morning with a sack from Granma's pantry.

She walked with him only as far as the last flower bed behind the house, and the whole time she held her left wrist in her right hand as though it was broken. Ulises walked slowly beside her and saw how, in her near-blindness, she was hesitant outside. He marveled at how well she must have known her home. She moved among the rooms of the house without struggle, had a place for all the pots and utensils, and she was quick. Outside, where the ground softened in the rain or hardened in the sun, she was shy in her steps.

Seeing her weak footing, he wanted to stay more than ever, to take her down to the river for lunch and back home again for an afternoon nap. She seemed a prisoner, though Ulises knew that was an exaggeration, but she had been so sweet, so kind to his foreign body and face, that he was indebted to her. Facing south, he saw the thin river leading up into the hills, toward the canopied forest. Ulises held Granma for a moment before he left, and she cried a little. She already missed him. Really, she missed Uxbal, but Ulises was more than happy to take Granma's wanting for his father as his own.

Roberto followed Ignacio, who followed José, who followed Gerardo. Isabel, renewed by her decision, by the idea of abandoning all fathers, zealously consumed the remaining rebel men. The sex she offered them was functional, but under the circumstances it was also glorious. These were men who'd not touched the other women in the camp in years, who could not see through their own grunge the pleasantness of skin anymore, and it took a will like Isabel's to ignore the stink of their armpits, the foul clothing they wore, and the situation of their rotting teeth. Her presence reminded them that they were, indeed, human. Her skin, her hair, her breasts, her legs, her lips—these were great and hidden things they had forgotten.

She found each of them in a different place, and she didn't bother as she had before in bringing them somewhere dark. They were all tucked away in the forest, and unless they fucked out in the open, in the clearing by the sabicu trees, privacy was not hard to assume. Isabel had the men behind trees, near anthills, amid a swarm of humming-birds, and at the mountain creek. She had them, that is, wherever she found them, and they relented like prophets in the Bible, as though her naked body were a burning bush. They were struck with a mixture of panic and excitement, and they suffered a choking fear when she spoke to them like children, her sentences all commands. They heard her voice, and though they did not know her, they followed. She asked for nothing. She no longer bit her lip or swallowed her moans, and she could be heard screaming with pleasure.

The months following her conquest were a strange time, when the camp seemed to resurrect itself. Revived, the men began to move about, to fix some of the shacks, to bathe more regularly, and to once again make the noise of human traffic. Their vigor was contagious, and the women, who hid even more secretly, even more quietly than the men, started to walk about freely in the daylight. Though they still spoke little and were rarely up after dark, suddenly Isabel did not feel like such a singularity. They looked at her as though she were a wild thing in their civilized world, but they were also not unkind to her. Some even left cleaner, newer clothes at the chapel for her, sometimes a bit of food.

Uxbal, like everyone, noticed this and, perhaps inspired by the hubbub, managed to escape from his shack. He even went to see his daughter in her chapel, which now had the makings of a Bible inside it. Isabel had told Gerardo to steal paper as well as food the next time he went to the markets south of the range, and he'd brought back with him two red notebooks. On the lined pages inside Isabel had begun to record what testament verses she remembered, though she wrote them down not in the order of the King James, but in the order of her memory; Genesis was still first, but Kings followed that, and then came Mark, John, Proverbs, Micah, Nahum, Leviticus . . .

Isabel was recalling Proverbs when Uxbal, walking stick in hand, blocked the light from the doorway. What have you done to this camp? he asked her.

I don't know what they're doing, she said. You're in charge of them.

I know you fucked those men. I hope you didn't do that in my name.

I did it for myself, she said. Now that I've seen what you've become, I'm learning to want for myself.

What have I become?

I don't know, entirely. I can only really say what you're not. You're not the man I was taken away from. You're not the man who spoke about God as though he were in your blood. You're not the father I took north with me. There are two Uxbals: the one I knew, and the one standing here.

I'm not well, he said.

You're not dead.

Did you come here to watch me die? Is that why you came back?

I came back because I made a promise to you.

I release you! Uxbal shouted. Be free!

That is the last thing I want, she said. Go away.

And Uxbal did.

Eventually, Isabel saw her abdomen stretch. A floating weight took residence between her hips, and her breasts swelled. She thought it had taken this long because of how little food there was, how hard it was to acquire any mass when she sometimes ate only once a day. But her pregnancy began to show itself, and the loose canvas shirts she wore, the ones left behind in abandoned shacks, began to lift at her stomach. If she raised her arms over her head, the smallish bump above her crotch slid out from below like an almond-colored crescent moon. She was more tired than ever before. But, tracing with her fingers the upper strands of her pubic hair, she was satisfied. The skin there was taut, and if she pressed against it, the stretched muscles pushed back.

The rebel men noticed first, and because they had begun talking again, it was not long before Uxbal found out. Since the camp's resurrection, he'd gotten accustomed to staying in his shack until dark, at which point he would venture out into the night and join some of the others who had begun building bonfires in the evenings. Those men caroused for hours, unworried about helicopters or patrol units in the way that forgotten men have few concerns. As they talked, they fried plantains or roasted corn over the flames. They drank also, and in the mornings Isabel could smell the remnants of liquor in the air.

One evening Uxbal came drunk to Isabel's door. She'd built a lean-to against the chapel shack, and there she slept at night with Adelina and Augusto. She awoke to the noise of a man walking very slowly in her direction, and she feared it was one of the men, blotto and aroused. But it was her father, and he carried a candle stump and a pail of water.

What are you doing? she asked. You're going to wake the children.

Kneeling at the opening of the cramped lean-to, Uxbal crawled as slowly as possible toward the foot of his daughter's bed. In the candlelight she saw that his pupils were as small as pinpricks. He had a sweat on his face that gave off a strange odor and washed the color from his cheeks.

This is why he's dying, Isabel thought to herself, and she wondered what, exactly, was the alcohol the men all drank. It was absurd that under such duress they would spend their energies getting drunk. But it was also understandable. She felt a surge of pity for Uxbal then, too cowardly to kill himself with a knife or a jump from a ledge. She also felt a fluttering affection, because maybe he'd been killing himself slowly as a way of leaving some door open, a death wish stalled by the hope that someone might return for him at the last possible moment.

She noticed that despite Uxbal's stupor, his beard was cleaner than it had ever been, and it was even trimmed. His clothes were not as dirty as usual, and, judging by the cleanliness of his fingernails, he'd recently bathed.

Why are you here? she asked.

He didn't answer. Instead, he motioned for her to stay on her cot, and then he gave her the candle to hold. Isabel sat up, and she watched as Uxbal pushed her blanket up her legs so that her feet were exposed. From the bucket came a washcloth, and in a moment Uxbal was cleaning her heels. The water was clear but smelled faintly of lemons, and her father's hands, which were stronger than she imagined they still could be, felt good on her tired soles. He washed between the knuckles of her toes, and he scrubbed at her nails with a bamboo stick wrapped in stringy coconut hair. He rinsed her ankles and squeezed her tendons. When he was done, he dried her feet with the loose end of his shirt, which was cleaner than Isabel's blanket. Finally, he spoke.

The Lord is not slow to fulfill his promise as some count slowness, but is patient toward you, not wishing that any should perish but that all should reach repentance.

Uxbal reached out his hand and lowered it onto Isabel's stomach.

God bless, he whispered. I'm sorry to be the grandfather but am overjoyed that you will be the mother. When it's born, I hope you take it away from here. I hope you tell it nothing about me, and I hope that you are happy.

Uxbal took back his hand and then lay down on the floor next to his daughter's cot. He put his head in his arms and fell asleep.

Isabel quietly cried; she mourned. Here was a descendant of Abraham, a man who was ancient by the time his first son came into being, which meant the man, the devout man, by rights, should have already given up on God. She considered the pain of waiting, the agony of expectation. Her father had been killing time, waiting for her to return, hoping she would come back. How could she, after so many years, think he had any faith left in him? Isabel also thought of her own child, the girl, and what she had accomplished, unknowingly, unwillingly, by simply being: Uxbal was weak and dying but now supplicant and apologetic. Isabel was free, though she never felt that she'd been imprisoned. Was it always the role of children to release their parents?

Isabel fell asleep next to her father thinking these things, and she did not wake until the next morning when the sky was gray and a familiar voice called her name from outside the lean-to. She left her cot and her father and Adelina and Augusto, and she entered the cool morning. There she saw, walking through the trees her brother, Ulises. He stopped when he entered the clearing and saw her face. He said, Ma is dying, to which Isabel replied, So is Papi.

Isabel told Ulises everything she knew. She told him there once had been other rebels, but they had left before she'd arrived. There had been a movement to slowly expand the group, but it had failed, and instead they had retreated, first to their homes in Buey Arriba and then up into these hills. She told him how they now stole from farms abutting the mountain range and sold their earnings to the quiet black markets in Chivirico, Uvero, and Comecará. For clothing and other supplies, they raided homes on the edges of town, basically stealing from the other poor. They often went days without food, and they drank from the nearby mountain stream. They were scared of being caught, first as rebels and now as thieves, so they rarely left the camp.

Their fear is irrational. It's entirely paranoia, Isabel said. No one is coming here for them. If someone is watching, if anyone even knows about this place, then they know they only have to keep waiting and everyone will die.

She told him the rebels barely survived, and most of the time they did not talk, though recently they talked more and more. There were men and women, and the men were like overactive sloths during the day, though at night they could chatter. The women were like shadows, and they watched the children for the most part, which was to say, they kept them quiet.

I know that this doesn't matter to you, Isabel said, but there's no sense of God here anymore. These people don't pray. Even Papi seems to have forgotten his voice, though sometimes it does come back. I'm building a chapel, which is a shitty hut, but in this place it feels like I'm re-creating the universe. I'm also teaching the two youngest children here sign language. They have no parents. In the camp, the children belong to everybody or nobody. But now they seem to belong to me. I didn't ask them to follow me around, but I think maybe they're too young to really fear the world as the other rebels do. Their names are Adelina and Augusto. They're malnourished, but I've been feeding them more and more.

If you worry that I've become a thief, know that I'm a vicarious one. I make the men share. They get me what I need when I ask, never immediately but always within a few days. They avoid me when possible, but if I call them by name, they listen. They don't bother me otherwise. They're terrified of me, and to some degree, so is Papi. He might think I'm a ghost, an angel come to get him. But no angel takes this long.

Isabel also told Ulises that Uxbal was dying from alcoholism.

I was dumb. I should have realized what it was when I first arrived. I could have taken him back to Buey Arriba, to the house. Our grandmother's sister, Delfín, is somehow there. They were twins, you know.

To all this Ulises said, Christ, you're talking again. You look like Ma, but you sound like that old woman at the house. How is it you're talking again? Tell me this means you're giving up all your promises.

I'm pregnant, Isabel said. I'm six months along, and my voice has changed.

Ulises looked at his sister and saw the slightest bulge in her abdomen. He thought she'd been starved, that she was suffering a distended belly, but not that she was pregnant. She didn't look as if she had the strength to carry a life beyond her own.

You're not exactly the brother I remember, Isabel said. You look like Papi, you're so tan and bald. Though you're much, much bigger. I forgot how large you'd gotten. You're twice his size now. When you came out of the forest, you looked like him from years ago.

Is the father a rebel? Ulises asked, pointing at Isabel's stomach.

His sister nodded.

I want to meet him, he said.

You can't, she said. I don't know who he is.

What do you mean? he asked.

I slept with six men. I don't know who the father is, and I don't want to.

Ulises didn't know what to make of that, but he heard in her tone a familiar distance. She had never felt the need to answer him, and she spoke in a way that made Ulises think she herself could not entirely explain what had happened. But she sounded and looked so different—her voice was much deeper, and she looked not frail but gaunt, though gaunt in a manner that revealed her bones as a rigid understructure, her frame as hard-edged rather than crumbling. She was taller and more severe, and Ulises realized that this woman was not really his sister but a young mother.

You should go see Papi, Isabel said.

Ulises said, You're not afraid I'd hurt him?

Not if you see him, Isabel said. Unless you've become the worst kind of coward.

You should come home and see Ma. She's had two rounds of chemotherapy, if you can believe it. The outlook isn't so good. And she blames all of this on herself. It might be nice of you to forgive her of that idea before it's too late.

Leave one dying parent for another? Isabel asked.

I haven't spoken to Papi in years, he said.

And I haven't spoken a word to Ma in a long time now.

It was evening, and the sky was gray again, which made Ulises think it would rain.

He said, There was a hurricane on its way when I left Havana. It's not safe up here.

There are small pits in each of the shacks, she said. They're shallow but wide. We take cover in them during the worst storms.

Doesn't it flood? he asked.

No. There are dry riverbeds on either side of the camp. Water flows around us. Most often the wind turns north of here.

Isabel crossed herself.

Why did you do that? Ulises asked. Haven't you broken your vows? All of them?

I've kept the promises I needed to.

Do you really not know the guy? Ulises asked. The rebel father? Don't you think the kid will look like him? But this was for Papi, wasn't it? You've finally gone and done it. Of all the promises you've kept.

The baby, Isabel said, is for no one but me. It was my choice, not Papi's.

The man sounds half-dead, but somehow he's not dying so much as learning how to survive on air. You think he's on his way out, but maybe this is his ruse, maybe this is the act he's put on for those who stumble onto this camp. Here comes the military to eradicate any threats to the magnificent government, and what do they find? An old man, a dying man, a useless, empty man. Better to leave him be. Better to simply let him waste away rather than drag him down the mountain, in front of a fake judge and a fake jury and have him tried for treason. What then? Execute a feeble grandpa in public for all the people to see? Wait for the international rebuke, the humanitarians to come and protest? For other governments to call for another invasion of the island? He knows they'll leave him be if they think he's barely there. If he looked any better, then he'd be fucked. It's an act, and you've fallen for it.

Have you ever touched the dead? Isabel asked. No, not once. Have you been at the side of a person who's not hungry because their brain has removed from its consciousness the idea of eating to stay alive? Of course not. Have you smelled a body that's half given up? Do you know how soft the skin gets when the insides begin a long shutdown? You tell me Ma is dying, but she's survived two chemo treatments. I'm not going to leave this place again because of something that is only partially true. She could live. What will be the story then? I'll be stuck there forever again. Are you going to drag me out of here if I refuse? I'm here with Papi, and you could have stayed in Connecticut with Ma, but you didn't. Don't be angry with me because you left her behind.

You can't see her anymore, can you? Ulises said. Ma is gone from your brain. You want to talk about forgetting, but you see my face, and the only thing reflected back to you is Papi. Can you close your eyes and even imagine her? You used to sit face-to-face for hours and talk through those insane notebooks. You used to touch her face with your fingers and trace her nostrils with your thumbs. If you think I'm angry, I am. But so are you. And it's because of this shithole on the mountain. This is the ridiculous dream. This is the promise you've been made to keep. And it isn't nearly enough. Maybe this is why the baby. There's nothing else here, so you're going to take from it what you can. Because leaving is the same as telling yourself that God and Papi were wrong.

If you have that baby, there's no chance on Earth of getting off this island. Don't you remember how hard it was to escape in the first place? Do you think they'd ever let you escape twice? That baby will be a part of the Cuba that was always, in its memory, this way. It won't know a different world, and it won't want to leave the way we did, or the way Ma wanted to. Papi wanted you to birth more rebels, but this kid's going to be nothing of the sort. He'll be a Cuban of the now, which isn't nearly as angry or desperate. Hungry and poor, yes, but a son of the revolution. You're going to give birth to the wrong kind of revolutionary. And he or she will never leave, which means you won't either.

If I have the child here and I can't leave, then I'll stay, said Isabel. And if we are found out, I'll also stay.

She got up from her chair and walked over to Ulises. She took his hand and put it on her stomach.

You're going to be here forever, Ulises said. You'll never come home.

I am home, she said. I never should have left.

Should I be feeling something? he asked. Has it started kicking yet?

It might, but maybe not. Don't press so hard.

You can't raise a child in a place like this, he said.

Papi won't last that long. I'm leaving here when he's through.

So it's the showing him that's important. You got here, and Papi told you to leave, and now you're having this kid out of spite. Would you really do that? This isn't about God or faith, is it, Izzi? You're just screwed up like the rest of us, and you need to fuck someone else up to make the world a little more palatable.

Ulises watched Isabel's eyes darken. This was the fissure that had begun in Hartford, the underground split in the bedrock that now crossed the Florida Straits and cut his sister's heart in two, the schism that made her ideal world—faith and family—all but impossible. Her pain, so much more evident than it had ever been, so much on the surface of her skin, reminded Ulises of his mother, whose pain had eventually manifested itself in her breasts, had at last needed to claim something real and substantial from the woman's body as opposed to just her psyche, heart, and soul.

I'm sorry, Ulises said. I told you that Ma is dying, but you're right. I don't really know anything. I lied to you. The farther away I've gotten from her, though, the more I think she won't survive.

Our family doesn't fare well across distances, Isabel said. I thought when I finally saw Papi, something would come rushing back into me. But nothing did. He was a stranger to me.

You sound ill, Ulises said.

I'm not. I'm just angry at myself for holding on to memories.

Ulises heard in Isabel's voice the end of things. Her face grimy and covered in a film of gray dust, she was an unclean spirit come to weakly portend the expiration of days.

Ulises asked, Which shack is he in?

Uxbal sat up in his cot, his back against a wall, smoking a hand-rolled cigarette. Though he was awake and puffing, his body appeared arranged, like a corpse exhumed, taken out for study in a lab or at a coroner's office somewhere and then returned to the casket, all the limbs reset at burial angles. The old man was thin under his baggy clothes, but his head was large and bald, and his neck had a fierce thickness to it. It was as if Uxbal had preserved the primary parts of his younger self, at a cost to his torso and limbs. But Ulises only had to look him in the eye to see the much-enduring father of his memories.

Ulises's first thought: I was right about his condition. It's an act, and the old man is fine. Or, he thought, this posture is an act. He's in terrible shape and sporting a face because he knows I'm here.

Ulises felt a trifle flattered, because here was the giant man of his Cuban myths, and he was putting on a private show. And Ulises was grateful then too, grateful to have this first moment with his estranged father alone. He realized he'd been anxious not just about seeing his sister, but also about seeing her and Uxbal side by side, and he wasn't sure he would have been capable of much in the presence of them both. The truth troubled him, because it made him think of God and Jesus and the devil, the last only ever speaking to the Father or the Son, never braving an appearance before the two together.

Uxbal flicked his half-finished cigarette. A collection of embers landed on the man's belly, singeing the thin fabric of his shirt. Uxbal either didn't notice or didn't care, or he couldn't muster the energy to do anything about it.

This is what I've been wanting, Ulises thought: the full sight of my father in daylight. Uxbal burning.

And then Uxbal's scalp wrinkled, and his eyes squinted, though his hands stayed still. You have your mother's knack for language, he said. But I never imagined that you'd speak Latin.

His voice was like a vapor exhaled from the earth.

Ulises said, No one speaks Latin. It's a dead language.

Your sister told me you loved school, which means your mother knew something I didn't.

It wasn't me you wanted to stay, Ulises said.

I wanted all of us to stay here, including you. Your mother had her ideas, though, and maybe it sounds unfair, but I was willing to let her go if she left me some bit of my family behind. It could have been either one of you, you or your sister.

Isabel needs to leave again.

I'm not keeping her here, his father said. I can barely keep myself upright these days. He coughed into his hands and then took several quick breaths.

What's wrong with you? Ulises asked.

I'm dying, Uxbal said. He added, somberly, I've drunk myself down. Or I've kicked myself loose of the earth. Depends on how I envision the going, whether it'll be a floating off or a terrible sinking down, and that depends on the day. Your sister knows. When she came, I could barely stand to see her. I cried for two days after she arrived. She is both your grandmother and your mother, and when I look at her, it's impossible not to see everyone here, almost the whole family. She is just as serious as I remember, which is wonderful, because I was worried that eventually I would forget. Then I was trying to forget. Less effort.

Ulises discerned a familiar jealousy flooding his chest. He expected Uxbal to say what he remembered of his son, but the old man, who really was not that old but had lived what seemed a rushed life, was lost in his thoughts.

Forgive me, he said. I don't sleep well, and sometimes I doze off.

Do you even remember me?

I don't remember that scar, Uxbal said. And you're darker than I imagined you'd be. You know what I remember? How quiet you were. How much you hated singing, especially at church. You never sang with us, and I teased you because of it.

Ulises did not remember that about himself, though it might have been true. The old man paused to rack his brain for something no longer there. He touched his forehead, the first time something besides his face had stirred, and his right hand looked swollen, as if it had been stung by a bee or a snake.

Your hand, Ulises said.

Uxbal shrugged.

I've seen the giant bees, Ulises said. Did one of them sting you?

They're hummingbirds, Uxbal said. You really have been gone for too long. I should ask you, do you remember me? Or has your mother helped you forget?

I tried on my own to forget, and it wasn't hard, Ulises said. Then I tried to remember, and that was much harder.

You left under traumatic circumstances. Probably easier to forget the whole island rather than just parts. People who've left and come back, they've suffered the same amnesia. It was a phenomenon for a while. I remember seeing it in the papers. I tried to remember you too, and it was also difficult. We never had much in common. Your mother claimed you.

She loved me, Ulises said. She loves Isabel. She'd like to see her before it's too late.

Before what's too late? Uxbal asked.

Ma is dying too.

Uxbal's face sagged, the skin of his jowls curling into mud. He closed his eyes and said, If you're going to take your sister, have her, at least, come say good-bye first.

She won't leave until you die.

I've been trying, Uxbal said.

Together Ulises and Isabel waited for Uxbal to die. Though Isabel had said she'd stay in Cuba, if necessary, for the child, Ulises thought she might not, that with Uxbal's passing might go all her affinities for the island, all her will to remain. He had to wait and see and hope.

Isabel, who seemed to be exercising again her old religious mania, continued work on her chapel. She taught Adelina and Augusto how to weave with palm leaves, and together they crafted baskets, decorative crosses, and book covers for the notebooks, which would become finished Bibles. That task fell to Ulises. He took on the duty of scribe as Isabel recited aloud what she remembered. While he wrote, he watched his sister with the children and admired how she guided their efforts. They too understood that she was pregnant. They often put their ears to her stomach, thinking they might hear something. And as Isabel's stomach grew larger, so did her presence in the camp. The women, normally stoic toward Isabel, began to bring her more food and clothing, and the men began lowering their heads when she walked by. Seeing all this, Ulises came to believe that their reverence was a consequence of the minor miracle of Isabel's conception; that anything should grow or sprout in a camp that had clearly suffered long near the edge of annihilation was a blessing.

And, truthfully, Ulises found himself smitten with his sister. He deferred to her in the making of the chapel and the writing of the Bibles, and he experienced a deep satisfaction in pleasing her. He'd not spent so much time at her side, so much time talking with her, in years, and her decisions were easy to predict. They were always the most practical, and she approached all her tasks with the same Catholic vigor Ulises remembered from her youth.

It reminded him first of Willems and then of himself. He recalled the afternoon hours back in Connecticut he'd spent sorting seeds, repairing greenhouse windows, tilling fields, and tying with twine bundles of freshly cured tobacco leaves. She was as diligent as he in the way she leveled the dirt floor of her chapel and in the way she taught the children new words to sign. She showed Adelina and Augusto how to move and spread their fingers, as though talking was a form of art rather than a necessity, a privilege the world outside the camp possessed. Isabel was relentless, and whereas this had been detrimental when it pushed her away from their mother, there in the camp it was a welcome sight, and she became a mirrored image for Ulises to revel in even though they had grown to look so unalike.

And maybe it was these two children, Adelina and Augusto, who offered Ulises and Isabel a pantomime of their own dynamic. The little girl, Ulises saw right away, was a sweet boss to the young boy, who was not so much scared as always skeptical. He would hesitate much longer than the girl would before trying new things, and she, obliviously stubborn, taught him by force, by dragging him to the chapel, by grabbing his still hands and flexing his fingers when he would not. Or maybe it was that the boy was more easily satisfied. Maybe Augusto did not want so many words to deal with. Perhaps he had enough, or what he considered enough, to be content, and it was the girl who kept asking for more.

It was a beautiful sort of education. Ulises saw that if Adelina learned too much too quickly, if her limb-driven vocabulary outpaced her brother's, then they ceased to communicate. She would speak not only more quickly, but also with a cadre of signs the boy had yet to understand, and the language they briefly shared became a mystery again to Augusto. While Isabel labored at the structure of the chapel and Ulises copied diligently the Psalm of Psalms, the two children would argue in a corner of the shack–cum–house of God. It was obvious that the boy was angry and felt left behind, but his only power was to leave. He would sometimes storm off, and the girl, precocious but in love with the only family she was mildly certain of, would wait ten minutes and then go retrieve him. She'd coax him back into the presence of Isabel, who, needing a break from the manual labor, would make up for Augusto's own brand of stubbornness with her saintly patience. Gently, she'd fill in the gaps of what he did not understand and reintroduce the young man to his sister, to whom he could now express himself again.

These moments were recursive, and eventually Ulises began to expect and hope for and cherish the instances when Adelina, her arms around Augusto's shoulders, or sometimes around his back, or even sometimes holding Augusto like a baby, carried him back into the chapel. It made his heart skip in time, and Ulises remembered that rarely are relationships built on equity, that some half, one person of the two, must always be dragging the other along, must always be teaching the other the new language, the new ways in which they should speak to each other. But Ulises also knew that Augusto was not without his purpose, and he saw how the boy's presence, his scowl or hurt eyes—they could transmit hurt like a television screen, meaning clearly and evidently, with the knowledge that the pain evidenced was happening elsewhere but was very real—kept Adelina's hands from lifting too far off the ground, from forgetting his world, meaning the world they had grown up in together.

Eventually, or perhaps as a result of what Ulises witnessed and felt, he asked Isabel to teach him sign language, and to his joy—the commingled joy of learning he'd always possessed paired with the joy of rediscovering, or reseeing, his sister—he found it fascinating. She made him sit and face her, and he was forbidden to talk. First she taught him the alphabet, and then she taught him the basics of making it through the day. She taught him the signs for *here, there, now, stop, more, yes, please, may I,* and *good night.* He caught on quickly in his mind, but his hands, more accustomed to the blunt motions of cutting, twisting, and pulling, took longer to remember the more delicate gestures. The children were not allowed in the chapel during lessons, because they were distracting, and so Ulises and Isabel were often alone together.

In the slanted light of late afternoon, Ulises spent hours studying his sister's face. He saw that she had their father's nose, which was more Mediterranean than Continental. Her eyes were Soledad's as well as her forehead. Her cheeks were a cross between the parents, and her lips seemed to come from no one, or maybe from a distant relative or grandparent they had not known. Ulises watched as Isabel spelled words and spoke sounds, each accompanied by a slow but deliberate and exact series of minor movements. There was a synchronicity to her hands and face, and it was mesmerizing to watch.

Some nights Ulises found himself dreaming about Isabel's hands. In his dreams they touched his face and stayed there, and the dream paused at such moments till he woke. They disturbed Ulises because they seemed illicit, as if to dream of his sister were the same as to dream of her naked.

Awake, Isabel was patient with him, perhaps more so than with the children, who had no other language and would assimilate easily whatever knowledge she offered them. There was a faith she had in him that he should and could learn to properly ask with his hands, *May I sit here?* and, *Will you bring me a towel?* She was teaching him to speak all over again, and every day he improved, he felt closer to her, more drawn into her world, and after some time he realized that he'd been expelled from the inner lives of his family since the start, since the boat trip from Havana to Miami, since his mother held a pair of sewing shears to his neck. Isabel had sunk down into her faith in God and her father, and his mother had found another love to whom she could devote herself. Ulises understood that he'd been alone all these years and that he'd grown used to his solitary lifestyle. He'd made no friends in school, had worked night and day in fields alongside migrant workers, and both his mother and sister, the two women of his life, had gone mute in conjunction with each other. And though he perhaps had done so to survive, he'd forgotten them. Yet here in Cuba, inside a makeshift chapel and amid the buzz of hummingbirds, Ulises remembered his sister. He felt a part of her again, and he felt wanted in her heart. The feeling overwhelmed him, and one afternoon he cried when she tried to correct one of his signs, a failed attempt at *Today will be sunny*.

What's the matter? she asked.

I'm sorry. I know now that forgetting is a sin.

Isabel said nothing, but she touched his face.

At the same time, Ulises had other dreams as well, dreams he was not so fond of. He dreamt of a man with swollen arms coming into his room and rubbing his back, and he awoke from these visions in a state of apprehension, realizing every time he opened his eyes that he was in a strange place. Ulises thought he understood the meaning of his reveries, his brain working over the proximity of his father, an oddity after such a long separation manifesting itself in his nightmares.

He did consider the vague possibility that Uxbal visited him in his sleep. The old man had seemed curious in their conversation, and Ulises wasn't sure if Uxbal believed what he'd been told about Soledad. He might have made his way to Ulises's lean-to—a second lean-to since added to the chapel—to watch the sleeping stranger, the prodigal son, for signs of truth on his face. He likely wanted to know if it was worth worrying over the news of his wife's imminent death. Uxbal, Isabel had said more than once, drifted in and out of consciousness, and Ulises had witnessed the vacillating attention. Maybe he'd come in the blue light of morning to simply touch Ulises and see if he was real. His son might have been an apparition or a hallucination brought on by his poor health, and perhaps Uxbal worried that he was seeing things. Perhaps Ulises was a manifestation of guilt. Uxbal saw every day his daughter living in squalor, and it was his fault. By continuing to live, he'd drawn her back to Cuba and to this poverty, but he couldn't admit it to himself, so his mind, clearly rotting along with his heart and kidneys, created a son who might tell him just that.

But Ulises stopped himself when he realized he was speculating a remorseful Uxbal, and that was not what he'd encountered. Also, the old man was obviously too ill to ever get out of bed more than once a day. He would have collapsed trying to stoop down into Ulises's tight quarters. Uxbal was barely a man anymore, and as Ulises thought about this, he chastised himself for considering the sickly creature a menace. Isabel, Ulises knew, had a large heart, a plainspoken and forceful heart but a brimming one nonetheless, and her plight now was one of sympathy, not obligation. He believed her when she said she would leave after Uxbal died. She would certainly leave.

Ulises's nightmares prompted him to ask Isabel about their father; she, unlike Ulises, would regularly go to the old man, and she had even begun bathing him again. Uxbal sometimes still got up at night to drink with the other rebels, but he didn't stay up as late, and he often fell asleep by the fire, leaving to whoever was still awake the responsibility of dragging his crumbled form back to his cot. His smell had also changed for the worse, Isabel told Ulises; she claimed that even after a wash he had a peculiar stench, a mushroom odor that seeped from the pores of his face.

He is beginning to fall apart from the inside out, she said.

What does that mean?

It can't be much longer now.

The psychologist said to Soledad, Soap operas are an interesting medium, aren't they?

What did Henri tell you? Never mind—I'm sure I can guess. Yes, I'm taking notes. No, I haven't really thought about why. I enjoy the game of keeping it straight. One sees a pattern after a while. I can guess about half the time where the story will go, who will die, who will live, et cetera. It keeps me occupied.

Why do you think Henri told me about the soap operas? the psychologist asked.

Because we're not fucking as much anymore, Soledad said, but then she apologized for her language. I'm drawing away from him. I feel it as much as he does. The sex has gotten boring. The soaps, they're not terribly exciting, but there's brainpower involved: Robert killed Madeline, who was sleeping with Joseph, who was Robert's bastard son . . . I enjoy how deep the story runs. There's an interconnectedness that's unavoidable.

The psychologist asked her to explain further. For instance, did she think there was a disconnectedness in her own life that led to her fascination with *As the World Turns*?

You're referring to my children.

Good, the psychologist said.

I'm dying, Soledad said.

You don't know that.

I don't want to spend my last days thinking about children whose lives I've mismanaged.

So you'll think about other families and their children? the psychologist asked.

I'll enjoy myself. Does that make me a terrible person? Does that make me disgusting? Reproachable?

Soledad waited for an answer, and then she said, Yes, I know it does.

She began to cry, but then she said to the psychologist, Henri was asleep one day, and he didn't see the special report that interrupted the show. It was about a hurricane in the Gulf of Mexico. They said it was going to pass over Cuba. Isn't it clear? My children are dead. Both of them. One I could not stop, and the other I sent there myself because I was too afraid to go. I've sent them both to their deaths.

You can't be sure, the psychologist said. Until you hear from someone, you can't be sure.

Bullshit, she said, and she started to cry again.

The psychologist sat up in his chair. Why are you afraid of going back? I think we should talk about that. I think maybe you should stop watching TV for a while. I think you should write about something else besides *As the World Turns*.

Like what?

Cuba, the psychologist said. Take some notes. Maybe create a list of your own family members. Remember as much as you can. I think we have to go there to make any sense of this.

A week passed. The psychologist said, Read me what you wrote.

My family was from the east, just a mother and a half sister. The half sister meant another man for my mother, but I never met him. She told me barely anything about him, my sister's father, and she said just as little about my own father. He died on a boat, according to her, and I always believed it was *his* boat, and I often asked my mother why we never got it back, whether or not it was at the bottom of the ocean.

A half sister, the psychologist said.

I've never met her either, Soledad said. Her father took her away before I was born.

What did that do to your mother?

Her mother had felt guilty about the separation, especially toward her. It was as though Soledad had been robbed of an essential person in her life, a counterpart who watched the same things happen from nearly the same perspective. She imagined it would have been nothing unusual until they were older, until they got curious about their fathers. Then she and her half sister probably would have spent all their time trying to figure out what parts of them belonged to their fathers and what parts they shared from their mother. But talk like that would have driven her mother crazy.

Did you write your way to your own children?

No.

Do you think Isabel and Ulises spend much time looking for Uxbal in their own features?

My daughter has her father's arms and his constitution. My son is different. I'm not sure he even knows what to compare. He does sound a bit like his father. I once heard Ulises shouting in a tobacco field. He was calling to some of the other workers in Spanish, and I could hear the little booms of his soft consonants—all his *d*s and *b*s—bouncing down the row.

When he was still in high school, I used to attend his Latin Club orations. These were readings meant to show off the boys' impressive but useless skills. They all wore white collars and dark blue ties, and they would take turns reciting classic myths in Latin. I would sit at the back and sip weak coffee. Ulises never went first, and I think that's because he was one of the best. He would take the stand last, and his thick neck would bulge against the collar of his shirt. He wasn't as big as he is now, but I should have seen it coming. He would stand perfectly still, and only his mouth would move. The times I am remembering now, he hadn't yet learned how to look up at the audience, but that didn't matter, because his voice was so strong. The audience, we would all together put down our coffee and listen. The room hushed as a room does when a truly wonderful song comes on the stereo. Or the way a theater suddenly darkens when the starlet, the one we've all been waiting to see, comes onto the screen with her hair bouncing at her shoulders.

Lovely memory, the psychologist said.

Sentimental, Soledad said.

That was how Uxbal sounded?

I suppose so, Soledad said, but that seems like something I should have been more conscious of. And now I wonder, am I mistaken altogether? Was Ulises really so talented? Did others really put down their drinks to listen to him? Looking back, it seems hard to believe.

Did you ever tell Ulises this?

No. I stopped going after a while.

Why?

Henri and I had started dating.

The psychologist scribbled on his notepad, and Soledad heard how grating the sound of his pen could be, how it turned to claws from a distance.

She said, Can I ask you, do everyone's actions, all the pasts of your other patients, seem so obvious and trite in retrospect? Is there any mystery in why they do the things they do?

I can't talk about my other patients.

I feel like such an idiot.

Why?

I thought I had let go of my husband.

The psychologist said, Well.

You're on the verge of telling me these things are natural. That of course we hear or see our loved ones in the bodies of others, especially our children.

Did you write about Uxbal?

Some.

Please.

They met at a New Year's Eve party. Soledad was working for an English family as a housekeeper and a nanny. She didn't know whom Uxbal knew at the party, but he came, drank but did not get drunk, and stole her away from them. He told her his family had some land in Buey Arriba. He said the government had taken away his family's farm but not all of it. A house and a plot remained, and though he had an aunt, she was blind and couldn't take care of the place.

What was your impression of Uxbal when you first met?

He was very convincing.

Anything else?

He was very alone.

The counselor escorted Willems to the couch.

How's the sex? she asked.

It's stopped completely, Willems said. She just watches television now, though she's also doing writing assignments for her counselor. She's been sick again recently. The doctors aren't sure if she's weak from the chemo or if this is a sign that she's about to take a hard turn. It's not that she's exactly without energy, but she seems trapped in her own mind. She walks around the house with a faraway look on her face. I've spoken to her about it, but she says she's just thinking. I ask her about what, and she says, Cuba. The children. I ask her if she wants to talk, and she says no. She says she's just trying to hold it all together in her head, all those thoughts and memories. And I know I'm not a part of them.

How? the counselor asked.

Because when she comes out of her daze, she looks at me as though I'm a stranger. It takes her a moment to recognize me. What do you make of that?

What do you make of that? the counselor asked.

I don't have a fucking clue. I'm beginning to think these sessions are worthless. I do all the talking, and I don't feel any better for it. And the last time we met, the only conclusion we came to was that I'm becoming a myopic, sex-driven monster. Sex is all I've got left. It's the only damn thing we even talk about in here, and I'm treating Soledad like a body that stumbled into my room.

We can talk about other things, the counselor said. When Soledad says she's thinking about Cuba, what do you think she means?

I'm not entirely sure, Willems said, but there are times she just sits at the kitchen table with a cup of tea, and the tea goes cold because she gets so lost in her head. I sometimes wonder if she isn't just re-imagining her life, wondering, maybe, what would have happened had she stayed.

Do you think she misses it?

You mean the time in her life when she had both her children? Willems asked. When everyone was under the same roof?

Willems looked out the window of the counselor's office and ignored the question, waving it off with his hand. It was an inane question. It had an obvious answer.

Your doctor tells me your recovery is starting to lag, the psychologist said. Are you eating well? Are you sleeping at night?

I try to eat whatever Henri makes me, and I'm awake all the time, Soledad said. Sometimes if I open the windows and let the room get cold, I can rest for an hour or two.

With your condition I would worry about a fever or pneumonia.

I'm not concerned about the cancer anymore. It's there. I'm living with it. I want to be comfortable when I can.

The psychologist said, Sometimes an illness, especially when it comes back, can seem permanent. It can feel as though it's become a part of us. Some of my patients have described their cancer as another organ, another limb.

They've only cut me up and taken things away.

How would you describe it?

I would call it a fog under the skin. Eventually, it will get to my lungs and choke me out.

That's very different from *living* with your cancer. It's more like waiting for it to take you over. I have to ask: are you experiencing any suicidal thoughts?

My body is not the problem. It's my heart. We haven't heard from my son in weeks, and the Cuban government isn't cooperating, which means Ulises and Isabel are still missing.

Your heart is part of your body.

I just want to see my children again.

You have to take care of yourself for that to happen.

Not if they're dead. If they're dead, then the longer I live, the longer it will be before I see them.

You think they're waiting for you in some afterlife?

I don't know, but I want to join them, wherever they are.

Willems canceled his next appointment with his counselor. He went walking through some of his tobacco fields east of the city. He walked for hours, staring at the ground, and if he kept his eyes on the leaves passing by his feet, then he swore he might as well have been in Cuba. Or Haiti. The dirt was just as dark. He went home.

Soledad was up and sitting at the kitchen table. Where have you been? she asked. I had a terrible session with my psychologist, and when I came home and found the house empty, I started to worry.

As she told him this, Willems watched her face, and he remembered something of the hunger in her eyes she once had for him. It made his chest ache, and he put his hand on her shoulder. He squeezed her neck.

That feels wonderful, she said.

Willems rubbed her shoulders with both hands, and Soledad moaned. They went up to the bedroom and had the slowest sex of their lives.

During the act, she'd been able to forget briefly about her children, about Cuba, and she found that tracing the hairs around Willems's nipples gave her some continued distraction from the bizarre constructions of her mind. As a result, she seemed alert, and Willems took the opportunity to say to her what he'd been thinking.

I think you might be losing your mind.

You think so?

Yes. Actually, the both of us. I'm starting to believe in my father's curse. I want to say it's breaking us. It took my mother from my father, and now it's taking you from me.

What's it responsible for? Soledad asked. Is it the cancer? Is it the sex? Or is it your bad luck? Is it having fallen in love with a woman who would die in front of you and leave behind a ridiculous family?

I don't know.

How does any of this fit with your family's past?

Who says these things are logical?

No one, she said. Except for you. Though you did tell me once that your grandfather eventually lost his mind. Perhaps we're headed in the same direction.

May I ask you something I probably shouldn't?

I don't think that's possible anymore.

What did you and the psychologist talk about in your sessions? What did you tell him?

Soledad pushed herself onto Henri's body. She pulled his head into the sweaty cavity of her chest.

I told him that Uxbal was a singer, that he sang at church, and that the first time we met, at a New Year's Eve party, he sang just for me. He and I had talked ourselves into a corner—not a standstill in the conversation, but an actual corner where we were alone—and the bells began to chime. The whole party began to sing. I only mouthed the words. Uxbal saw, and he said he wanted to kiss me, but only if I sang with him. I said I was too embarrassed, but he said it was fine. The point was many voices together. So I sang, and it was terrible. We kissed after the last refrain. I told the psychologist that being invited into the song by Uxbal was intoxicating. He had a sort of optimistic charm, and it made a space where he sang over me, but somehow my own voice still helped. It made the song a little more interesting, even though I was such a terrible singer.

Henri put his lips to Soledad's scar. He spoke into her purple skin.

You're stretching yourself across the Atlantic. The result is a body in Hartford and a heart in Cuba. You can't live in two places at once.

I think the psychologist is just making it worse, she said. What should I do? I think I agree with what you're saying.

Willems said, I think we have to go to Cuba.

Soledad, because she had once loved Henri with almost all her being, waited a moment before saying, Would you take me there? I don't feel quite so strong these days.

Yes, of course, Willems said, and they both knew they'd begun to say good-bye.

There came a night that Adelina and Augusto went to sleep in Ulises's lean-to. Isabel, herself unable to sleep for nearly a week and feeling a coldness in her throat, woke the children and told them to take their bedding out of her shack and put it into her brother's. She told them to be extremely careful not to rouse Ulises but to sleep near him as though they'd always slept at the foot of his bed. The children did not understand, and Augusto began to whine, which made Isabel shiver and close her arms around her shoulders.

She said to him, *My sheep hear my voice, and I know them, and they follow me.* Augusto stopped fussing, and he and his sister did as they were told.

When they were gone, Isabel covered her ears and held her breath. She thought, *The word of God is living and active, sharper than any two-edged sword* . . .

It was God, she believed, who had kept her awake the past few days, and He'd done so with the grating breath of the two mute children. At first it was Augusto whose snoring seemed heavier than usual, and one night Isabel sat up by his side thinking he was sick, because he made sounds like a tide drawing back from the beach too quickly. She worried that his spirit was leaving his body. She grabbed his shoulders and shook him. Suddenly conscious, Augusto eyed her suspiciously, as if she were the one experiencing an illness. Through the low light of the moon he said her face was blurry and pale like a grub. He counted accurately the fingers she held up to his nose, and Isabel thought, He's just tired, and she told him to go back to bed.

More nights passed, and Adelina began to breathe her own strange noise, something like a whistle from a boat from across a lake. Isabel couldn't understand how Augusto slept so soundly so close to his sister's face, his nose just inches from Adelina's cheek.

Isabel's head began to ache. Her muscles were tender, and her body was slow to move. Always awake, she spent hours in the chapel reading through Ulises's Bible scrawl and praying for relief, but the noise, even away from the children, seemed to follow her. She also felt a turning in her abdomen, and there was blood sometimes when she urinated. Isabel cried, thinking she'd teased God with her thoughts of Sarah, and she began to worry that He had come ironically through the mouths of Adelina and Augusto to take her baby away.

In Leviticus she read, *If a woman has a discharge of blood for many days . . . all the days of the discharge she shall continue in uncleanness . . . Every bed on which she lies, all the days of her discharge, shall be to her as the bed of her impurity.*

Isabel purified her lean-to as best she could, washing the clothes she slept in and tidying the space. With a rock, a shard of soap, and a bucket of water, she scrubbed the canvas of her cot until the fabric strained clear liquid. She bathed herself twice a day in the mountain creek, and on the days she saw a beige discharge in her underwear, she kept clear of the chapel.

But eventually the noise settled into Isabel's bones, where it throbbed tectonically, and she relinquished the children to her brother.

In the hours after they were gone, she listened to the swifts and mosquitoes and goatsuckers outside the lean-to's door, and after some time the night took on the kind of blackness only possible under clouds and jungle canopy. The dark offered Isabel a sense of solitude, but that was temporary, and the space of the shack soon felt cavernous, which made her feel small and pitiful, a fish in the ocean. At first Isabel had thought she'd removed the children from her presence, but she realized that what she'd really done was ban herself from their company.

She was alone for three nights, the children at the foot of Ulises's bed, before her brother asked, Why do you keep sending them to me?

I can hear Him again, Isabel said.

Who? Ulises asked.

God, she said. He's using the children now. He's using them against me.

What does he say?

He says that I should be alone.

Is this the baby? Ulises asked. Are you feeling unwell? There might be something wrong, and it's causing you pain.

Ulises reminded her of the geriatricians at St. Anthony's. They had a talent for speaking evenly to the distressed, for hearing the irrational pains of the elderly without blinking. Then they would start moving backward, trying to carry with them the old, worried mind that saw ghosts in arthritis, karma in broken hips, and penance— some manifestation of guilt—in a clogged ear. He was being kind, Isabel thought. And, like the doctors, he wanted to know first that she wasn't dying, that her body was sound, before he entered the space of her thinking.

I don't think so, Isabel said. I feel all right otherwise. There's just a noise that comes with them now, and it's unavoidable. Maybe you're right, and it's a phase of the pregnancy. Maybe it will pass.

Ulises let her be, and he kept the children away from Isabel during the day as well as the night. This surprised her, because her brother had only ever doubted the things she'd heard or thought she'd heard. But in his distance she found a change in Ulises's being: he had given her the space to follow what signs she perceived. It made her throat tighten in a sickly way and her depression deepen, because the more she meditated on the noise flooding her ears, the more she felt her separation from the children as a break from all things. She had once imagined being in Cuba with the father of her dreams, and now she was in a jungle with the father of her dreams, the brother of her America, and the children of her rebel promises. She was surrounded. But suddenly she could not stand these people, her father's words, or even the children's sour breath, and the pain made a quarantine of her lean-to. She was alone, and the loneliness got worse as those who could cure it hovered at the edge of her vision. I'm a leper, she thought, and she felt acutely the baby turn inside her. Isabel wondered if the girl, once she could hear, would hear the same things. She wondered if bringing the girl into this camp, where there were so many creatures making so many different sounds, was as dangerous as leaving her alone on the side of a mountain. At once she understood the terrible noise: she had to leave this place and these people behind, including her brother.

Not much later Ulises listened as Isabel said to him in her beautiful voice, When Uxbal dies, I'm leaving here. I'm leaving you as well. I've already left Ma. I can't stay behind, and I can't know you anymore, neither for my sake or yours, but especially for this kid.

I don't understand, he said.

If I know you after this, Isabel said, or if I keep taking care of Adelina and Augusto, there will be a path back to this camp. If she wanted to, my daughter could trace her way back to this place and back to these men. Then she'll know how she was made. She'll know how I abused her. She will know how I abused you, how Uxbal abused me, how we both left our mother in America to die. If I leave when Uxbal dies, and if she doesn't know you or these children or Ma or Willems, then I can tell her that I had a family once but I lost it. I can tell her the truth, which is, I don't know who her father is. She can grow up without my mistakes hanging around her neck. She won't have to ask herself the questions about her parents, why they were so ruined, and is that a part of who she is.

She'll want to know, Ulises said. She might go looking still.

Not if there's no reason to, Isabel said. Not if I ruin this place in my mind and refuse to speak about it.

You're ashamed, he said. That's all. You're ashamed of how she was conceived. She'll forgive you if you tell her.

I can't tell her these things. They're too painful. It's too much to ask a person to understand.

It's easier to disappear? To forget us?

I won't forget you, Isabel said. Not with that face, which looks like Uxbal's more and more every time I see it. I could never forget that chin, that nose, those lips. But I can't give those eyes to my daughter.

In Ulises's mind, history had collapsed into an echo; the Encarnacíon family was dismantling itself once again. His sister claimed she was the one slipping into isolation, but Isabel's child would carry her blood, so it was Ulises, in the end, who would be without kin, who was losing father, mother, sister, and future in the same scythe of time.

He got drunk. Specifically, he couldn't sleep at night following his sister's revelation, and, leaving Augusto and Adelina alone in his lean-to—abandonment was also part of the cycle—he was drawn to the fireside conversation of the rebel men who sometimes stayed awake sipping liquor, which he quickly learned was *guaro,* the same transparent liquid Granma had given him. There, in a fog of gray smoke, he drank more than his fill.

It took Ulises some nights to realize that Uxbal was also present at the bonfires. The old man was still killing himself with drink, as Ulises saw firsthand on evenings when his papi crawled out into the darkness to guzzle the booze. Saying nothing, Uxbal reached for the jug, and the other men ignored him until he fell asleep. When the embers faded, they drew sticks to see who would put him to bed. Uxbal made an appearance once every three nights, and in his sadness, Ulises could not help but stare into his father's glazed eyes, to dwell again in the anger he'd spent most of his life harboring for the man. He thought terrible things: holding his papi's face into the fire, beating him senseless with a stone, cutting his wrists, biting off his ears, even crucifying him on the royal palm behind his shack.

But the more he watched Uxbal, the more Ulises saw an old man who'd spent the majority of his last years abandoned, who'd not really known his family, who had a vision of the people he said he loved—mother, son, daughter—but whose ideal he could never reconcile with the truth. What Ulises understood when he was drunk, when he was too hazy to plot the murder of his father, was that Uxbal's life was somehow his own: Ulises had been alone for so long, so distinct from his mother and sister, that he also could not call himself part of a family. When they'd left the father in Cuba, they'd left Ulises as well.

We're tomatoes on the same rotten vine, he eventually thought.

Consequently, Ulises experienced a brief but ecstatic period of self-destruction. He began sleeping during the day like his father, remaining unwashed like his father, cursing God like his father, and wishing he would die like his father. The alternative—to live alone or, at least, be left behind—seemed more miserable. This public self-abuse led to one particularly wet night when a few of the rebel women ventured from their shacks. It seemed like the first time Ulises had laid eyes on them; truthfully, the women might have been there all night and every night before that. As a group, they had a tendency to cut their hair short, almost as short as the men's, which kept Ulises from telling them apart most of the time. Also, it didn't take much *guaro* before Ulises's world began to blur, and the faces he saw in the flickering darkness dissolved into gray or blue masks adorned with wide black eyes. The clear liquid had a way of distorting Ulises's recent memories, so that he awoke mornings-after with a throbbing jaw, swollen knuckles, and only the firm recollection of his first days in camp, which, as a result, made him sadder, because, at least then, he had just recently found his lost sister. On the other side of raising Cain, he awoke to the painful realization that he'd come so far only to lose Isabel for good. He carried this melancholy with him throughout the day, throughout his hours with Adelina and Augusto, until it was night again and he could sterilize his brain with another dirty milk jug of *guaro*.

On that particularly wet night, the evening on which Ulises noticed that both sexes sat around the fire, he felt something familiar to the attraction he'd held for Inez. The rebel women were smaller than he remembered—or maybe it was that their size shrank in the shadows of the firelight—but just the same, he drank with them for some hours. Then, later, when he was truly drunk, when his brain had been washed and his mind was blank again, he reached for them. At first they kept a distance, but as the embers dimmed, they yielded to the sexual energy of the camp, to the carnal undercurrent Isabel had started long ago with Efraín. More so they gave in to Ulises's face, which was actually Uxbal's, which they perhaps remembered as strong once, which they liked seeing again on a younger man, which gave them a false sense of hope.

Eventually, Ulises went with two of them, a Sofia and a Lena, to an abandoned shack, where he kissed them both. They asked about his sister and her child, and they wondered why he and Isabel had come to the camp. They wanted to know why they stayed when Uxbal was nearly gone.

Ulises said, It should be obvious. We're starting over. My sister and I will repopulate the mountains, and when there's enough, we'll return to Buey Arriba. We'll take over the town.

Sofia asked, Is your father done?

Zeus and Hera were brother and sister, Ulises said. Zeus destroyed Cronus, who was the son of Uranus, and he became the father of the gods. Hera was the goddess of marriage, and my sister has married all your men. She gave birth to countless deities.

What about Zeus? asked Lena.

I told you, Ulises said. He was the father of them all.

Lena and Sofia laughed and then began undressing him. But Ulises was too drunk to become aroused, so he spent the first half of the night kissing and licking the women, satisfying their reignited wants. At times he would move back from the two of them, and they would kiss each other. Then they would take turns trying to stiffen his penis, and it became a game they played, Lena first kissing softly his scrotum and massaging his ass, Sofia then fingering his anus while plunging her tongue into his ear.

You two are marvelous, Ulises said, but still he couldn't get an erection. They resorted to rougher tactics, Lena slapping at the tip of his penis while Sofia ground her clitoris unkindly on Ulises's face. He could barely stand it when Lena forced her fingers into his rectum, and for a moment he seemed to feel something in his groin, but the sensation, a shot that went up his spine rather than down his length, dissipated.

Thankfully, he was also too drunk to smell their bodies, to notice the dirt under their eyes or crusted into their nostrils. They had hair everywhere as well, and Ulises kissed their oily armpits while pulling tenderly at the dense curls blanketing their crotches. No one asked what the others wanted, and they could not stop themselves, though their energies did wax and wane, which meant Ulises experienced brief moments of unconsciousness during which he imagined having his own children, seven of them, seven boys. Each of them he would send out into the world to find his sister, their aunt.

When Ulises awoke, he told Sofia and Lena that an army was coming, but really what he wanted to breed was a search party that would retrieve his missing loved ones, even the niece he'd already lost. He kissed the women long after they fell asleep, and later, much later, when the *guaro* had worn off, he woke them up again, and they took proper turns with him, his at-last erect member a minor miracle, until he was too exhausted to sit up or keep his eyes open. He fell asleep on Sofia's stomach with Lena's hand in his, and he slept through the next day.

When he finally awoke, he hurt like a man who had wounds beneath the flesh. He knew the entire camp had witnessed his bacchanalia, because the eyes of the other women, the older ones, looked away when he passed by, and the men kept a wide berth around him. He went to see Isabel, but she sat alone and silent in the chapel, and she would not answer him.

I suppose it doesn't matter if I'm already alone, he said to her.

Ulises went to bathe in the mountain creek. He let the water run over him until he was cold. The water numbed his hands, and he could barely flex his fingers. He thought of Adelina making the sign for water, a w tapped against the mouth, and he touched his fingers to his lips, which were also cold and, as he imagined them, blue. He thought of the three ways he could speak, two with his mouth, one with his hands, and he wondered whom he would speak to for the rest of his life. Willems? Orozco? Professors? Prostitutes? He couldn't imagine the world beyond the time of his parents' deaths, which was also, in a way, the time of Isabel's death. He could not foresee a way to survive. He decided to go to the only person he knew who might tell him how it was a person lived alone, and how it was a person had a life after his family had abandoned him. He went to Uxbal.

The old man was in poor condition. He seemed not only to have lost more of his sight, but to have gone somewhat deaf as well. He had a terrible color to his skin, a thin yellow, and his breath filled the shack with a bitter air. Ulises moved to wake his father, but instead he scared Uxbal, who sat up in bed and asked him, Who are you?

Your son, Ulises said.

My son? My son was a boy when he left. He lived in his own world, always in his own head. He had a sister, but he ignored her. He was outside a lot, trying always to catch small animals. It took me some time, but I figured out he was trying to catch a hummingbird, one of the zunzuncitos. He built all sorts of little traps and hung them on trees and bushes. He hung them from our windowills. I kept stepping on them. He did that until he was seven. Then his mother taught him to read, and that was that. There were stranger animals in his books than the hummingbirds. He went outside less, only when I made him pick tomatoes with me. He was slow as shit. Took forever to fill a basket. But he never bruised a single tomato. He was too careful. The same with church. He wanted a Bible, so I got him one, but during service he would just read the Bible. He wanted to make sure no one missed a word, so he wouldn't pay attention to anyone else. He had a sister, though. She sang at church, loudly. She loved to sing. She had a wonderful voice.

I still read all the time, Ulises said.

Uxbal rubbed his eyes and touched his forehead. He said, You look just like me when I was a young man. How old are you?

Twenty-one.

Nineteen sixty-one, Uxbal said. The year I was twenty-one. Do you remember it? A terrible year to be a young man. The island was a mess. You couldn't get a drink, we were all so poor. But it was exciting then too, very exciting. A new nation, we all thought. A great new country coming up. We were attacked—do you remember? But we won. We defeated the invasion. We all had very high hopes. I met my wife a few years later, and we moved to Buey Arriba. We grew tomatoes. Whatever you do, stay with your wife. You might be tempted to leave her sometime, to go off and be with the men and explore another way of living. But that's a terrible idea. You can't go wrong following a good woman. I went with rebels. We met in the packinghouse for church and other things. We had a plan, but there was an exodus at an embassy, and the government sent the army, like wasps, through the countryside to squash any more dissidents. They destroyed our packinghouse, and we went to live in the hills. We made *guaro* for a while and sold it on the black market, but then stealing sugarcane became too dangerous. The government started sending the army to ship the stalks to the processing plants, and those caught stealing were shot in the fields. Uxbal yawned. We hid, he said.

You wrote me a letter, said Ulises.

We couldn't build outside of Buey Arriba without communicating with one another, Uxbal went on. The government has communication. They had—still have—the telephone lines and the electricity. They had the mail too, but the mail was vulnerable, even if they were censoring it. You still needed men and women to sort the letters, to box them up, put them on the right truck, and send them to the right towns. In those towns you still needed individuals with individual backpacks to carry letters from door to door. Those people had to be locals. The maps we had of the country, the few of them, were old, and half of them were incorrect entirely. And the Leader wanted to rename so many towns and places that the good maps wouldn't last. They'd have to be redrawn with the new names, the new places. He was defacing the country with the legends of Martí, using the old poet's name to make Cuba seem new when it was the same old. But that was all on the official maps, which didn't mean anything to anyone who wasn't in Havana, especially not the local *correos,* which were staffed by people who'd never left their towns, let alone kept track of what the government was calling them. But they knew where everyone lived, and there weren't many lists. When a new carrier came to train on a route, he or she just walked around the neighborhood all day with the retiring carrier. They did this for months until the new person had a clue. They had maps, and they looked at them sometimes, but from the 1970s on, it seemed like a new map came out every other week. The whole town renamed, or parts of it renamed, in honor of some dead Communist from Russia, or some smaller city erased because the land, sunk low in a pretty valley, could be used for sugarcane. What I am saying is that there were men we could talk to, and young women, who delivered our mail, who might carry mail secretly for us between Buey Arriba and anywhere else.

But everything is slower here, so we had to wait a long time to even start recruiting a carrier. The idea was to get one man in one *correo,* and he might then turn another and another and another until we owned the post office. Then we could make outreaches to nearby towns, to those carriers who make the slightly longer trips. It was not a terrible plan, but it was a tedious one, especially since neither I nor the others received much mail then. Who was sending us letters? Who could we write to? And we never knew where the censors might read our letters. We didn't know if there were censors in Buey Arriba or if they only worked in the larger cities. We wanted to believe they were concerned only with the mail that left the island, especially the stuff heading for Miami, but we were also too scared to test those theories, for someone to drop off a red-hot warning flag and see who came to town asking about the unsigned missive begging for money and complaining about the regime.

But I had the house still—I'm sure it's still there, though who knows who's inside now, whether or not someone's taken it, whether or not there's an old lady still guarding it for me—so I was the one to wait every day for the post, for a *guapo* with a lip that had clearly once been cleft. You could see the scar below his nose, which is not to say the surgeons hadn't worked a miracle, but in the sun all day, I imagine, walking from door to door, the tissue hardens and darkens. He wore an old baseball hat, but the brim was cracked, and it only ever covered his eyes. I used to offer him lemonade, which he always declined. And the mail that came was so little, I had to make up reasons to write to folks. I had to give people reasons to write me back. I wrote to newspapers praising the new names of towns or suggesting other ones. Sometimes they would print my letters and send me a free issue. I wrote to cousins I thought still lived in Santiago, sure that if they were dead or gone that, at least, the letters would come back. They never did, nor did I ever hear anything. I wrote to Russian musicians. Sometimes in Buey Arriba the radios would snag signals for long enough that we could listen to operas or the music of the ballets happening in Havana. I'd send them fan mail, and once I did get a letter back from a conductor on tour in Holguín. He said he'd love to take his music to the country and have people sit on the grass and listen. I wrote him again and again after that, but, nothing. Eventually, though, maybe after a year of those charades, the *guapo* learned my name and took a glass of lemonade.

And eventually he saw my wedding ring and asked about your mother. I told him she and you all were gone and that I was afraid to write a letter because the censors would see it headed to Miami, to your mother's cousins, and they'd come for me.

The *guapo* said to me, You're right. They would. I wouldn't feel right about carrying such a letter for you either. It would be like carrying your death sentence, and you would have written it yourself.

He was nice like that. The *guapo* himself was not from Buey Arriba but a town near Manzanillo and the coast. I asked him which place he thought was more beautiful, his seaside city or our farmers' plain.

He said they were both beautiful. The plains, he said, are easy and close, and you can see the end of things. It's sometimes nice to witness the edge of a place. Manzanillo slipped into the ocean, and that was nice too, because then it felt as if the city had crawled out of the sea, which gave everyone a reason to spend most of their time at the beach. Houses in Manzanillo, he told me, were mostly for sleeping. I knew then that I could trust him. I gave him a real letter, and he took it.

Uxbal looked spent. He shifted in his cot. He rubbed his eyes with the tips of his fingers and spoke through his palms.

Someone read my letter, and they came back, he said. They brought me a response. It's here above my head. He looked up and touched his lips. I should sleep.

Uxbal slept, and Ulises waited by his bed.

When Uxbal awoke again, Ulises asked, Do you know when you're awake?

It's difficult, Uxbal said. Sometimes the pain is really bad, and sometimes it's just an ache. It confuses me, and that's what I am sick of most. I think I want to die.

You're ready to die?

No, said his father. But I want to go. I want to be done with this. You're my son, aren't you?

Ulises nodded.

That's confusing, because you look like me with a little more hair. And you've been out in the sun, and I don't wander around much anymore. I can't keep track of time. Too many hours in this bed. I don't know who's outside that door anymore.

Isabel has been here for months, Ulises said.

Uxbal coughed. Maybe, he said. You say her name, and I think of someone who's very sad. Is that true?

Yes, Ulises said.

I have dreams of her. She washes my face for me. In the dreams, she touches my cheek as though it were a brown eggshell.

I followed her here, Ulises said. Ma asked me to.

Is your mother really ill? Is she going to die?

Yes, Ulises said. I think so. I'm supposed to bring Isabel home so she can see Ma one more time.

It seems a really terrible thing just now, asking your child to come home to you so they can watch you die.

I imagined watching you die, said Ulises. I imagined killing you myself someday if I had the chance.

I thought the same about your mother, his father said. All the ways

I would hurt her if she ever came back. How I would teach you and your sister to hate her. How I'd never forgive her even if she came crawling back to the door in Buey Arriba. Then I started drinking, because it took a lot of energy to think that way. They were the worst fantasies, but every day you were gone, I thought more and more about them. I held on to them more than I did my memories of you or your sister. I had to be drunk to enjoy them. You have to be drunk to hate so freely. When I die, don't hate me. Or your mother for taking you away. Or your sister for coming back.

Should I forget everything? Ulises asked.

No, his father said. That would be just as bad.

What do I do?

I don't know. I never found the answer.

Ulises sat with his father in silence for an hour, and they both fell asleep. They awoke to someone calling Ulises's name. The accent was strange, the Spanish spoken in a peculiar way, and it got louder. Someone had found the camp. Ulises cracked the door to his father's shack to see outside, to see who'd come for them, and after his eyes adjusted to the late-day sun, he saw that the screaming man was Willems. Behind him was Simón. They walked slowly into the clearing, and Simón held a machete in his hand. Ulises stepped outside.

Your mother has come, said the Dutchman. She's not well.

Before Ulises could answer Willems, he heard his father's voice behind him.

Take me to her. Take me to my wife.

How did you find the house? Ulises asked Willems.

He stood with the Dutchman and Simón at the edge of the camp, just beyond the clearing. Uxbal stood at the door to his hut and strained to hear. Willems looked thin and out of place, uncomfortable in the heat, and Simón could not stop looking over his shoulder back toward the circle of shacks.

Your mother remembered everything, Willems said. As soon as she saw the lake, she knew exactly where to go.

Ulises turned to Simón. Where did you come from?

I sent a man to Buey Arriba to find you. When he couldn't, I told him to go back every three days. Two days ago he found your mother, and I came.

How is she?

Exhausted, the Dutchman said. He hesitated a moment. I wasn't sure we would make it this far.

We'll send for a doctor when we get back, Ulises said.

We already have, Simón said.

Soledad had come against her doctor's orders. She wanted to see her children before she died. According to Willems, it didn't really matter, because her mind was already in Cuba.

She has lost some of herself already, he explained to Ulises. Or maybe it's that this half of her has been dormant for a number of years, and it's now awake again. It's consuming everything the cancer left behind.

Ulises tried to imagine his mother's face, but he could only see the gaunt cheekbones of Isabel. She looked painfully unwell when Ulises went to share the news that their mother had returned to Cuba. He found her sitting rigid in a pew in her makeshift chapel, looking hungry, undernourished, and weak.

He said to her, Ma is here. She's come to see you, which is a miracle. But she can't make it up the mountain because she's so weak. Come down with us. Come see our miraculous mother.

Isabel didn't answer, and Ulises was unsure of what to do. He toyed with the idea of threatening to steal Adelina or Augusto if she didn't come. But those were desperations born of anger—had she been serious when she said she'd already left Ma behind? Was this part of her zealous promise-making, to say she was done with her mother and then pretend not to hear her name spoken?—and in the end, his greatest desperation was to see his mother, with or without having brought the wandering Catholic home to her.

Ulises walked around the pew and stood in front of Isabel.

You're not a mute anymore. You can't hide behind your vows.

Isabel lifted her head, and Ulises saw that she was crying, but the sight of his sister in pain didn't compare with the urge to hold his mother's hand.

It's not safe, said Isabel.

For whom? Ulises asked. For your plan? For your guilt? It's safe for you to live in this shithole, but not to leave it? It wasn't safe for Ma to come, but she did.

I told you before, Isabel said. It's not a matter of love. Will you remind her that I love her?

No, Ulises said. Then he left his sister alone in the chapel, but not before saying, Don't forget that forgetting is a sin.

Ulises did not mention to Isabel the other miracle he'd witnessed. Uxbal had been temporarily resuscitated, returned to a fully conscious, mostly alive human being. And, unlike his daughter, Uxbal demanded that he be taken to Buey Arriba with Ulises. He demanded to see his wife, above all else. Ulises was reluctant to move his father, but the old man was already gathering what clothes he had and shouting for his bamboo walking stick. Ulises observed the cringing face of Willems.

We don't have to bring him, he said to the Dutchman. She came here with you.

I couldn't be so petty, Willems said, though he was remembering all the terrible sexual fantasies he'd imagined over the past few months.

Yet seeing the stiff knees of Uxbal, his sunken cheeks, and his cloudy eyes meant, at least to Willems, that there were no villains in the world, only the caricatures we draw of people upon whose backs we wish to thrust our own deficiencies. So they took Uxbal with them, Simón shouldering his shaky weight the entire way down the mountain, and they moved so quickly that they beat the doctor to the house.

Ulises rushed to Delfín's room, where Soledad lay asleep in her marital bed, in the first house where she'd raised her children. She lay like a wooden board under humid air, her body curled into an unnatural position that, at first, made Ulises fear she was dead. Delfín sat vigilant in a rocking chair in a corner, and she wouldn't let him near Soledad. The old woman slapped Ulises's arms till he left the room, and she shouted after him to bathe himself—something he'd not done in many, many days—before he came back.

She's probably right, you know, Willems said to Ulises. Your mother's not at full strength. She could catch something from you. Better clean up first.

That night Ulises soaked in the tub for three hours. He refilled the basin seven times, the water as hot as he could stand it. He rubbed his skin raw with a dingy gray washcloth, and he dug under his toenails with a boiled roofing nail. In front of the mirror he saw what a tremendous animal he'd become over the last few weeks. He had all the parts of a body, but they were so worn and haggard, they didn't seem to add up to a person. Ulises searched for and found a straight razor in the bathroom cabinet, and after washing it twice, he shaved his face, first chopping at the longer hairs along his jawline and then dragging the blade from neck to chin to cheek. When he finished, he touched his scalp. The hairs there were soft from the long soak, but they were ugly, and he decided to shave his head as well. He felt and eventually saw his scar, and when he finished, he finally noticed how thin he'd become. His skin was a layer of volcanic shale settled over his bones, dry, flaky, ready to come off, and his eyes were as wide as olives, as cloudy as rainwater. He did not look so large anymore but, like his father, resembled a wilted palm.

Willems and Simón had prepared for Ulises some food, but of course he wanted to see his mother instead. They said that while he was in the bath, the doctor had come. Soledad had awoken, had spoken to the physician, had taken a morphine pill, and was asleep again. He went to her anyway, stopping at the bedroom door and watching her face as she slept. Her skin, in her illness, was retracting some. Miraculously, she'd kept her long eyelashes after the chemo.

Willems and Simón told him to be patient, so in the kitchen Ulises sat down at the table and ate slowly the meal they'd made. With each bite he was more tired. He asked Willems what the doctor had said. He'd prescribed only the drug for Soledad and not said much else, which Ulises took as bad news. The doctor hadn't had much morphine, but Henri had bribed the man, and they were left with half a bottle of tablets, maybe twenty in total. Ulises asked about the treatment back in Connecticut.

Was the cancer gone? he asked.

They thought so, Willems said.

Why does she look so terrible?

I don't know, Willems said. She's ill. She's looked this way for a time now.

Ulises left the kitchen and went to one of the spare bedrooms to be alone with this non-news. After an hour, he crept to the door of his mother's room and sat against it. He had not seen Delfín and assumed she was still inside guarding the bed. He was clean now and did not have to wait, but he did anyway, because there were no more excuses, no other means to avoid walking through the door and seeing his mother and discussing with her the last days of her life. Ulises had gone to Cuba because she'd asked him to, because he'd felt as if he was waiting for the mission of his life. Now he understood that the mission was no such thing, was an act of cowardice; he'd been waiting to escape, which meant he wouldn't have to watch her die. He leaned a little lower against the door to his mother's room, and then he fell asleep crying.

He awoke to the humming of bees. In the hallway was an open window, and the morning sky was white. Quickly, though, Ulises realized the sound was not of bees but of the zunzuncitos. He saw two or three of the birds streak past the wire mesh meant to keep the bugs out, and he thought for an instant he could recall a wicker basket he'd once used in an attempt to capture a hummingbird. It had held his mother's underwear, and he'd dumped the clothes onto the bedroom floor before going outside to hunt. He'd been caught by his mother and spanked. He'd cried, and then she'd rubbed his back. The bedroom door clicked open, and the humming went away. It was Delfín. She motioned for Ulises to enter.

Soledad was on her side, in the same position as the night before when Ulises first saw her. She looked immeasurably small, as if the radiation had shrunk her body as well as the cancer. Delfín, or someone else, had covered her in several blankets, and Ulises thought the weight of all that fabric kept her from being blown away like a topsail torn from the mast during a squall. The drapes on the windows facing east were open, and shadows from the royal palms outside covered Soledad's face, which was why Ulises did not see her lips move when she spoke.

Come sit next to me, she said.

Ulises did as he was asked. He also placed his hand on Soledad's shoulder, but after a minute it was not enough, and he lay down next to her. He wrapped his arm around her waist and pushed his nose into the back of her neck. She did not smell the way he remembered.

Is she alive? Soledad whispered.

Very much so, Ulises said. But she's still up in the hills. She won't come down. She's given up on us, all of us. But, yes, she's alive. Papi is not well, but he came. I don't know if you want to see him.

What's wrong with him?

He's going to die, Ulises said.

Soledad took her son's hand and squeezed it. I missed you dearly, she said.

I tried to write. I'm sorry. I haven't forgotten you.

This place is beautiful, isn't it? I'm sorry I took you away from it.

Together they slept.

Later Ulises was roused by the midday heat, though Soledad's body seemed cold. She was still breathing, though her breaths were slow, impossibly slow. Ulises let her be, and he went and found Willems in the garden, inspecting the tomato plants. The man looked terrible, red in the face and overwhelmed, as if the air were too heavy to breathe.

Where's my father? Ulises asked.

Sleeping in the other bedroom. He hasn't woken up since we got here. These are fine vegetables. I don't know how the blind woman keeps them.

What does my mother want? Ulises asked.

To die here, the Dutchman said. She's not said anything to that effect, but I can't imagine her making it home again. I think she wants to die on the island with you and Isabel by her side. I think now she's trying to forget she ever lived in Hartford.

The Dutchman walked around a trellis sagging from excessive

fruit, the same trellis Ulises had fixed when passing through those weeks ago. He touched the wood and then plucked six tomatoes from the upper half of the vine. The wood straightened a tiny bit.

I have lost your mother, Willems said.

You have not, Ulises told him. She came here to find us, or at least one of us.

She told me once she'd never return. She told me Cuba was a dream she'd had, and she hoped never to dream it again. I don't think she lied to me, but in the past few weeks it's been as if the dream has taken over her mind. The drugs and her illness, of course, have something to do with it, but I think more than anything she wanted to close the wound she opened between Hartford and here. It's been open much too long, and now she's ready to give up.

Ulises thought that Willems was himself exhausted. He was being cruel because of what he also stood to lose. But there wasn't any anger in his voice, and Ulises had to admit that his mother seemed more at peace here in the old house, more centered in Buey Arriba, than when she was sick in Hartford.

My mother loves you, Ulises said.

I know she does, the Dutchman said. But she hasn't forgotten this place, and she can't forget your sister. They're the same, you know. I used to think they were different, but they've always been the same.

You're driving yourself insane with this talk, Ulises said.

Willems sighed. Your mother will stay alive until she gets to see Isabel again. She wants to tell her daughter how sorry she is more than she wants to walk on Earth. Then she's going to leave us, you and me.

When he awoke, Uxbal was in desperate need of a bath, among other things. Here Delfín emerged from her protective stance by Soledad's side and followed the men into the other bedroom. They were deciding who should wash Uxbal. Ulises took a swollen hand and lifted it. The bones felt hollow, like a bird's. This, he knew, was worse than a week ago, and though Ulises had not aided his father nearly as much as Isabel had, here he discovered a physical intimacy between them: Ulises possessed a working knowledge of his father's body, and if he were to die this minute, Ulises might claim he understood best the man's last hours of physical life. He felt like a midlevel authority over Uxbal, a deputy minister or a floor manager.

Delfín, however, did not want him to touch the old man, and she tried, with her hands and her low, butting head, to push Ulises away from his father's body. Only after a long, muttering rant did she allow him, under her supervision, to first carry and then bathe his father in the basin. Ulises remembered his own visit to the house not so long ago, and he knew this was somehow Delfín's territory, the bath and the bathing, Delfín something like a priestess at a forgotten oracle. Ulises would have liked to let the woman take Uxbal herself, but it was clear she was too old, though at one point she did help, scrubbing the man's backside as Ulises lifted Uxbal out of the water so that all his sacred parts could be cleaned. They also dried his body together, and before putting him back to bed they fed him water and orange juice. He was in a daze, and he touched his skin perplexedly, and Ulises knew he'd forgotten the feeling of soap and clean water. By the end of the day, husband and wife slept on opposite sides of a wall.

Simón watched the whole process. This is hurtful, he said that night, but I think we should dig a grave. It's only going to get hotter. Once your father goes, it will be difficult. He seems closer than your mother.

Ulises went to Delfín and tried to explain to her as much, but she seemed to already understand what he wanted to say. She brought him close.

You changed on me, she told him. But now I've got you. You've come back to bury yourself. You don't want to rot out in the open.

Ulises took Delfín's words to mean that he was, in her mind, the future ghost of Uxbal. Uxbal's body, in contrast, was emptied of spirit. The ship has no captain, Ulises thought.

He and Simón found two shovels in a closet. They followed Delfín out to the garden. She led them away from the river, afraid that a grave near water could be washed out. She brought them to a patch of wild portulaca, the leaf being what Delfín had served Ulises the first night he'd stayed with her. The patch was as wide as six men, and there Delfín instructed them to dig.

They were glad to work in the dark, because the air was already damp, and, come morning, the rising sun would boil the heat from the ground. Ulises felt as though they were digging atop a volcano, and at any moment they would unearth a stream of lava. They took turns, because the grave they dug was narrow. They made only enough room for one body. Ulises saw this and said something to Simón, and the two agreed they should make the ditch wider despite the hours it might add.

We should leave room for, at least, a modest coffin, Simón said.

He and Ulises dug until all the insects—the mosquitoes, the gnats, the ants, the horseflies—were awake and biting at their shins. They dug until the sun came up and the sky was blue. The sky, in Ulises's mind, had not been blue for weeks, but he was back down on the plain, the watershed of the mountains, and the clouds that huddled over the range dissipated into vapor once they slid past the peaks.

After washing, Ulises went to see Uxbal, but he was fast asleep. He went to his mother and found her sitting upright in her bed with her eyes closed. The gown she wore lay flat across her chest, and Ulises's was struck, then, with the idea that he knew Uxbal's hands better than his mother's new body. Opening her eyes, Soledad caught him staring. She unwrapped the red scarf that Delfín had draped around her head.

We have the same haircut now, she said to Ulises.

Ulises watched the scarf fall across his mother's left shoulder, and on her scalp was stubble like that on a man's face.

Come touch it, she said.

Ulises walked over to his mother and placed his hand at the back of her skull. He allowed his fingers to graze the skin, and to his surprise the hair was downy, like burst cattails in a swamp.

It's growing back, she said. The doctor said it would, but I didn't believe him. I don't know why. I think I was preparing for the worst. The air here, it's heavier, but I like it. Not so biting. And the humidity helps with my breathing.

Ulises said, You look wonderful, Ma. He asked, Do you know who is in the other room?

Your father, Soledad said. I heard you and Delfín bathing him last night. It sounded slow, if that makes any sense. I mean the time, not the image I saw in my mind of your father being washed. It's hard to explain. What I really mean is that I feel his body settled against the wall, and that took a long time. That's the movement I'm referring to, so I don't know why I mentioned the bath. Maybe it's because the bath reminds me of children and then of having a child, and his body against the wall is like a boy growing inside me. The boy is finally settled. Do you see?

I'm not sure what you mean, Ma.

Ulises thought Soledad was reacting to the morphine, but she was wide-awake. He was also reminded of Isabel, alone on the mountain and absurdly pregnant. He thought to tell Soledad just then, but he did not.

I've carried him with me, your father, Soledad said. I told you I'd never forget him, and I haven't. So he's been growing. That's what happens when you don't forget. I should have divorced him, but instead I've been seeing him through poor Henri, which makes me a liar and a thief. I've stolen things from Henri.

What things? Ulises asked. If he's given them to you, it's not stealing.

So much time, she said. Do you know I can hear your father

breathing? Not through the wall, but in my chest. Your father has spent a lifetime willing us home.

You're speaking nonsense, Ulises said. He is an old man. He's closer to death than you are. You're saying these things because you feel guilty, because you don't want to die having driven away your daughter and having left your husband.

Do you know why I came here? Soledad asked.

No, he said.

To see you. To tell you to go home. I shouldn't have asked you to come here, not for me or for your sister. I saw the hurricane on TV, and I knew that if you didn't come back then, that you had found her. I knew that you wouldn't come back without her, but I think I also knew, in some way, that she'd never come home. All of which meant *you* weren't ever coming home.

Ulises began to cry.

You should leave all of us, Soledad said. You should leave us all here.

That night Ulises got drunk with Willems out in the garden, the loamy expanse of which curled around the house from front to back. The tomato vines—buoyed by the patchwork of low, A-frame trellises— slunk in all directions, but yellow wildflowers choked the grass near the forest, and the cabbage beds closest to the brook had gone entirely to seed. In the kitchen they'd found a jug of the fermented cane juice, but it smelled rancid, so Willems paid a man to go to Bayamo for some decent cigars and two bottles of rum. Together, they drank and smoked and picked tomatoes to eat when they were hungry, spending most of the dark vigil in the abandoned, mushroom-scented rows by the stream. Willems periodically went to check on Soledad, and, contrary to what Ulises might have thought, the Dutchman seemed stronger for his belief that all was lost or, at least, that his and Soledad's affair was coming to a close. He was not necessarily in good spirits, but he was not a wreck either. He'd slept for most of the afternoon, and his skin had returned to a thin cream color.

The island is good for me, the Dutchman said. I haven't been back in a while. These cigars are second-rate, but they're better than what we grow in Connecticut.

Ulises had told Willems about his mother's ramblings. At one point Ulises called them delusions, and the Dutchman reminded him that delusions pass unless they are believed. His mother seemed firm in her statements. Willems then poured Ulises another glass of the rum and told him he was a better man than most, the best son he'd ever come across, and the only brother to really ever give a damn. Ulises saw that the Dutchman's flattery was superfluous but also genuine. The man had entered into an off-balance clan—which he said more than once—and he drunkenly congratulated Ulises on being the sole survivor of an insane asylum. Sympathizing with the Dutchman, Ulises told him, not unkindly, that to fall in love with another man's wife was no consolation.

I thought I was cursed, Willems said. It took your mother's insanity to bring me back here. You're older than you look.

It was sometime before or after midnight when the two of them, half in a daze from nicotine and alcohol, heard a confluence of voices coming through the windows of the house. They stumbled inside and stopped in the hallway, and what they heard was two people singing. Simón had left for the night, staying somewhere in town, and Delfín could not possibly sing with such clarity. It was Uxbal and Soledad. They were serenading each other through the walls, singing a *danzonete*. It was a slow song about Jesús Cristo feeding some peasants some fish. As Soledad's voice gained momentum, vibrations registered in Ulises's throat. Her sound was not great, but it was melodious, and it made Ulises jealous. What he wanted, then, was to curl up at the feet of his mother and fall asleep to her song. But, slightly drunk as he was, he made to enter his father's room and tell him to shut his mouth and let Soledad rest. Willems grabbed Ulises by the arm before he could take a step.

Let them be, the Dutchman said. This is what your mother has been dreaming about in her sleep. I've lain awake next to her and listened to this for weeks. She's consumed by it, so let her have it.

She's not insane, Ulises said.

Her mind and her body are finally in the same place, is all, Willems said. She doesn't know Hartford anymore. Thinking she never left Cuba will be the nicest way for her to die. And she's his wife.

It was the truth, and it made Ulises unbearably sad, because it meant Soledad had first been a wife and a mother only after—he had no claim on her. He looked at Willems, who had brought her back to Cuba. He seemed to have even given her back to Uxbal. He could make no claims either. The Dutchman was clearly flustered, pained to have to listen to this, but he seemed to know that holding on was a worse fate than letting go. Ulises retreated to the kitchen, and somehow this woke Delfín, even though the singing had not. The old woman came out of her room and told Willems to go and get some water, but he ignored her and went back outside.

The body is going, she said to Ulises. It sounds strong, but it will be done soon. You can bury yourself proper.

Eventually, the singing waned and became a murmur. Ulises, sitting at the kitchen table, listened as his mother and father spoke to each other through the wall. Uxbal told Soledad what his life had been like after she and the children left, and Soledad spoke of Isabel's faith and Willems's tobacco. She mentioned Ulises's green thumb. They were like old friends but less, like two people who'd happened to share nearly the same life and had only just stumbled upon each other. And though they were in different rooms, Ulises could tell that they spoke as if from across a pillow, which meant they were suddenly talking again like old lovers whose thoughts ran together, who shared secrets because it was like speaking into a mirror. Ulises listened as his parents rebuilt the past, talked their way back toward 1964, when they met, four years before he was born. He heard them erase time and forget whole decades, and he began to sob.

Are you afraid of dying? Soledad asked Uxbal.

No, he said. Just impatient. I've been dying for too long now. I wish someone would come and take me.

Don't say that, Soledad said. You've never had chemotherapy. You don't have a clue what it's like to suffer through a living day.

What do you hope for from the afterlife? Uxbal asked.

One of the beds creaked. Ulises imagined his mother pressing her lips to the wall.

A nice tomato garden, she said. But no worms to dig out. No mosquitoes to swat. An outdoor bed.

That's wonderful.

Are you imagining the same? she asked.

No, he said. The ocean. I haven't been there since I was a boy.

You die and go to the beach.

There is a woman there with me. She is beautiful, and she has a full head of hair like on the night I met her at a New Year's party when she wore an ugly brown skirt. At the beach she's dressed the same.

Why would she wear a skirt to the beach? Where's her swimsuit?

We swim naked, Uxbal said. There are no swimsuits in heaven.

Ulises thought, They are dreaming of a different Cuba.

Willems appeared in the kitchen and motioned for Ulises to come outside. There, the Dutchman pulled him to the edge of the garden.

Do you see it? he asked.

What? Ulises asked.

The light.

Ulises squinted into the dark. His pupils widened, and he eventually saw the faintest glow bobbing in the distance. Coming down from the mountains and nearing the house. A flame burning yellow, orange, and red.

It's a torch, Willems said. Someone is coming.

Isabel had come down from the mountain.

For the first and only time in his life, Ulises would watch his sister, the Death Torch, assist another person into the afterlife. Hollowed out and wearing more clothes than the warm weather demanded, Isabel bathed, just as Ulises had, before paying respects to her dying mother. When she dressed, however, she dressed in Uxbal's old clothing, ignoring what Delfín had brought her. Then Isabel and Soledad talked for some time alone. Halfway through the night Isabel called for Ulises to join them. In the room his sister stood by the bed, holding their mother's hands. Soledad seemed asleep but opened her eyes every few minutes.

God bless, Soledad said. You're here.

Isabel turned to Ulises. Can you remember the song Faithful We Shall Come?

I don't know, Ulises said. It's been forever.

I'm only going to hum it. When you remember the tune, hum it with me.

Isabel began, and the song was entirely foreign to Ulises. He watched in silence as his sister, still humming, pressed her lips to their mother's bald head. Though he didn't know the melody, Ulises listened as well as he could, and when he was sure he understood the highs and lows, he made a sound in his throat like singing. His sister looked at him, and he saw some fear in her eyes, and maybe they both understood that it wouldn't be long now. The song moved toward an end, and Ulises watched his sister's lips drop the melody and kiss Soledad's skin. Isabel took in a long, slow breath, and he swore he saw something pass from his mother's body into his sister's mouth. But then Isabel exhaled, and whatever had left their mother's form floated into the air and was carried out the open window by a slow, humid breeze.

Ulises remembered a time when he and Isabel were eight years old. A stovepipe, damaged during a recent hurricane, fed flames to the roof of a neighbor's house, which, in the early morning, burned to the ground. Most of the family escaped, but someone, Ulises was certain, had died. He could not remember who.

In the days that followed, the Encarnaciós and other towns-folk helped the grief-stricken family salvage what they could. Uxbal wrenched hot nails from charred siding. Soledad scrubbed blackened pans pulled from the ash. Isabel and Ulises gathered from the garden vegetables the smoke hadn't touched. They worked as long as there was light.

At dusk they walked home, and one evening they left Uxbal behind to continue the work. Halfway down the road, Ulises remembered, Isabel tripped on a stone, her body—then still the mirror of his own—collapsing like a cut sail. Soledad lifted her from the ground, and her face was clay, the dust of the road clinging to the skin wet with tears. Soledad hushed her daughter and with her hand wiped Isabel's chin. Seeing the dirt on her own fingertips, Soledad slid her thumb across Isabel's dirty cheek and then touched the girl's head. She turned to Ulises and smiled. She asked him to come closer. He came to her side, and she reached out. On Ulises's forehead Soledad made the sign of the cross. She brought his hand into her own and took the children home.

At Delfín's insistence the mourning lasted seven days: a three-day wake before the interment and a three-day vigil afterward. The public came during the first seventy-two hours, because word had spread that a bald woman had died and her husbands—she was rumored to have two—were feeding any and all visitors. Soledad's body, after the mortician had finished his work, was displayed in the main room of the house. The coffin was blue, because it was the only color available that was not white or red. Guests lined up at the front door, and they were allowed into the house six at a time. There were whole families, groups of young men, single women, and old crones. Hungry boys came to the house by foot or on their bikes, and the yard was a mess of rusted two-wheelers.

Willems, the gentleman that he was, had gone to tell Uxbal the news, but the old man was already standing at the edge of his bed when the Dutchman gently tapped open the bedroom door.

Will you help me bury her? Uxbal asked.

The family wore whatever white they had. Ulises took shirts from his father's moth-ridden closet and found clothes for himself and the other men. He dressed Uxbal, taking great care to make the old man presentable. He trimmed the few hairs still trying at the back of his neck, and, borrowing soap and shaving cream from Willems, he used the straight razor on his father's face. Ulises splashed him with after-shave, tucked in his shirt, knotted a tie for him, and managed even to buff his shoes. In the end, Uxbal appeared like an aging ambassador. Delfín dressed Isabel in a white skirt and light blue blouse, which was too large for her and swallowed her torso entirely. They stood as a family just beyond the casket and the makeshift kneeler where visitors bent down to pray. They shook hands with the people of Buey Arriba and kissed strangers on the cheek. Even Uxbal did this. For the entire wake he and Henri stood side by side in front of the casket, and not a person could tell who was the lover and who was the husband.

By the second day, Ulises and Delfín had achieved a passable rhythm between cooking and accepting guests. Breakfast was skipped in favor of lunch: meats, tomatoes, cheeses, coffee, bread, and dates. For dinner each night Delfín roasted fish and potatoes, which could be cut into thin slices and served on hard rye with red peppers, tomato paste, and vinegar. There was coffee in the evening as well, and neither Delfín nor Ulises slept for more than four hours a night.

Oddly, Isabel was only awake four hours a day, from noon till late afternoon. She told Ulises she'd not been well on the mountain. I didn't think I could bear this, she said. But then I was afraid if I came down, I might break my promise to myself to leave.

But you won't? Ulises asked.

We will see.

Ulises examined Isabel's pale face and saw a life barely tethered to the world. She was trying to buck the compulsory love of parents and children, and Ulises imagined this to be an arduous, perhaps impossible, effort. He heard his dead mother saying, I left my voice in Cuba, which reminded Ulises of Isabel's unborn child, a forgotten thing or, if he was honest with himself, a person he willfully forgot.

How are you feeling now? he asked Isabel. He eyed the baggy canvas shirt she wore. Is everything all right with the kid?

It's hard to tell, she replied.

This was the edge of a confession. She thinks she's lost the child, Ulises thought, and it made him feel the worse, guiltier, as if his sister's past and future had dissolved all in a night. The child's conception had been something of an impossible phenomenon, but every other plan of hers had come to fruition, and Ulises had assumed the child would be same: the baby, by the will of his sister, would, of course, be born. For the first time he thought that Isabel's desire to escape was perhaps not the worst thing ever, that maybe it was even necessary, considering what she'd seen and suffered.

He wanted to take her in his arms then, but she looked on the verge of shattering, so, instead, Ulises kissed her on the cheek and said, Go back to bed. Sleep. The procession will take all day, and it's going to be hot and sunny.

The funeral procession wound through Buey Arriba, turning around corners and cutting through alleyways erratically. According to Delfín, there was a traditional path through the streets, and the casket had to be carted on a makeshift gurney the entire way. Two family members at all times had to be touching the wooden box. The wreaths from the house were carried by volunteer children twenty meters ahead of the procession, and a boy on a bike was hired to ride ahead and call out the coming of the dead. The townspeople seemed slow and tired, sluggish with all the food they'd eaten in the last three days. They came lazily to their front stoops. As the casket passed by, Ulises led the way. Isabel was on his arm, and Delfín was a step back with a Bible in her hand. Miraculously, Willems accompanied Uxbal behind them all, their hands touching the blue lid.

The people from Buey Arriba gathered the flowers from their houses and tossed them at the casket. A few young girls laid palm leaves in front of the procession, and they dried quickly under the sun, crackling under the feet of the pallbearers. Delfín told Ulises where to turn and take the procession, and halfway through the day they'd arrived at the nameless lake. Delfín went to the water and soaked the scarf she had worn around her shoulders. She returned to the group and squeezed the lake water over Ulises's hands and then over the casket. She said a prayer that reminded Ulises of the baptismal rite. Delfín knelt and crossed herself, and then she told Ulises to lead them all home.

They sang the body into the grave that Ulises and Simón had dug for Uxbal. Uxbal asked when and who had dug the hole, and Ulises lied to him, saying Simón had hired some men from the town. The grave was big enough for a man in a modest coffin, which meant it was wide enough for a woman in a beautiful coffin, which is what Willems had purchased for the woman he'd come to Cuba with. The lowering of the box by rope took twelve men and ten minutes.

When called forth to recite a eulogy, Willems tapped Uxbal on the shoulder, signaling him to speak. But the old man simply kissed Willems on the face. I did not deserve her, he said. Or my children.

It was as fine a thing as Ulises could imagine him saying.

Isabel was the first to throw a palmful of dirt into the grave and onto the coffin. Ulises was next, then Willems, then Delfín, and, last, Uxbal. The men who'd helped lower the casket began to fill in the rest. It grew dark out. Isabel went to lie down. Simón took leave of the family. Willems, realizing perhaps for the first time that he would sleep alone for the rest of his life, began to weep, and Delfín took him aside. Ulises and Uxbal, who was still standing, who had not sat down the entire day, watched as the grave was filled to the brim with rusty soil.

You dug that grave for me, didn't you? Uxbal asked.

Yes, Ulises said. We thought you would die first.

My sorries, Uxbal said. I've failed you again. The old man hobbled away.

Delfín came out of the house with a bouquet of chalice vine in hand. She walked to the place where the headstone would eventually be set, and she brushed the flower heads across the dirt. She did this around the entire grave, in a long oval.

She said to Ulises, The hummingbirds will come. Good luck.

The next three days were for the family to pray together for their lost love, but only Delfín spent hours in front of Soledad's grave with a rosary in hand. Willems stayed mostly in his room or went walking in the direction of the mountain range. He came back sometimes with wild tobacco leaves and a calm look on his face. Isabel prayed quietly next to Soledad's deathbed. Uxbal remained in his room, and with the funeral ended, he seemed devoid of all his strength again, though he was still coherent, and sometimes Ulises could hear him to talking to Isabel. He wanted to know where she had come from. Had he been in a coma? Had he been hit on the head? Delfín told Ulises that on the seventh day of mourning, the third night after the interment, the family would eat a meal together. They would break bread and eat veal. Ulises asked Delfín where she would get the calf, but the old woman ignored him. Ulises told Uxbal about the dinner, and the old man nodded.

Do you still pray? Ulises asked. Or did that die with the revolution? He said this kindly, as if he too had suffered a great loss with the disintegration of the rebel camp.

God is only as tall as the tomato vine, Uxbal said.

Ulises understood his father in this way: God lives only where there is life. Then his father cried, and Ulises did not know how to console him.

The meal was somber but sprawling. There was veal, as Delfín had promised, as well as lamb. But there was also guava paste, knuckle bread, mint jelly, yams, a white bean soup, baked carrots, garlic yucca, white rice, goat cheese, small bits of sweetened ham off the bone, deviled eggs, and fried plantains. There was so much, Ulises could not catalog it all. Sitting down at the table, he stared bittersweetly at the feast, neither hungry nor interested, and he saw a similar look on his sister's face. Willems was smoking a cigar, and, despite Delfín's nagging, he would not put it out. Uxbal either stared at his own lap or was asleep.

But Delfín was undaunted, and she served first a spinach salad and then a sprout casserole. She ate the food in front of her in silent bites and told them it was tradition that every member of the family taste every dish offered. Ulises couldn't tell if this was true or if Delfín's pride had been hurt by his slow mouthfuls; regardless, he shoved more casserole and spinach into his mouth. Isabel did the same. Willems, still smoking, said the casserole was delicious.

Uxbal did not lift a finger. This was a problem, because dishes had to be served in order, and one course had to be finished before the next began.

They would wait, Delfín said, for Uxbal. To eat ahead was bad luck for the dead.

Papi, Ulises said, try the sprout casserole. It has tomatoes in it.

Ulises, sitting next to Uxbal, held a fork in front of the old man's mouth for fifteen minutes before he finally took a bite. Ulises did the same with the spinach salad.

Uxbal nodded after the salad, as if to say he liked it, and Isabel said, There's plenty more, Papi.

The mood at the table lifted, and each dish Uxbal tasted was another miniature cause for celebration. In this way they moved through seventeen plates, through all the cheese and rice and ham and, finally, the veal. After the meat, though, came the bread, and Delfín, splitting a loaf into fifths, recited the *Our Father*. She passed the bread around, and this alone Ulises did not have to feed to his father, who took the piece in his palm as though it was the body of a dead bird. He kissed the bread before eating it, and Ulises, seeing this, did the same. They had finished the meal. The ordeal was done.

It was only in the silence that followed the feast that Ulises heard footsteps trudging through the garden. He stepped outside. In the twilight he saw four men and a boy. The men were dressed as soldiers, and the boy looked familiar.

Is this him? one of the soldiers asked the boy.

Ulises squinted in the gray light. It was the boy with the bike from the first time he'd worked in the garden for Delfín.

What's going on? Ulises said.

The boy didn't answer.

The soldier turned to Ulises and said, This boy saw a bald man at this old woman's house who'd not been here for a long time. Then there was a large meeting here.

There was a wake and a funeral, Ulises said. My mother died.

We are looking for Uxbal, the soldier said. We know he's come back to the house. He used to live here.

What do you want him for?

He's a counterrevolutionary, the soldier said.

Ulises turned and looked at the house. He saw Delfín at a window. She watched through the glass.

Let us into the house, the soldier said.

The boy stepped back behind the soldier. Ulises heard a humming by his mother's grave. He thought of his father in the dining room and the bites he'd taken during the meal, small and finicky like a child's. In his mind he saw his father naked after a bath, his hands swollen and red. He saw his sister walking not toward the house but away from it, one hand bearing a torch, the other touching her abdomen, the last place she'd gone to for hope or faith or whatever, the last place that had failed her. He did not see Willems. He imagined Delfín dead. He knew then, no matter what, that he would never see them all again, that to stay himself was to witness the final sinking of their lives into the soft red soil behind the modest country house.

Ulises said to the soldier, You've come for me. I am Uxbal.

THE ISLAND

For two years Ulises lived and worked on a sugarcane plantation outside Santiago alongside other dissidents, army deserters, accused homosexuals, true homosexuals, embezzlers, political adversaries, freethinkers, students, and thieves. During the first three months of his incarceration, he attended a weekly class meant to rehabilitate his broken socialist spirit. The instructors, as they were called, interrogated him each time with the same questions: Where are your other men? What was your plan? What is your revolution?

Each time Ulises answered, I'm alone. I had no plan. I'm poor. I want to survive. I could not conquer a child. The revolution is over, and I have lost.

The instructors had never seen a spirit so broken on arrival. They deemed him rehabilitated and dismissed him from the class. Still, he was part of the dissidents' ward and kept in solitary confinement. He was not allowed to write or send letters. He was not allowed to have visitors, except charitable nuns or government officials.

In the fields Ulises was twice worked nearly to death. Both times he had been uprooting foul cane stalks blighted by beetles. Both times he was taken to the infirmary and given saline, cold packs, and aspirin because he was such a good worker. By the middle of his second year he'd been placed in charge of a small gang, and the fields they oversaw produced the most consistent crop.

When the camp began to swell with new inmates, Ulises was put in charge of more men. He asked where the prisoners were coming from, and a guard told him that the Berlin Wall had fallen. Socialism was dead in Germany, which meant it could die elsewhere, and the president wanted any remaining counterrevolutionaries, confirmed or rumored, detained.

The influx also resulted in Ulises's transfer to the general population, where at last he was placed in a cell with three other men, all of them new to the prison. They acted tough, eyeing him meanly and stealing his bedsheets, but Ulises ignored their bravado. That, coupled with his size—the consistent food and work had returned width and muscle to Ulises's depleted frame—meant they took him for something like a disinterested murderer and let him be. The quiet ones, they said, are always the craziest.

It was another year before Ulises realized he could write a letter to someone now that he was out of solitary. He did, but then he wasn't sure where to send it. In the end he mailed it to the United States, to Willems's offices in Hartford, with the help of a guard who had a sister up north. Six months later he received a reply in the form of an unsigned business letter: Uxbal had died three weeks after Ulises was taken. He was buried next to Soledad. Isabel left Buey Arriba shortly thereafter and disappeared.

The letter, though on Willems's stationery, was not written by Willems, but by the acting manager of Henri's tobacco operation. The Dutchman had taken an open-ended leave of absence from the company, and the manager—the only person in contact with Henri—was handling his correspondence. According to his reply, Willems had departed Buey Arriba after Soledad's death, though not without first leaving behind some money for Delfín, who somehow managed to live on. Presently, Willems was traveling the world collecting rare tobacco leaves, and every few months a small box arrived at the Hartford offices with a carton of cigars hand-rolled by Henri himself. The carton came with instructions to sell the cigars, which, the instructions stated, breathed a blue smoke purer than air, at ten thousand dollars apiece. The labels on the cigars were also handmade, and the

stogies were called Imperial Soledads. The letter finished quickly
with an apology for Willems's inability to respond directly, and it included a cream-colored insert that Ulises presumed would come with
the cigars, should someone be carelessly rich enough to purchase an
entire box:

> These cigars are of the finest quality and meant for travelers.
> They should be smoked as a way to remember something
> familiar, something left behind; they should be smoked in
> such a way that a traveler never becomes accustomed to
> a place, that a placeless nostalgia overcomes him, and he
> is forever traveling, which is the plight and joy of the trav-
> eler, removed always from friends, family, familiar terrain,
> acquainted mountains and hills, beloved faces, a river of a
> man always.

Two more years passed. The Soviet Union collapsed, and Ulises was
released from jail. He was let out not for his good behavior, but for his
growing skills. With the dissolution of the European socialist bloc,
Cuba was on its own economically, and the government moved swiftly
to subsidize its people. More than anything it had lost a trading partner, and the price of sugarcane plummeted. An official from the Min-
istry of Farms and Agriculture met with Ulises to discuss his role in
what the president was calling the Special Period in Time of Peace.
He wanted Ulises to run a new farm, or a series of new farms, that
grew something besides sugarcane. The official wore burgundy wing
tips with delicate stitching along the sides, and they reminded Ulises
of his steel-toed dress shoes, his first gift from Henri, his first boots.

Ulises said, I can grow tobacco.

We need to feed our people, the official said.

Ulises suggested tomatoes.

Fine, the man said. Then he asked, Where would you like to go?

Ulises thought of the whole island, but then he was exhausted by the idea of learning some new place, relearning another Cuba, so he said, Buey Arriba. The soil is fine, and it gets plenty of rain.

Upon his return to Buey Arriba, Ulises miraculously discovered Delfín—who looked exactly the same—living with two children. In strange accents, they asked her who the stranger was. Ulises saw their hands flutter when they spoke, even when they whispered, and after some discussion he realized they were the mute orphans, Augusto and Adelina, from the rebel camp. They must have been six and seven years old, respectively, and though they were much taller than Ulises remembered, they were still very thin. Delfín told Ulises they had shown up in her garden one day like moles out of the ground. This happened a year after Uxbal had died. At the time they still could not talk, but now they sounded like Delfín, which meant they could communicate but were barely intelligible. Ulises told Delfín he was moving in, to which she replied, Thank God. The next morning Ulises found her dead, lying faceup, arms crossed, eyes open, mouth set in a frown, atop her bed quilt, the sheets clean and unwrinkled.

She waited for you, Adelina told Ulises, her gray eyes wide and searching.

Me? Ulises asked.

Augusto grunted.

Ulises began to teach the children to speak a better Spanish, and after some time, he even started teaching them English. Apparently, Delfín had read to them from the Bible every night, even the gruesome bits regarding fire and brimstone, and Ulises continued this tradition, because it made the children feel safe around him. They fell asleep faster, sometimes all of them falling asleep together in the same bed. When Ulises translated the Spanish Bible stories into English, they were twice as fascinated. They did not know God could be heard another way.

At the same time Ulises went about constructing a tomato farm. With government funds, he procured six hectares of the Buey Arriban plain west of the nameless lake and just north of the national forest's boundary line. He hired men in the town to build trellises, and he took from Delfín's garden roots with which to start fresh vines. He drew water from the lake and contracted local pig farmers for manure. He grew only oxhearts. In a year, he had his first harvest, which was small but consistent. He spent his most of his hours in the field or with Augusto and Adelina, and he had no other companions.

At night he began leaving the children alone in the house so he could visit Buey Arriba's one bar, which was little more than a room filled with the lonely men who worked his farm. They were good-humored, but they wanted to fraternize away from the boss, and many of them came and went, because the work was hard. If there were any women left in Buey Arriba, they did not socialize at the bar. The women, Ulises had been told more than once, were leaving the island again, escaping with their families and daughters to other countries.

On the anniversary of Delfín's death, Ulises and the children decorated her grave with flowers and small wreaths woven from palm leaves. They beat the ground around her headstone with fresh petals to attract the zunzuncitos, and they ate roasted swordfish. The meal reminded Ulises not of his mother's death, but of Delfín herself. As Adelina and Augusto forked flakes of white meat into their mouths, Ulises saw the old woman scurrying about the kitchen, filling pots and cutting bread. The spices on the fish also stirred in Ulises's nose the memory of Delfín's scent, and he began to cry in front of the children.

Augusto said, Do you miss Granma?

Yes, Ulises said, but really it was more than that. Ulises missed not just the presence of the old woman, but the presence of all women. He felt an ache in his body, and he counted the days since he'd last seen a pair of hips shaking through the house, his house, any house.

From a pig farmer in town Ulises rented a shabby pickup truck. With it he drove all the way to Havana. He parked off of Avenida de Santa Catalina and ignored the jeers from passersby who called him a bumpkin. He walked up and down the street searching for a building with white paint and gold trim, but he found none. He drove home. For the next four months, Ulises went to Havana once every four weeks.

When Adelina asked, he said he had business in the city. Augusto wanted to come, and Ulises promised him another time. During his visits he slept in the bed of the truck, and if it rained, in the cab. During the days, he visited cultural centers and museums. He saw art shows and bought tickets to historical exhibitions. On a Sunday in April, Ulises toured the Arabian House in Old Havana, which was when he finally found Inez.

She was more than startled but said to him, You look really well, but I thought you would have gone back to the States by now. Did you find your sister?

Yes and no, Ulises said. And I live in Buey Arriba now. I want you to come stay with me.

Impossible, she said.

Then let me, at least, sleep with you.

Inez had moved. A hurricane had come through Havana a year ago and flooded the basement of her old building. The trapped water, which was never pumped out, eventually rotted out the foundation. Now she lived in a much smaller studio, much closer to the ground, and the space was lined, floor to ceiling, with books. There was barely room to stand and even less room for sex, but the two of them managed. Ulises paid Inez without asking.

I will see you again, he told her.

The next time he visited, he paid for the entire day, though they only slept together once. Ulises did this for several weeks, and he eventually began purchasing her entire weekends. Yet one Sunday Ulises returned to Buey Arriba and, while undressing in his room, found his money returned to his shirt pocket. He drove back to Havana.

You can stop paying me, Inez said.

There's plenty of space for your books in Buey Arriba, Ulises said. We can add on to the house. We can build you a library.

This Ulises also did without asking, and soon enough he convinced Inez to come visit his home.

She told him, This is no different than the town I grew up in.

Except here I'm a king, and you're not a whore. He said this lovingly.

Inez met the children, whom she liked. They can be yours, Ulises told her, which he knew was a cruel trick, but Inez didn't seem to mind.

They're bizarre, Inez said. Augusto sounds like a caveman priest, and Adelina—she never flinches.

You will love them, Ulises said.

Why do you love me? Inez asked.

Because you don't adore this place, Ulises said. If someday I should say, let's go, I think you would come. Then Ulises proposed to her, but Inez, after some moments, said no.

She told him, This is moving backward. Your house is lovely, but it's a dream I had a long time ago, and it seems like too much work learning to want an old fantasy.

Ulises was, at first, heartbroken, and for a while he tried to forget Inez. But then he felt the urge to explain to her that he wasn't angry and he understood her position. This led Ulises back to Havana, where he spent an entire night sharing with Inez all that had happened to him and his family: his time in Connecticut, the Dutchman's tobacco farm, his mother's dissipating chest, his sister's orgies and religious awakenings, his own sexual episodes, the children he might have somewhere in the world by way of Sofia, by way of Lena, and Uxbal's swollen knuckles. In the end Ulises knew he might have been capable of making Inez happy, but the more he thought about it, the more he found his attraction to her grounded in the way they spoke to each other, which was candidly, without the hint of false satisfaction. Satisfaction—contentment—was a mystery for others to chase. This became the foundation of their subsequent discourse, which some might have called a version of love, and following that long night they made a habit of weekends spent in conversation, interrupted only occasionally with sex. In this way they lived a sort of marriage on the Saturdays and Sundays they were together.

A few months later a superfluity of nuns visited Ulises's tomato farm. They had come to distribute paperback Bibles and pray with the workers, since there was no priest in town. One sister approached Ulises, but he told her he wasn't interested. He said he'd prayed enough for a lifetime. The nun, however, stood fast, and when Ulises eyed her more closely, he realized it was Isabel. She looked beautiful in her vestments, more beautiful than Ulises remembered. He had been, perhaps, as a young man, too annoyed by his sister's decisions to see how well the veil framed her face, how lovely her skin looked against the starched white of her blouse and the dark blue, almost black, fabric of her habit. The contrast softened her olive skin, which seemed firm and hydrated. He thought she looked healthy, though perhaps not happy. They both wanted to cry but could not.

Where have you been? Ulises asked her.

I don't want to tell you, Isabel said. But isn't it obvious? I'm with the religious again.

What church? Ulises asked.

A parish somewhere in Cuba, she said.

Did you know I had come back?

Yes, but I haven't known for long. I visited the work camps to look for you. I asked every prisoner I met about a bald giant doing time. Some of them said they had seen you before, but they could never remember where. Where did they hide you?

Somewhere not far from here, just outside Santiago. I was in solitary. They thought I was a threat. How did you know I was here?

A month ago I met some military at a church in San Luis. One of the sisters introduced me to a private who'd been a guard at a prison she'd passed through. He said that he'd seen you but that you'd been released. That you were sent home to grow food for the state.

Tomatoes, he said.

I didn't think I would see you again, she said.

I thought that's what you were after, which makes me wonder why you looked for me. If I was so hard to find, why not take that as your excuse?

I came to tell you that my daughter was born, she said.

You have a daughter, Ulises said, and he felt the need to lie down and close his eyes.

He was overwhelmed by two things: the tender fact that his sister would find him to share this news, and the realization that children can sometimes make their parents human again. Despite Isabel's veil and her hard eyes, she was suddenly a mother to him.

He managed to ask, When?

The day before I came down the mountain, Isabel told him. I would have come to see Ma sooner, but the girl came when I wasn't expecting her. She was early, dangerously so.

You wanted to see Ma but couldn't.

Yes and no, Isabel said. I wasn't sure. Then I had her, and I was terrified that my last image of Ma would be her crying for me as I left on a mission. I felt this desire all the way inside my bones to see how she'd changed, how she was different. I wanted to know as much about her as possible and not just what I remembered from Hartford. And then I decided I should be there when she went.

I remember that kiss, Ulises said. He paused. Why didn't you bring the baby with you? What if she'd died?

I was afraid, Isabel said. So I left her with the women at the camp. They said she would be fine, and I saw Adelina and Augusto and thought, yes, she will be fine. But I was also superstitious. I didn't want her to see anyone's face in case she might remember something. In case one day she got curious about a memory.

What's her name?

If I tell you, you might try to find her. Cuba isn't so large. There are only so many convents.

I could ask one of your sisters right now, but I'm done chasing after you, he said. I was already convinced I would never see you again.

Isabel gathered her hands into a knot. She said, To me she is Yerma Soledad.

That's beautiful, but what do you mean *to me*? Does she have another name? Does she have an alias? Do you really not trust that I won't come looking for you?

Isabel's eyes reddened, and she placed a hand on her throat. She wiped her face and tucked her veil under her chin.

Yerma is an orphan, Isabel said. She lives with other orphans at an orphanage. The parish runs the orphanage, and we look after the children who are there, including Yerma.

But she's not on orphan, Ulises said. She has her mother.

Everyone else, Isabel said, calls her Lucia. They tell her that I found her during my mission work in the countryside. They tell her I knew her mother but that she died in childbirth, and I brought her to the orphanage so that she could be taken care of, which was her mother's dying wish.

Why do they tell her that?

Because that's what I told them, Isabel said. The moment we're born, we begin to want. If we're lucky, satisfaction follows. But Yerma won't ever be satisfied, not with this family. Not if there's someone, especially her mother, who can only give her half answers. Not if everything I tell her leads to more questions.

Then Isabel said, Promise me that you'll never try to see her. Promise me that you will leave her alone.

This is why you came? Ulises asked. Because I could ruin Yerma's life by finding her?

Ulises stepped closer to Isabel. Suddenly he could smell her odor, which was something of the body and something from a cheap washing machine, and he knew without thinking it that the nuns did not wash their clothes often, nor did they shower with expensive soap— two inclinations toward vanity. Being a nun is giving things away, he thought. Being a nun is being chaste, which is the same as renouncing motherhood. Under the veil Isabel's hair was long, and Ulises could see how it had to be rolled together and pinned up so as not to drop beneath the cape of the fabric. If it was pulled back any tighter, she would look as bald as a woman suffering chemotherapy.

Ulises asked, Did Ma know? Did you tell her?

I don't know if she knew or if she really understood. She was so close to the end by the time I arrived. But, yes, I told her. She squeezed my hand. She didn't ask any questions.

Isabel touched her face. The way her hand moved looked as though she were forming a sign, albeit a mysterious sign no one but she understood. She looked at her brother and said, I wanted her to know me just then. I think she did.

Ulises thought, *He who has an ear, let him hear what the Spirit says to the churches. The one who is victorious will not be hurt at all by the second death.*

He took his sister's hand in his. Yerma will never know me, he said.

Isabel embraced Ulises, and he felt her breath on his neck.

Nearby, the other sisters had gathered to go. They stirred without speaking, and their skirts churned the air beneath them.

I'm sorry, Isabel whispered into her brother's skin. I've come and gone as I've wanted to. I can't imagine what you think of me.

Ulises said, When I wake in the morning, you are my first thought. When I go to bed at night, you are my last. You haven't fallen out of grace.

She kissed his cheek, and they said good-bye.

Early the next morning Adelina and Augusto found Ulises alone in the kitchen, sitting in his dirtied work clothes and drinking coffee.

You should be gone, Adelina said.

I'm not going to Havana this weekend.

Why not? Augusto asked.

I don't feel like it.

You're sick, the boy said.

No, Ulises said. My sister came to see me yesterday, and we haven't spoken in a long, long time. It wore me out.

We have an aunt? Adelina said.

No, not exactly, Ulises said.

You said she was your sister, Augusto said.

She is.

You're not our father? Adelina asked.

Well, no, Ulises said. Not in a biological sense.

Do you know what happened to him? Adelina asked. Or our mother?

Augusto added, Do you know where they are? Are they farmers like us? What language do they speak?

Ulises did not know what to tell them, and he said as much to Inez the following week when he returned to Havana.

You can't lie to them, Inez said. Even if your sister would.

Ulises felt the same way, but still he said, If I tell them who their parents were or might have been, then I will have to tell them about the rebel camp. If I tell them that, they might run up into the hills to see the old shacks. If they see the camp, they might want to know about my father and what he did. I would have to tell them about Isabel, and then they might want to find her. They don't know that they might have a cousin, or maybe three cousins, and maybe they'd run off looking for her or them.

What you tell them might also be a reason for them to stay, she said. Or to come back to you. You're the only one who knows their histories. But probably they're just curious children who have an itch to scratch.

They might abandon me to see about their real family.

It sounds as though you've grown to love them, Inez said.

Eventually, then, Ulises gave in to the children's demands for answers, knowing how powerful the draw of the past was and how dumb it was to fight it. Saying first, Know this above all: fate is family, and family is fate, Ulises began the arduous task of explaining to Augusto and Adelina where they had come from. He began with his own childhood, what he could remember of it, and told the children about Isabel, Soledad, and Uxbal. He told them where the tomato vines on his plantation originally came from. He told them about the packinghouse church and his sister's singing, the old guava crates men used to sit on, the hummingbird traps his father used to step on. He explained what it was like to ride a train for the first time and how much colder it was up north than it was on the island. The story, Ulises quickly understood, was much too long and possessed too many details, so after a while he limited himself to one or two hours a night alone in the garden with the children by the gravestones. In this fashion he made his way toward the distant end, which was only Augusto and Adelina's beginnings, but he hoped, after a while, that hearing everything was enough of an answer as to why the two of them lived with a perfect stranger in Buey Arriba. Some nights he forgot where he had left off or what he'd already told them, but the children never forgot; they knew exactly what his last word had been, and this should not have surprised him. They were good, obedient children, and though they spoke with odd accents, they listened extremely well, perched as they were, like bee hummingbirds, on the various strands and branches of the account of their creation, of Ulises's life, and of the manner in which he eventually returned to Cuba.

Acknowledgments

All my gratitude and appreciation to:

PJ Mark, for the tremendous time, patience, insight, and energy you gave to this book.

Marya Spence, for your careful readings and criticism.

Tim Duggan, for shepherding this novel into the world and for helping me to discover its final form.

Will Wolfslau, Rachel Rokicki, Sarah Grimm, and everyone at Crown Publishing, for their extraordinary support.

Erin McGraw, for the endless wisdom you have shared and continue to share with me—if there is any soul in this story, it is because of your intellect, friendship, and dedication.

Andrew Hudgins, for teaching me how to read and write another way, and for your mostly funny jokes.

Michelle Herman, Lee K. Abbott, and Lee Martin, for your teaching and guidance.

All my peers, friends, and colleagues of The Ohio State University MFA program.

My truly remarkable friends and first-readers Bill Riley, Clayton Clark, Daniel Carter, Alex Streiff, and Gabe Urza—I am wildly fortunate to have found and kept as confidants such funny, intelligent, and compassionate folk.

My supportive and loving friends Morgan Lord, Abraham Stein, Peter Harrison, Daniel Beaulieu, Stefanie Carrabba, Lindsey Pryor, Jessica Corey, Chris Markunas, Joe Scapellato, Dustyn Martincich, Erica

Delsandro, and, of course, the incomparable duo of Christopher and Erin Maskwa.

My friends and colleagues at Bucknell, Susquehanna, Sewanee, IAIA, Nouvella Books, and the University of Michigan.

My incredible parents, Debra and Carlos.

My wonderful siblings, Aubrey and Dan.

All the joyous new members of my clan: Keri, Selena, Ava, Lise, Adam, Delilah, Nic, and Gaylyn.

The entire Palacio family.

My wondrous creature of a daughter, Esmé Ofelia.

Lastly, there is a love in my life I will never deserve but still get to call my own—te quiero mucho, Claire Vaye.

ABOUT THE AUTHOR

Derek Palacio received his MFA in creative writing from The Ohio State University. His short story "Sugarcane" appeared in *The O. Henry Prize Stories 2013,* and his novella, *How to Shake the Other Man,* was published by Nouvella Books in the same year. He is the co-director, with Claire Vaye Watkins, of the Mojave School, a free creative writing workshop for teenagers in rural Nevada. He lives and teaches in Ann Arbor, Michigan, and is a faculty member of the Institute of American Indian Arts MFA program.